Praise for BROCK'S AGENT

"… a propulsive historical novel … this ripping yarn."
— *The Globe and Mail*

"Taylor spins a well-rounded and riveting tale of war,
love of country, and friendship …"
— *Historical Novels Review*

"… breathtaking intensity."
— *The Ottawa Citizen*

"… Taylor writes with a passion, power, and pace that will leave you
breathless and thirsty for more. A born storyteller, Taylor weaves
a gripping yarn with the very strands of our own history."
— Terry Fallis, winner of Canada Reads and the Stephen Leacock Award
for his book *The Best Laid Plans* and author of *The High Road*

Praise for BROCK'S RAILROAD

Book of the Year Award ForeWord Reviews,
2012 Historical Fiction Finalist

"Taylor paints an unforgettable picture of the War of 1812 in all its
glory. With an appealing hero, Jonathan Westlake, and a dynamic
legend, Isaac Brock, this is rip-roaring storytelling at its best."
Jill Downie, award-winning historical fiction novelist,
and author of the Moretti/Falla mystery series

"This riveting and potent tale of freedom tears asunder
historical stereotypes in favor of three-dimensional characters
that leave indelible marks on the reader."
— Cindy Vallar author of *The Scottish Thistle*

Tom Taylor is a Canadian writer who graduated from York University with a B.A. majoring in history. He once served in the militia with the Toronto 7th Artillery. He resides in the Greater Toronto Area.

BROCK'S TRAITOR

BROCK'S TRAITOR

TOM TAYLOR

HANCOCK AND DEAN

Hancock and Dean
6 – 80 Citizen Court
Markham, Ontario
Canada L6G 1A7

Published by Hancock and Dean

A Division of GIFTFORCE INC.

Brock's Traitor is distributed by Auralim Gift. For information about
special discounts for wholesale purchases, call 1-800-265-9898.

Cover and text designed by Tania Craan
Cover photography of soldier by Elizabeth Woodley-Hall
Background images by iStock Photo

Manufactured in Canada

ISBN: 978-0-9868961-2-5

For my teacher and wonderful friend,
Professor Brayton Polka.

"We create ourselves every day."

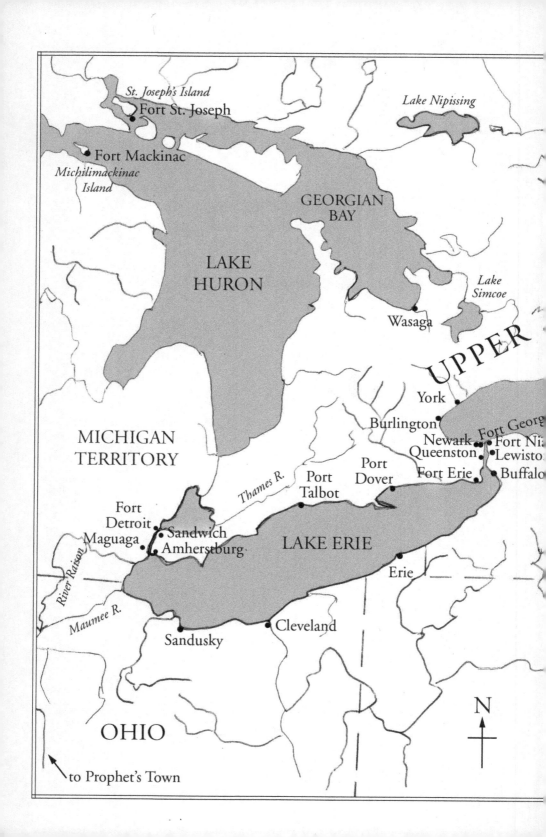

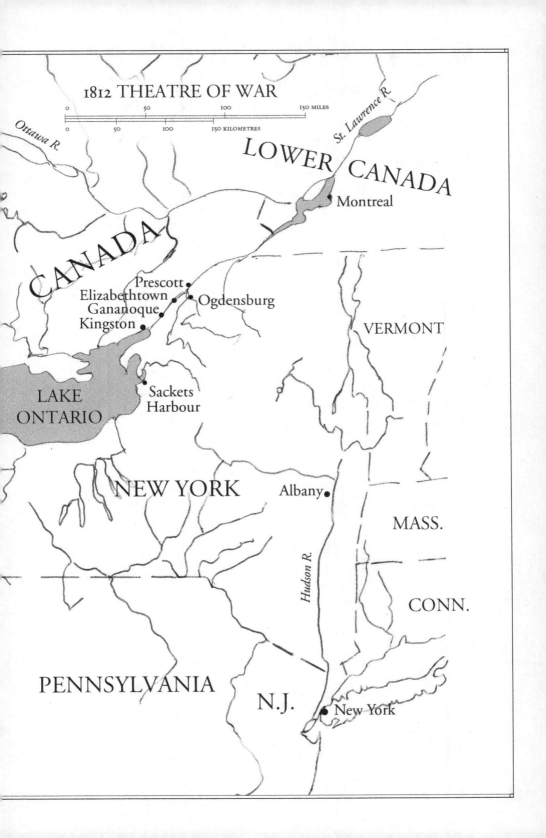

1
. . . . . .

The Americans were coming to kill him.

Young Willie Robertson stood to attention at the end of a long line of Leeds County Militia, his Brown Bess musket clasped tight at his side. He forced himself to take a deep breath of morning air but found it impossible to relax his shoulders. An artist of immense talent, something known only to himself, he wondered what he was doing here about to fight his former countrymen. In fact, he doubted if he even could.

A galloping horseman had shouted the news that hundreds, perhaps thousands, of American riflemen were marching south on the little village of Gananoque. The United States' war against Britain, declared in June, had taken barely three months to reach the Canadian shores of the St. Lawrence River. As he peered toward a bend in the road, waiting to see the enemy appear, Willie couldn't believe this was actually all happening to him.

On his right, two ranks of thirty militiamen fidgeted at attention, in anticipation of the enemy's approach. Most wore only civilian blue and grey homespun, under brown leather cross-belts. A few men were dressed in faded redcoats, cast-off uniforms of the regular army. The young artist gripped his musket hard enough to make his fingers ache. The extra money earned from joining the army now seemed like a bad bargain.

His old sergeant slid his feet together, coming straight to attention in front of the ranks. Playing the soldier, Willie reckoned. After a few parade-square drills, if that miserable man thought these scared militiamen could hold off thousands of enemy soldiers, he was out of his mind.

"At your own time, prime and load!" the sergeant commanded.

Willie fumbled his Brown Bess before ramming the ball down the barrel and sliding the ramrod back in place. The two ranks blocked the road. Directly behind them stood the colonel's storehouse rich in supplies, and farther back rose his beautiful residence. It was the kind that Willie liked to draw, with a big white veranda encircling half the house. Willie figured that the approaching riflemen would pause to ransack the storehouse, thereby giving him time to run. If he could just get himself over to that residence, he'd be safe as a groundhog in its hole.

He heard the low rumble of feet, and there, thrusting around the curve in the road, marched a column of green clad American riflemen. Not only could he barely breathe, but now his throat refused to swallow. It didn't matter that he'd just turned fifteen; if he ran off right away, everyone would know him forever as a stinking coward with no honour. He had to figure a way of standing still here without peeing in his trousers.

I'm an artist, not like these other lesser likes. Just paint the picture.

Willie slid on his spectacles to better study the enemy, first looking for any of his pals from New York. Not long ago, he'd waved goodbye to them as his intensely Loyalist family had left the new republic behind, and set out for British North America. But instead of familiar faces, these men looked older and more hard-boiled — a phrase his mother often used.

Eighty yards away, they marched straight down the road four abreast, as if Willie and the other militiamen weren't standing there ready to oppose them. They wore dark green uniforms with yellow trim, and great black plumes bounced above their leather caps. *Good for a painting, indeed.*

"You will fire one volley and then immediately prepare to make ready for the second." The sergeant's order brought Willie back to the imminent danger. At fifty yards, the American riflemen veered off sharply to either side of the road, spilling out across the clearing directly in front of the Leeds Militia.

Willie noticed how even his veteran sergeant looked worried, his eyes darting from the enemy riflemen back to his own two murmuring lines. They really needed the colonel to command them, and quite a few more men too, because now the riflemen kept marching fearlessly off the road and into the field. There must be thousands of them, Willie figured, but he wished he knew for sure what that many looked like.

"Present!" the sergeant bellowed.

Willie raised his musket just as a single rifleman stepped forward. The man wore a long green coat that clung tight to his body, and unlike the others, white plumes floated above his wide-brimmed hat. *A strong face to draw, calm in its bearing.* He had a pistol tucked into his belt and a riding crop clamped under one arm. The officer advanced ten yards in a free and easy manner, drew a sabre to seemingly point directly at Willie, and then shouted, "Prepare to advance."

"Present!" ordered Willie's sergeant. "Fire!"

In the early morning light, in the quiet stillness, Willie pressed the trigger and the Brown Bess recoiled hard into his shoulder. Sixty muskets crashed out, spitting flame and balls, but Willie saw only two of the riflemen fall to the ground before the smoke obscured his view.

"Prime and load!" His ears ringing, Willie heard someone hollering, but it sounded far off, the voice unsteady. Through the drifting smoke, he saw the sergeant's lips move.

"Prime and load, I say," the old sergeant repeated.

Willie raised his musket to begin the prime-and-load drill. When he was calm, it took him thirty seconds to load and fire again.

He heard that officer with the white plumes yelling, "Charge!"

The enemy riflemen could easily cover forty yards in less than thirty seconds. *No time to reload.* Willie was about to be stabbed, run through with an officer's sabre as easy as poking a pincushion. The musket smoke from the volley lifted, and he caught a glance of that officer's grinning face. Willie felt a bump to his arm as the militiaman next to him turned and bolted. He glanced to his right. No one. He was the only man still standing in line.

Willie threw down his Brown Bess and ran to save his life.

Lieutenant Abraham Tasker laughed and adjusted the white plumes on his hat. There wasn't a chance on earth of these bumbling militiamen holding fast against experienced riflemen. For the most part, the enemy had fired too high, a sure sign they were nervous. His only worry was the sight of a handful of redcoats. Regular British Army didn't run — they might die — but they didn't run. No matter, there were too few of them to cause any real concern to his own two hundred trained soldiers. Now, as he peered through the smoke, the militiamen fumbled trying to reload.

"Don't worry, lads. Show 'em your steel will." Calm in his approach to his own men, Tasker knew this enemy in front would run at the first sign of his advance.

"Advance!" he shouted. "At the double! Charge!"

The entire front line surged forward as his men leapt from a quick march into a dash. Within seconds, the militiamen's two ranks had collapsed into a retreating rabble. Most flung down their muskets even as they turned to run. A few men at the far end just threw their hands in the air and sat down.

"Seize their muskets and all the ammunition you can get your hands on," ordered a heavy-set man from the back of the regiment. Captain Benjamin Forsyth, fifty-two years of age, stepped forward wearing his green coat with a white vest visible underneath. He pointed with his sword. "Go surround that residence, Lieutenant. Demand that any fools left inside surrender to us immediately."

Forsyth held up his gloved hand and counted off against his fingers: "Take cash, jewellery, weapons, and ammunition. All mine. Kill anyone that resists. Then hurry back, the whole damn British Army could be marching on us." He waved his sword to get the lieutenant moving while he stared nervously down the road.

Tasker ran forward to the storehouse, where the riflemen had formed up as planned. He divided the regiment into two groups before signalling forward his smaller company of fifty men to the two-storey home with the extensive veranda. The Leeds County Militia was either long gone or hiding inside. Either way, that house and all its contents now belonged to him.

He made a circle in the air with one arm, indicating for his riflemen to surround the building. Then he cupped his hands around his mouth and bellowed, "Surrender your weapons and step outside immediately. We mean you no harm. You have one minute to comply."

From inside the house there came no answer and no sign of life, with the exception of one curtained window on the lower floor that swished briefly to one side. Tasker dropped into a crouch lest a musket appear from behind the drapery.

"They're watching us, sir," warned a sergeant, pointing to the same window.

"We'll give them a stiff volley, and then charge from all sides. Pass the word, Sergeant."

"There could be children inside, sir."

Tasker's face grew stern. "Then their parents should have surrendered when they had their chance," he commented quietly. "Remind all the men that the valuables and weapons belong to me and the captain. And they're on their goddamn honour, so no stealing from me!"

The sergeant ran off to spread the word. Tasker lifted his hat, brushed back his brown hair, and wondered what exactly he would find inside. He glanced over his shoulder at the storehouse, where Forsyth was already loading barrels into the wagons. *So far, so good.*

"Ready, sir." The sergeant puffed out his words and came to attention.

"Time's up for these idiots." Tasker whispered every word distinctly. "No second chances. Order the men to fire."

"Present!" the sergeant bellowed. "Fire!"

The rifles erupted, shattering the glass windows. The soldiers stormed the entrances. Darting in front of Tasker, his sergeant kicked in the front door. The adjoining parlour proved empty. Tasker sprinted toward the kitchen with his drawn pistol. On the floor lay a middle-aged woman groaning while she clutched her bleeding arm.

"Make sure this floor is clear first, then upstairs to the bedrooms," Tasker ordered his sergeant. "You know what to look for."

Tasker reached down to slowly lift the small woman up and onto a chair by the kitchen table. He yanked open a drawer beside the washbasin and found a broad strip of cloth.

"You're the colonel's wife?"

The woman nodded, holding her forehead in one hand. She'd already turned the colour of snow.

"This is going to hurt."

She nodded again.

Tasker sat down beside her. He tore the cloth in half, tied the two ends together, and then wrapped it tight around the woman's arm. She made no sound but simply leaned back in her chair and sighed. Tasker glanced at the washbasin, where a wedding ring rested on the counter.

"Feel better?" He grinned.

"No thanks to you and your merciless savages." She choked out the words as if about to cry.

"You could have come straight outside and avoided that arm." A crash from the dining room told him the silverware was now under attack.

"You're stealing from civilians." The woman's voice grew stronger now as she regained her composure. "There are rules that honourable men follow ... even in war. What you do is *disgusting*." She hissed the last word.

"It doesn't have to be." Tasker touched the soft skin on the back of her hand.

"Don't touch me. Ever!" She pulled her hand away, wincing at the sudden movement.

"If I was your husband, madam, I would never leave you alone here to fend for yourself."

"Take what you want and get out."

"Have it your way," he said with lips compressed. He stood, stepped over to the washbasin, and with a quick swipe snatched up the gold ring. "Tell the colonel you'll be needing another one of these."

"Bastard." She spit at him.

Tasker raised his riding crop to strike her just as the sergeant appeared in the doorway. His hand gripped the collar of a bespectacled boy who didn't appear too happy. "Look what I found hiding upstairs under the bed," he exclaimed.

"Willie." There was sadness in the woman's voice. "I warned you not to hide there." She put a hand to her cheek and sobbed.

Tasker tucked the riding crop back under his arm and peered through the broken window to see black smoke billowing out between the storehouse doors. "Did you find what we came for?" He turned back to the sergeant.

The sergeant patted his bulging pockets with one hand.

"We're done here. Tell the men to get out," Tasker ordered with a jerk of his head. "Ma'am, it's been a pleasure. Another time maybe?" He grinned.

Tasker grabbed the boy's collar from his sergeant's grasp. "I saw this little bugger aiming right at me from one end of their line. He's coming with us." He hustled the unfortunate Willie out the front door.

The last of the wagons made its way down the track just as the storehouse roof erupted in flames. Tasker jogged to catch up to the wagons, dragging his captive behind him. The sergeant stumbled alongside, loaded down with three confiscated muskets and two extra pouches of ammunition.

"Found a beautiful hunting knife as well, sir." The sergeant grinned at the weapon suspended on his belt. "Not much drink for the men, though." He piled the muskets into the back of the lumbering wagon.

A section of Tasker's riflemen formed up in column behind him while others helped push the laden vehicles. Now they just had to make it back to their boats before the British Army arrived. The heat of the mid-September day increased as the sun lit the open roadway in front of them. He thought about the woman's wedding ring in his pocket before stepping up sharply beside Captain Forsyth. "Any count, sir?" he asked.

Forsyth shifted himself along behind the last cart as if going on a mid-afternoon stroll. "Of course I know the count. Thirty barrels of flour, twelve enemy prisoners, not including him" — Forsyth indicated the boy still gripped in Tasker's hand — "forty-one muskets, as many ammunition pouches — and the plunder from the house, as yet uncounted. That'll teach the colonel of the Leeds County Militia a damn lesson. He's no more a civilian than I am. I heard a volley fired at the house."

"Just this boy ... nothing serious. One woman shot through the arm." Tasker grinned. "She didn't appreciate my advances."

"Maybe she didn't like being shot at. Canadian women are odd like that."

Tasker fingered the wedding ring in his pocket. "Excuse me, sir." He turned around to address the sergeant. "I need to borrow your knife."

He stepped out of the line, pulling Willie along with him. The sergeant followed. "Do you know what the French did to English archers?" Tasker asked the boy while holding the knife to his throat.

Willie shook his head, eyes wide with fear.

Tasker grabbed Willie's wrist and laid the knife across the extended fingers. "They cut off the archer's fore-fingers so they couldn't shoot an arrow again."

"Please, sir," Willie cried. He looked up through spectacles that sat crooked across his nose. "I'm an artist from New York. They jail us if we won't fight just 'cause we happen to live here."

Born in New York himself, Tasker's family had moved to South Carolina when he was still young. He wondered if this boy's father had regularly beaten him too, and in that instant he experienced a type of empathy. Willie's parents probably forced the kid to travel north with them and leave behind all his friends. Tasker knew what it was like to be friendless in a strange town. Still, Willie had fired his musket, and that meant the lad had to be punished so that he'd never fight again.

The boy tried to pull away.

Tasker looked at the boy's hand, then slowly into his eyes. Finally, he shifted his gaze to the boy's trousers and quickly slit a hole in the pant leg — before stabbing hard into his thigh.

The boy screamed.

"Keep your fingers, Willie, and paint your pictures, but don't ever let me catch you fighting against Americans again." He held on tight to Willie's wrist and pressed down on the wound while the boy squirmed and whimpered, waving his free arm like some mad thing. Blood streamed down onto Tasker's hand as extracted the knife, then reached in his pocket and took out the wedding ring. He slid it over one of the boy's fingers.

"You take this ring back to the colonel's wife. She'll bandage your leg." Tasker let go of his wrist. "Tell her I might be back for a friendly visit." The lad turned to limp away, and Tasker booted him in the arse.

"Very gentlemanly of you, sir, to leave the boy with all of his fingers," the sergeant remarked.

"My father was a right bastard, too." Tasker sighed and handed the sergeant his blood-stained knife. "Seems the men didn't do too well on this trip, Sergeant." Only a few men carried any loot: a bottle of wine or a small piece of furniture. "I think we need to persuade Captain Forsyth to undertake another raid soon. Meet some more Canadian women?"

"Suits me, sir, but forget their women. Too stuck up for my liking." The sergeant put the back of a finger under his nose and flicked it twice. "Stick with the devil you know, I always say. As for another raid, I've been thinking about a visit to that little village just upriver — Elizabethtown — heard of it, sir?"

"Heard of it but never been there. Women?"

"Some beautiful Canadian women there, sir. Just waiting for you." The sergeant raised his eyebrows and grabbed his crotch.

The U.S. brig *Oneida* tilted into a stiff westerly breeze on Lake Ontario, and Commodore Isaac Chauncey shifted his weight slightly to keep his balance. Now aged forty, his entire professional life had been spent around ships — sailing, building and administering them. He glanced up at his commodore's pennant to gauge the brisk November wind.

"Helmsman," he called out, "can you not sail her closer to the wind? At this rate, we'll be zigzagging all over the damn lake."

"She won't stand for it, sir. Built too shallow, so as to avoid the shoals, you see. Sailing close only drifts her downwind."

As he felt the ship begin to drift under his very feet, the commodore nodded his understanding, even though he didn't like it. Despite her limitations, armed with eighteen thirty-two-pound carronades, the *Oneida* ranked as the U.S. Navy's most powerful fighting vessel on Lake Ontario. Aware that such short guns would be deadly for fighting in close, he also knew that any British ship possessing long guns would blast the hell out him before he could get close enough to return fire.

"Ease her off two points, if you will."

"Sir."

He stared back across the water at his struggling flotilla of six armed schooners tacking against the prevailing westerly. In formation with the *Oneida*, they made up the largest U.S. naval force ever to sail the Great Lakes. But his mind questioned whether these ships could both sail and fight at the same time.

"The Ducks ahead, sir," the helmsman announced.

"I have eyes," Chauncey replied sharply as he squinted at the Duck Islands — small but treacherous for unsuspecting sailors — sitting thirty miles due west of his head-quarters at Sackets Harbor.

"Deck there, sail off the port bow," an old gravely voice in the rigging shouted down to the quarterdeck.

Chauncey raised his dimpled chin, extended his glass, and stared across the water until the other ship sailed into view.

"British flagship, *Royal George*, sir, unescorted," the man announced in a gleeful tone, surprised at their obvious luck. Standing in the rigging, he wrapped one arm around a ratline and pointed with the other at the enemy. "She's already altering course, sir, due north for the Bay of Quinte."

"Midshipman," the commodore hollered. "Up the halliard, now, signal the schooners to make chase! By God, we'll have some action yet, on this late afternoon." Chauncey raised a fist in the air and glanced westward toward the last red curve of a sinking sun. His ship, positioned farther downwind, had already forced the enemy to change course, but he wondered if the *Oneida* could outpace the British vessel before darkness ended the chase.

"Get the t'gallants on her," he bellowed to a lieutenant standing close at hand, as other men ran and scurried up the rigging to set more sail.

Caught unawares, the *Royal George* was soon heading at speed into the bay, making all sail for the North Channel. The commodore studied the smooth tacking of the enemy vessel. *The man can sail a ship, I'll give him that.* The *Oneida* and its six schooners followed close behind as they approached the Bay of Quinte.

"We could get off a shot, sir," the helmsman suggested.

"When I want your opinion ..." Chauncey snapped his glass shut and looked away. "Too damn far for these short barrels. At least we're sailing with the wind. That shallow hull of ours should protect us from the worst of the shoals," he thought out loud before his face brightened. "Lieutenant, make signal to our schooner, *Conquest*. Take the lead and prepare to open fire." The long-barrelled thirty-two pounder on the *Conquest* would do his fighting for him.

The breeze lightened and the last of the sun's orb had long disappeared. By the time *Conquest* positioned herself, the *Royal George* had faded from sight. "Damn!" Chauncey stared after the enemy and slapped the rail in disappointment. As darkness spread over the water, he risked disaster to continue blindfolded. He had no choice but to take in sails and signal his entire flotilla to drop anchor while they could still see the outline of his signals.

"The *Royal George* can't risk sailing in the dark any more than we can, sir." The helmsman risked stating the obvious once again. "If we've anchored, then so has she, which means that ship of theirs remains just ahead."

"And if I can't carry on sailing, I might as well sleep," Chauncey replied. "That goes for you as well. Six hours, helmsman, not a minute longer — then you and I are back where we stand to resume the chase." Chauncey nodded and climbed down the companion ladder to his quarters in the bow, pleased to have some action. The chance for victory lay with the morrow.

The November sun rises ever later in the morning as winter solstice approaches. The anxious commodore had been pacing the quarter-deck at least two hours before the first light barely touched the water's rippled surface. Then, to his delight, that same gravelly voice shouted down from the topmast, "Sail ho!" Chauncey glanced up at his pennant barely fluttering in the breeze. His chest rose in anticipation. *The hunt begins.*

"All sails, Lieutenant. Signal to make chase." Chauncey bellowed his orders after peering through his glass. He had a pudgy, not unkind face, and scratched his hooked nose before addressing the helmsman. "You were correct, sir. There lies the *Royal George.*"

The helmsman nodded his appreciation modestly, while a midshipman bawled out orders through his brass trumpet.

The *Royal George* enjoyed the Bay of Quinte as her home waters and, confident of avoiding familiar shoals, must have continued to sail through the near dark. She had gained several cables length at dusk so that when the chase renewed, the schooner *Conquest* was pressed to make up the lost distance. Both ships were quick off the mark, like two racehorses at the starting shot. The finishing line would be Kingston harbour.

Several hours into the afternoon, *Conquest* had closed enough water to signal a request to engage the enemy. Chauncey answered back immediately to his schooner: "Open fire!"

Boom! The cannon blast split the afternoon air and the seamen cheered. A white spray blew up behind the *Royal George.* Even with the *Conquest*'s long thirty-two-pounder, the iron balls continued splashing just short of the enemy ship. Chauncey pounded one fist into his palm out of frustration. His flotilla fast approached Kingston harbour and would soon come within range of its shore batteries.

The *Royal George* swept around a point of land, and for the moment it was out of sight. The instant the *Conquest* approached the same point, the harbour defences crashed out, their cannon shots throwing up a shower of lake water around the schooner. Chauncey stared aghast, wincing as a ball punched through the *Conquest*'s sail.

Then came the turn of *Oneida*. In the light breeze, Chauncey gritted his teeth, as it seemed to take forever to pass the point and sail into the harbour. "Get some men in the bows to keep a lookout for shoals," Chauncey called to a lieutenant. "This is getting too damn close."

At first the enemy balls miraculously skipped passed his ship, without causing a splinter's damage. Then enemy cannon found their range, and two balls in quick succession tore through the main sail. Musket fire from the shore joined in, so that the *Oneida*'s deck regularly tapped to the thud of lead balls. As the harbour itself came into view, the *Royal George* sat in its centre and she opened up a ragged fire even as she proceeded to anchor.

The sporadic blasts told Chauncey that either the enemy wasn't trained in gun drill or they found themselves undermanned as they took in sails, anchored, and tried to fire their cannons all at the same time. He counted ten thirty-two-pound carronades facing him from the vessel, yet they barely touched the *Oneida* until one ball suddenly crashed in and blew a man clean through the rail.

The schooners, led by the *Conquest*, wore round for another engagement with the *Royal George*, but the enemy ship dragged her anchor enough to sink deeper into the protective umbrella of the harbour defences. Chauncey saw a man go down on the closest schooner, and immediately afterwards, three of his own men slumped to the deck, felled by musket fire.

"We could sail in right beside her, sir," the lieutenant suggested.

The helmsman winced and rolled his eyes skyward … it would be a matter of seconds before their luck ran out.

"Not this time, Lieutenant," Chauncey said, as a musket ball clipped the wheel, dislodging a sliver of wood. He gestured toward his flotilla. "Every single vessel of ours has holes in her sails. Signal to wear ship and close on Flag."

"Sir." The lieutenant saluted and ran off, barking orders. As the ship answered the wheel, he returned to Chauncey's side.

Kingston harbour had filled with the drifting grey smoke of cannon fire. The commodore swallowed its taste. He pointed up toward the hundreds of redcoats lining the hills along the shore. "To try to lay the *Oneida* alongside the *Royal George*, we'd all be cut down by the damn shore defences before we could engage." He nodded to the west and slapped his hands together. "Better to live to fight another day. I've now learned what I needed to know."

"And what may I ask, sir, was that?" the lieutenant inquired.

"That the British flagship can either fight or it can sail, but she can't do both. And also she has no long guns. We now have command of the lake and can transport troops and stores to any part of it without serious risk." Chauncey grinned. "That's enough good news for one day."

The commodore glanced westward toward a sun long disappeared and began pacing the quarterdeck, oblivious to the musket fire from shore as the *Oneida* exited the harbour. The wind increased with the sun gone, and the darkness spread farther with every passing second. While the British captain had saved his ship through some smart sailing, the engagement told a vital story.

Chauncey judged that his flotilla needed one more brig, one that could be built over the winter in the relative safety of Sackets Harbor. With that extra ship, he could successfully invade anywhere he chose around the lake and not worry a shred about losing an engagement. He had only to pick a juicy target. Perhaps he'd attack Kingston again, with its rich store of government supplies. Newark and Fort George, in lush Niagara, might be a better prize.

"I need a damn army to fight alongside my ships," he said out loud to no one. Or if his fancy pleased him, he'd pay a friendly visit to the capital of Upper Canada, a muddy little town called York.

2
· · · · · ·

LIEUTENANT JONATHAN WESTLAKE gripped the axe in his right hand, his eyes studying a horse and rider some fifty yards away at the bottom of the hill. In summer, the maples that lined both sides of the lane leading up to Maple Hill almost touched branches full of foliage, offering visitors an overhead canopy, but now, in early December, their frozen grey limbs remained stiff with snow and ice. The rider slowed the horse to a walk as it began to climb the long slope in the sunshine. A flash of a red showed underneath the man's greatcoat. Westlake's stomach tightened into a small knot.

He stared at the firewood scattered around his feet, kicked the blocks into a rough pile, and headed to the barn behind him. The bar holding shut the large door swung over with a thud. Westlake's horse gave a low whinny in his darkened stall.

"Let's go for a little ride, you and me." He patted the horse's nose and began to tack up. As his tenth birthday present, his father had given him Warman when the animal was still a colt. Although that was seven years ago, he'd never forgotten the great sense of freedom he enjoyed that first time as he rode the horse away from their new sugar shack in the woods. The old shack was only a mile away to the north, but it was beyond his parents' control, a mile of freedom he'd never forget.

By the time the rider from the lane appeared in the light of the barn's entrance, Westlake was almost finished. He glanced up and gave the man a single nod.

"You don't look pleased to see me, Lieutenant," the officer remarked. "Staying out of trouble, I hope — not killing anyone lately." His narrow face grew into a grin. "You're not shaved."

"Doing my best, Captain." Westlake rubbed his chin. "Have another bloody mission for me … so why should I be pleased?" He cinched up the last leather strap, tucked it in place and led Warman out of the barn.

"We're in better circumstances now than the last time we stood on a hill together. And the view is better too." The captain coaxed his horse back along the path following Westlake. "No dead bodies at least."

Westlake cringed at the memory of a battlefield. He looked down beyond the lane and over the garrison town of York hugging Lake Ontario's northern shoreline. As far as he could see, except for along the water's edge where ice had already formed, the lake glistened under a crisp blue sky. He mounted up.

The captain had started for the laneway. "No, not that way, sir. Follow me, if you please." Westlake tugged his reins to the right and Warman trotted past the great oak door forming the main entrance to the stone house called Maple Hill. Untouched by winter's snow, a Christmas wreath hung on the door itself.

"I'd invite you in, sir, but I fear my mother and father are somewhat at odds just now." The path narrowed and Westlake spurred his horse through a gap in the trees. "So how have you been, Captain Nelles? Miss him much?"

"Upper Canada misses him. I worked with General Brock every day, so I'm bound to notice the change."

"Who do you report —"

"Sheaffe," Nelles interrupted. "I report to Major General Sheaffe. Although he doesn't quite know what to do with me … being Brock's man and all." His long face broke into another smile. "He's put me to work gathering intelligence on the enemy. Thinks it'll keep me out of the way."

Westlake rode his horse up a snow-covered incline until he reached a rocky crest and halted. Well out of earshot from the house, he turned his horse back to view the sparkling lake. From every rooftop in York, ribbons of grey smoke drifted skyward. Nelles rode up and stopped beside him. A thick stand of pines cupped the ridge, so the faint wind blew only lightly on Westlake's face. Overhead, a lone goose quacked, banked its wings and then continued flapping the way south.

Whether the scent of the pines, or the soft bed of needles on the ground, or perhaps just the tranquillity, Westlake always relaxed in this spot, gazing out at the lake. He tucked a couple of strands of blond hair under his black tuque and tugged it down, covering the bottom of his ears. Then he sighed, watching his frosty breath dissipate in the air.

"You didn't stay for the funeral, Lieutenant. A grand affair, full of fifes, drums, speeches. Thousands of mourners travelled in from all over. With Sheaffe allowing another armistice, there was no threat of action on that day." Nelles shook his head, remembering.

Westlake said nothing and simply stared across the water toward Niagara. The barest outline of Lake Ontario's south coast made itself visible — the enemy's shore. The war had been raging since mid-June, after the United States had declared war on Great Britain and invaded first at Sandwich and then at Queenston, along the Niagara River.

"They buried General Brock under a bastion in Fort George. I would have preferred Queenston Heights myself, but I guess it doesn't matter." Nelles glanced skyward. "Even the Americans honoured him. A seventeen-gun salute roared out of Fort Niagara. One old girl in the line even fainted, thinking another invasion had commenced." He chuckled. "So how are you?"

"Do you mean am I ready for duty, secret duty, sir? Arm's healed and the limp's now gone. Nothing like a good soaking in that freezing lake to fix a wound." Westlake nodded toward the water below and shivered. "Takes the swelling down in minutes, if you can stand the cold. Yourself?"

"Stiff as hell, but the pain's gone." Nelles held up his left arm and stretched it out straight with a grimace. "I gave you a letter from General Brock, written on the eve of the Queenston battle."

"I still have it … unopened."

"Why haven't you read it?" Nelles demanded. "My God, it's been almost two months, Lieutenant."

Aware that others would have reacted differently, Westlake liked the idea of leaving it unread, retaining the feeling that Brock still had something new to say to him. The second he finished reading the last word in that letter would be the moment his hero had nothing more to say ... finally dead. He slid a hand inside his fur coat, unbuttoned the buckskin jacket, and touched the letter itself. He took it out and glanced at Nelles. Brock had once held this paper in his own hands.

One corner of the folded page flipped up exactly where Westlake had once started to break the seal and then stopped. He slipped his finger under the flap and stopped again. "I'd prefer not, sir, ... not to read it today."

"Listen carefully to me." Nelles's tone grew markedly sharper. "General Brock believed that a traitor is working in York garrison. He wanted you to find him."

"I once told him that myself," Westlake replied.

"I'm here to ask what you've discovered since mid-October and the answer is nothing — because you weren't looking." Nelles had raised his voice.

Westlake tucked the letter back inside his jacket. A gust of wind blew up, and Warman sidestepped as the pines swayed around him. Westlake's mind wandered into the ugly thoughts of battle, of killing, conjuring visions that he worked hard to push away.

"I'm sorry, sir, but I don't want to do this agent business anymore." Westlake tapped his chest where the letter rested. "Makes me feel sick in the stomach just thinking about it."

"I can't see you in a redcoat and cap on a drill square." Nelles nodded toward the lake. "When the ice retreats in the early spring, the fighting will recommence with vigour. And now that we've dilly-dallied, there's some bloody urgency in finding Brock's traitor."

"Even if I wanted to, I wouldn't know where to begin, sir." Westlake shrugged. "I'm the wrong man for this job."

"Start with a tavern or, better still, attend church tomorrow... be good for your soul. Either way, see what you can learn." Nelles squinted across the lake to the American shore. "No one in York except your family knows you're officially a lieutenant with the militia, so that's why the general believed that you were in the best position to go nosing around. Read his letter first, then decide. Send me word by Monday morning, no later: yes or no." Nelles demanded. "There is still a question of duty, Lieutenant."

Westlake urged his horse off the crest and back down to the path of hardened snow, Nelles following close behind. As their horses reached the stone house, the oak door swung open to reveal Mrs. Elizabeth Westlake standing on the threshold. Since the news of Brock's death, Westlake had watched his mother's radiance fade. As the weeks passed, her cheeks had shrunk and her normally fine features appeared drawn, and often angry. Lack of sleep had left her appearing worn, so all that remained of her beauty were her striking blue eyes and wavy blond hair. Westlake guessed that her relationship with Brock went deeper than other people knew. Since the great man's death his mother needed a constant diversion, something else to think about.

"Captain Nelles, how good of you to call," she said. "My husband is taking me for a sleigh ride, but you are welcome to stay for a while. You should meet Richard."

"Pleasure to see you again, ma'am, but I was just on my way." Nelles touched his hat in salute to her. "Perhaps another time."

"What are you doing for Christmas dinner?" she asked. "You would be most welcome to spend it with us. We have a number of guests coming."

"I should really —"

"Please, Captain, consider it, for old times sake." Elizabeth peered up at him, seeing here a connection to Isaac Brock. For a moment, a pleading smile lit up her face again.

"Of course, ma'am. I'll be here." The change in her countenance registered a shock in Nelles. "I'm looking forward to it. See you in a week or so, Lieutenant. Ma'am." Nelles touched his hat politely, then nudged his horse down toward the lane.

"It's odd he should ride here all the way from the garrison, only to head off so soon," Elizabeth commented, gazing after him.

Westlake stared at Nelles's retreating back as the officer rode away. "Remember when I was in school … before I got thrown out?" His mother frowned at the thought. To Westlake it felt like a lifetime ago, though it was less than two years previous. "Anyway, you and I often debated religion and politics."

"We had wonderful discussions," Elizabeth agreed.

"But in a serious way." Westlake saw his mother's face grow sombre again. "I need your help once more. Right after your sleigh ride, we'll talk. Just you and I, like before. I have a letter to show you … from a good friend." He gave a slight smile and turned Warman toward the stable.

Elizabeth Westlake stepped down from the sleigh and waved goodbye, as her husband snapped the reins and the horses pulled away.

"I'd like to talk now, Mum, while Father's gone." Westlake stood waiting in Maple Hill's doorway.

"You weren't joking when you said *right after* our sleigh ride. Something must be bothering you." Elizabeth strode into the house, took off her fur cloak, and hung it on the rack.

Westlake closed the door behind her and made his way into the parlour where the fireplace blazed with new light. While she was gone, he had counted the minutes chopping the remainder of the wood. After piling it all in the shed, he had spent the last half-hour staring out the front window, wondering if he would have the nerve to go through with it and actually break the seal.

"I have a letter to show you, one that I'd prefer us to read together." The quicker this conversation began, the less chance of his turning back, of keeping the letter for another day. "On the eve of the battle for Queenston Heights, and of course just before his death, General Brock handed Captain Nelles this letter for me. He'd already put the forces on alert, knowing that a battle was imminent."

Westlake rubbed the paper between his fingers. His mother's face stiffened as she bent over to unlace her boots. She didn't rush herself removing them or taking her seat on the sofa beside him. Her emotions, as always, were kept under strict control, and Westlake knew she expected no less from him. That is not to say that his mother didn't show affection as she now put her arm around his shoulder and gave him a hug. But at the extreme, any public display of feeling, any outbursts, were not considered proper.

Elizabeth sat erect, her hands folded in the lap of her black dress. Her breathing steadied, her eyes drifted down to the page in his hands. She didn't even question why he wanted to read the letter together, which told him that perhaps his guess was right: his mother may well have been in love with Brock.

Westlake slid his thumb under the seal and slit it open. He unfolded the letter, and placed it face up on his knee closest to his mother so they could both read. On seeing the handwriting, his mother drew in a sharp breath.

"Would you like to read it out loud, or should I?"

"Begin." His mother nodded.

Westlake looked at Brock's last written words to the world and started to read.

> *"Dear Mr. Westlake,*
> *Congratulations on your promotion to lieutenant. While you have experienced your difficulties, you've earned this promotion. Remember that, in achieving anything worthwhile, everything is hard; nothing is easy. Life's progress does not run in a straight line. We believe a battle is approaching. This will not be like your individual trials up till now fought mainly in the forest. Stay close to your friends."*

Westlake paused and stared at his mother. He almost heard Brock's confident voice as he read the man's words. "He knew something terrible was coming."

Elizabeth looked away briefly, twisting the fingers in her folded hands. "Pray continue, Jonathan."

Before resuming, Westlake inhaled deeply, like he was climbing a steep hill. He flattened the paper and started reading again.

"You once warned me that you think a traitor is working inside the walls of York garrison. I now have reason to believe that you are correct. After this affair at Niagara is straightened out, and you subsequently return to York, I wish you to find this traitor and bring him to justice. Again, be careful, for my guess is that he does not operate alone.

Yours truly,

Major General Isaac Brock

P. S. Please give my kind regards to your mother, on your return."

His very last words. A traitor in York and a remembrance to his mother. Westlake had delayed receiving Brock's order and now the general spoke to him from the grave bestowing a final mission. At first Elizabeth's face remained impassive, but when a tear rolled down her cheek and grew into a sob, she had to admit the emotion behind it.

"Look at me. Silly." She waved a hand in front of her face, as if she could shoo away her feelings.

"It's not silly if you truly cared for him," Westlake said. "See how he thought of you on the eve of his demise."

Elizabeth stood and marched to a drawer where she withdrew a fresh handkerchief. Her chest rose and fell markedly as she dabbed the tear away. "And what about your traitor?"

Westlake respected her desire to change the subject. "I've told Captain Nelles that I feel sick about this whole agent business. I've decided I'm finished with it and I'll join the ranks of the regular militia, like normal people." The fire had dimmed and Westlake reached down to throw on another half-log. Too many people had already died around him, and just the idea of living a secret life now seemed too great a burden. He wanted to make some new friends and gradually forget about the war. But Brock's letter and Captain Nelles were pulling him back in.

"What would Isaac say to you if he was in this parlour right now?"

Westlake paused, remembering. In his mind, he could see Brock smiling at him, encouraging him on with that infectious confidence.

"He'd remind me how I once told him I wanted to make a difference. He'd talk about protecting my home — about duty and honour — the same stupid things that got him killed." Westlake almost spit out the words, surprising himself at how angrily they left his mouth.

Elizabeth returned to sit beside him. Like she always did, he knew that she was thinking through her arguments, choosing her words carefully, until she looked up into his face. "I agree that there is a foolish type of honour ... rushing in knowing you will probably be killed. But defending one's home entails a different kind of honour, or a duty, if you prefer. There is nothing stupid about that. All *honour* is not the same."

And it had been that easy. Westlake knew he was defeated. He had to defend Maple Hill and his family. He might say no to Nelles, but not to both Brock and his mother. "This is the part where I would tell him that I'll do my best." Westlake smiled at his mother, but that sick feeling in his stomach returned. "He encouraged me to believe that I could do anything, although this time I don't know how to begin."

"You can start by coming with us to church tomorrow."

He laughed. "That's what Captain Nelles advised. Very well." The decision made, he began to fold Brock's letter. "I'm taking Warman for a ride. Get some fresh air and think."

"Can you leave that with me? I'll read it again while you are out, then put it in the top drawer in your room."

Westlake saw the pain in his mother's eyes as she stared down at the letter he held. "I want you to keep it. Please." He thrust the paper into her hands and then clasped them together. "I know how he cared for you."

"Thank you, Jonathan." She gave him a hug. "Now go for your ride and figure out how you can save us all from this damn traitor." Elizabeth slapped a restraining hand over her mouth.

It was the first time in Westlake's life he'd heard his mother swear.

Horse-drawn sleighs rested on the snow surrounding the Episcopal Church in York. Westlake tied Warman to the back of his parents' sled and paused to listen to the muted tones of the parishioners' Christmas carol filling the winter air. On Saturday night his father had gone to bed early after drinking a glass wine in the parlour. Westlake had stayed in front of the fire, slowly consuming the rest of the bottle. Well late for Holy Communion and suffering from a hangover, he dreaded meeting the Reverend Doctor John Strachan again.

The young man ran up the church steps, opened the door, and removed his black wollen hat. The Advent season had brought out a packed congregation in preparation for Christmas. He stood among the crowd at the back while the choir across the front of the church, dressed in white surplices over black cassocks, finished the last bars of "Joy to the World."

Inside the little church, two aisles divided into three sections the rows of eight pews running straight toward the raised alter. Painted grey with brown railings around the top, each row ended with its own little gate. Westlake gazed up at the square windows that threw light across the parishioners dressed in their best Sunday garments. Trying to find a traitor in a church was like thrusting your head into a bushel of apples in the hope of finding the single rotten one.

The Reverend Strachan rose to speak and stepped into the pulpit. He stared out over the congregation and immediately spotted Westlake standing at the rear. "Ah, Mr. Westlake junior has arrived — late," he announced as if he'd caught a criminal. "Come and take your place here at the front in your parents' pew. You've missed communion, but at least you're in time for my second sermon."

Reluctantly, Westlake edged through the parting crowd and headed for the front pew in the centre. His father, Richard, rose and stepped out into the aisle, holding the gate open. In public, Westlake noticed his father always wore his business face, stern and knowing, developed over years of trading in furs. That is until he needed to impress, and then his face changed into a grin, a trader's smile. Now his father stood, looking down the aisle with a pleasant expression, before he stepped aside to allow Westlake to sit between him and Elizabeth.

"I prefer the aisle, sir. Too much travel in wide open spaces, I suppose." Westlake offered his own half-smile. He genuinely hated confinement. Already he found himself tugging at his collar to loosen its grip and wondering how long the sermon would drag on. *This was a bad idea.*

His father stepped back into the family pew. A woman Westlake didn't recognize greeted him with a charming grin from the row behind. Westlake nodded to her and plunked himself down, closing the pew door so that the latch locked him in. *Just what I need, to be confined in a room packed full of firm believers.* A drop of sweat trickled down his spine, and all he could think about was escaping.

"Are we finally ready?" The clergyman stared down at him.

Only twenty-one months ago, Westlake the student at school had suffered the wrath of this same Doctor Strachan. He thought back to his classmates and the laughs they'd had at schoolteacher Strachan's expense. A stern Scot with a broad forehead and dimpled chin, he fancied himself a leader, or if need be a bully … exactly the type of person Westlake despised.

"Open to the Book of Job," Strachan instructed.

The congregation rustled through their Bibles until they found the correct page.

"Why do you suppose we need this story today, so close to Christmas?" Strachan asked his flock. "It's because we are all going to be tested just like Job in the coming weeks. You've heard the rumours, I'm sure. The Americans are coming, and every man here will be counted on to do his duty. Anything less is treason." His black vestments rippled as he shot out an arm, pointing toward the heavens.

"You will defend the Crown, the Church of England, and your home." The Reverend Strachan raised his voice. "Get ready, for like Job, you will feel deprivation and you too will witness death."

"Better not be too many deaths," a man behind Westlake mumbled. "Many hereabouts would rather be Americans."

Richard turned. "Shut up," he ordered. The man went silent. Mounted on the wall at the end of each row, the tapered candles fluttered.

For another twenty minutes, Strachan read out passages from the story of Job; he railed against the Americans, reminding the congregation that all things British were decent and good. The collection basket gradually filled to the brim as it passed up and down the pews. Finally, the service ended with the Lord's Prayer.

"Thanks be to God," the congregation repeated.

"I have one more item of business to announce," Strachan declared. "The ladies of the Loyal and Patriotic Society will now gather at the back for a short meeting. In case you don't know, this Society has sent one hundred and eighty-four flannel shirts, and numerous other items of clothing, to the less fortunate militia based in Niagara. Miss Liz Selby would now like to add a word."

The female greeter sitting in the pew behind Westlake rose. He had not seen Lizzy Selby since his childhood, and the young woman proceeding to the lectern looked nothing like the girl he had once known. Although hardly dazzling in looks, she had grown into a woman of confidence and maturity.

"Good morning," she began. "The Society would first of all like to acknowledge generous donations from two of our most honourable and loyal citizens: Mr. Richard Westlake for one hundred pounds and Major General Sheaffe for two hundred pounds."

Led by the Reverend Strachan, an enthusiastic round of applause and cheering rose up. The clergyman smiled, clapping vigorously, and nodded to Richard Westlake, who rose briefly and bowed his head.

Lizzy continued. "As you may have also heard, the last supply ship delivered bolts of material instead of finished shirts and trousers. The Society is asking for volunteer seamstresses to turn this material into clothing suitable for our fighting men. I'll meet all who are interested at the back of the church presently, and will myself be the first to offer my services. Thank you."

"And I will be the second." Westlake's mother waved her hand as she rose to volunteer. Another ovation followed from the parishioners, and it continued when one after the other, more women stood to present themselves.

"I've just donated a hundred pounds," Richard chided his wife in a whisper. "Isn't that enough from one family?"

"I need to do this, Richard," she replied sternly. "Not just for the common good but also for my own conscience."

Immediately following Lizzy's announcement, Strachan marched down the aisle as if off to battle. Westlake stood quickly and jumped into the aisle behind him, not waiting for the others to parade out. At the door, Strachan turned and with a self-satisfied smile extended an arm ready to shake hands with the departing congregation. He stepped back on seeing Westlake, leaving his hand dangling in the air.

Westlake seized Strachan's hand and shook it vigorously. "Good to see you again, sir."

"Why would that be?" Strachan replied flatly.

"Reminds me of how pleasant my life became after leaving your classroom. Expel all the boys, did you?"

"Just you." Strachan's eyes narrowed.

"Too bad, I thought there were a few others in that school who could think for themselves." Westlake clapped Strachan on the shoulder with his free hand, aware how much this man would like to wring his neck.

"You're still nothing but a troublemaker."

"And you preach the gospels but don't live by them." Westlake spoke softly, as if they were having a pleasant conversation. Strachan tried to step backward, but he was already up against the doorframe.

"I'll see you condemned to hell!" Strachan said in a strained voice, his face flushing red.

"You've done enough scaring for today." Westlake finally let go of his hand. "This story of Job … remember, sir, only the faithful can be tested, so you're preaching to the choir. Go easy on them. Those who are treasonous are already traitors, and they have no loyalty to test." Westlake grinned and strode on toward the sleigh, leaving Strachan with a puzzled frown.

The congregation poured down the church steps onto the snow-covered path where many began tramping homewards. They pulled up their collars and braced themselves arm in arm against the sharp wind. Others pulled away in horse-drawn sleds, leaving behind piles of steaming manure.

The meeting of the Loyal and Patriotic Society lasted only a few minutes. Soon joined by his mother and father, who climbed into the sleigh and sat on the rear bench, Westlake took the reins in hand. He gave a flick and the horses jerked the sleigh forward. *Thank God that's over.*

"What did you say to the Reverend Strachan?" Elizabeth asked. "He looked like he'd been poleaxed."

Westlake turned in his seat. "That traitors are already lost to us and he should go easy on those remaining loyal."

"Be careful around the Reverend Strachan, he wants power and has the friends to give it to him," Richard advised. "Next Sunday, be on time. I don't want any needless trouble."

3

. . . . . .

Prescott, Upper Canada

Lieutenant Colonel George Macdonell stretched his short frame upwards and peered through his telescope trained straight south across the St. Lawrence River, toward Ogdensburg, New York. The brief message he received, scrawled in a sloppy hand, had read: "Boats — early evening — south beach." Another damn raiding party, or perhaps smugglers friendly to the British cause? No one could tell from such an inadequate choice of words.

He snapped the glass shut and cursed. Nothing to see, nothing but the dull grey waves of mid-December.

He'd arranged his anxious redcoats behind a thick curtain of cedars, and now he jerked one arm down. Positioned on the landside of a knoll running the entire length of the Prescott beach, his troop of eight dozen soldiers immediately dropped flat onto to their bellies. Seventy-two Glengarry Light Infantry held the centre, while a dozen Leeds Country Militia jostled for position on each flank, completing a thin defence of some hundred and thirty yards in length.

At the southern end of the line, and just forty paces from the water's stony shore, Macdonell waited with his hands tucked inside his greatcoat. Under a sky the colour of lead, a nasty wind blew hard out of the west and cut cleanly through his clothing to touch his skin. He removed his hat and brushed a hand through his carrot-red hair. He knew the men affectionately called him Red George on account of its colour and that of his bushy eyebrows. Now, Red George prayed that the enemy would show themselves soon before his men half froze to death. The colonel stepped behind a tree, out of sight of any searching eyes over on the American shore.

The United States had declared war on Great Britain in mid-June, and by July the fighting had commenced brutal and furious — but except for a few nuisance raids nothing much on the St. Lawrence River between Kingston and Cornwall where Macdonell patrolled. There, only peace and goodwill could be found between the local residents on either side of the river. They didn't care about Orders in Council or the politics of sovereignty; feeding their families and business trumped any inclination for war. The idea of killing each other seemed ridiculous.

Macdonell fingered the pouch on his belt that held the gold for payment of smuggled goods, and wondered if he'd it need this day.

Vital for the British Army, trade between the Americans and Upper Canadians continued at a similar rate as before the war. The sustenance that kept his men in the field had to continue arriving regularly across the river or the people of Upper and Lower Canada would starve. And, for the Americans, British gold and manufactured goods allowed their farmers to repay the town shops who advanced them credit. Macdonell shivered and kicked at the stones as he thought about this great circle of commerce that disgusted him. Trading with the enemy had swelled into a normal way of life here on the St. Lawrence River, and he was as much a part of that necessary system as any willing accomplice.

"Shouldn't be long now, lads. Be patient," he said. "It's either beef in your own belly or lead in theirs." He scanned along his line of men to the far end, where a militia colonel remained hidden while keeping watch on the river.

Three months previous, led by a tough-minded captain called Benjamin Forsyth and his lieutenant, Abraham Tasker, a company of U.S. riflemen had attacked Gananoque, pillaging the same colonel's residence and burning his storehouse. They'd wounded the man's wife after Tasker had ordered a volley fired at the house. Macdonell wondered how the colonel felt at this very moment, preferring grain from the smugglers for his flourmill, or more likely praying for the raiders to attack again and offering him a chance at revenge on his wife's behalf.

Following that attack on the colonel's compound, the American riflemen had continued their raids along the river, stealing horses at every opportunity. The entire St. Lawrence Valley trading arrangement fell into jeopardy. Macdonell sent word to Captain Forsyth to stop such raids or else the British Army would destroy his headquarters in Ogdensburg and let loose the Indians. Forsyth replied by returning the messenger with a shaved head and the words *"Go to hell,"* written on the man's scalp.

Not for the first time, Macdonell's faced had flushed bright red. Now Red George stood firm against the buffeting wind, hoping that Forsyth would row into his trap. These rotten apples would be crushed so that the honest smugglers could make a decent living. He hoped he'd get his chance but wasn't sure it would be today.

For all the good it would do, he posted signs along the beaches to remind the regular American traders of their arrangement. One such message read IF YOU DON'T SCRATCH, I WON'T BITE! On a sign near Gananoque, young Willie Robertson, the militiaman who fancied himself an artist, painted an American eagle over the word *scratch*, and a British lion under the word *bite*. Macdonell glanced down at the men lying flat out on the knoll, their chins in the grass and reflected that if the raiders attacked today, some of these same men would die.

Robertson half rolled over and raised his head, adjusting his glasses to sit straight on his nose. "Do you think they might bring women with them this time, sir?" the boy asked in his high-pitched voice, a fool's grin covering his face. Only fifteen years old, the spindly lad held the unfortunate distinction of being the youngest soldier in the Leeds County Militia.

Scared stiff and showing off to the adults. Macdonell chuckled, remembering his own first time in battle. Now, some thirty years after the American rebellion, peeing his pants never occurred to him, but his stomach twitched ever the same — like the devil had jumped straight into it to make him puke.

"You wouldn't know what to do with a real women if she sat in your lap, laddie," his sergeant replied as he stood behind the troops. With the butt end of his musket, he nudged Robertson in the back of the head. "Before you give us all away, shut up and keep your head down." A few other men laughed nervously until the sergeant held up a massive fist to threaten the next one who made a noise. Macdonell watched as Robertson shrunk back into the near-frozen grass.

The scudding clouds directly overhead had grown darker, and Macdonell glanced skyward as the first large snowflakes struck his cheek. When he turned his gaze back to the water, the distant movement of oars seemed to wave to him from the river's midpoint. A dozen longboats, packed with men and straining at their oars, rowed toward the shores of Upper Canada. He counted twelve bodies in the first boat, but when they drifted downstream, past his own position, Macdonell wondered if the note had given him the correct beach.

The snow fell ever thicker, slanting horizontal in the fierce wind, then melting as it hit the water's surface. Macdonell's vision grew hazy after a hundred yards into the breath of river, making it near impossible to discern more than the barest outline of the boats. *Let them come. This is what I've been trained to do.* He felt the devil give his stomach that familiar twitch.

"Lieutenant," Macdonell whispered hoarsely against the weather, "pass the word: everyone get up and under the trees." He gestured to the row of cedars behind them. "Fix bayonets, then order each man to put his firing pan beneath his armpit."

The lieutenant looked puzzled so Macdonell continued. "I want the firelocks kept dry. We'll need every available musket spitting lead today."

He stepped up onto the knoll and peered between a couple of cedars, putting a hand above his eyes though it made little difference. Through the big flakes of falling snow, he couldn't distinguish any barges full of supplies trailing the longboats. Soon, he couldn't see a damn thing but snow.

"If they don't carry the grain, it means they're here to kill you," Macdonell declared in a hushed tone, once again pacing along behind the line. "But we have a surprise for them, don't we?" He needn't have whispered. No one could hear anything but the wind in their ears.

He turned next to the lieutenant waiting on his orders. "One volley when they stand up to disembark, but wait for my signal. Then we charge and kill the rest of them still in their boats." With at least a dozen men in each longboat, the enemy easily outnumbered him, but Red George assured himself that surprise and superior British training evened out the odds for victory.

"Sergeant, take a man along with you and make certain that our bloody horses and wagons remain secure." Macdonell again glanced up at the storm. "And be quick, man. I want you back here before the fighting starts."

"Sir." The sergeant shouldered his musket, dragged up a soldier by the collar, then turned and ran toward the train of carts waiting well back from their position.

Macdonell drew his sword. A white blanket of snow had descended on the lake, and for a moment the vessels and their oars completely disappeared. Nothing moved, only the snow. His heart pounded in his chest.

Then the longboats suddenly materialized through the falling blanket, pulling closer with every tug on the oars. He searched for the green uniforms of Forsyth's riflemen, which would confirm that these boats carried the enemy. The snow began to thin and the wind slackened.

"Colonel Macdonell, sir," Robertson squeaked out and then pointed northwards to the far end of the line of longboats. "I see barges."

Macdonell ran his eye along the line of boats, and sure enough, there floated the barges. *Thank God.* As the boats had rowed toward the beach, the barges had drifted on their ropes farther downstream. A quiet cheer rose from the men, and instantly Macdonell ordered silence, but Robertson had spotted what every man there prayed for — barges loaded with grain and live cattle.

"Good eyes, Robertson," Macdonell congratulated him.

"Observation is part of my artistic talent, sir." Robertson grinned, obviously pleased with himself.

"Carts and horses secured, sir," the returning sergeant huffed. His barrel chest rose and fell with every panting word.

"Lieutenant," Macdonell called to his subordinate, "take a dozen men and stand guard at the north end. And be awake for any bloody tricks. I'll be watching here myself."

On seeing the barges, the militia colonel had raced to Macdonell's position for orders. "Your militiamen will assist with loading our carts, Colonel," Macdonell instructed. "Sergeant, bring the smuggler's boss-man to me." He nodded in the direction of the lead boat.

Before fetching the carts, the colonel, dressed in a tailored bear-skin coat, approached Macdonell even closer. A Loyalist, originally from Connecticut, and the richest resident in Gananoque, the colonel owned the flourmill, a blacksmith's workshop, a thriving retail store, and a small lumber mill, all of which extended over an eleven-hundred-acre grant of Crown land. Red George would listen to his protestations if only to appear polite.

"Do you not think I should greet our visitors instead, sir?" the man asked. "After all, I probably know most of them quite well."

"Thank you for your suggestion, Colonel," Macdonell replied and paused.

The man bowed modestly, thinking he'd won his case.

"But the Leeds County Militia needs their leader present to command them and I myself need your sharp eyes for counting the supplies. You will load our carts, as ordered. Make haste to do so, sir, and return the wagons here, if you please."

The colonel said no more but turned and solemnly marched away, shouting orders at his men. Rich and poor alike would do their duty together this day.

The longboats crested in toward the shore and men jumped out to haul the vessels up and onto the stony beach. Then they began the arduous task of reefing in the barges that tugged on their guide ropes, until they too were grounded on the beach. The animals aboard bellowed as the gates swung open and the oarsmen began prodding them off the barges.

The sergeant escorted a pair of tall strangers to where Macdonell watched and waited in the drizzle that followed the snow. Each wore a type of white canvas poncho and held a wide-brimmed hat to his head with one hand. "This is Colonel Macdonell of his Majesty's Glengarry Light Infantry." The sergeant extended his arm to make the formal introduction. "You will show him your papers now, gentlemen."

The more heavy-set man of the two stepped forward and offered his hand. "Joseph Rosseel, sir. Pleasure to make your acquaintance. This is my partner, John Ross." Standing at least a head taller than his host, Rosseel lifted up his poncho, yanked a small leather valise out from under his coat, and handed it to Macdonell. "I'll think you'll find everything in order, sir."

Red George untied the drawstring and took out the sealed single page. He then withdrew from inside his breast pocket a similar sheet of folded paper. He carefully compared its list of contents to the one supplied by Rosseel. "Looks to be in order, gentlemen." Macdonell gave them a thin smile.

"There is the matter of payment, sir." Rosseel stepped forward, aggressively looming over Macdonell.

"Now why would I trust a smuggler to deliver all the goods he claims?" Macdonell demanded. "You betray your own government, so why wouldn't you cheat me?"

"You offend too much, Colonel." Rosseel raised his voice, the steam from his breath almost touching Macdonell's face. "My employer would never short-ship a paying customer."

This man thinks he can bully me, Macdonell decided.

Red George quickly stepped back, unsheathed his sword, and held the tip to Rosseel's throat. "And your employer is … ?"

The sergeant slowly lowered his musket to point at the chest of Ross, who stood perfectly still.

"You know very well who you are dealing with." Rosseel tilted his head away from the sword and mumbled two names. He squealed, trying to retreat, but the colonel kept the sword's point to his neck.

"Of course I know them both." Macdonell laughed. "Stay just where you are." He sheathed his sword with a sliding snap. "Now let's see if your barrel count is accurate. Only then will I hand over to you the King's gold and your wagonloads of teapots. God knows what you plan to do with them all."

Could there be honour in trading with one's enemy? Macdonell prayed for a truthful count.

The militia colonel arrived next with the creaking wagons. Fearing the ruts on the beach, he arranged the column of vehicles parallel to the treeline and allowed a narrow gap just wide enough for the groaning cattle to be herded through. While smugglers rolled barrels across the pebbled beach and then lifted each of them onto the wagons with a thud, militiamen lugged crates of teapots packed in straw to the barges. Boatmen worked alongside the militiamen as the barges and wagons were emptied and then began to fill again.

"Sergeant, tell the good Colonel to wave if his numbers agree with these." Macdonell handed the sergeant the single sheet.

"Sir." The sergeant saluted and ran off to the colonel.

Macdonell surveyed the transfer of supplies as the loading continued apace. *Almost finished. Don't lose any time.* "You may sound the recall, Bugler," he ordered. At the bugle's sharp signal, the dozen redcoats guarding the north end of the beach, began marching south.

"You were expecting visitors other than us, sir?" Rosseel asked.

"Your Green friends, perhaps," replied Macdonell.

"No friends of ours, sir — common thugs more like. Bastards would kill us for trading with the British and then strip our homes of everything we owned." Rosseel peered down the beach to where the militia colonel continued counting with a finger outstretched. "Captain Forsyth is recalled to Sackets Harbor, for now, but when he and his damn officers return you can bet your life they'll start their raiding again, serious like."

"So no raids on Prescott for the time being?" Macdonell inquired.

"I myself watched them marching away this morning." Rosseel looked to Ross, who nodded in confirmation.

Macdonell squinted as the colonel gave an expansive wave with his arm, and a thumb up still holding the single sheet of paper in one hand.

"Thank you for that, Mr. Rosseel," Macdonell said. He handed over the pouch of gold. Ross produced yet another valise, only this time thicker and obviously holding a number of pages.

"Been our pleasure, sir," Ross said. "The contents of this are intended for the addressee's eyes only." He offered his hand and Macdonell shook it. "Goodbye."

"Good day, gentlemen. Until the next time." Macdonell nodded and then spoke quietly to his lieutenant. "You will escort two of the wagons, along with twelve men, to Prescott, and I will take the rest with me to Kingston. Their boats may have been followed, so get moving. I want this area cleared in minutes."

"Sir." The lieutenant saluted and hurried off to carry out his new orders.

The militia colonel appeared particularly pleased with himself, as most of the grain was destined for his own mill in Gananoque. Everyone seemed to be making money out of this war. Red George placed a foot in one stirrup, then swung his leg over the saddle. He sat up straight, circled his hand in the air, and pointed south, the signal to move out. The bugler sounded out the order to the assembled troops.

After waiting there briefly, Macdonell gave a deep sigh and stared down the empty beach that had been crowded with activity only moments ago. He imagined the battle that never happened: the volley of shots erupting through the cedars, the gun smoke burning the back of his throat, the charge across the slippery pebbles ... and then the killing. They'd been lucky this time, but he remained feeling cheated, perhaps even somewhat disappointed. *You can bet your life they'll start raiding again, serious like.* Rosseel's words stayed with him, as if hanging in the frosted air. He'd get his chance soon enough at bloody Forsyth and his Greens, and the delay wouldn't kill him.

The boats had now pushed off, towing their full barges behind them. Slowly they disappeared amid the returning snowflakes. He glanced down at the heavy valise in his hands and wondered what might be inside. Inscribed right into the smooth leather was a notation.

Contents Secret
Deliver to York Garrison
Compliments to Captain Edward Nelles:
For your eyes only.

Printed in a confident hand, the inscription might as well of told him to mind his own business. He'd never heard of any Captain Nelles but wished him luck in this disgusting game of cat and mouse. Red George spurred his horse on toward Kingston, wondering how long it would be before Forsyth returned.

At the entrance to the Jordan Hotel, an old man dressed in tattered clothing held his hand up but stared at the ground. Westlake peered to one side to get a better look at the haggard face.

"Mr. Forbes?" Westlake observed. "The drink's got you again."

The man looked up and studied his face. "God save me! It's young Master Westlake all grown up now."

"Look at your clothes. Come in out of the cold." Westlake lifted the old man under the arm and guided him into the hotel. An old sailor thrown up on the beach, as Westlake's mother had once described him, Forbsy had been the town drunk for as long as Westlake could remember. They made their way to the bar, where welcoming candles burned at each end.

"Stables don't need cleaning yet, Forbsy," the barman said. He wiped the bar in a sweep with a grey rag. "Out you go."

"A very hot tea for Mr. Forbes." Westlake slapped a coin on the counter. Forbes gazed at him with sad eyes. "And a single glass of wine, sir?"

Westlake added two more coins to the first.

"God bless you, sir." Forbes used both his hands to grip Westlake's in a vigorous shake.

"Drink it slowly and get warm, Mr. Forbes." Westlake turned around to find a seat in the barroom.

The Jordan Hotel regularly spread fresh straw on the dirt floor to soak up any damp and to keep the establishment clean. A fireplace crackled at the far end of the room, so Westlake chose a table with a bench near the hearth, to keep warm. Tall candles flickered on every occupied table. He passed by four men huddled together at the centre table and heard the word *redcoats* spit out of one man's mouth, before silence quickly descended.

A slender barmaid with a wooden tray soon approached and asked his pleasure. Her low-cut dress, trimmed in a loose white lace, had Westlake thinking of more than just beer. He cleared his throat. "Good afternoon, ma'am. Just a pint of your best, if you please."

The barmaid smirked. "Oh, aren't we respectful like," she said, then turned and sauntered back to the bar, swaying her hips with each step.

Westlake felt the warmth of the fire on his back. The straw rustled under his feet as he stretched to better view the bar's interior. A few well-dressed patrons drifted in, preferring to stand at the counter rather than take a seat. One of them raised a hand to the bartender and proceeded to order a round of ales for himself and his friends.

The barmaid returned to place his beer on the table. She smiled, fluttering her eyelashes over large brown eyes, then held out her hand.

Westlake put the coins in her palm and then added another. "And that's for you, ma'am, thank you."

"A gentleman, I do perceive." She stared down at the amount in her hand and her eyes widened. "Blond hair and blue eyes, to boot. Thank you, good sir."

Westlake caught the hint of a Scottish accent. "You're most welcome," he said. "It can't be easy for a pretty girl to work in a place like this."

"You're pulling my leg, you are. No one calls me pretty unless they want something from me. You can just paddle down a different stream, you can."

"I see you're also smart." Westlake laughed and leaned back before taking a sip of his beer. "Actually," he lowered his voice, "I want to know who are those men in the middle of the room. Don't look."

Westlake had reached for her hand and held it softly in his. Too late, she had turned to look at the four men before hearing his last words. They stopped talking again and glared at her.

"My, my, I've forgotten what it's like to have a gentleman hold my hand." She peered down at her hand in his and smiled sadly. "The little man's named Elias Hendrickson," she said quietly. "And they call his big friend Archer. You can keep the pair of them, for my liking. Anyway, I don't know the other two."

"Thank you," Westlake replied, grinning. "You're an angel."

"Be careful with that lot. They'll mess up those lovely white teeth of yours." She turned and strolled off to the next table.

The tavern began to fill quickly until customers occupied all the tables. Three men jostled their way through the crowd searching for an empty bench, and seeing Westlake at a table on his own, they sat down without invitation. The fire sparked and an ember landed on the floor. As the straw began to smoulder, the large man seated closest to the fire casually stamped on it.

These fellows didn't look as desperate as Archer and his friends, but Westlake's body tensed and he checked for the knife carried inside his boot. Satisfied, he took a sip of beer.

"You don't mind us sitting with ye?" The broad-shouldered man scratched at his thick neck, the Scottish accent betraying his birthplace like so many others in York. He leaned forward almost threateningly, and the others did the same.

"Is there any reason I should object?" Westlake shrugged. "Something maybe you need to tell me."

"We cramped your table without asking 'cause we're feeling what's known as disgruntled," said another in the same accent. He brushed back some curly brown hair with one hand and scowled.

"Yes, disgruntled, that's me," said the third man. "Sounds good, but what the hell does it mean?" He frowned and looked to his friend for an answer.

"It means you're unhappy," Westlake interjected, "and you think you can therefore be rude. Why are you unhappy, gentlemen?"

The three men looked at one another, and Westlake wondered if they were about to set upon him. "My schoolteacher was a Scotsman," he blurted.

"Educated, are you? And you think if you're friends with a Scotsman in these parts, it'll save you," said the big man.

"I don't need saving." From under the table he drew his knife with its broad foot-long blade and pointed it at the big man beside him. "And that miserable teacher wasn't my friend."

"Christ, young laddie, we're just joshing with ye." The curly-haired man grimaced. "We're homesteaders, not killers!" The men leaned back as the barmaid brought their tankards of beer.

"Is there going to be trouble?" She'd spotted the knife and nodded in the direction of the counter. "The proprietor keeps a loaded musket back there."

"No trouble," Westlake said. "These men were just about to tell me why they're so unhappy."

"Pay up, first." The barmaid held out her hand and each man placed a coin in it before she turned away. They watched her hips as she moved to the next table.

"Well, you're disgruntled," Westlake said. "Why?"

"Farm implements," the big man replied straight away. "The Crown promised farm implements along with the provision of our land."

"But they hold on to them for their friends, instead of distributing them to deserving settlers like ourselves," said the man with the curly hair. "Do you farm? We don't even know your name."

"I'm in the fur trade … not a farmer," Westlake replied. "But I don't understand. Who holds them?" He reached under the table and slid the knife back into its sheath.

"The Reverend Strachan and his committees won't distribute them like it was promised," another man continued. "I know the warehouse … if the Americans invade, it'll be the first place I show 'em."

"Christ, keep your voice down," Westlake said in a harsh whisper. He lifted the beer mug to his lips. "That's treason talk, man."

"And that's on top of the Clergy Reserves, which drives everyone crazy." The big man finished and took a sip of his own beer. "The church keeps the best land for itself."

Most citizens willing to brave condemnation by the church had complained about the unfair practice of reserving one-seventh of all land for the Anglican Church. In the centre of York, great fields of rich farmland lay fallow, pushing farmers farther away and on to less arable land. Westlake had heard such dissatisfaction expressed throughout his entire life.

The three farmers raised their tankards and nodded to one another: "Cheers." They slurped down some beer, then slapped their tankards on the table as the man with the thick neck continued quietly. "No need to worry in here, mister. Every man jack of us has a grievance of some kind." He swung his mug around at the room like a man at a family gathering. "See those men up at the counter … building that new ship in the harbour, they are. Well, the *Sir Isaac Brock* ain't ever gonna be built."

Westlake turned slightly to see seven well-dressed men in animated conversation over tankards of ale. Four friends had joined the first three. They kept waving their hands about and didn't seem to care who knew what they discussed.

"They haven't been paid on time, so they've withdrawn their services. Do you know the new dockyard storekeeper, Superintendent Thomas Plucknett?"

Westlake shook his head.

"Can't organize his shoes, that one. Rumour is they'll burn the ship down if they don't get their money … and soon."

"Are they not loyal to the Crown?" Westlake asked. He began to wonder if anyone in the room was genuinely faithful.

"Loyalty! Don't speak of loyalty to me. I'm devoted to my stomach first." The big man nodded to the room. "I have a wife and child to feed, like most here."

"Two months ago, men much like yourselves died at Queenston Heights so we could enjoy this pleasant conversation," Westlake said and took a drink from his mug. "I would hate to think —"

"That they died for nothing," the curly-head interjected. "I agree, but the militia best ask themselves what they're fighting for: the Crown or —"

"For themselves. They fight for each other, just like you do," Westlake said, remembering the frightened faces, the musket fire, and the groans of the dying. He began to feel his anger of that day returning. "Not for the Crown," he added with determination, "but for their own homes, and because the soldier standing next to you is ready to give his life. If the enemy does invade, it will not be as pleasant as you imagine."

The man laughed. "Do you think the Americans will come and we'll get those implements?"

Westlake downed the last of his beer. The barmaid had disappeared and so had Hendrickson, Archer, and their two friends. "We're at war, so what do you think?" He stood to leave.

"They're coming," the man insisted.

Westlake shrugged.

Outside, in the fading afternoon light, Westlake stood on the hotel's porch, the crisp air freezing the moisture in his nostrils. Good men whose talk bordered on treason, the farmers had departed angry and confused. The Reverend Strachan's fierce loyalty was clearly driving men into the arms of the enemy. He reached into the pockets of his fur overcoat for his gloves, but before pulling them on, he heard a voice cry out from around one side of the hotel. Gloves still in hand, he ran toward the noise.

The barmaid lay on the snow with the four men from the bar's centre table standing over her. She was covering her head with both hands in anticipation of the next blow.

"Stop!" Westlake shouted and stepped forward.

"Look what we have here. Just the man we need to talk to." Hendrickson, the little man with bushy eyebrows, gestured to one of his partners to move up beside the intruder. Westlake noticed the thug's reddened fist and the pair of pistols tucked into his belt. He had been the one to strike the girl.

"We're going to beat you senseless unless you tell us why you're going round asking questions." Hendrickson grinned, arching his thick eyebrows to form a couple of up-side-down Vs.

His friend Archer cleared phlegm from his throat and spit.

Already angered by his encounter with the farmers, Westlake's heart quickened as he tried to keep his rage under control. "But there's only four of you." He chuckled. "So I hope those pistols of yours are loaded."

"Of course, you idiot," the man snarled, "and any one of us alone could wipe those pretty-boy looks off your face."

Westlake made to reach down to help the young woman to her feet. He tossed his gloves in the air. The man beside him glanced at the flying gloves. Westlake grabbed onto the nearest pistol and pressed the trigger. The weapon exploded in the thug's pants, sending a ball through his thigh. Before the man could collapse, Westlake twisted the second pistol on his friend and squeezed the trigger.

Both men collapsed, groaning on the ground in seconds. Each pistol shot had sounded like a cannon echoing between the close-set buildings. Westlake yanked the barmaid off the snow and drew her behind him. He glanced around to see Hendrickson standing with his mouth open, while Archer, his square features contorted, was tearing at his own overcoat, presumably to uncover a weapon.

From his boot, Westlake casually extracted the knife. "Stand still or I'll kill you both right now."

The men froze in position, reaching their hands out to either side. Their friends on the ground writhed in pain, squirming to clutch their legs in a vain effort to stem the flow of blood.

"You'll leave this woman alone from now on or I'll hunt each of you down and kill you, one at a time." Hearing his own voice, Westlake surprised himself at how frightening it sounded. His deep breaths blew a white mist as he brandished the knife level with their throats. He backed away slowly after the men nodded in turn. "Don't let me hear otherwise. Now, get."

Hendrickson glanced at the two men still writing on the ground. "Leave 'em be," Westlake ordered.

Hendrickson grabbed Archer by the arm and the two of them ran to their horses. Meanwhile the other patrons came running out of the hotel entrance. "We'll be back for you, girl," Archer growled as his horse galloped by.

Westlake picked up his gloves, then supported the girl by the arm as they made their way through the crowd and back toward the bar. "I think some fool had his pistols go off in his pants," he remarked to the first man. "Shot himself *and* his friend." He chuckled and kept walking.

Once inside the tavern, Westlake turned to the barmaid. "Feeling better, I hope."

"My whole head hurts, but I'll live. I need to sit down." She touched her bruised cheek and glanced up the stairs. "I have a room."

"I'll help you." Westlake began to ascend the steps.

"No customers allowed upstairs," the barman shouted, reaching for his musket. "That's not the house I run here."

"If you even touch that weapon, you'd best be prepared to use it," Westlake hissed before marching up.

"Five minutes," yelled the barman. "That's all — just five." The returning customers stood and stared at Westlake and the girl.

Once inside the barmaid's room hidden at the end of the hall, Westlake sat the girl down gently on the bed. The walls were unfinished, showing the exterior logs with wind blowing through the cracks. Clearly this room was not considered suitable for hotel patrons. He took a chair from a small table, twisted it around to face her and sat himself down.

"Why on earth would you risk going outside with men like them?" he demanded.

The girl's rounded chin began to tremble, and Westlake guessed at the fear underneath.

"You warned *me* yourself how nasty they were," he continued.

"Archer claimed he needed just to ask me a few questions in private." The girl pleaded, before looking away. "They saw me talking to you and wanted to know what you asked about. They planned to wait outside in the alley for you."

"Then why not just wait for me? They didn't need you for that." Westlake frowned and shook his head. "No. They wanted you for something else as well. I can't help you unless you tell me more. Remember, they'll be back; Archer said so himself." Westlake stood to leave before the barman began to get suspicious.

"It's best you don't get involved. I can take care of myself." The girl put her hands to her face and sobbed.

"You're joking. I've just lamed two of them and you tell me not to get involved." He opened the door to leave. "What's your name anyway?"

She wiped the tears off her cheeks and reached down to rub at each knee nervously. "Lucy Dunbar." She tried to smile.

"Please to meet you, Miss Dunbar, my name is Jonathan Westlake." He smiled and studied this woman on the bed, now rocking back and forth as she continued to rub her knees. She appeared so alone. "They won't be back tonight, I reckon, so you're safe ... for the time being. Get some rest now and I'll be back to see you as soon as I can." He closed the door and listened to the soft sound of her weeping.

4
• • • • • •

THE AROMA OF ROAST GOOSE wafting through the family's stone house on Maple Hill made Christmas Eve Jonathan Westlake's favourite night of the year. The fireplace crackled with burning logs and lit the parlour in a shimmering light. In the dining room, a green wreath surrounded the candelabra holding three tapered candles that rested in the centre of a white linen-covered table. The entire atmosphere served to wrap him up in a blanket of warmth and goodwill.

Westlake fidgeted with the fire, knowing that Captain Nelles would soon be joining them. His father, dressed in waistcoat and neckcloth, stood by the hearth rubbing his bony hands together. He'd been away on the Continent for more than a year, like so many times in the past, arranging the sale of furs in London and Paris. On his return in early November, Westlake noticed how his black hair had begun to turn grey above the ears. The man was growing older, but he still remained thin and hard. If he loved his family, it never showed in an affectionate way.

Westlake wondered about his own feelings for his father. He hardly knew him but more than anything wanted his respect. As if the stern man could read his mind, Richard began, "I read the long version of your report. Of course, it's almost a year old now, but your assessment of the situation in the old northwest has turned out to be precisely correct." His father then nodded. "You should be proud of that report. Seems getting tossed out of the Reverend Strachan's school didn't do you much harm at all."

Westlake grinned in appreciation.

He recalled the image of his teacher standing outside the school door with cane in hand. Strachan's black robes had flapped in the

47

wind as he raised his voice to permanently expel the troublemaker from his school. With idle time on his hands, Westlake had proposed to his father a scouting expedition to Ohio and Illinois, to be followed up by a written report on conditions there in the fur trade. With his parents reluctant agreement, he'd set out full of energy and anticipation and not yet sixteen years old.

Westlake's mind drifted to his happy times among the Shawnee and the fur traders. He chuckled on remembering the things they had taught him — riding bareback, trapping, and combat – the best time of his life.

His report detailed the conditions of the powder keg ready to explode in the northwest. The Americans were trying to shut out the Canadian fur traders, and the Indians would fight to the death to keep their land. They had little or no choice; without land, the natives had no place else to hunt for food. No land meant certain starvation.

"I knew before you departed they'd all be fighting for their miserable livelihoods," Richard said. "The Americans and British just want that territory for expansion, but take away an Indian's land and he starves. Of course" — he paused and looked directly at Westlake — "we still need the furs. Just be careful the work you do for the damn redcoats doesn't get you killed."

"Their aim is to *protect* Upper Canada." Westlake moved over to the front window and spotted Captain Nelles approaching on horseback.

"Believe me, the more we antagonize the Americans, the worse it will become for us." His father continued, "We, — you and I both — need your Indian friends to continue bringing us furs. That's who you should be befriending — *for the furs*. This is our business."

Before Nelles could knock, Westlake opened the door and stepped outside to join him in the fresh air. The smell of smoke from the fireplace reached his nostrils and he inhaled deeply. Arguing with his father inevitably caused unwanted tension. Joseph, the stable hand, came and led Nelles's horse away.

"An indoor fire always smells better outside than in." Nelles laughed. "Merry Christmas! How are you, young man?"

"Beautiful night for a Christmas Eve." Westlake stared up at a night sky packed with stars, then reached out to shake Nelles's hand. "Merry Christmas to you too, sir." He glanced up once again at the heavens and took a step closer to Nelles. "Please remember that my father doesn't entirely support this war," he said in low voice. "I only hope we can get through dinner tonight without a blowup."

"Perhaps this will cheer him." Nelles brandished a bottle of red wine. "A generous gift from General Brock's wine collection. I thought I'd share it with you all and we could raise a toast to him."

Westlake's smile instantly faded.

"Come on, young man, we can't mope about the man's death forever. He wouldn't want that. Just be happy you knew him. Besides, now that you're with us again, I have a small assignment to assist you on your greater mission!"

Westlake's chest tensed at the announcement and he supposed it showed.

"It's not for conversation now," Nelles continued. "Later, after the Christmas week is over. Tonight, let's celebrate the birth of our saviour."

Westlake opened the door just as his father arrived on the other side. "Step in out of the cold, sir," he invited before turning to his father. "This is Captain Edward Nelles," he explained. "My father, Richard Westlake."

After shaking hands, Richard took a step back, his face impassive.

Westlake hung Nelles's greatcoat on the rack. In his captain's dress uniform of red and gold, Nelles made an imposing sight. His long and narrow head, retained an erect bearing that told any observer this was a man not to be trifled with. Westlake supposed that his many days spent working with Brock had instilled a seriousness of purpose on the man's character and countenance. Brock's man, indeed.

"Welcome to Maple Hill, Captain. And Merry Christmas to you." Richard beckoned him forward. "Join us in the parlour for a drink."

"Thank you, I can smell the apples cooking. Wonderful!" Nelles exclaimed.

Westlake was relieved. All day he had dreaded the meeting between these two men. Now, his father seemed genuinely pleased enough to entertain this visitor from the British military.

Westlake's mother entered the room with a silver tray carrying glasses, each of them filled with red wine. He remembered seeing her wearing the same dress, for a dance she attended with General Brock almost a year previous. The deep-blue gown with ruffled cuffs and bunched shoulders was otherwise plain, but when combined with the single strand of pearls about his mother's slender neck, the effect was stunning. At least for tonight, the sadness resulting from Brock's death had vanished from around her eyes. Now they shone as piercing blue as ever before.

Westlake was sure he heard Nelles catch his breath.

"So nice of you to join us for Christmas Eve, Captain. Please take a glass."

Westlake picked up two of the glasses and handed one to his guest.

"Thank you, ma'am, my pleasure." Nelles held the glass up to his nose. "Lovely. Medicinal you know ... does wonders fighting off the damp." He laughed.

"The kitchen needs my assistance if you'll excuse me," said Elizabeth as she left the room.

Westlake put the glass to his lips and let the wine slip down his throat. Perhaps the evening would be joyous as planned. He held out an inviting hand, to draw Nelles toward the fireplace.

When Elizabeth had departed the room, Nelles immediately turned to Richard. "Major General Sheaffe sends you his kind respects, sir." He bowed politely. "He particularly apologizes for the great loss of your furs in that Buffalo warehouse — especially after you provided such valuable intelligence on the enemy. Alas, our artillery was poorly sighted."

"You're acting as a spy for the army!" Westlake exclaimed in astonishment. He'd always assumed his father opposed the war.

"We have people in Westlake Trading operating on the other side of the water who hear things. I pass that information on to Captain Nelles." His father shrugged. "That hardly makes me a spy." He took another sip from his glass. "And I'm still against the war, all wars, as everyone of any sense should be, but that doesn't mean a man shouldn't help out wherever he can be of use."

Westlake had heard of U.S. raiding parties near Fort Erie and the British bombardment of Buffalo, but he had no idea that his father had used his trading company to spy for the British Army. The news made him question his own judgment: did he really know what was going on in Upper Canada?

Elizabeth re-entered the room with a comment on the unusually heavy snows. A safe conversation about the weather ensued for several minutes, until a servant girl entered the parlour and whispered something in the hostess's ear before disappearing back toward the kitchen.

"Dinner is served, gentlemen," Elizabeth announced, smiling.

As head of the household, Westlake's father sat at one end of the table made for eight. His mother occupied the other end while Westlake sat directly across from Nelles. The candles in the table's centre wavered until everyone settled in their chairs. Richard then said a short grace, and with the clink of cutlery, the entire party began to eat.

"This is wonderful, thank you," Nelles commented after several mouthfuls.

"It's very nice to be home," Richard said. "Wretched weather held up my Atlantic crossing a good two weeks. I see the new ship they're building in the dockyard is taking its sweet time. In church there was grumbling about some of the men not being paid on time."

"I visited the quay yesterday morning," Nelles added. "All too chaotic for my liking. It's obvious the *Sir Isaac Brock* will never be ready for a spring launch if they don't shift themselves sharply. That could have tragic consequences for our fleet."

For a time the conversation paused while the party concentrated on eating. Westlake realized in that moment his own home could become a plum target for the enemy. After the servant girl cleared away the empty dinner plates, Elizabeth arrived next with the pudding and began serving out the generous portions.

"I should tell you, sir, that not all the grumbling is confined to the new ship's construction." Westlake took up the conversation where Nelles had left off. "Local residents complain about other issues too."

"Such as?" Richard inquired as he dug into his pudding.

"The distribution of farm implements is favouring only a select few," Westlake replied. "And the Clergy Reserves lie fallow, yet they contain the best farmlands. It's the total control of everything by the Reverend Strachan and his cronies that is making men angry."

"How widespread is this discontent?" Captain Nelles asked.

Elizabeth interjected, "Surely not everyone is unhappy."

"They're mostly just complainers," Westlake said, "Perhaps some might turn traitor if given the opportunity, but it's impossible to judge."

The servant girl carried in the opened bottle of wine Nelles had brought and set it down in front of him. He proceeded to pour it into four fresh glasses for distribution around the table.

"Let's have a toast now, shall we," he announced. "To a man who never failed to do his duty. To Sir Isaac Brock."

Westlake looked to his father, who took a sip. His mother's expression had turned sullen as she put her glass to her lips. A few more toasts were proposed, but Elizabeth went strangely quiet.

"Perhaps we could retire to the parlour and enjoy the warmth of the fireplace," Richard suggested.

Westlake and Nelles rose from their chairs, as Elizabeth suddenly added, "I have a Christmas present for you there, Captain." Finally a tiny half-smile returned to light her face.

Westlake followed Nelles to stand in front of the fireplace. "I'm afraid I have only brought the wine," Nelles confessed.

"Your presence is gift enough," replied Elizabeth. "I knitted this for you myself." She handed Nelles a dark blue scarf, tied around with a red bow. "Merry Christmas to you and thank you for coming." She stepped forward, and gripping each of his arms, kissed him on the cheek.

"My goodness, this is a merry Christmas indeed." Nelles had flushed red. "Thank you, ma'am, but I suppose I should be pushing off," he continued. "I've a chilly ride ahead, back to Government House.

"I'll come out to the stable with you," Westlake said, handing Nelles his coat, then grabbing his own.

Nelles turned back. "Mr. Westlake, it's been a pleasure. Thank you for your kind hospitality. Merry Christmas."

"Same to you, sir," Richard replied, offering his hand.

Westlake and Nelles passed through the front door out into the crisp night air. A heaven packed with stars and a bright moon over York lit the rutted path leading to the stable. Westlake sighed in relief. "That went much, much better than I expected between you and my father, sir." The horses stepped nervously in their stalls at the sound of visitors.

Nelles winced. "In a way, he has a right to be angry at us." He placed a blanket over his horse before Westlake heaved on the saddle. "We managed to blow up his furs after he'd provided the very date and time of the American raid — and, I should add, at great risk."

The thought of his father acting as an agent had completely shocked Westlake's senses. He never imagined the man indulging in skulduggery for the British Army. His mother would be proud.

Westlake cinched a leather strap tightly in place before Nelles mounted up. "Are you going to say what task you have for me, sir? My own search for this traitor has me suspecting every single person in York."

"First, enjoy your Christmas week and do the rounds of the taverns for me," Nelles replied. "My courier has not arrived yet, but come to the garrison the third day of the New Year. I should know the details by then."

"Merry Christmas, sir." Westlake reached up and they shook hands. "January third, then. For a new beginning."

"Merry Christmas, Mr. Westlake, and thank your mother again for a lovely dinner." Nelles gently kneed his horse and it trotted off down the hill in the moonlight, leaving Westlake wondering where this assignment might take him.

Once Christmas was over, time passed slowly for Westlake. For the first couple of days, regular snowfalls kept him and the stable hand digging outward from the doorstep. The path cleared to the outbuildings, his father asked him to ready the sleigh. They set off travelling a little-used trail that led northeast from Maple Hill, and as a consequence, the horse pulled knee-deep in powder snow.

"I have a little surprise for you," Richard declared. "When we reach the Don River, head south a ways. Our destination is that new sawmill owned by Mr. Alex McMullen."

Westlake listened to the wind whistling through the maple trees as it bit into his face. The family sleigh dashed over the snow's surface, and he pointed out where a herd of deer had crossed their path. "I suppose you won't tell me the surprise until we get there?"

"Sometimes you are so insightful." His father laughed, and Westlake laughed along with him: father and son finally doing something together. Westlake felt like he was part of some great outing, or a close family enterprise. He turned the sled south onto the path that followed alongside the Don River. A few minutes later, they stopped in front of a building constructed only the previous spring.

"Behold, the McMullen sawmill ... but now the Westlake mill!" Richard announced. "We are moving away from furs and into the lumber business."

"When did you do this?" Westlake asked in amazement. "You've only been back home a month!"

"I had a rough tour selling our furs in Europe this past trip," Richard replied. "So I thought I'd cash in some of the furs and diversify." He gestured up the lane. "Here comes Mr. McMullen himself."

A middle-aged man marched toward the sleigh followed by a red-coated officer that Westlake had once met in Niagara. Major James Givens, assistant superintendent in the Indian Department, was a robust man and this morning he looked like a fellow in a hurry.

"Good morning, gentlemen." McMullen's wind-beaten face smiled like he'd just caught a fish. "Welcome to your new mill. This is Major Givens, who has just informed me that for the defence of the town I've been made up to lieutenant in the 3rd York Militia." His chest swelled and he almost came to attention.

Westlake jumped down out of the sleigh. "Hello again, Major Givens. This is my father." All the men shook hands with one another in turn.

"Congratulations, on your promotion, Mr. McMullen," Richard said, "though I doubt the Americans will come here. Major Givens, you've met my son?"

"Another time, another place, sir," Givens replied. "But don't be so sure the enemy will forget about us. York is the capital after all and there is the matter of the half-built *Sir Isaac Brock*."

"Then let's hope our ships sink theirs first," Richard added.

"That's the spirit," Givens said. "You'll have to excuse me, gentlemen. I should be off to see my Ojibwa friends. Pleasure meeting you both."

McMullen stepped forward. "Unless you need me, I came simply to hand over the key and to welcome you." McMullen put the key in Richard's hand. "It seems being a lieutenant entails extra responsibilities."

Lieutenant Westlake thought about his own recent activities and wondered what McMullen referred to. He was about ask when McMullen turned and waved farewell as he walked away.

"Pleasure doing business with you, Mr. Westlake," McMullen called out. "You've paid a fair price for the mill, of that you can be sure."

"I may need your assistance as I begin the operation," Richard shouted.

McMullen either didn't hear or purposefully kept walking. The major and the new lieutenant mounted their horses and made their way toward town.

"That was over fast," commented Westlake.

His father walked to the mill's front entrance, slid the key into the lock and opened the door. Even in the winter, without the saws running, the expansive interior smelled of fresh-cut wood. Built on a hill beside the Don, the mill drew its power from the river where its water narrowed and plunged downwards, increasing its speed. "A three-foot drop of water will give you seventy cuts a minute," Richard explained. "These are all new Sheffield blades and gears. The whole place cost me fifteen hundred dollars so that bandit made off with a profit of three hundred."

Westlake stared at the huge saw blades resting idle, and the logs piled on the floor waiting to be cut. He glanced out the front window to see Givens and McMullen riding off downhill toward York. "Why did Mr. McMullen decide to sell?" he asked.

"When the water flows heavy in the spring, this mill cuts lumber for the construction of warships." Richard lowered his voice. "McMullen thinks the Americans will burn it down if they invade. Worries too much about the risk." Richard gestured him toward the stairs leading to the floor below, and they descended.

"The water-wheel drives these huge gears, which in turn pull the belts that spin the blades." His father pointed out the workings of the machinery. "A customer brings twenty logs in the spring, we charge him two dollars per thousand feet, and he leaves ten logs behind for the mill. Twelve inches square is standard building timber." His father clearly had every figure in head as if he'd been in this business for years. "Now, if the customer is the government, we charge six dollars per thousand feet. That's where there's real money to be made."

The men exited at a back door of the basement where a feeble latch was all that held it in place. "I should install a lock," Richard commented as they struggled up the narrow path between the river and the building. Once seated in the sleigh and on the way home, Westlake's father began spouting numbers again. Floorboards were cut two inches thick while roofboard ran to an inch and a quarter, all in twenty-foot lengths. In York, new houses were constructed with post-and-beam framing, so the mill would work constantly during the months when the Don River flowed at its height.

"The river's deep and fast above the mill but widens and runs shallow just below," Richard added.

"Have you told mother yet?" Westlake asked him.

"I only got the key a few minutes ago, and I thought you and I would do this together. When the wind dies down and the weather warms, I'll bring your mum over to see it."

"Mr. McMullen could be right." Westlake warned. "The Americans might burn it down."

"General Sheaffe thinks they are more likely to hit Kingston than York. Besides, there's pressure for launching an attack on Sackets Harbor before the enemy fleet breaks out of the ice."

"If I've learned one thing about war, it's that no one can ever be sure what might happen," Westlake replied.

The following day, Westlake decided to pay another visit to the Jordan Hotel and speak to Lucy Dunbar, as he had promised. He tensed slightly as he opened his dresser drawer to find the sheath holding his hunting knife. He drew out the weapon, scanned its foot-long blade, then snapped it back into the sheath. A violent image flashed through his mind: the beach at Detroit and a red line across a man's neck as the skin peeled back to ooze blood. Westlake shook his head, willing himself to think about something other than killing. He breathed in deeply, strapped the sheath inside his right boot, and set off for the stable.

Even for a horse the size of Warman, the ride to the hotel was slow going as the animal struggled in the deep snow. Westlake expected to see only a few patrons, but to his surprise the barroom was packed. Extra candles and new straw on the floor gave the place a fresh appearance.

He ordered a pint of ale from the barman, and while standing at the counter, he surveyed the room for Lucy but could see no sign of her. More than a week had passed since his previous visit to the Jordan, but many of the rough faces present were the same he'd seen on his first visit. At the back of the room, sitting alone in Westlake's former seat by the fire, a man he couldn't forget ran a finger around the rim of his glass. Hendrickson slouched over his beer.

Westlake walked over to the table and sat down. "Good afternoon, Mr. Hendrickson." Already his heart began to beat faster.

"You've got a nerve," Hendrickson snarled, his bushy eyebrows angling as he spoke.

"I told you never to come back here. Where's your pal, Archer?"

Hendrickson stiffened, and something in his eyes told Westlake that Archer was close by. *Lucy missing and so was Archer.* Westlake jumped up and darted for the stairs. He took the worn steps two at a time and ran down the dark passageway to the farthest door. He kicked it open and charged through to find Archer gripping the girl by her throat.

Archer turned his square jaw toward the door just in time for it to meet Westlake's fist. The blow knocked the man to the floor.

"Close the door," Westlake ordered Lucy. But, instead of moving, she stood perfectly still. "Now!" he shouted.

Startled, she stepped to the door and pushed it shut.

Westlake drew his knife from its sheath. He lifted Archer to his feet, and grabbing his collar, he held the edge of the blade to his throat. Pounding footsteps hurried down the hallway. He pushed Archer right up to the door just as it collapsed off its hinges, crashing down on Archer, with Hendrickson landing on top of it and his partner.

A dazed Hendrickson peered up for a second before Westlake's boot caught him sharply under the chin. His head snapped backward, and he rolled off the door to lie unconscious on the floor. All was silent.

"My God!" Lucy blurted out, holding both her small fists to her chest.

Westlake sheathed the knife and led Lucy by the hands to the bed where he sat down beside her. They listened to the rumble of feet charging down the hall. Her chin trembled slightly and her fingers gripped his hands like a vise. "Look me in the eyes." Westlake urged, smiling calmly into her face. "Everything will be fine. Just go along with me."

When the footsteps stopped, the long barrel of a musket slowly protruded around the doorframe. The barman and two others peered into the quiet room to find two young people chatting on the edge of a bed. The men then stared down at the broken door under which

Archer's legs stuck out at an odd angle. Their heads jerked from one scene to the other, and their eyes travelled together to gawk at Hendrickson. Then they stared at each other, as if one of them might offer an explanation.

The heavy set barman shrugged and demanded, "What the hell's going on in here?"

"Every time I visit this establishment, these same two ruffians prove how they can't hold their liquor," Westlake complained indignantly. "Either fix this door immediately or move the lady to another room. They broke off the hinges and this room is barely inhabitable as it is."

"Get out of my hotel!" the barman shouted. He trained the musket on Westlake and spoke to Lucy. "Did they really break down the door?"

She nodded, unable to speak.

"Looks to me like one broke the door down on top of the other fella and knocked both of themselves out," suggested one of the other men.

"That's exactly what happened." Westlake declared, pointing at the man. "The pair of them should be jailed."

"Get my tools and fix this damn door," the barman ordered the men. "Lucy, girl, you get back downstairs and start working."

Lucy stood and rubbed her neck. She nodded a thank you to Westlake. Without a word, she pushed her way past the intruders and out the door. The men followed her, leaving the barman and Westlake with the fallen.

The man still had his musket trained on Westlake. "What am I going to do with these two?"

"First, lower that bloody musket, then throw both of them out into the snow," Westlake demanded. "When they come to, they'll have terrible headaches, but that's not your problem."

The barman swung the weapon to one side. "You're going to help me," he insisted. He laid the musket on top of the dresser and bent to lift the door off of Archer. "Come on," he urged impatiently, "shift yourself."

"I'll need a word with the girl before I leave. Fine with you?"

"Help me get these brutes out of here and you can have five minutes with her, no more. And only downstairs where I can keep an eye on you."

"Deal," said Westlake.

The barman shook his head, studying the two men on the floor. "There's something going on with that girl."

Westlake dragged Archer away by the armpits, his boots banging against each stair while they descended. The customers stood and stared. Someone shoved open the front door and Westlake pulled Archer into the street, the man's heels dragging parallel lines into the snow. He tossed him to one side and let go. Archer plunked down to lay face up.

The barman arrived directly behind and dropped Hendrickson on top of his unconscious companion. "When they come round, I want you gone. Go get your five minutes."

Westlake nodded, then hustled back through the front door of the bar, and scanned the murmuring crowd. Lucy was in the middle of the room. He caught up to her, taking gentle hold of a wrist. In her other hand, she balanced a tray with two tankards of ale. "We have to talk," he whispered. In normal circumstances, Lucy's bosom alone had most of the men there watching, so now leading her by the arm, Westlake felt like he was on a theatre's stage.

They edged their way between the tables, heading toward the bench by the fire. "Well, explain yourself," he insisted. "Both times I've come in this place you're in trouble with those men."

Lucy hesitated and looked away. The bruises on her face from the alley fight had mostly healed. "I tell them anything I hear." She shrugged. "They give me a pound a month." She spoke in a rising whisper. "Satisfied?"

"A *pounding* is more like it." Westlake held up his fist. Patrons in the bar continued watching them. It made him feel uncomfortable, and he wished he had a beer. "I'll buy this ale." He gestured to the two tankards on her tray.

"It's their order." She pointed to the table where the men stared at them. "I'll fetch you another." Lucy delivered the beer and the men watched her sway between the tables. She returned to Westlake with a single mug.

"That pound is a lot of money to me, and I don't have to do much for it. That's why I went outside with them the other day. But today" — she poked the table with a finger in anger — "I had nothing, no information to give them, on account of it being slow at Christmas. They got annoyed."

"They were going to beat you for having nothing to report?"

"Archer was. He seemed kind of desperate but wouldn't pay me without some bit of information."

"Their interest in your reports probably means they're spies, as I'm sure you've guessed," Westlake declared emphatically. "Once you get involved with men like that, one day they will want more."

Everyone in York appears to be spying for someone.

Lucy leaned her face closer to Westlake. "This tavern is known for its American sympathies, so everyone comes in to complain." She looked away. "That's all I ever tell them – the complaints I hear — mainly from farmers whining about the militia duty they have to perform. Nothing sinister."

Westlake noticed the barman holding up a finger to signal he had only a minute remaining with her. There was something more that Lucy wasn't telling him, but he'd run out of time. "Here is your pound." Westlake turned her palm upward and put the note in it. "Now you work for me. You know old man Forbsy? Keep a look out for him."

The young woman's brown eyes grew large on seeing the money. "You don't have to pay me to take care of Forbsy. I often sneak him hot tea out the back door, by the latrines." She grinned.

Westlake stood to leave, but Lucy quickly stepped toward him. She put both arms around his shoulders and he felt her slender frame pressing against his own. Her body, warm and soft, reminded him of an earlier time with another woman.

"Hey, hey!" a man at the next table shouted.

"Thank you, again for everything, Mr. Westlake." She hugged and then kissed him on the cheek before picking up her tray. "There's something dangerous about you, yet reassuring as well." She smiled mischievously. "Maybe you're a little odd that way, but I still like you."

Westlake watched her saunter off in the special way she moved. *And you are definitely not telling me all you know.*

5

· · · · · ·

CAPTAIN EDWARD NELLES sat behind a plain wooden table in a room otherwise almost bare of furniture. To one side, the fireplace crackled with a stack of burning maple logs. A small portrait of King George III adorned the wall directly behind his chair, where the Union flag hung from a pole. Westlake stared at the chair, a large, buttoned-down, black leather affair.

"General Sheaffe wanted to keep his own chair, so I swiped General Brock's," Nelles explained. "I thought if I sat in it long enough, I too would have some great thoughts. Seems our minds don't work that way, however." Nelles shrugged. "Even so, I feel his spirit." Nelles glanced over his shoulder at the old flag Brock had always kept nearby.

"I'm sure he'd be pleased for you to have it, sir," Westlake replied quietly as he turned to close the door.

Nelles gestured to the wooden captain's chair placed in front of the table. "You can sit if you wish, Lieutenant."

On the table between them lay a large map weighted down at one end with a sheathed sword and at the other end with two pistols. In the centre of the table flickered the flame of an oil lamp. The map showed both shores of Lake Ontario, and the St. Lawrence River extending all the way to Montreal.

"I suppose I'm going somewhere on this map, sir," Westlake remarked, his eyes scanning the details.

"Here." Nelles jabbed his finger at the name Prescott. "I understand that you know the area well."

"The school I once attended in Cornwall is a bit farther downriver, sir, but I've visited everywhere along here." Westlake gestured up and down the course of the river.

"On the American side too?"

"Not so much, sir … just in winter, travelling by sleigh across the ice."

"Excellent. You're going to Prescott now to meet Lieutenant Colonel George Macdonell, otherwise known as Red George by the troops. He will give you a man to take you across the ice to Ogdensburg, where you'll be introduced to a merchant named Mr. Silas Sterling." Nelles drew his finger across the river to a point where the map read "Ogdensburg."

"And Silas Sterling will do what, sir?" Westlake grinned. "Tell me the name of our traitor."

"Not quite." Nelles leaned back slowly in the black chair, folding hands on top of the table. "No one knows this traitor's name. However, I'm told our agent Mr. Sterling can at least describe him. Sterling does business down in Sackets Harbor, and it seems someone there knows what our traitor looks like."

"Why do traitors risk it, sir?" Westlake asked. "My mother thinks it's probably ideology — you know, republic versus monarchy — but I think it's more likely just for the money."

"You're forgetting human emotions and base desires, Lieutenant, two other powerful motivators," Nelles explained. "People can betray their country after falling in love, or sometimes simply a matter of thinking with the wrong head … if you follow me. As for Mr. Sterling, hand him this package but only after he gives you the information. Under absolutely no circumstances do you hand it over until you have the traitor's description."

Westlake clutched the cloth bundle, feeling a wad of pounds notes inside. He wondered how much money it contained and how much this traitor had already been paid? His mind settled on one thing for sure: *Mr. Sterling sold out for cash.*

That prompted him to ask about the fellow's reliability. If Sterling's services went simply to the highest bidder, then he could easily bite the hand that fed him the package. No side in a war could ever trust a man without honour or principle.

Nelles proceeded to tell him that this same agent kept Lieutenant Colonel Macdonell abreast of all the developments in Sackets Harbor, where Commodore Chauncey had anchored his fleet. Sterling reported that a new ship, the *Madison*, a twenty-four-gun man of war, had finished construction of its hull and slid into the bay in less than sixty days. The shipwrights would mast and arm her, and complete the inner furnishings during the long winter ahead. With that vessel added to the other schooners Chauncey had purchased, the balance of naval power on the lake, like water on a tilting pan, had shifted in favour of the American side.

Westlake thought about the chaos surrounding the construction of the *Sir Isaac Brock*, whose hull was not scheduled to be in the water until May or June. No wonder the shipwrights in York felt frustrated. They knew the stakes as well as anyone. Every life in the town now stood exposed to the whims of the enemy's navy.

"Tomorrow the necessary paperwork will be drawn up for you to requisition supplies from the quartermaster. Sergeant Puffer will assist you. Say your goodbyes to your family tonight, leave Maple Hill at first light, and I will meet you in this office immediately on your arrival." Nelles stood up and offered Westlake his hand. "Ready for this?"

Westlake chest tightened. "My father's sister, Aunt Evelyn, lives this side of Elizabethtown, sir, with my Uncle Adam." He tried to look on the positive side of the ledger. "She'll be surprised to see me again."

"Adam and Eve?" Nelles gave a skeptical grin.

"I know, sir. They get kidded all the time." Westlake shrugged. "They've got a particularly lovely garden."

"There have been recent raids up and down the St. Lawrence so your aunt will have stories to tell no doubt. Keep alert as you travel to learn all you can."

The following morning Westlake waited anxiously at the long green counter fronting the quartermaster's store. Though keen to be on his way, he'd yet to have his meeting with Sergeant Puffer. The entire storeroom smelled of animal feed. After another rap on the counter, Westlake cleared his throat loudly, hoping Puffer might hear.

Behind the counter stood six wooden racks that had been painted black. Filled with supplies, they each ran thirty feet down a storehouse floor swept clean. A sign in white lettering posted on the two racks to the left announced BARRACK STORES. Farther down that aisle Westlake could see an array of hanging mops, cooking utensils, washing tubs, and all kinds of other items useful for garrison life.

The sign on the middle two racks read COMMISSARIAT, where the animal feed in cloth bags lay piled up. Also filling those shelves were candles, lantern oil, and an iron strongbox marked Cash. The troops are probably paid from that very box, Westlake reflected.

He walked farther along the counter to the right and peered down the last two aisles labelled QUARTERMASTER STORES. At that moment, Sergeant George Puffer's chubby face appeared around a corner, and he jerked his head up as if surprised. In one hand, he held a flat board to which a supply list was attached.

"What are you staring at and how did you creep in 'ere past the guard?" Above his right eye a savage scar shone pink-red as that same eye gave a nervous wink. Behind him the long racks in perfect order held stacks of uniforms, haversacks, and a line of canteens.

Puffer stepped directly in front of Westlake to block his view. He motioned with the board. "I asked you a question." He winked involuntarily again.

The man known as "winky" to the troops was always rather cantankerous, but no one knew more about the workings of the British Army than Sergeant Puffer. He was at least twice Westlake's age and a lifer in the armed forces. Like all quartermaster's everywhere, the sergeant protected the King's storehouse as if it belonged to him personally, and he had a reputation of being the best in the business.

Silently, Westlake handed him the folded sheet of paper listing the supplies necessary for his journey. Puffer shook the list open roughly, staring down at the scrawled signature of Captain Edward Nelles at the bottom of the page.

"Don't have time for all this. They've taken my three men to Niagara." Puffer gestured up at the three signs and winked again. "Doin' everthin' meeself here, aren't I. Come back tomorrow." He threw the paper on the counter and turned his back to continue checking his shelves.

"I need those supplies right now, Sergeant," Westlake said. "I have urgent business."

"Everyone demands my goods, now!" Puffer winked and turned his back to check off an item on the board. "Ain't fair. I'm even doin' payroll and the payouts to contractors." He winked yet again and gestured to the strongbox.

"I'm very sorry for that, Sergeant Puffer, but I need to be on my way." Westlake remained firm.

Even in his tailored redcoat, the scruffy sergeant looked out of place here amid his neatly arranged supplies on a storehouse floor swept clean. Westlake knew that this man had worked previously in Halifax, Montreal, and recently in Niagara. He ignored Westlake for a while until he turned and put the board on the counter.

"Why are you so special, then?" He leaned forward with both arms extended along the counter, as if proving this was all his.

"I'll give you one last chance," Westlake announced. "Give me those supplies, now."

"Go to hell." Puffer winked and snatched up Westlake's list. "Come back tomorrow and maybe, if you're real nice to me, you'll get whatever I'm prepared to give you."

Westlake turned and marched out. Within the hour he was back with Captain Nelles at his side. To his astonishment, the items on his list were already spread across the countertop. Puffer stood smiling behind them.

"I could strangle you, Puffer," Nelles snarled, "making me march here like this. Why do you have to turn every requisition into a contest?"

"Just joshin' with the lad, sir." Puffer winked. "You see." He waved at the counter. "I was already getting him what he wanted, but he stormed out on me."

"That's a lie," Westlake yelled.

Nelles took hold of Westlake's forearm and frowned at him.

"Being a gentleman, I didn't hear that." Puffer winked.

"I appreciate it, Sergeant, and that's just as well for the both of you. Load up your horse, Mr. Westlake," Nelles instructed. "While there's still daylight, I want you on your way."

Zebulon Montgomery Pike, colonel in the US Fifteenth Infantry, opened his eyes and struggled to remember his exact location. The mountain peaks of Colorado floated hazily through his mind. He remembered nearly freezing and pulling the blankets tight under his chin. But sweating now, he kicked off his covers, imagining the heat of the deep south he had experienced once visiting a Spanish settlement. He watched his chest rise with another breath, closed his eyes, and then drifted off. *A Spanish patrol had him under arrest. A soldier seized his files and had ushered him to the very line in the sand of the Louisiana border. "Give me back those papers, damn you. They're mine!"*

"Wake up, dear." His wife's voice echoed in the distance, breaking his confusion. "You've been dreaming again. It's just the fever." A cool cloth wiped his face.

Yes, it was his wife. Home. He reached slowly to take her hand. "Clarissa, are we home? Where …"

"Back home, dear."

He glimpsed her beautiful face, briefly closing his eyes again as the cloth swabbed his forehead.

"No more exploring for you. You're at home in Plattsburg, with the army. Just sleep now, darling."

The colonel opened his eyes again, suddenly lucid, remembering everything. Pleurisy. He was sure that pleurisy had been the doctor's diagnosis. "I've been here too long." He barely coughed out the words. "General Dearborn needs me. The invasion … we're going." He threw the cloth aside and attempted to sit up, but his arms gave way and he collapsed heavily back onto the pillow. "My strength … what's happening?"

His wife clutched his hand, but he lost the sound of her voice. *Rest ... just let me rest a little and we'll see things right. Clarissa.*
Thank God, I'm home.

The Lynde Inn and Tavern in Whitby rose up to cast a long shadow as the January sun disappeared below the horizon. Known for offering a good night's sleep to weary travellers, the inn provided the last place of comfort and safety all the way from York to Cobourg. Previously, Westlake had always sped through Whitby, but the delay involving Puffer had cost him more than an hour of travelling time, and although he wasn't tired, he decided on a quiet evening and an early start the next morning.

He dismounted and walked his horse to a large barn, where an eager stable boy took the reins. Westlake inspected the stalls to find where his horse would be kept. He took the lad's wrist and put a coin in his hand.

"Unburden the animal, feed and bed him down for the night. Don't try to steal anything, I warn you. Have him ready to travel at first light and there's another coin for your purse."

"Thank you, sir." The lad grinned at the coin. "He'll be ready as a bear in spring, count on it."

Westlake entered the hotel through the back door and paused in the barroom doorway. Straw lined the floor, but unlike the crowded conditions at Jordan bar, only two customers sat at a single table, their backs turned toward him as they watched a low-burning fire. He didn't have to strain his ears to overhear their boisterous argument.

"Not bloody fair," said a burly man wearing a black hat. "I came here for the free land and tools, like what they promised, and what have I got to do but join the goddamn militia. Not me. I won't do it, I tell ye." He gulped some beer and slammed the tankard on the table.

"We have no choice," said his friend. "I'm not giving everything up to the bluecoats."

"So you're gonna fight, then. Get your head blown off." The man took another large swig, well on his way to drunkenness, and loudly smacked his lips. "Well, I'm not. I'd just as soon help the Yankees as fight them."

Westlake stepped into the room and cleared his throat. "Something warm, please, barman." He claimed a table one removed from the customers and placed his fur coat on a chair. The barman, an older man with stringy grey hair and a face distorted with worry, brought over a steaming mug. Westlake paid on the spot and sipped the strong tea that warmed the back of his throat.

"Where the hell did you come from, laddie?" demanded the fellow in the black hat. He swung around in his chair to get a proper look at Westlake. "Who do you think you are, creeping up on us like that?"

The two men stared at him, waiting for an answer. Westlake and the barman both knew they had just heard bare-faced treason. If they didn't immediately report it to higher authorities, they could face the same miserable punishment as this traitor. Hanging.

"I'm a fur trader, friend. I don't ask other men their business because I like to mind my own. But if anyone wants trouble ..." Westlake let the words hang in the air while his heart raced.

"You're mighty young to be a trader," black hat remarked. He folded his arms across his chest and leaned closer.

"Be happy I'm not serving with the army and can't hear too well." Westlake flicked the back of his ear twice and winced. "Got too close to a ship's cannon fire, so my hearing's nearly gone."

The man lifted his black hat and brushed back his hair while still eyeing Westlake. He downed the rest of his beer and dropped the empty tankard to the table. "We be on our ways, then." Both men rose slowly, nodded to the bartender, and made their way to the front door.

The door had barely closed behind them when Westlake jumped up from his seat. "Stay here!" he directed the barman as he raced for the back door, and then out to the barn beyond. He opened the great door just a crack and slid inside.

A single oil lantern hung from a vertical beam, casting deep shadows in the stalls. The stable boy was about to unsaddle his horse when Westlake snatched up his musket resting on top of the supplies the boy had already piled on the floor. "Say nothing and keep to your work," he instructed while quickly loading.

The barn door swung open and two figures entered. Westlake stepped into the shadow, standing silently behind his horse. He hadn't had time to replace the ramrod, and now it stuck out the end of the barrel.

"Get out, boy," the man in the black hat ordered.

"I have a job —"

"Git, and don't you go anywhere nears the bar, or you won't live to see tomorrow." The burly fellow raised his fist and the boy ran outside.

"We shouldn't be doing this," advised his friend. "It's wrong."

"Let's see what this bastard is really up to."

The boy had left the door open, and a cold wind whistled through the barn before exiting out through spaces in the walls. In their stalls the horses nervously shifted themselves. The big man hurried forward, but with his hand about to touch Westlake's haversack, the warning click of a musket froze him stiff.

Westlake stepped out from the shadow, the musket level with the man's chest. The other one threw his hands in the air, his eyes bulging in fright. "We mean no harm, mister," he said. "We're only farmers, not thieves."

His big friend twisted around in desperation for a weapon of some kind. "This is the second time you've crept up on me," he growled.

Westlake laughed. "Take your horses and get on your way. Be thankful that I don't tie up both of you and leave you out here till morning."

"You can't even load a musket proper," the man sneered, "so maybe you don't know how to shoot one either."

"You don't *really* want to take that chance. Have you ever seen a ramrod sticking out of a man's chest? Painful way to go." Westlake exaggerated a wince. "Move." He gestured with the musket toward the other stalls, where their horses snorted. The man seemed about to speak again until Westlake raised the musket as if to fire. "Be gone! Muskets have a nasty habit of going off."

The men hurried to a couple of old horses and mounted up. They spurred the animals while still in the barn, then galloped out through the open door. "Bastard," one of them yelled as he charged by.

The young lad raced inside and slammed the barn door behind him. "That was amazing, mister. There was even two of them and you weren't scared one bit. I heard you laugh at them."

Westlake smiled. *If it were only that easy.* He hurried to the door and scanned the lane to make sure the two scoundrels were really gone. "Don't you believe it for a second. I'm still sweating buckets."

The boy stared at him in awe as he slid the ramrod back in place, picked up his haversack, and surveyed the lane again before returning to the bar. This time he kept the loaded musket close at hand.

The barman approached his table with fresh cup of tea. Westlake lifted the cup to his mouth with a shaking hand. He stared into the fire, wondering if he would have shot the ramrod into the man. An image of a fellow on his knees gripping a ramrod lodged in his chest jumped into his mind. *Queenston Heights will be with me forever.*

Is every tavern in Upper Canada bursting with traitors? He thought back to the customers in the Jordan Hotel, speaking openly of treason, yet so few voicing their loyalty to the Crown.

Westlake and the bartender were now alone in the barroom. "So many with treason in their hearts," Westlake said out loud. He put his hands around the cup until it scalded his fingers and he stopped shaking.

"Aye, you're right about that, laddie." The old man brushed back his stringy hair. "Every barman in Upper Canada could be hanged by the neck for what we've overheard and not reported. Remember that more than half the folks hereabouts are less than a few years arrived from the United States."

"Then what chance have we got in this war?" Westlake let go of the cup and threw his hands in the air. The fifteen hundred redcoats currently in Upper Canada could not defend the entire province from the Americans without the help of the militia. For that matter, both forces also needed the assistance of the natives, or the war was lost.

The barman interrupted his thoughts. "Because half of those that come here despise what the new republic to the south is doing. No King, just a mob; every man for himself, they claim." He pulled a Brown Bess from under the counter. "I'm from Boston, I am, but I've joined the Durham Militia." He raised his musket in the air. "They won't be bloody winning this time."

And so Westlake had his answer.

6
. . . . . .

IF THEY WERE ON A SHIP, every officer aboard would be a mutineer.

Captain Edward Nelles leaned back in the great leather chair and rubbed his narrow chin, considering his situation. A cabal of disgruntled officers had come together with the aim of undermining and replacing Major General Sheaffe. They expected Nelles to join them, as if it was a foregone conclusion — "Brock's man" and all.

In the beginning, immediately following the general's death at Queenston Heights, it boosted his ego to be considered Brock's man. Even senior officers sought his endorsement of their plans and projects, as if Brock himself were giving approval. They soon asked for more than he could deliver, more than his meagre authority as a captain would allow.

His relationship with Sheaffe remained cordial but strictly professional. There would be none of the camaraderie that emanated with Brock's style of command. In fact, Nelles was sure that each and every time Sheaffe set eyes on him, the new commander thought of Brock and the man he himself wasn't. "He's no Brock," the common phrase used to describe Sheaffe, must have grated on the general profusely.

At the best of times, Sheaffe had always kept his subordinates at a distance, but now he seemed downright hostile. Instead of playing such politics, Nelles wished everyone would simply concentrate on winning the war. Hadn't they learned that already? With London willing to totally surrender Upper Canada, and Governor-in-Chief Prevost acting in compliance with London, who would stand against their enemy if they fought more among themselves? Surely, at this moment, unity was paramount.

"Damn you, Isaac, where the hell are you when we need you?"

Nelles stroked the armrest with his fingers and recalled Brock's fall on Queenston Heights. On receiving the sudden news of Brock's death, the rumour spread that Sheaffe had been stunned, unable even to talk or move, let alone issue a command. He had rallied, however, and organized the militia, regulars, and Indians for an assault that drove the Americans into the Niagara River and carried the day. Sheaffe's finest hour.

But only an hour. Nelles shook his head. General Sheaffe, the former Bostonian, had followed up his victory by granting the enemy an armistice. Then he paroled most of the American militia, and a good number of their officers. Even Governor-in-Chief Prevost had been outraged by such conciliation. Little wonder that Brock's officers turned on the general shortly after the victory. And now they expected Nelles to join them.

He pulled from his pocket two notes received from a lieutenant colonel friend and reread the salient message: *We are no longer commanded by Brock, and our situation is most materially changed for the worse.* But this wasn't the worst of it. Nelles shuffled the sheets of papers to read the second note.

When the enemy tried to cross the Niagara River in November, General Sheaffe had written to his British commander on the scene, advising him that his men "ought not to be exposed incessantly" and to take "measures best adapted for a retreat if your force be inadequate." To suggest a retreat to the victors of Queenston Heights was like telling the King to abdicate: simply treasonous.

"God's teeth," Nelles exclaimed out loud to his empty office. "That man's his own worst enemy."

A sharp knock at the door startled him. "Enter," he called.

An aide stepped into the room. "Your appointment, sir." The man came to attention. "Three gentlemen to see you, sir: Mr. McLean, clerk of the Legislative Assembly; Major Givens, assistant superintendent of the Indian Department; and the Reverend Doctor John Strachan."

Nelles gestured for the men to be brought in as he turned the insubordinate letters face down on top of his desk.

"Mr. McLean, good to see you again. Major Givens. Doctor Strachan." Nelles reached across the table to shake their hands. "Please take a seat." Strachan's wide forehead furrowed, the only expression Nelles had ever seen him wear. The man's stern countenance matched his cold handshake.

"Captain Nelles." McLean nodded. "We don't see you at any of our social gatherings, not even at Sunday service, sir, and our business is too serious and too urgent to wait any longer."

"I've been rather busy." Nelles pointed to the maps on the table. "Who is we and what am I needed for?"

Donald McLean's distinguished features also set themselves in worry. His fingers rubbed the edge of the table, his nervousness evident in every movement. Suddenly he jumped up and walked toward the fire, hands outstretched. He clapped them together, indicating a resolution for this soft-spoken man to begin.

"I represent a group of gentlemen who believe we must strike first at Sackets Harbor, for the good of Upper Canada. You see, the other magistrates ... well, we've all heard the tales about the gathering American fleet." He paused and turned back to the fire. "And I'm not willing just to have others do my bidding, sir. I've purchased a musket."

Nelles nodded in approval, a commendable act for a magistrate exempt from military service. "That's most honourable of you Mr. McLean, but why come to me? You yourself have access to General Sheaffe." He glanced at Strachan. "And I dare say even to Governor-in-Chief Prevost, if you so choose." Major Givens shifted in his seat and managed to clear his throat.

Nelles rose and went to a side table bearing glasses and a decanter. He filled four goblets with wine. Without asking, he walked over to the fire and handed one glass to McLean and the other to Strachan, who simply put it on the table. Major Givens picked up his own glass and immediately took a sip.

McLean nodded his appreciation before guzzling down half the contents. "I saw Brock sit in that same chair. You're known to be his man, so we expected you to be bold. And there's so little time. When the ice goes out in the spring, the bloody enemy will be right on our doorstep. Count on it."

"You don't know that for sure," Nelles replied. "I concede it's possible they may attack here, but the Americans have far more to gain in Niagara or Kingston than a little place like York."

"But why take the risk they might come here?" the Reverend Strachan interjected. "In any event, it would be a great achievement to stop them from attacking anywhere. Surely you must see our point?"

"And you want the British Army to strike while the American ships are ice-bound," Nelles postulated. "Burn the lot while they're still frozen in."

All three men nodded in unison.

"A thirty-five-mile hike from Kingston, cannons transported on sleighs, and blast their ships while they can't move," McLean explained. "We don't have to take the town, just destroy a few ships." McLean made it sound so easy.

"But Mr. Sheaffe and Mr. Prevost aren't cooperating with that suggestion, are they?" Nelles added. "That's why you've come to me."

Strachan raised his eyebrows. "Those men do not know how to win. It takes a certain boldness — and doing one's duty." He fingered the bottom of his glass but still did not drink.

"Be careful who you say that to, Doctor." Nelles glanced back at the leather chair. "Boldness can also get one killed." Everyone in the room knew he was speaking about Brock.

Major Givens cleared his throat to speak. "If there's anything I've learned in my time with the natives, it's to get to the point. In Niagara, fighting against the enemy, all General Sheaffe would consider was retreat. He is not the right man to take our case for an attack to Governor-in-Chief Prevost. On the other hand, we know the governor listens to you."

"And besides, General Sheaffe is too ill back in Niagara to consider anything at present," McLean acknowledged. "He should come here to see how poorly York is prepared to confront the enemy."

"And Governor Prevost won't consider anything other than

defensive measures," Strachan interjected. "I speak for the Anglican Church, and we only ask that you put our suggestion before the two of them. Coming from you, the idea will carry weight. So we have your agreement?"

Nelles had heard rumours of Strachan's persistent methods, his constant efforts to wield power. Now he saw him in action.

"Let me consider it."

He clinked his glass on McLean's, wishing him the best for 1813. McLean downed the rest of his wine after the toast, shook hands, and departed with a modest bow. The Reverend Strachan followed him out.

"I'm sorry to put this burden on you, Captain, but you are the only one to make our case." Major Givens shook hands and withdrew.

Nelles slumped into the chair, knowing that his visitors were right. A quick strike against the enemy was indeed their only chance. He leaned forward, put his elbows on the table, head in his hands. When the ice went out, the enemy would have a possession of the lake. He had two months, perhaps three, to pursue an attack on Sackets Harbor before the Americans could attack anywhere they pleased.

Lieutenant Westlake pushed his snowshoes heading northeast along the north shore of the St. Lawrence River. He tugged at the reins in front of his horse, inching the animal forward, as it struggled through knee-deep snow. The driving wind and snow stung his face until his cheeks had lost all feeling. Through his thick fur coat, deerskin jacket, and homespun shirt, the wind's fingers caressed his body as if he walked naked. Inside his gloves, the fingers of his left hand had slowly grown numb. Westlake tightened his lips and drove his feet onward against the attacking elements.

He had pressed on doggedly through atrocious weather, averaging twenty miles a day. The taverns visited along the road, where men grumbled about life, held no further surprises. The authorities had begun arresting all those who tried to escape their duties as militia-men. Even if those same men had only recently arrived from the United States, the law showed no mercy.

Westlake knew every inch of the area on Kingston's east side, where the river turned sharply north. In his early teens, while his parents travelled around Europe arranging the distribution of furs, he had attended the Reverend Strachan's school in Cornwall, well upstream from Kingston itself. When school finished in the spring, he worked through the long summer days on his uncle and aunt's farm. Now, he stood peering down a long-sweeping hill where a road would have been visible but for the snow. Less than quarter a mile away stood his Uncle Adam's farm.

A genuine frontiersman who demanded that everyone carry their fair share of the load, his uncle stood firmly erect and gave the initial impression of sternness. In reality, the man laughed and joked more than anyone else Westlake knew, always seeing the funny side of life. Long before other farmhouses in Leeds County had wooden floors, Uncle Adam had laid one down for Aunt Evelyn. "Cleanliness is next to godliness and I won't have us living here like cattle. Straw floors are meant for the barn," he declared. Westlake looked forward to his visits because with no children of their own, his aunt and uncle treated him like a son they never had.

He trudged on downwards until the barn's snow-covered rooftop finally revealed itself, grey smoke billowing out behind from the farmhouse chimney. The family dog, her nose raised expectantly in the air, bounded over the snow to greet him.

"Cherry, how are you, old girl."

Although now barely midday, the dark clouds made it appear more like early evening. Westlake approached the barn with growing excitement. He passed the trunk of an old oak tree that still bore the scars of a thousand hours of his target practice with knives and tomahawks. He tried to speed up, but the snow wouldn't let him. Then he realized something was not quite right.

The barn door rocked on its hinges, restrained from flying open by the deepening snow. And no light shone through the farmhouse windows. Westlake stopped in his tracks. The undulations of a thousand footprints flattened the snow all around the barn entrance. He reached down and released the strap on his snowshoes before dashing back to his horse to fetch the musket.

Westlake ran quietly up the sidewall of the barn, loading the weapon as he moved. The view from the space around the door's hinge revealed no humans inside. He stepped around the creaking door and walked into the barn. The horses were gone and only the three milk cows remained.

Westlake hurried out and ran toward the rear of the house. He slowly pressed down on the back door's worn handle, just as he had done a thousand times years earlier. The door wouldn't budge an inch. "Uncle!" he called out. "Uncle Adam! It's me, your nephew, Jonathan." He put his ear to the door.

Westlake heard the click of a musket hammer and then the voice of his aunt. "Is that really you, Jonathan?"

"Aunt Evelyn, don't shoot!" He stepped to one side lest she fire. "Of course, it's me," he shouted. "Open the door."

"The back door's blocked up. You'll have to come round the front."

Westlake sped around the house to the front entrance where his aunt stood on the threshold with a musket resting across her arms. She had the figure of a stooping pear, and except for her longish nose, his aunt looked nothing like her older brother, Richard Westlake. Though only in her mid-thirties, her hair had already gone grey.

"Why are you holding that musket … and where's Uncle Adam?"

"I can't tell you how good it is to see you, boy. Come in out of the cold." She laid the musket on a small table and stepped forward to give him a hug. "American riflemen in green jackets came and took your uncle away," she gasped. "Said he was a prisoner on account of him being in the Leeds Militia. Seems his name was on a list. How they knew he was in the militia, I'll never know." His aunt shook a warning finger at him. "Someone's telling tales."

"You mean giving information to the Americans."

She nodded, her face contorted in anguish.

Westlake stepped farther into the house and immediately noticed the floor covered in smashed crockery. The windows were boarded over, explaining why he'd seen no light inside. One chair lay on its side with a leg broken where obviously a struggle had occurred. "Did they hurt him?"

Evelyn nodded and put a hand over her eyes as she started to cry. "It was terrible. They beat him awful."

"How about you?" Westlake tensed expecting the worst. "Did they touch —"

"No, they left me alone."

"At least that's something." He scanned the room again and clenched his fists. "My God, Uncle Adam would never hurt a fly. When did this happen? Do you know where they took him?"

She shook her head. "In the middle of the night, when we were asleep."

"I should go and shut the barn door before the cows freeze to death. You know they've stolen your horses."

"They also took all our money and my jewellery, such as it was. But they missed that musket hidden in the cold room. Stupid common criminals, that's what they are." Her chin began to tremble. "A big man with white plumes in his hat ... oh, did he think he was something special ... he opened the closet and even stole your uncle's boat cloak." She put her head into her hands and sobbed.

"Aunt Evelyn, I'll put things right in the barn, and do what else I can around here. But I can only stay a day or so."

She nodded and flopped down in a chair, the despair evident in her face. "Can you find him?"

"I'm seeing some men who can help."

Westlake shut the front door behind him as he ventured out toward the barn. He felt the old anger rising in his chest. Cherry greeted him at the door with a lick to his hand. Nelles had already warned him of the raids but this made his fight personal. He only hoped his uncle would still be alive by the time he reached Ogdensburg.

From atop his horse, Lieutenant Colonel Red George Macdonell surveyed the assembled troops: more than one hundred men of the

8th Foot, at least three dozen soldiers of the Royal Newfoundland Regiment, a Company of Glengarry Light Infantry, and a couple of hundred militiamen. Dressed in furs and greatcoats, knitted caps, scarves and gloves, the soldiers crammed themselves onto the main street of Prescott, exactly like they had so many other cold winter mornings. A great white cloud of frosted breath hung in the air above the parade.

"We're marching out on to the St. Lawrence ice again," the colonel announced. "Only this time, instead of cowering so close to home, we'll march three hundred paces out from the riverbank to practise the prime-and-load drill. The enemy in Ogdensburg should get to know that we can deliver the business end of a Brown Bess if they push us too bloody far." He referred to the recent kidnapping of farmers, ransacking of farms, and theft of horses. A murmur of agreement rumbled through the troops.

"The assembled companies will form four deep!" Macdonell bawled out his preparatory command. The entire rear rank of the parade took one step back. Macdonell then stood in the stirrups to give the executable: "Form four deep."

Every second man took one step back and then slid over to his right behind the soldier previously standing next to him. While the men shuffled into position, young Willie Robertson glanced up at the colonel with a bright face lit with a morning smile.

"To your right, face!" Macdonell bellowed.

Each soldier pivoted on his heel so that the column now faced the roadway leading down to the river. They held their position, anticipating the next command as Macdonell rode his horse to the head of the column. They were operating like one machine now, and inwardly he smiled to himself, proud of his men.

"Captain Jenkins, take the Glengarries to the right, if you please," he ordered. "I'll take the 8th and the Royals to the left. The militia can split up at the rear." Macdonell paused to look over the assembly.

"At the ordinary, march!" he hollered.

The column jolted into their stride. The colonel guessed the men were happy just to get moving in the cold. Willie Robertson stamped his feet hard as he marched. After the first column had descended the embankment onto the ice, Jenkins veered it slightly to the right, as ordered.

Macdonell gestured to a lieutenant. "Take two militia companies to the left of the Glengarries," ordered the colonel.

With the balance of the militia in tow, Red George marched the 8th Foot and Royal Newfoundland Regiment to the far left. Large snowflakes began to fall as he ordered the entire force to form into two ranks. He rode in front of the troops now spread across the ice and all standing at attention. The sergeants meanwhile pressed the men together and straightened the lines.

Captain Jenkins rode up to report. "Everyone's ready, Colonel."

Red George shielded his eyes from the snow and stared out across the St. Lawrence River. "How far do you think it is from where we stand now to Ogdensburg, Captain?" he asked.

"Not far, sir." Jenkins grinned. "Just under a thousand yards, I suppose. But armed with a musket and loaded down with a fur coat, that distance is a good run. You're not thinking of a giving old Forsyth a surprise today, are you, sir?"

"I have orders to the contrary, sir, — and I always follow orders," Red George stated indignantly, as if he'd never think of attempting such an action. "Give the orders for prime-and-load and have the men aim right at Ogdensburg. The enemy won't know we're firing blue cartridges." He rode slowly along behind the lines, toward the militia, where Willie stood awkwardly at attention.

"Prepare to load!" The order travelled down the lines. Willie brought his Brown Bess up across his chest and opened the musket pan. The colonel counted off the seconds as the drill proceeded.

"Handle cartridge!"

From a small box resting against his right hip, Willie withdrew a blue paper cartridge, a blank with no ball, and bit off the end.

"Prime!"

He poured some powder into the firing pan and snapped shut the frizzen.

"Cast about!" The orders had come seconds apart.

Willie swung his musket to rest on its butt and poured the remaining powder and paper down into the barrel.

"Draw ramrod!"

He pulled the ramrod from under the musket and slid it a few inches inside the barrel.

"Ram down cartridge!"

To jam the cartridge in firmly, Willie pounded the ramrod twice down the bore. As Red George watched, he smiled on noticing Willie's progress. The young man concentrated on the task at hand and was growing into a fine soldier.

"Return ramrod!"

"Shoulder arms!" The entire line snapped the muskets up to their shoulders.

"Make ready!"

The colonel urged his horse along the line to where the regulars were running through the drill like the working of a giant clock.

"Front rank, present!" The men pointed their weapons upriver.

"Fire!" More than two hundred Brown Bess muskets banged out their charges, the blast echoing off the riverbanks on both sides. Twenty-four seconds, the colonel told himself: not bad for the first time through the paces.

"Rear rank, present!"

"Fire!"

"Prime and load!"

The men would now run through the drill themselves without being given the individual orders. Colonel Macdonell counted again and this time the prime and load took only twenty-one seconds. And so it would go on and on, until either the officers or their horses became too cold to continue. After ninety minutes, the lines were firing better than three rounds a minute.

As the morning wore on, the snow came down harder and the Brown Bess had less chance of firing in such damp conditions. "Captain Jenkins, that's enough for today," the colonel announced.

"Time to return to shore — our side, of course. You may have the honour of taking them home."

"Sir." Jenkins saluted and rode slowly back behind the lines, giving the troops the order to shoulder arms and about-face. Again, he formed the men into fours. When he reached the column's far end, he shouted, "At the ordinary, march!"

The assembly followed the captain as they wheeled round off the ice and headed for Prescott's shore. The snow fell thick and heavy now, blurring Macdonell's view of the American side. He rode up beside Jenkins.

"Well, that should give Forsyth and his cowards something to think about, sir," Jenkins remarked. "First time for prime-and-load drill on the ice. I have to admit, sir, I'd love to have a go at those bloody scoundrels. It's despicable what we've let them away with so easily."

"Tomorrow morning, I want the same drill in the same order, with the Glengarries on the right," the colonel declared. "Only, this time, advance to the very centre, midway between the riverbanks. The enemy should get used to seeing us out on there the ice."

"Are you perhaps planning something that I should know about it, sir?" Jenkins inquired.

"Nothing that you should know about," Red George replied sternly.

7

· · · · · ·

THE TWELVE-MILE RIDE SOUTH from Ogdensburg to the little village of Morristown had been cold enough, but out on the bare ice nothing stopped the fierce weather cutting clean through a man. Lieutenant Abraham Tasker peered through the darkness toward the Canadian side of the St. Lawrence River and pulled his new boat cloak tighter around his neck as it flapped in the wind. He hunched down against the wind and hoped his freezing fingers would still be able to work when he next needed them.

Along with two hundred American riflemen and other militia, Tasker's horse slid down the embankment on to the ice itself. Under the leadership of recently promoted Major Benjamin Forsyth, the troop headed toward Elizabethtown, Upper Canada, less than two miles across the river from Morristown, U.S.A. The unmounted militia rode bundled up in furs packed onto sleighs, and right now Tasker eyed them with envy. *Bastards probably even have flasks tucked under those furs.*

His orders were to set free twelve jailed Americans, late Loyalists who had gallantly refused to join the local militia and fight against their former country. At the same time, his riflemen would capture local militia commanders and as many supplies as the sleighs could carry. And maybe, Tasker prayed like a thirsty man in the desert, he'd grab a few good Canadian women who fancied a turn with a real Carolina man.

His horse snorted a cloud of frosty breath, and he wheeled the animal around to find the owner of the local Morristown tavern right behind him. It had been Tasker's idea of snatching the tavern keeper and using him to guide the entire force of raiders across the ice to the Elizabethtown jail. But the barman didn't have the same enthusiasm for the mission.

"It's kidnapping, that's what this is," the barman complained from atop the horse he rode. "I've been kidnapped."

Tasker's sergeant held the reins as he tugged the barman's horse forward. "Just as you ordered, Lieutenant," Sergeant Shaughnessy reported. "Mr. Delaney here is more than willing to help us. Aren't y'all?"

"Just remember our deal," Delaney replied. "I'm not having Sean's tavern ransacked on my account. He's my goddamn brother, and don't forget it. I don't care if he is in enemy territory."

Lieutenant Tasker rode his horse up beside the sergeant and took the reins from his hand. He pulled out a riding crop and held it firmly under Delaney's chin. "We'll post two strong fellows outside your brother's door to make sure nothing untoward happens inside his tavern," Tasker said. "Now guide us over to Elizabethtown and that jail." He handed the reins to Delaney.

Sleighs pulled by anxious horses, skidded on to the ice and snow under the barest glimmer of light from a moon half covered by cloud. Men grunted and the horses checked their step, and out of every living creature blew a white stream that quickly dissipated in the breeze. The wind whipped the snow into small tornadoes that grew up from the frozen river only to disappear again into the ice.

Tasker coaxed his horse on and nodded to the sergeant. "Shoot him if he tries to run."

"Suits me, sir." The sergeant grinned and gave Delaney a shove in the back. The carbine slung through the ring of his saddle wouldn't fire anyway. Under threat of instant death, no one carried a loaded musket lest it accidentally go off and give away their whole enterprise. If the force met sudden resistance, then everyone would have to stop and load before they could defend themselves.

Tasker prayed for total surprise as they approached the shoreline of Elizabethtown. The little village loomed ahead in utter darkness, and his heart beat faster. If the British were there waiting in ambush, they'd surely open fire about now. Tasker held his breath, staring at the dozen or so houses along the shore. So far, they remained quiet.

All two hundred men left their sleighs behind on the ice, divided themselves into platoons, and began to climb the sloping riverbank. The platoons separated to the left and right, preparing to surround the town. Trailed by Major Forsyth and three-dozen militiamen, Tasker followed Delaney on horseback up along Main Street and directly to the front of the jail. There, the party quietly dismounted and tethered their horses. They had achieved total surprise.

"Now what about my brother?" Delaney demanded.

"Shut up and knock politely on the door," Tasker ordered. "Sergeant, load your weapon and get behind him."

Delaney knocked as instructed, but all remained quiet inside. He looked questioningly at Tasker, who gestured for him to knock again. A lock turned and the door creaked open slowly to reveal the yawning jailer still in his pyjamas. "Delaney?" he asked. "What's going on here?" His eyes widened as he found himself looking down the barrel of the sergeant's rifle.

"I'll take over this now." Major Forsyth stepped forward and pushed the jailer back through the entrance. He took off his fur coat and pressed it into the jailer's outstretched arms. "Keys!" he demanded.

The man nodded to the wall where a ring of skeleton keys hung from a peg. Forsyth grabbed the keys and motioned for the jailer to follow. "Bring that lantern, Lieutenant. And shut the damn door."

On either side, farther along a short aisle, four barred cells held the prisoners. Three of them held four men each, while in the fourth slept a solitary occupant. Beside a narrow bed, a wooded bucket stood upright in the corner of each cell. Bins full of clothing sat at the end of the aisle.

"Americans, on your feet!" Tasker ordered. The light cast shadows through the bars as men woke and began to pick themselves up off the floor. "I said Americans, let's go!"

"We're here to take you home, boys." Forsyth beamed. A ragged cheer went up as the men rushed over to grip the bars of their cell.

"Who's he?" Forsyth pointed to the man sitting in the fourth cell by himself and now fully awake.

"A murderer," said the jailer.

"This true?" Forsyth asked the fellow prisoners.

"True as your pecker shrinks in the cold, sir," another inmate said.

"Want me to shoot him, sir?" Tasker asked, drawing an unloaded pistol from his belt.

The lone man jumped to his feet, his eyes bulging in the flickering light. "You can't just shoot a fella like that. I has to get a trial and what have you."

Forsyth stared at him for a moment, deliberately making the fellow sweat. "Leave him be. He's more trouble to them alive than dead." Forsyth unlocked the three cell doors and motioned to the bins full of their outer garments. "Get dressed. Then we're paying a visit to the home of every militiaman in town."

From inside his coat pocket Forsyth produced with a flourish a sheet of folded paper. He cleared his throat before speaking. "These are the names and addresses of every bastard that would dare fight against us."

Tasker heard the room go quiet. No doubt everyone was wondering how Forsyth got such a list. "I'll see to the rest of our troops, sir," Tasker offered. "They can round up all the horses in town so our men here can ride on the return journey. We'll fill every sleigh to the limit with booty."

Tasker placed the oil lantern on a counter and opened the front door. *So far, so good.* He mounted his horse and pointed with his riding crop to two of his men. "You two, and Delaney, you're with me. Let's go visit your brother. Lead us."

Reappearing from behind a drifting cloud, the full moon lit up the road. The Elizabethtown tavern lay a block of houses over to the east. A two-story log building, freshly painted white, with glass windows and a green door, gave Tasker the impression of a prosperous business. But he saw no light behind the panes of glass.

Delaney pulled a key from his pocket, unlocked the front door, and pushed down on the handle. "Sean," he called out, "wake up. It's your brother, Joe."

The door opened wide into the main barroom, and in minutes Sean himself, dressed in a robe and carrying a candle, clambered down the stairs. "What the hell do you want at this time of night?" He rubbed an eye and raised the candle to better see the others visitors.

"The American Army's come," Delaney explained. "This is Lieutenant Tasker. He's promised to protect your tavern."

As the light flickered across Tasker's face, he snatched the candle from the man's hand and strolled to the bar's counter, where bottles of whiskey waited. The proprietor grabbed Tasker's arm, and out of nowhere, the riding crop shot down hard across Sean's forehead and nose.

The innkeeper cried out and dropped heavily to the floor. A thin cut opened above one eyebrow and a stream of blood gushed from his nose, rolling down his chin. Sean put his hand to the wound and moaned.

Tasker turned his back. "I prefer nice wooden floors like these," he commented, "instead of that damn straw. Much cleaner-looking and they keep out the damp better." He took a sip of whiskey, then another, and let it burn down his throat. "Now get up and don't ever dare to touch me again."

Tasker handed the bottle to one of his soldiers who immediately took a large gulp. "That's enough, now. Don't let our major catch the pair of you drinking on duty." The man passed it to his companion for a drink. Tasker snatched back the bottle and handed it to Delaney, who had hurried to his brother's side.

"You just didn't know the rules." Tasker grinned and patted Sean on the arm, but the man shied away. "These good fellows will stand guard outside. You see, Delaney, I keep my word."

"Thank you, sir." Delaney stared at the floor.

"When we depart, they each get two full bottles, understand?" Tasker pointed the crop at Sean, who nodded silently. "And feed them something hot for their trouble."

Tasker glanced up the stairs. "Any female lodgers here?"

Sean shook his head.

"Don't try to lie to me." Tasker warned, waving the riding crop in his face. "You must have some lodgers. Names." He ordered sharply.

"Just one man — a fur trader. Name's Westlake."

"Let's pay him a nighttime visit, then." Tasker reached for the candle and started climbing the stairs.

At the sound of voices on the floor below, Westlake opened his eyes and yawned. He'd departed his aunt's home a few days earlier and now laid still, trying to assess the noise … voices again, sharp and angry. He leapt silently out of bed, lit a candle, and pulled on his pants. Men shouted outside in the street.

From the side of his window, he watched two long files of soldiers march past, shoving prisoners in front of them. The military wore greatcoats, furs, and blankets. Then an officer shouted out an order in a southern accent. *Christ, the Americans!* He grabbed the first shirt from the top of his bag, slipped it on, and did up the buttons.

A man cried out from the bar below. Westlake jammed on his boots and strapped the knife sheath inside the right one. He grabbed his musket from the table and loaded it. A last look out the window showed the street had emptied.

What could he hope to do, certainly not take on a whole army? He wouldn't accomplish much in an American prison either. The mission and rescuing his uncle had to come first; no sideshows, Brock had once told him. He lifted the candle and tucked the musket under his arm. Just as he reached for the door handle, bootsteps echoed along the hallway. A hard knock rapped next on the other side of his door.

"Open up," a man ordered. The banging continued.

His shoulders tense, Westlake stepped back and quickly returned the loaded musket to the table. "Coming, I'm coming." He undid the top buttons of his shirt.

"Open this damn door or I'll break it down."

Westlake unlocked the door and his stomach clenched. The man in front of him stood a good head taller and wore a familiar item of clothing: his uncle's boat cloak. He pushed past Westlake into the room. The proprietor followed and was himself accompanied by a man who by his looks had to be his relation.

"This is Lieutenant Tasker, of the United States Rifle Regiment." A warning note had crept into Sean's voice.

Westlake noticed the bloody gash over the innkeeper's eye and the blood staining his nightshirt. "Pleased to meet you, Lieutenant Tasker," Westlake said. "Odd hours for making house calls."

"And this is my brother, Joe, Mr. Westlake," Sean added quickly.

"Joe." Westlake acknowledged but didn't take his eyes off of the lieutenant.

Tasker took up position in the centre of the small room, his eyes pausing to stare at the musket. He reached out and picked it up, unaware it was loaded.

Westlake inhaled sharply.

"Expecting to hunt down a beaver here in your room, no doubt," Tasker remarked sarcastically as he replaced the musket on the table. Downstairs someone slammed the front door.

Westlake took a few steps toward the table where Tasker stood. "One has to prepare for any emergency these days — such as unexpected visitors in the middle of the night," Westlake replied.

Sean pushed past Tasker, bumping his arm in his anxiety to place himself between the intruder and Westlake.

"Not learned your lesson, yet." Tasker spit out the words, raising the riding crop again. But as his arm rose to strike, so did Westlake's, who simply snatched the crop out of Tasker's hand. "Yes, that's a very nice article, sir, thank you. I've never found use for one of these before."

More footsteps echoed down the hall until the sergeant came bursting through the door. "Sir, sorry for the interruption," he exclaimed. "Major Forsyth demands your presence."

Tasker remained standing with his mouth open. Westlake handed him back his riding crop and smiled. "Is there anything else I can do for you, Lieutenant?" Inwardly, he felt his heart pounding.

Tasker hesitated, anger flashing in his eyes. "You travel awfully goddamn light for a fur trader, Mr. Westlake." He glanced around the room.

"I'm on the administrative side of the business, sir. Westlake Trading has pelts waiting in New York ready to sail for Paris and the French Emperor's court." He coughed the last words from a suddenly dry mouth.

"Sir, we have to get going. The major's waiting," the sergeant insisted. "We can arrest this fellow if you like."

Westlake watched Tasker carefully, lest he try again to strike out. From behind, the sergeant shoved Joe Delaney to one side.

"For what, sleeping in his bed?" Tasker demanded of his sergeant. "There will be another time, Mr. Westlake." Tasker shook his riding crop as if a warning, and marched out the door. The sergeant immediately followed his lieutenant. Westlake watched the boat cloak disappear and felt a pang of anxiety at this reminder of his uncle. He stepped to the door to see Tasker and his sergeant depart down the hall.

"I could have just run him through with my bayonet, sir," the sergeant proposed as they hustled away.

"Somehow I think he'd get the better of you," Tasker concluded. "And you'd end staring up at the ceiling, with the bayonet in your own throat."

Westlake tried to relax and breathe normally, quickly closing the door.

The two riflemen had clumped down the stairs when Delaney announced how close they'd all come to being prisoners of war. He reckoned it was only the goodwill he'd purchased with his cooperation that saved them. "I never saw anyone with faster hands than yours, Mr. Westlake, but you risked your life taking that crop away from Tasker. No one dare touch the man. Just ask my brother."

Westlake stood slightly back from the window to see the first detachment of riflemen marching away in column, followed by the captured Leeds militiamen, fifty-two by his count, all shuffling along, huddled together. He clenched his fists, peering at the parade through the falling snowflakes. A final batch of riflemen marched past, some guarding their new prisoners while others carried stolen furniture or bulging canvas bags. A few enemy soldiers even rolled away barrels of flour toward the river.

Perhaps Delaney was right and he had been lucky not to join the captured. One thing for sure: when Tasker raised his arm to strike, his Uncle Adam's cloak flapped open and underneath was a green jacket of exactly the type described by his aunt. If the stolen cloak didn't condemn him, the green jacket certainly did. Tasker and his cronies had kidnapped his uncle.

As the last of the invaders disappeared from view, Westlake turned away from the window. "Delaney, where exactly does this bugger Tasker and his men make their headquarters?" he asked.

"Ogdensburg, Mr. Westlake. About twelve miles farther down-river, right across from Prescott."

"Isn't that convenient of them," said Westlake. Now he had another reason to visit Ogdensburg. "I have to get some sleep before I travel. Any chance for breakfast in a few hours?"

"Absolutely," Sean said, rubbing his face where the riding crop struck. "The least I can do is send you on your way with a full belly."

Captain Nelles raised his collar, hunching his skinny frame down inside his greatcoat. A sharp wind off Lake Ontario still cut through the cloth to chill his flesh. The banging noise from inside the newly constructed grand magazine grew louder with every step toward its concealed entrance. At the request of the lieutenant in charge, this was a courtesy visit designed to please the officers and artificers who had laboured on the building.

Approaching from the lakeside, Nelles could barely make out the doorway, as the magazine itself seemed to be built into the ground. He walked up an embankment to find the building sitting in a hollow that had been excavated to at least thirty feet. Twenty paces away stood the old wooden shed that sufficed as York's original magazine for more than a decade. Governor-in-Chief Prevost's decision to make York a provincial marine depot had rendered the little shed obsolete.

The new depot required an expanded magazine to hold the vast quantities of extra cannon powder and musket cartridges.

Nelles slid on the snow back down the hill and entered through a great oak door that creaked open to his pull. He closed it behind him against the wind only to face another door of similar weight inside the vestibule, this one sheathed in copper. Once inside, he peered up at a vaulted ceiling and noticed a square black vent located on the back wall that offered ventilation to keep the powder dry.

A wiry, hard-looking man, Lieutenant Alex McMullen of York's 3rd Regiment of Militia, aged thirty-seven, snapped to attention along with the other men working inside the room. "Nice of you to join us, Captain Nelles, sir." He wore a proud smile on his weather-beaten face.

Nelles returned the salute. "Stand easy, gentlemen. Pray continue." He extended his hand to McMullen as the others returned to their work. The smell of fresh-cut lumber filled his nostrils.

McMullen gestured toward the cavernous room with an expansive wave. "General Brock would be proud of his idea coming to life. Better than that bloody old shed out the back, eh? Nothing could blow up this baby, sir."

Brock again. He wants Brock's approval, so he's invited me.

Nelles stared up again at the vaulted ceiling. "Yes, Lieutenant, he would definitely approve. He always wanted a new magazine built; you and your men have done a fine job. How's the family?" A good man, McMullen had moved to Upper Canada in 1795 with his parents as part of the late Loyalists tide, meaning Americans who arrived from the United States long after the revolution, seeking free land and the tools to work it.

"Sophia's wonderful, sir. The three boys are a handful, but I wouldn't know what to do without them." He laughed. "Our two girls are just as pretty as all get-out, and the eldest is learning to spin yarn." McMullen had once owned a tavern, done some farming, and of course, he knew the sawmill business.

Scattered on the floor in front of Nelles, great squares of timber lay waiting to form the end supports for the racking yet to be assembled. McMullen had obviously used his expertise to pick out the choicest pieces from his former sawmill. A box full of wooden nails caught Nelles's eye, and his surprise must have showed.

"No sparks allowed down here or kaboom." McMullen threw his hands in the air. "So we use wooden nails instead of steel," he explained. He bent down to the box, selected a nail, and handed it to Nelles. "When I get these racks up, this place'll store over three hundred barrels of gunpowder," he continued proudly.

Nelles carefully surveyed the ceiling while feeling the nail smooth to his touch. "Three hundred! No wonder you have to be cautious. How long now to get these racks up?"

"That's the darnedest thing, sir. We've only just got the timber, and I've an order signed by the assistant quartermaster to immediately start moving in the barrels from the old shed. But I can't do that with no racks built." McMullen screwed up his face and furrowed his brow. "I was wondering, with your influence, if you could help us out by getting a slight delay." Out of his vest pocket, McMullen handed Nelles his orders.

My influence? I'm not General Brock.

The men continued hammering at the racking supports while Nelles read the instructions in the formal order. Obviously, General Sheaffe didn't know of the conditions in the magazine or he wouldn't have pushed the quartermaster's department to hurry up emptying the shed. Signed by Mr. LeLievre, assistant deputy quartermaster, the order proved to Nelles that the officers' complaints about Sheaffe held some truth; the left hand didn't know what the right hand was doing.

"Steady there," McMullen called out to the men now quickly raising the first supporting H in the rack. The lieutenant gestured for other men to assist them.

"Mr. LeLievre is presently at the docks," Nelles replied. "I'll see what I can do for you. Just get these racks up sooner rather than later."

"I knew you'd help us, sir." McMullen smiled. "I guarantee you'll be proud of what we achieve here. This magazine will last long enough for your great-grandchildren to see it."

8

· · · · · ·

WITH THE WIND of a hard snow pushing from the north, the twelve-mile hike from Elizabethtown took Westlake the better part of the next day. Sean Delaney had made him a large breakfast, served in front of a roaring fire. The brothers had warned against travelling during the storm, but he knew a report of last night's raid was too vital to keep from the garrison at Prescott. Besides, keeping pace with the raiders would likely lead him to his uncle.

Westlake packed up everything on his horse, strapped on his snow-shoes, and said goodbye to the two Delaneys. He'd travelled only a few miles before wishing he'd followed their advice and remained in front of that fireplace. The branches on the pines sagged under great pillows of snow, and the drifts all but blotted out his path running between the trees. Even his horse struggled, nodding its head as he reached forward to pat its neck.

At the southwestern approach to Prescott, a slight twist in the road brought him abruptly in sight of two sentries ahead, stamping their boots in an effort to keep warm. "State your business," the younger one demanded.

Westlake only had to mention Colonel Macdonell's name. The junior man immediately volunteered to act as escort and guide through town. They proceeded along streets where buildings were under construction around every corner.

"Willie Robertson, Leeds County Militia, sir. Most pleased to make your acquaintance." He held out a gloved hand and Westlake shook it. "I'm going to be a well known artist one day."

"I'm very happy for you, Mr. Robertson." Westlake did not offer his name. He noticed that the lad walked with a distinct limp and had a boyish face. "You should still be in school."

"Kicked me out of that Cornwall school." Willie laughed. "Didn't think my drawings of the headmaster funny at all. I hated the place."

And Westlake knew then why he had instantly liked young Willie Robertson. He clenched his fist, remembering his own hatred of the same school, before Reverend Strachan had once ordered him to leave.

They turned downhill toward the river, and before long they'd reached their destination. A small man, his back toward them, watched a dozen men who were hammering away at what appeared to be a new barracks. Lieutenant Colonel Red George Macdonell stood motionless with his hands planted on his hips.

"Please hand him this," Westlake requested.

"Sir."

Westlake stayed back while Willie marched forward, came to sharp attention, and saluted. He placed the sealed letter from Captain Nelles in Macdonell's hand and in the gusting wind leaned forward to say something in his ear. When no reply was forthcoming, he marched to stand beside Westlake. Macdonell swung around to glimpse the visitor and then turned back to study the work in progress.

An hour later, his teeth rattling and his toes gone numb, Westlake waited in the cold with Willie Robertson at attention beside him. His patience was quickly coming to an end. Red George had shouted a few terse orders to the workers, but Westlake had yet to speak to the colonel. Perhaps the man had forgotten him. He finally decided he'd waited long enough.

"Please tell the colonel I'm off to find myself some lodgings," Westlake said quietly to Willie. "I'll return later in the day when he has more time for me."

The young fellow limped the several paces to Macdonell and passed on Westlake's message. Red George immediately spun round and tore off his hat angrily. He glared through gargoyle-like eyes under thick red eyebrows. "Don't you move a muscle, young man," he shouted. "I'll tell you exactly when you can leave."

The colonel's red hair had sprung out to the sides and now he brushed it back into place with one hand. *Fiery* was the word Nelles had used to describe the man, but at this moment Westlake thought *explosive* might be more suitable. He did as told and remained in place.

"I have orders to carry out, sir," Westlake spoke up. "My superior answers only to Major General Sheaffe himself, who is under direct instructions from Governor-in-Chief Prevost. Are you going to read the note he sent you, sir?"

"Damn ye, you're a cheeky fellow."

"I fulfill my orders, sir." Westlake persisted. "I should add that I'm also here to tell you that American riflemen struck Elizabethtown in the early hours of this very morning."

"God's teeth! You should have spoke to me before this!"

"I've been waiting for over an hour, sir." Westlake folded his arms defiantly across his chest. "The raiders left as fast as they came. Perhaps I could offer you the balance of my report indoors, sir?"

"Back to your post," the colonel ordered Willie. Then, with his hands cupped around his mouth, he called out to an officer standing in the open doorway of the new barracks under construction. "Another half-hour, Captain Jenkins, and then call it a day." The officer delivered a token salute before the colonel turned back to Westlake. "Follow me, young man." He did not offer to shake hands, but Westlake was just as pleased to keep his own inside his glove.

Red George led him into a log cabin whose single large room extended the full board length of twenty feet square in each direction. "Make yourself comfortable," the colonel growled.

The dimly lit interior offered warmth at least, and Westlake breathed a deep sigh of relief. He dropped his pack in a corner before pulling off his outer garments, including his boots, and then stood in his stocking feet on the loosely planked floor. *Heat at last.* He helped himself to three pieces of wood to place on the fire and then stretched his bare hands above the shimmering coals.

Red George lit a candle and placed it on a table big enough for two, which rested against one wall. He plunked himself in a chair and gestured for Westlake to take the other. Finally, the colonel tore the letter's seal. Westlake waited in the hope that Nelles had explained the objective of his mission sufficiently for Red George to help him track down Silas Sterling in Ogdensburg. The colonel's eyebrows suddenly rose and a smile spread over face. He pushed back his chair, stood up, and stepped over to Westlake with his hand outstretched.

"So you want to go to Ogdensburg, do ye?" the colonel began. "Well, Lieutenant Westlake, you're a man after my own heart, you are." For such a wiry fellow, a head shorter than Westlake, the man's grip was like a vise. "Your captain's note says that you were present at the surrender of Fort Mackinac, the fall of Detroit, and the battle of Queenston Heights. You must be the only man alive who fought at all three."

"How I can get across to meet Sterling, sir?" Westlake gestured toward the river with his thawing hand.

"You're persistent, if nothing else. Silas Sterling's currently in Sackets Harbour so you'll have to bunk in with me here until he returns to Ogdensburg. Accommodation's at a premium in Prescott right now." Red George looked down at the letter again. "And besides, I want to hear your personal account of each battle … minute by minute. But first, tell me all you know about the raid on Elizabethtown."

Westlake related how the raiders struck in the early hours of the morning, broke open the jail to rescue a dozen men, and then retreated with fifty-two prisoners of their own. "They seized whatever booty they could stuff in their pockets and carry on their sleighs, then withdrew across the ice. I set off at dawn this morning for Prescott." Westlake kept the kidnapping of his uncle to himself. He would see his uncle free, but first he had to get himself to Ogdensburg. "Before they left, I had a run-in with a bastard of a lieutenant named Tasker and his miserable sergeant."

"One day, I'll catch up with those two." The colonel grabbed a fistful of air. "Unburden your horse and put your things over in the corner. Three bearskins on the floor will be your bed. Join me for dinner and then you can finish your report."

"After breakfast, I'm off to Cornwall, sir. If our spy Mr. Sterling's not in reach for a couple of weeks, I should make good use of my time." Westlake intended visiting some old friends from his school days, but even torture wouldn't force him to reveal that to Colonel Macdonell.

Red George eyed him skeptically.

"Best not to ask, sir. Secret," Westlake lied.

"Damnable doubledealing, eh. All this agent stuff; there's no honour in it if you ask me. I thought I had you tomorrow morning for some prime-and-load drill out on the ice."

"Sorry, sir. Next time, for sure," Westlake volunteered. He turned to his pack on the floor. "I look forward to it," he lied again.

Through a glass trained on the ice of the St. Lawrence River, Lieutenant Tasker scanned the manoeuvrings of the redcoats and wondered exactly what they were planning. He shivered and glanced up at the grey winter sky. Every morning from his perch on a wall in the ruins of an old fort, he studied the British, stamping through their drills.

Major Forsyth had put his entire force on high alert, and the men now cursed him for it. Except for the cleaning of their own rifles, individual discipline in the company didn't exist. Even Forsyth could not expect a man drunk at midnight to be up before dawn the next day. Impossible, thought Tasker. As the days wore on, fewer and fewer men were showing up for the early parade. Tasker heard it said among the troops that old man Forsyth had lost his marbles if he expected anything more.

The British fired and the blast echoed across to Ogdensburg, where Tasker ducked behind his crumbling wall. Still, no balls peppered the American shore. Behind his back, Forsyth arrived and chuckled. Tasker readjusted the glass.

"You needn't fear," Forsyth said. "They're using blue cartridges … blanks. If they switch back from blue to white, we know they're coming. I've half a mind to charge them out on the ice just to see if they have any white cartridges with them."

"I count about five hundred men there, sir," Tasker commented. "They drill sharp enough but can they fight, that's the question." He glanced behind him to where only a hundred of his own rifle-men stood freezing in the bleak weather. If the British launched a real attack at this instant, he'd not have a chance in hell of holding Ogdensburg against them.

"You can never tell for sure until a man is actually in combat," Forsyth replied. "That's why our raids have been such good practice for the men."

Tasker had kept a steady watch on the enemy's lines. Each morning the British columns had sortied closer to the American side of the river. Now they were more than halfway. "Do they think we don't notice them creeping always nearer?" he asked. "Stupid British bastards. We'll shred their fancy redcoats to pieces on that open ice long before they reach our bank."

"Check out our cannon to make sure they're ready," Forsyth ordered. "And tell our rifles I'll shoot any man who can't wake up promptly because of drunkenness on whichever morning the British choose to attack."

Tasker paused, wondering if Forsyth would follow through on the threat, and decided better not to test the will of his major. "Do you think they'll be coming, sir?" He nodded to the river.

"They want us to grow complacent. Then one day, it won't be blue cartridges they'll be firing."

A few days later, the northeast entrance to the little town of Prescott, a dozen sentries stood guard on the approach from the road. Behind them a company of redcoats marched sharply followed by a troop of dragoons circling north of the settlement. The riders eyed Westlake carefully as they trotted off. A sentry approached, snapped to attention and demanded a password from him. The certain tension evident in the guard's eyes revealed that things had changed in Prescott since the last time he'd been here.

Westlake did not know the current password, but on the mention of Colonel George Macdonell's name, the ensign in charge of the sentries this time assigned two redcoats to accompany him to Red George himself. With the reins of his horse firmly in hand, Westlake pushed his snowshoes downhill toward the river. The sound of saws cutting logs was loud on every street. A small army of tradesmen hammered away at the buildings under construction seemingly with renewed vigour.

Red George stood in the same position as before, hands on hips, only this time Westlake received a more cordial reception. The colonel dismissed the two sentries before he spoke. "Ah Mr. Westlake, you're just in time for dinner again." He grinned. "Never did hear all of your battle stories. There's a special guest in town I'm sure you'll want to meet. You must join us for dinner and be sure to wear your best shirt."

Westlake watched as the same troop of dragoons he'd seen earlier came circling along the shoreline. They were obviously guarding something, like they were waiting for an imminent attack. Their activity brought an excitement to Prescott, and just for a moment the men working on the barracks stopped to gawk at the horsemen.

"What's going on?" Westlake asked.

"You'll find out soon enough. Keep your wits about you tonight," Macdonell warned. He turned back to the construction site. "That's enough standing about. Back to work, the lot of you."

Of the two dozen buildings in Prescott, Lieutenant Colonel Red George Macdonell and Lieutenant Westlake entered the one that boasted the most recent construction. Once inside the front door, a narrow hallway divided the house straight down the middle. Westlake peered into a room on his right where a dinner table held cutlery set out for three. The rattle of pans and the aroma of cooking chicken floating down from the far end of the hallway suggested that dinner was soon on its way. His stomach growled.

Red George vanished for a few moments, then reappeared and gestured for Westlake to follow. They turned left into a parlour where bearskin rugs covered a newly planked floor. A roaring fire at one end of the room offered warmth to two stern-faced gentlemen dressed in red coats with gold facings. On seeing Westlake, the pair ceased their conversation and stared at him, clutching their wineglasses still in mid-air.

Pleased he'd worn his only white dress shirt, Westlake hastily fastened the top button of his waistcoat. He wondered who these people might be as he made his way over to the hearth, where he too looked forward to getting warm. Red George stopped in front of the two men and offered a modest bow.

"Gentlemen, let me introduce you to the remarkable Lieutenant Jonathan Westlake of the York Militia. He has travelled all the way from York, and I'm sure has many fascinating stories for us."

"I'll be my own judge of that, thank you, Colonel." A man with a cherubic face and curly brown hair thrust out his hand. "Lieutenant Colonel Thomas Pearson, officer commanding ... You've had an uneventful trip, I hope. What exactly do you do in this army of ours, Lieutenant?"

Red George poured two additional glasses of red wine and handed one of them to Westlake.

"I'm afraid not so quiet a trip, sir," Westlake replied. "American raiders struck Elizabethtown in the early hours of the morning less than a fortnight ago. I'm sure Colonel Macdonell will have given you my report."

"Forsyth and his bloody Carolinian raiders," Pearson burst out. "You already know of my plan to wipe them out." He hissed the last words to Red George, but Westlake sensed that the words were actually meant for the other man by the fire, who still sipped at his wine as he studied Westlake.

The opulent gold braid on his uniform suggested some grand authority, a messenger of the King perhaps, but one who had yet to say a word. From the expression in his light brown eyes, Westlake guessed that this man saw everything and listened to everything intently. His hair was loosely parted in the middle and he occasionally scratched at his wide sideburns. A rather weak-looking dimpled chin accompanied a broad forehead, but the assertive voice that now emerged offered no hint of weakness. He turned away from examining Westlake and faced the fire as he spoke.

"You're Brock's agent, aren't you?" The room fell silent at the mention of Brock's name."

"Sir?" Westlake tensed.

"You needn't play coy with me, Lieutenant." The man gave a log in the fire a nudge with his boot and a dormant slice of bark caught flame, brightening his cheeks before he turned back to face Westlake. "I approved your lieutenancy, young man, and I congratulate you on your daring exploits to date. Captain Nelles has no doubt since found good use for you."

Surprised that this stranger knew so much about him, Westlake hid his confusion under a passive expression. And, remembering the lessons learned from drinking on an empty stomach, he took only a small sip of his wine to calm himself. Then he stared at Red George for help but found only mischief in his eyes.

"Mr. Westlake, you needn't look so dour. Your secret is completely safe in this company." Macdonell finally chuckled. "Let me introduce to you, Governor-in-Chief, Sir George Prevost."

The governor smiled and offered his hand. Westlake shook it, reflecting. So this was the one man who had restrained Brock, who had held tight the leash that tugged him back from attacking the American Army that had threatened them across the Niagara River. Westlake had lost count the number of times officers had complained, "If only Prevost would allow" — allow them to do this or that. In private, officers claimed that given the chance, they'd ring the man's neck like a chicken. At least now he knew why little Prescott was crawling under the dragoons' blanket of security.

"Perhaps then someone would tell *me* about Mr. Westlake," Pearson requested. From inside his jacket, Red George produced the letter of introduction received from Captain Nelles. Once put in Pearson's hand, he offered it first to Prevost, who shook his head. A soldier wearing a red coat and white gloves entered the room to whisper into Pearson's ear.

"Set another place setting," Pearson ordered him. "The lieutenant will be joining us."

Dinner proceeded unhurried under a single portrait of the King. A fire blazed in the dining room and Westlake's feet and hands finally felt warmed. He sat beside the governor, directly facing the two officers. Under the light of several lit candles, the white-gloved soldier served them formally with the aid of a young woman from the kitchen staff.

All three officers questioned Westlake about his experiences at the fall of Fort Mackinac, and the sudden capture of Detroit by Tecumseh and Brock. Eventually, their inquiries came round to the battle of Queenston Heights. Westlake's stomach twisted into the familiar knot that reoccurred each time he thought of the uphill charge that saw Brock meet his end. It pained him to remember cradling the dead man's head on the way to the hospital, hoping his eyes would open; indeed, expecting them to. Westlake dropped his fork.

His heart raced while he felt his face flushing crimson and his dinner do a somersault in his stomach. Then, just as fast he went cold. He put a hand to his clammy forehead, feeling about to faint.

"Are you all right, Mr. Westlake?" Prevost asked, and Westlake felt a hand touch his shoulder.

"None of it needed to happen if we'd been allowed to attack them on their side of the river," he managed to say before the room disappeared and Westlake's head dropped toward his plate. Feeling Prevost's hand grip his arm, Westlake caught himself in time, took a deep breath, and sat up straight.

"Don't you dare question the judgment —" Pearson began, but Westlake barely heard a word.

"It's fine, Colonel," Prevost interrupted. "No doubt he's been through traumatic times. Take a drink, young man. You'll feel better." He put a glass in Westlake's shaking hand.

Westlake gulped at his wine and inhaled. Red George nodded at him with a reassuring smile. Westlake pushed his plate to one side lest his head fall straight into it. *I've made an ass of myself!*

"It was difficult for us when General Brock fell, sir, ... like the world itself had died," he blurted out. "In a way, it did too. At first sad, the men grew angry. Some of that anger directed at yourself, sir. I'm sorry."

Pearson leapt to his feet, his chair flying out behind him. "Damn your eyes, Lieutenant. This is the Governor-in-Chief you're speaking to, and you will mind your tongue or face the consequences."

"Sit down, Colonel," Prevost ordered coldly. "You are more offended than I. The man speaks only the truth. I'm not oblivious to the sentiments of our troops — and some of the officers." He glanced at Red George, who sat listening quietly. "How did the enemy manage to get up that cliff and behind General Brock?" Prevost asked.

"The rumour is a local fisherman led them, sir," Westlake explained. "But Captain Nelles has found no trace of any such man. The night before the battle, General Brock wrote a letter to me and gave it to the captain for delivery. In it, the general stated clearly that he believed a traitor is at work inside York garrison. This is why I must go to Ogdensburg."

"Ogdensburg?" asked Pearson.

The room went silent as the young woman cleared away the dinner plates and the soldier placed a dish of apple pie in front of each guest. For a moment the sweet smell of it distracted Westlake, reminding him of his family's dinner table and Maple Hill.

"To meet a man called Sterling," Westlake explained. "Apparently one of his associates there in Sackets Harbor knows what this traitor looks like." He picked up his fork to scoop some of the pie into his mouth. Pearson's eyes cut knowingly to Macdonell.

"The 8th Foot could escort him safely across the ice before dawn, sir." Red George cleared his throat and added, "Fifty men would do nicely."

Pearson looked to Prevost, who shook his head. Red George then suggested a smaller force of a dozen, and again Prevost shook his head. There was no way that Red George would be allowed to antagonize the Americans. At close quarters, Westlake was now observing Prevost's infamous leash in action.

"Send just one man who knows that shoreline. Captain Jenkins will suffice," Pearson suggested.

Prevost nodded approval. "Mr. Westlake, you risk your life for us and so deserve an explanation." He rubbed a sideburn and grinned. "Both these officers want to wipe out Forsyth's raiders squatting across the river, and I stop them for the same reason I restrained General Brock. You want to know why?" He tilted his head in anticipation of Westlake's curiosity.

"My orders from the secretary of war are to take defensive measures only — do nothing that might excessively antagonize the Americans. Through smuggling activities, here and mainly along New England's coast, their farmers feed our army in British North America as well as His Majesty's forces serving under Wellington in the peninsula … thousands and thousands of bushels of grain and beef. Understand?" The governor promptly reached out for the wine bottle and divided its remaining contents between Westlake's glass and his own.

Thinking through what he had just heard, Westlake nodded and picked up his glass. Smuggling? He'd had no idea it was the lifeblood of Upper Canada. He glanced at Red George while Prevost sipped at his glass.

"That's mostly what I do," Macdonell said. "Swallow my pride, deal with these smugglers, and feed our troops."

"On top of that, every man we lose in the Canadas is irreplaceable," Prevost added. "General Brock started off with less than fifteen hundred men to defend an area larger than England. If he lost a few a hundred of them on some adventure, they could not be replaced, and therefore we could lose the war on one throw of the dice."

"But, sir, surely there are times when it's prudent, even safer, to attack first, perhaps a surprise assault to save your own men from a concentrated blow."

"You sound just like your fellow officers here." Prevost smiled at Pearson, who began drumming his fingers on the tablecloth. "As long as the enemy are perceived to be the aggressors, the New England states will continue to support us with their produce. The very second the British Empire attacks America, there is every chance these traders, who are, after all American, will turn their backs on us. We just can't risk it. Even if we could do so, I have my orders."

The soldier with the white gloves re-entered the room and handed Macdonell a folded paper. In an effort to change the subject, Red George interjected, "If you don't mind a suggestion, sir, a quick start to the morning might be best." He looked down at the message on the page. "We lost two deserters tonight, who'll probably go and tell the enemy of your presence here."

Prevost raised his eyebrows, nodded agreement, and looked to Pearson, who readily concurred. The dinner came to a rapid finish, and Westlake had yet to receive a plan to reach Ogdensburg. "I still have to cross that river, sir," Westlake persisted. "Captain Nelles is counting on me."

"I can see why he does," Prevost said. He wiped the corners of his mouth with his napkin and stood up while pushing back his chair. The others stood with him, but Westlake didn't stir except to lift the last morsel of pie to his mouth.

"We have some knowledge of this Sterling, and he is not due in Sackets Harbor until tomorrow morning at the earliest," Pearson explained. "But, of course, one never knows in this damn skulduggery business. If he sends his usual signal, Captain Jenkins will escort you across tomorrow evening, after dusk." He looked to Red George, who nodded his concurrence.

"That should make you happy, Lieutenant," Prevost announced with some satisfaction. He tapped Westlake on the shoulder twice. "Join me for an early breakfast. I have another question for you."

Westlake stood immediately. "Thank you, sir. I appreciate your assistance. The sooner I meet this man, the sooner we'll all know the identity of Brock's traitor."

9

....

THE FOLLOWING MORNING with breakfast over, everyone rose from the table together. They said their goodbyes and stepped out to the horses, whose breath hung in the air. Prevost let Pearson and Macdonell go ahead, then he pulled Westlake back inside for what the young officer considered an odd inquiry. "Will the dissatisfaction among the officer corps serving with General Sheaffe affect our defence of York?"

Still half asleep, this question took Westlake by surprise ... he was only a lieutenant after all. He remembered Red George's warning to keep his wits about him. "I took some time off to recuperate from wounds I suffered at Queenston, sir." He tapped his leg where a bayonet had pierced his thigh.

Prevost didn't react, obviously expecting more.

Westlake considered a further reply, aware that any negative response from him would implicate his closest associate, the good Captain Nelles. "What I mean is, I've been out of the conversation somewhat, sir, ... but I can tell you this. Immediately after the battle, General Sheaffe offered the enemy that armistice and also paroled the entire New York State Militia on our side of the river. Our officers, including myself, wanted to finish the battle in American territory. There was much dissatisfaction then directed at the general, but that will have absolutely no impact on their loyalty, or indeed the defence of York."

"Hmm," was the only reply from Prevost. They shook hands goodbye and he exited the room.

Westlake stepped outside to overhear Colonel Pearson make his farewell. Before departing, Pearson ordered Macdonell that under no circumstances, excepting an outright attack by the enemy, could his demonstration on the ice that morning turn into an attack against

Ogdensburg. Both men knew that the other craved an opportunity to charge straight across the river and give Forsyth a proper thrashing, so it was odd to hear Pearson mouthing the instructions received from Prevost.

"You won't let me down, will you, George?" the senior officer murmured.

The two men shook hands vigorously. "Of course not, sir. I follow my orders like the next man."

Pearson simply nodded goodbye to Westlake. With an entourage of cantering dragoons and sleighs piled high with supplies, Governor-in-Chief Prevost and Lieutenant Colonel Pearson departed for Kingston in the dim light of dawn.

From the doorway, Red George waved slowly as the sleighs pulled away, leaving a trail of lines that marred the snow. The colonel wore no overcoat, as if he intended returning to breakfast, but instead he turned to Westlake the moment they were inside. "Get that fur coat on, Lieutenant. Find Captain Jenkins and give him the message to load the six-pounder on a sleigh." Red George reached for his greatcoat. "I'll speak to ordinance myself about the ammunition today. Tell the captain that we'll be using white cartridges this morning."

"White cartridges carry the King's lead, sir," Westlake said with assurance. "The blue ones fire blanks."

"You have a naive habit of stating the truth at the wrong time, Lieutenant." The face of Red George switched from friendly to fierce in seconds. "Get your feet moving and keep your mouth shut." Westlake suddenly understood, just as the colonel added an emphatic, "Now!"

A plate crashed to the floor in the kitchen as Westlake grabbed his coat and gulped down the last of his tea. He snatched two rolls from the breadbasket and stuffed them in a pocket before hurrying out the door.

February 22, 1813, dawned with a grey sky offering a hint that more snow might be on the way. On the march down the hill, halfway to their new barracks, Captain Jenkins beckoned to Westlake, calling him over. "The signal from Mr. Sterling showed itself before dawn,"

Jenkins announced in a whisper. "I'll take you across there tonight as instructed, Lieutenant. Meet me by the barracks at midnight."

"That's wonderful, sir, but we now have a different matter at hand." Westlake quickly relayed the latest orders from Colonel Macdonell. Jenkins's eyes grew large at the news of white cartridges and a wide smile spread over his face. He slapped Westlake's shoulder heartily as if he'd just received a gift.

"Arm yourself, lad," said Jenkins. "I'll see you soon enough in the town square." He hustled off.

A militia sergeant ran past toward the river, tugging the reins of two horses following behind him. The fast-spreading news brought soldiers stumbling out of their quarters at a run. One man grasped a musket in one hand while still buttoning up his tunic with the other.

Westlake dashed across to the cabin where he had bunked with the colonel. *What the hell is going on?* Surely Red George could not be planning to attack Ogdensburg. Westlake had heard express orders given to the contrary. However, he reasoned that if the army charged across the St. Lawrence, the opportunity to rescue his uncle would have to present itself. At the same time, Sterling would probably disappear.

Inside the cabin, Red George's sword and greatcoat were missing. Westlake grabbed his own musket and slung his ammunition pouch over his shoulder. He sheathed his knife, strapped it in his right boot, and darted out the door. By the time he reached Prescott's main street, he found the town square packed with jostling soldiers in a haze of steaming breath.

Captain Jenkins appeared on his horse shouting for the Glengarry Light Infantry to form at the front followed by a company of Leeds County Militia and another of Dundas Militia. This force didn't wait for the rest of the troops to form up but simply began marching off toward the river. Late to join the parade, Willie Robertson limped in behind, nodded to Westlake, and then attached himself to the tail of the column pounding off down the hill.

"Lieutenant." Red George had ridden up beside him. "I would have you go with Captain Jenkins, if you please."

"My purpose, sir?"

"Any messages he needs to send to me, you're his man. And one more thing, Mr. Westlake, watch young Robertson for me. I know his parents and he's craving revenge for Tasker stabbing him in the leg."

"Sir." Westlake grimaced, touched the brim of his hat, and hurried after the militia column. As he caught up, he found Willie Robertson marching at his side.

"Good morning, sir." Willie smiled. "I've got something here for you." From inside his jacket, he produced a small charcoal sketch of Westlake himself.

"Willie!" Westlake studied the image. "I don't know what to say. That's bloody fantastic!"

"You didn't really believe I was an artist," Willie commented reproachfully. "I've cleaned up the frightful parts of your appearance, so my drawing makes you appear more handsome than you are." Willie burst out laughing, and Westlake rapped him on the shoulder.

"Stay close to me today, Mr. Robertson," Westlake ordered as the American shore came into sharper view. He unbuttoned the top of his greatcoat and slid the picture safely inside. "How fast can you run on that leg?"

"Like a deer," Willie boasted.

The lad was an accomplished liar as well as a good artist.

They reached the edge of the river in time to see the sleigh carrying a six-pounder slide off the bank onto the ice. It tilted dangerously to one side, threatening to tip over before Westlake and Willie joined the struggle to keep it upright. Two horses hitched to the sleigh began to pull it forward while two artillerymen pushed from the rear.

Willie eyed the cannon with a raised eyebrow. "What's going on here?" he questioned.

"You will do yourself a favour to keep quiet this morning, Mr. Robertson," Westlake advised with satisfaction.

Captain Jenkins veered his column off to the right, until the troops formed two ranks directly opposite the western end of Ogdensburg. They soon marched passed the midpoint of the river, where the cannon sleigh came to a halt on the left of the line, and waited there for further instructions. Westlake's boots crunched on the snow and ice coming to attention beside the six-pounder. He fixed his gaze on Ogdensburg, less than six hundred yards away.

Colonel Macdonell rode ahead of the 8th Foot and Royal Newfoundlanders, leading them left so that he faced the eastern side of Ogdensburg. Westlake counted at least two hundred militiamen trooping behind the colonel's regular force of more than a hundred. Again, the men formed into two ranks. If Red George genuinely had thoughts of disobeying orders and launching an attack on the town, no outward sign of haste showed itself. Westlake glanced up at a dull eastern sky, reckoning it was now just after seven o'clock.

Macdonell and Jenkins proceeded to ride alone from each side to the centre between their two columns. Their horses circled each other. Someone somewhere, perhaps from the midst of the larger column, fired a pistol.

Immediately, Red George called out: "You hear that, lads. The bastards are attacking us." His horse wheeled around as the men gave a great cheer. "Captain Jenkins, do your duty," he bellowed for all to hear.

"Gladly, sir." Jenkins galloped back to the front of his own ranks and ordered, "Prime and load!"

He counted fifteen seconds before hollering, "Fix bayonets!"

Standing in his stirrups to be better heard, Jenkins gestured toward Ogdensburg and shouted to his men, "These damnable thieves have attacked Gananoque and Elizabethtown, kidnapped our farmers, burnt our barns, and stolen our property. They think Prescott and your home will be next on their pillaging list, but this morning we're going to surprise the lazy bastards in their beds. At the quick, march!" He drew his sword and pointed toward the enemy shoreline.

Again, he paused, then finally shouted an order the men had all been hoping for, "To victory! Charge bayonets!"

"Huzzah!" the men yelled in eager response and bolted forward.

One of the horses pulling the sleigh gave a sudden whinny at the uproar. Westlake rushed over to assist the artillerymen push the sleigh before rejoining the stampeding line alongside Willie. He stared at the trees lining the American shore. When would the Carolinian riflemen wake up from their daydream? Their rifles could pick off any target they chose on the open ice. He could no longer tell if his heart pounded from exertion or fear.

Westlake glanced down the river at Macdonell's troops, also storming across the ice. They were already three-quarters of the way across when he heard the boom that shook his body. *Cannon fire!* He shoved Willie from behind as he dove to the ground himself.

Beside him, the sleigh and the two artillerymen exploded into a shredded tangle of metal and blood. Westlake jumped back to his feet. Others stood and gaped. The once picturesque scene now resembled a vision of hell.

The up-ended six-pounder had crushed one man's chest while the other soldier had been torn nearly in half by the ricocheting cannonball. The pair of horses reared up on their back hooves, finally bolting upriver with the shattered remains of the empty sleigh bouncing every which way behind them. Willie stared at Westlake, his mouth dropping wide open.

"Don't look," Westlake warned.

"I've never seen …" Willie tried to say more but stopped and jerked his head away.

Captain Jenkins wheeled his horse around to view the carnage and shouted, "Don't stop. Just keep going!" He waved his arm forward.

Westlake ran on a hundred yards before his paced slowed, his mouth gone totally dry. He stared over at the American shore, aware that his only safety lay in reaching its snow-covered riverbank. His heart heaved as he pumped his legs forward. Willie limped behind him.

"Come on, Willie!" Westlake hollered encouragement against the wind that tore over the ice. "We're dead if we stop here."

Captain Jenkins rode a few paces off to his right. "Keep the lines moving!" he demanded.

Still three hundred yards from shore, and a good twenty yards ahead of surging lines, Westlake turned to see Willie dropping back.

Then the first sporadic fire of rifles ripped through the air. He ran back toward the exhausted youth and yelled, "Down!"

Willie dropped flat to the snow. Westlake slid in beside him and grabbed his arm. "Are you hit?"

Willie shook his head, puffing frost.

Thank God.

"Listen carefully." Westlake squeezed his arm. "A rifle takes longer to load than a musket, so we'll make a dash immediately after they next fire, counting to twenty as we go." He scanned along the river where Macdonell's lines charged forward. He had not yet heard a single shot fired against them. He was surprised that it had taken so long for the American riflemen in front of Macdonell to realize they were under attack.

Another volley erupted from the American shore.

"That's our cue, Willie." Westlake lifted him under the shoulder. "Just twenty paces. You can do it." He pulled Willie along and counted off the steps before diving back on the ice in a slide. Right on time, the riflemen fired again. "See, nothing to it. They'll always aim for the easier targets."

Still puffing, Willie grinned and jumped up for another dash forward. At twenty paces he slid down onto the snow and again the riflemen fired. Westlake heard a scream of pain. Twenty yards to his right, Captain Jenkins slumped over in his saddle.

Lieutenant Tasker had been studying the British soldiers drawn up in two ranks standing rigidly on the windswept ice. They must be freezing, he reckoned. Through a telescope at his parlour window, the round eye of the lens focused on the redcoats as they formed in two separate divisions. Every day they had bored him with the same drills performed at the same time each morning.

If he was intent on attacking Ogdensburg today, the lieutenant figured he'd do exactly as the British had done — divide his troops in two and come at the town from both ends. So today would be like all the other days. The enemy soldiers on the western side directly facing him would begin their drill first, followed by the eastern division.

Tasker yawned and stretched, thinking wistfully about the barmaid he almost had in his bed last night, wishing he'd moved faster before her father arrived to fetch her home. *Christ, there's no justice in this world.*

He had passed the telescope over the lines one last time and then moved the lens back an inch to the centre. That cannon was new, and surely men didn't need a cannon for a marching drill. His shoulders tightened as the two commanders met in the centre, the pair of them alone on the ice between their two divisions. They circled around each other once as the sound of a single shot echoed over the ice. Then they each galloped away to take up position at the front of their men.

Prime and load — nothing unusual so far.

Fixing bayonets! That's new.

Tasker watched as the commander directly in front of him rose up in his stirrups and drew his sword.

Christ, they're attacking!

Tasker stared for just a moment longer, disbelieving what his eyes were seeing. He jerked the glass toward the eastern division, where the enemy also started to charge. "Sergeant! Wake up Major Forsyth in the back room. Now!" Tasker turned but found Sergeant Shaughnessy wasn't there. He ran to the back room himself and shook Forsyth urgently by shoulder. "Sir, wake up! The redcoats are attacking us."

Forsyth groaned and opened one eye.

"The British, sir!" Tasker pleaded desperately.

"I heard you, Lieutenant, no need to yell." Forsyth clutched his head but didn't rise. "It's probably just another type of drill."

"They've fixed bayonets — sprinting across the ice — and they're well past half way!" Tasker replied tersely. "I'm off to our nine-pounder. God help those men attending it if they're not at the ready."

He charged out the bedroom just as the sergeant quietly came through the front door. "Where the hell have you been?" Tasker shoved the man to one side as he ran for the door, tugging on his greatcoat.

"Taking a piss, sir," Sergeant Shaughnessy announced as if he didn't see the problem.

"Well, don't! Assemble the men, now!" Tasker pointed to the window. "The British are coming to kill you," he snarled.

Thirty yards from the same house in the ruins of the old fort, seven artillerymen manhandled the truck that held their cannon close to the river's edge. "Lower the elevation, for Christ's sake," one man bellowed in excitement.

Lieutenant Tasker slid to a halt as another man carefully selected a nine-pound ball from a stack of others as if he were choosing a tasty melon. "Can you hit that damn sleigh carrying their six-pounder?" He shivered in the cold, putting a hand to his forehead as riflemen flooded into the ruins to take position behind the walls.

"Exactly what we were aiming at, sir," the artilleryman said. "Like shooting ducks in a barrel, having them out there on this open ice." The man's grin revealed his one remaining yellow tooth. "First shot, guaranteed." He laughed before his face turned serious-looking as he gazed down the barrel of the cannon. His men had now stuffed the charges home and stood quickly to one side.

"Fire!"

The enemy sleigh carrying their cannon shattered under the initial blast. Tasker couldn't believe their luck. "Good show!" He pumped a fist in the air above his head and slapped a gunner on the back. "You all deserve a medal for that. Keep firing. They're mostly just stupid farmers," he lied, knowing full well the soldiers they faced were in large measure British regulars.

Sergeant Shaughnessy had raised sufficient alarm to ensure that when Tasker raced back toward the house, the green-jacketed riflemen were jamming themselves in between the buildings that lined the riverbank. Many of them wore partially buttoned-up overcoats and looked as if they were still asleep.

"Seen Major Forsyth?" Tasker asked.

"No, sir," replied Shaughnessy.

"Christ, look at them. They're not ready, Sergeant!"

One stupefied rifleman gazed across at the enemy. A few of the rest fastened their jackets against the cold. Others began firing independently. "Prime and load!" Tasker ordered in a shrill voice, trying desperately to assert some order.

"Make ready and take aim!" Tasker turned to see the advancing enemy line only three hundred yards away. "Fire!"

A sheet of flame spit forward from the riflemen's barrels. The smoke drifted out over the ice, obscuring his view. Once it cleared, he saw their volley had produced little effect. In their nervousness, his men had fired too high. His cannon roared to life for a second time, but the enemy, sprawling like so many black dots lying on the snow, remained untouched. They were soon up and charging again.

"Imbeciles, you've fired high!" Tasker screamed. "Prime and load!" He marched out in front of them, his riding crop jabbing the air. "Make ready and take aim. This time pick a target and aim lower. And you, man, shoot that goddamn officer on the horse." He gestured toward the redcoats.

"Fire!"

The enemy officer slumped in his saddle. "That was better. Teach these buggers a lesson for waking you up! Prime and load. Give it to them again." His troops fired, and the British checked their advance.

"Good start, Lieutenant." Major Forsyth stood at his shoulder and pointed down-river, where the more numerous eastern division surged in neat lines across the frozen white expanse. "Our militia can't stop those bastards from getting ashore," he warned. "This gang here will try to get behind us to cut off any retreat. I'll put a stop to that while you take half our men into town. Meet that division head on. I've already sent a six- pounder and the twelve over to Main Street to give you a hand."

"Sir." Tasker saluted, the edges of his mouth lifting slightly. In just a few minutes he'd turned the tide in their favour, though he'd yet to draw his sword. He looked forward to personally killing the other commander, and grinned as he sped away. "Sergeant Shaughnessy, you're with me." Tasker thrust out his riding crop. "All these men from this building on can follow us to Main Street. Move your arses. There's more killing to be done in town."

The crack of rifle fire echoed periodically across the ice of the St. Lawrence River. After reminding Willie to stand up and run again after each volley, Westlake darted back to where Captain Jenkins slumped over his horse. Beside the wounded captain, another lieutenant stood, waiting for instructions. With every blast from the enemy riflemen, more soldiers of the western division fell to the snow. Both ranks were hesitating to move forward as their comrades dropped around them.

"Push on, damn you," Jenkins groaned. "We can't stay out here in the open or we'll all get cut to pieces. I'll be fine, so just push on." He made a further effort to sit up straight.

"The riverbank ahead must be over ten feet high, sir," Westlake panted. "There's no way up it without ladders. Even if we get to the top, those rifles won't miss us at only twenty feet."

Another volley exploded from the enemy. Jenkins's horse whinnied and fell to the ground with the captain still in the saddle. His lieutenant spun round, gripping a hand in agony. Westlake crouched low beside Jenkins, who looked as white as the snow.

"Sir, may I suggest firing a volley from both our ranks to diminish the enemy's boldness," Westlake gasped. "Then an orderly retreat."

"Do it," Jenkins instructed his lieutenant. "Call out the order, now. Mr. Westlake, get over to the colonel and tell him of the mess we've made of things here."

Westlake beckoned a couple of men to assist the wounded captain to his feet and begin the retreat. "Hardly a mess, sir. We've done well to get this far. I'll inform the colonel you're wounded and falling back."

Still clutching his own hand, Jenkins's lieutenant turned on his heel and choked out the orders: "Front rank, make ready!" Westlake was sure that gut-wrenching fear gripped every man, yet they all stood on the order "Present!" In one motion, like a giant machine, they lowered their weapons pointing at the American shore.

"Fire!" All along the line, Brown Bess muskets poured lead balls and orange flame across the snow-covered river. Westlake fired with them and instantly began to reload. Dense smoke and the stench of burnt powder soon hung in the morning air.

"Rear rank, present." The lieutenant stepped forward to holler the orders at the top of his lungs. His face turned red and the muscles in his neck bulged. Westlake suspected that the louder the man yelled, the less his hand hurt.

"Fire!" The crack of musket fire echoed across the snow and ice.

"And withdraw!" The two lines of soldiers began to run, their eyes focusing squarely on the Canadian side of the river. Westlake peered toward the American shore that seemed so far away and wished he could dig a tunnel to Red George.

10

· · · · · ·

A THICK SCREEN OF SMOKE from the discharged muskets now curtained off the enemy shore. Lieutenant Westlake jumped up and ran, bursting through the smoke to find that the volley fired by the retreating Glengarries had done its job. The American riflemen had cautiously hidden themselves from view.

Legs burning, lungs heaving, Westlake's eyes cut across the shoreline for the first sign of a weapon. He had only seconds before some enemy rifle blew his guts out from thirty yards away. A single shot cracked out, the bullet plucking at his sleeve. He slid hard onto the ice, jamming his shoulder into the high snowbank that lined the edge of the river. His entire body tensed as his fingers probed his coat, expecting to feel blood. A neat hole ran through one side of the sleeve and out the other. The enemy ball had missed the flesh of his arm by only an inch.

Some men of the Glengarry Infantry, those who had advanced farthest, had clearly not heard the orders to retreat and clawed at the snowbank as if to make themselves part of its wall. Westlake motioned to them, pointing at their retreating comrades. After a few moments of rest, they too turned and began the long flight across the open ice.

Willie limped in beside Westlake. "Now what?" the lad asked.

"For Christ's sake, Willie, you should've gone back with the others." Westlake shook his head. "Prime and load, they'll be coming," he puffed, still trying to catch his breath.

"I meant, how do we get up there," Willie replied as he used his ramrod to stuff a cartridge down the barrel.

A scruffy American rifleman poked his head over the side, searching for his quarry. His eyes grew wide on seeing some of the enemy right below him. Before the man could raise his weapon, Westlake aimed his own musket and squeezed the trigger. The man blew back out of sight in an instant.

"Run to your left, Mr. Robertson. Go!" Westlake loaded his musket as he ran too, hunching his shoulders in the expectation of a bullet and the pain that would follow. The river snaked its way northeast, and after they had gone fifty yards, he turned to peer back along the shoreline.

No enemy visible. Thank God.

Gradually the snowbank sloped down to meet the frozen river. Westlake grabbed Willie by the arm and gestured upwards. He'd run for three hundred paces, and once off the river's ice, he fell back with relief onto the snow, gasping for breath while staring up at a brightening sky. Willie dropped to all fours, himself heaving for air. The intermittent firing from the riflemen was concentrated on the retreating lines of Glengarry Infantry and their militia.

Westlake gave himself one minute to rest. He sat up straight and hung his head between his legs. "I was also thrown out of that Cornwall school," he revealed.

"I knew there was something I liked about you, Mr. Westlake." Willie grinned and huffed.

"Be proud, Willie. That's a bloody tough run you made." Westlake stood. Time to find Red George and inform him that his western division was heading home.

Red George Macdonell had ridden back to the river and surveyed the withdrawal from atop his horse. While the two ranks attacking Ogdensburg from the west retreated toward Prescott, his own larger force made steady advances through the town against minimal fire. Aware that the race to get across the river had exhausted his men, there was still precious time to lose if he hoped to catch up with Forsyth and Tasker. He prayed the riflemen opposing Captain Jenkins would make their way over to confront him.

From Prescott, a ragged stream of women ran across the ice toward him. *Plunder.* In anticipation of victory, they were hurrying to carry their husbands' plunder home. *To the victor go the spoils.* He'd have to hang every man and women to stop it this time. The enemy had done too much to enrage the otherwise peaceful residents. Better to let that anger burn itself out and teach the local population to hate their own army for bringing such destruction to their doorstep. Behind the women crossing the river, a single uniformed rider made a cautious approach across the ice.

Red George urged his horse away from the shore when a welcome sight came into view, running straight through the town. "Ah, Mr. Westlake, wonderful to find you alive. And I see you've brought young Robertson with you."

"Safe and sound, sir," Westlake replied, trying to catch his breath. "Captain Jenkins's compliments, sir, but he's severely wounded and retreating with the Glengarries to Prescott."

"I hope the good fellow lives," the colonel replied seriously. "Back to town for us." He gestured. "And urge our lot on."

"We just came through the edge of town, sir, and found our sentries guarding several doors, sir," Westlake commented. "Looks rather odd?"

Macdonell gestured with his thumb over his shoulder toward Prescott. "Those women go running about to collect plunder." He turned in the saddle to study their progress. "So our sentries guard the houses of our particular allies, plus the slaughterhouse and the storehouse that contain beef and flour. All of it destined for smuggling across the river into my hands."

"So we protect their traitors," Westlake commented.

"Our allies," repeated the colonel.

"And their food supply?" Westlake questioned.

"Soon to be our supply, so long as those women don't get their hands on it." He squinted, to make out the face of the approaching rider. "And don't go anywhere near those sentries, Robertson, or they'll shoot you. Let's go."

The rider galloped the last few yards on dry land, reared to a sliding stop, and saluted. The dragoon leaned forward in his saddle and handed a sealed letter to Red George. "Compliments from Governor Prevost, sir, I am to ask that you read the letter forthwith."

Red George sighed and tore open the seal with his thumb. He gripped the page on both sides as the wind buffeted the flimsy paper. "Hmm, seems the governor is worried that I might attack Ogdensburg, Mr. Westlake. His written orders are that I am to desist from any serious offensive operations." All four men stared toward the town itself just as the sound of musketry exploded. Red George continued, "Yet, they attacked us first, didn't they? Now the town is ours." The colonel exaggerated, of course, but he wanted rid of any interference.

Westlake nodded sharply to the dragoon. "I heard the firing myself, sir. They attacked first."

The dragoon saluted. "I will report such to the governor." His horse swung around and headed back toward the river.

Red George spurred his horse toward the musket fire, with Westlake and Willie jogging along behind him. In two minutes they came to the centre of Ogdensburg itself, where two dozen men of the 8th Foot were assembling behind a log cabin. As he slowed the horse to a walk, the colonel felt a tug on his stirrup.

"I came here on a special mission for Captain Nelles, sir." Westlake reminded him. "May I ask where to find the home of Mr. Silas Sterling?"

"Have you noticed we're in the middle of a battle? You seem to have a one-track mind, Mr. Westlake."

"Focused, sir." Westlake laughed. "I prefer focused. General Brock instructed me more than once that the mission always comes first."

"You had a good a teacher. Unless Sterling is unafraid of Forsyth's wrath, he probably went to ground at the first sound of the shooting. His is the end house on the last street at the southwest corner of town. Look out for the green door."

He watched Westlake nod and peer down the main street where some enemy artillerymen appeared, pushing their cannons into place. "Since you're heading that way, you could support the 8th in a charge to overrun that battery for me before they get set up. I'd owe you a big favour, so I would."

Westlake stared down the street. "A big favour, sir?"

Red George nodded.

"Then, I'll take the guns."

Red George reached down and looked Westlake in the eyes. He shook hands firmly as always, knowing Westlake would never forget him or his handshake. Then he straightened up in the saddle to shout the orders.

"You men will sweep those cannons before they can fire." He raised his voice louder. "Fix bayonets!"

He coaxed his horse forward a few paces to see down the street. "Willie, stay with me."

Led by a subaltern and accompanied by the men of the 8th Foot, Westlake rounded the corner and like a mad fiend he ran with all his strength toward the guns. Young Willie must have chosen not to hear Red George calling out his name again. The lad kept up his tired run down the street in an awkward limping gait.

"Oh, Christ," the colonel muttered under his breath.

Lieutenant Tasker was running hard to catch up to the guns in the village centre. This had been a good day by any standard. The old stone fort had held firm, and the retreating enemy on the ice was now target practice for Major Forsyth. Tasker grinned to himself as he glanced over his shoulder. The hundred riflemen behind him had to hold the centre or the town would fall. At least Forsyth had his back along the shoreline, and he had a way out. *A way out.*

"Sergeant Shaughnessy, I want twenty men on my far right, five men with me, and the other seventy-five to guard our left by the shore," Tasker ordered. "Do not let the enemy get between us and the river, understand?"

"Yes, sir." Shaughnessy nodded. "We'd all be cut off from Major Forsyth."

"So you do have a brain, Shaughnessy. Go!" Tasker watched the fellow's back as he ran off to instruct the men.

By the time Tasker rounded the corner to see the guns wheeling into place, he could barely stand upright from lack of breath. The twelve-pounder was refusing to budge in the deep snow, and he ordered four of his five rifles to assist the artillerymen. The six-pounder manhandled easily enough, so he and the other rifleman assisted its anxious crew in preparation to fire.

A howl erupted from the far end of the street as dozens of redcoats came pouring into view. Tasker frantically urged on the gun crews. The six-pounder was already in place, but he needed the damn twelve loaded immediately with grapeshot. He cursed himself for not bringing more men to assist with the guns. The twelve finally rolled into position.

"Can you not move yourselves?" Tasker demanded, watching the crew of the twelve fumble its charge.

"I need one more minute, sir. Elevation's all wrong. We're not going to make it." The man pleaded with his eyes, knowing full well that if he turned and ran Tasker would shoot him as readily as one of the enemy.

"Goddamn it, then fire the six and make them pay!" Tasker yelled.

Shaughnessy arrived just as the six banged out its ball. Two of the enemy were blown back, but the others kept on coming. White smoke from the gun drifted from the barrel, obscuring Tasker's view of the attacker's leading edge.

Willie Robertson! Thirty-five yards away, the enemy ran with Willie hobbling along on the far left of the street. *The cheek of the little bastard!*

There was no hope. The guns would be overwhelmed, the day lost.

"Run!" Tasker yelled. "Run!"

He grabbed Shaughnessy hard by the elbow and spun him around. "Shoot that little bugger, there." Tasker pointed at Willie, who ran toward them, only twenty-five paces away and grinning like a madman.

The sergeant raised his rifle and pressed the trigger. At twenty-five yards, he couldn't miss. Tasker was already running before the lad hit the ground. He and Shaughnessy turned down the first side street to avoid receiving a ball in the back from the overrun battery.

"Pull all the men from the riverside," Tasker panted, "and head them back toward the old fort."

He heard a ragged cheer go up from the enemy in possession of the battery. "Shit," he cursed out loud. The day lost and all for the sake of one damn minute – just one more minute and he'd have swept the street clean of those bastards. "I'll see to the other men." Tasker nodded inland.

"Major Forsyth has sent word he's abandoning the old fort," Shaughnessy explained, his chest heaving. "The enemy's other division is now recrossing the ice. We're to meet up with him south of here."

"Get on with it, then. I'll gather my company and meet you," Tasker explained. "Goddamn it, this day should have been ours." He spit out the words, angry with himself and the entire world. *Never again.*

The immediate crash and vibration from the cannon's mouth had left Westlake feeling weak at the knees. Then the battery's crew had begun turning, running, and he sensed the elation of a man just released from a hanging. He glanced over his shoulder. The fellow beside him had been blown backward in the air, his arm completely gone. *Get to the guns! Kill!* The rage surging inside him burned like an old fever returned.

Ten paces from a twelve-pounder, he raised his bayonet to stab forward. Through the smoke, he vaguely saw the outline of man raising a rifle. Westlake cut to his left and dove for the ground. The rifle fired. His ears still ringing from the cannon fire, he jumped to his feet and advanced. The Americans were all gone. The guns were his, the battle finished. He raised the musket over his head. "Huzzah!"

The rest of the 8th Foot poured into the makeshift battery, jostling and cheering at their victory. Relieved to be alive, Westlake felt their jubilation. His shoulders relaxed and strength flowed back into his knees. He peered back down the street and waved triumphantly to Red George, who came trotting along as if on a Sunday afternoon outing. Then he spotted a familiar face of a body crumpled on the snow. "No!"

He ran over and lifted the lad's head. "Willie, where did you get hit?"

Willie slowly opened his eyes. "Am I done for, sir?" He clasped his chest and grimaced.

Westlake undid the boy's coat to reveal his chest. On the right side, he saw a small hole through his tunic. Willie's face now flushed crimson red. Westlake had seen this look before following a chest wound. The thrill of victory vanished. Willie Robertson would die.

"You're going to be fine, Willie," Westlake lied as he fought back the tears. "Why did you have to try it?"

"My honour, sir." Willie let out a groan. "Had to do my duty."

"Not when it makes no sense, Willie." He cradled the boy's head and brushed back the tangle of his hair.

"You're one of us, aren't you, sir — a militiaman like me?"

Westlake nodded his head. "Just like you, except I couldn't draw to save my life." He laid Willie's head back gently on the snow and took hold of his hand. Red George paused his horse beside them.

"I knew who you were all along 'cause you're smart," Willie whispered, forcing a grin that soon faded. "Tasker stood at the guns, the man who stabbed my leg."

"You beat them, Willie," Westlake said. "And helped take their guns."

"Get 'em now, sir." Willie closed his eyes as he coughed blood. It ran down off his chin and discoloured the snow. "I'm counting on you, Mr. Westlake." He reached inside his coat pocket and put in Westlake's hand another charcoal sketch. It was a perfect likeness of Lieutenant Tasker, with that distinctive sneer. "So you don't forget who you're hunting," he explained.

"Lay still, Willie." But the boy's hand had lost its strength and fell away from Westlake's. Willie Robertson stopped breathing. "Damn it, Willie." Westlake bowed his head.

"Bloody hell!" Red George spat. "He was a good lad ... his whole life ahead of him. I'll need to tell his parents."

The crack of musket fire down toward the river drew Westlake's attention. One day Tasker and his sergeant would pay for this. The anger must have been evident in his face as he looked up at Macdonell. It made the colonel straighten on his horse.

"Why did you join our attack, Lieutenant?" Red George asked. "You're here on a mission. No one would have blamed you for coming across later."

Westlake paused. "I believe my Uncle Adam is held captive in the jail here, sir. Captain Jenkins tells me it's somewhere near the old fort. Tasker seized him off the farm in a raid." He shrugged before folding Willie's hands across his still chest, then stood up to gaze down at the body. Westlake shook his head. "Such a waste of a life. It makes one wonder why the hell we do this to each other."

"Go find Sterling," Red George urged. "I'll release your uncle. Sounds like my men are making good progress along the river, so you'd better hurry."

Westlake reached up to shake the colonel's hand and winced under that familiar iron grip. Meanwhile, at the end of the street, the women from Prescott rounded the corner and attacked the first empty houses they came to. The looting had started though the battle hadn't even finished.

Lieutenant Westlake passed a well kept house with a veranda running along three sides. Painted entirely in white, the building boasted two floors and more windows than any structure he'd ever seen. Four sentries, their bayonets fixed, were posted on guard on each side of the house. Westlake guessed that some important traitor living there, or ally as Red George described him, must warrant these extra guards.

The young officer had started off at a sprint, but since he'd been running for most of the morning, his pace soon slowed. Westlake carefully advanced to a part of town the British had yet to penetrate. Militiamen darted in and out of houses, running down the streets ahead of him, but for many of them, he couldn't distinguish friend from foe. Almost every man wore a similar greatcoat.

The southwest corner of town was less densely populated so it wasn't difficult to locate the last street. He soon discovered a cabin with a green door sheltered under a small awning. Since it was the only house on the street, he knocked firmly and stood back with his musket at the ready, the tip of the bayonet poised inches from the entrance. When no one answered, Westlake knocked again.

The door opened halfway to reveal a middle-aged man with shoe-polish black hair that was greying about the ears. He stood in black snowboots, clutching a fur hat and wearing a greatcoat that suggested he was either going out or had just come in. The man frowned at the sight of a bayonet. Strangely, his face appeared as if he was about to cry. Westlake lowered the musket until it rested on its butt end.

"Sorry to disturb, sir. My name is Jonathan Westlake and I'm here on behalf of ..." The man's brown eyes grew as large as chestnuts while his trembling jaw dropped open further. Westlake hesitated, "... the Westlake Trading Company. I wonder if I might have a word." He heard the movement of feet and a child wailing somewhere inside. "That is, if you are Mr. Sterling."

"Are you mad? Yes, I'm Sterling, but have you not noticed we're being invaded today, young man?"

Westlake nudged the door open with the bayonet's tip to reveal a young woman seated at a table with a child in her arms. She must have been a dozen years Sterling's junior, but pretty in a plain, almost dainty sort of way. The child wailed again on seeing him while its mother rocked the baby quiet. The way she moved reminded him of another face buried in his deepest memories.

He stepped into the room's centre and apologized for his imposition to the woman, with a modest bow. His eyes searched each corner of the cabin but found nothing threatening. "We have only seconds Mr. Sterling and I've come a long ways on direction from Captain Nelles." Westlake reached inside his coat and shook a cloth bundle in the air. "If they catch us, you'll lose all this, so describe the traitor. Now."

Sterling stared at the package and then looked anxiously to his wife, who merely gave a slight whimper.

"Now!" Westlake repeated and stepped forward with his bayonet touching Sterling's ribs. Westlake's heart pounded, knowing the man in front of him could identify someone Brock himself wasn't able to find. "Tell me immediately or not only will you lose the money, but I'll run you through."

Sterling stepped back quickly. "He winks."

"What?"

"He winks a lot, like this" — Sterling did his best to imitate — "after almost every sentence he speaks. Must be a nervous twitch or something. The courier said it was annoying as hell."

Puffer! Winky! Sergeant bloody Puffer! As quartermaster, Puffer would get to know the details of every job and from that he'd soon guess the mission. In his position he could acquire the names and addresses of every official and militiaman that came to requisition supplies. No one in Upper Canada could hide from his reach — the quartermaster perched at the heart of all military transactions conducted in York.

Westlake recalled the first time Puffer had asked him a probing question. It was February 1812, and he wanted to know what the supplies were intended for and where he was heading. Had Puffer been a traitor even then, or was it simply the natural tendency of all quartermasters worldwide to show a jealous interest in the use of their precious supplies? Either way the job provided a perfect cover for treasonous activities.

Westlake remembered his own capture outside Fort Detroit; it had been as if the enemy was deliberately searching for him. Only Brock and Nelles would have known where he was going. And Puffer. Now that he thought of it, he'd also seen Puffer at Niagara. No one had ever identified the mysterious local fisherman that led the enemy up Queenston Heights to a reach a position above General Brock. Something to remind Nelles of when he returned.

Even before Westlake's departure on this current mission, Puffer had exercised his God-given right to be inquisitive. Then remembering the man's attempts to delay him, a new level of fear gripped hold of Westlake. Puffer was giving away the very secrets that endangered his home and his parents. Yet the sergeant couldn't just leave the garrison whenever he felt like it. There had to be others helping him. It must have been these same men that had let Puffer down, forcing him to show his face.

"Another question Mr. Ster —"

The door crashed open. Westlake turned toward the seated woman and she gave out a squeal. Lieutenant Tasker was standing in the doorway, legs apart, slapping the riding crop across one hand. He stepped confidently into the cabin and flipped the cloak over his shoulder in a grand gesture. Sergeant Shaughnessy and another soldier pointed rifles at Sterling's chest.

Westlake's clenched his teeth and his stomach tensed. *This day only gets worse.*

"We meet again, Mr. Westlake. That doubles my catch today: a suspected spy and a … what do I call you … another suspected spy." Tasker grinned and gestured with his riding crop. "Drop that Brown Bess. Working with the British, are you?" Sergeant Shaughnessy quickly stepped around Sterling and approached with his bayonet point at the ready.

Three against two, though Westlake doubted Sterling would be of much use. He stared at Shaughnessy, thinking in that instant of how he would kill him. He looked back to Tasker, who had opened his coat further and now stood with one hand on a pistol. If Sterling were killed during this encounter, there would be no more questions answered about Brock's traitor. He took a deep breath, knowing he had to go along. His only hope was to stay close to Sterling until gaining the rest of the information.

A simple fur trader would have no need to carry a British musket with bayonet and he knew it. "I found this in the street today, beside a dead soldier boy," he replied to Tasker. He tossed the musket hard so that Shaughnessy had to catch it across his body. "Some coward had shot the lad in the chest."

Shaughnessy grimaced, trapping the musket in his arms. His expression grew into a snarl as he stepped toward Westlake. Shots rang out in the street, and Tasker jerked his head in the direction of the door.

"Let's go now, the both of you!" Tasker ordered. "I've no time for games this morning." He pushed Sterling ahead of him through the door with the sergeant and Westlake following close behind. "Make for the forest."

"I'll be back," Sterling said over his shoulder. The woman sobbed and the child wailed again.

"I doubt that very much," Tasker snarled. "But I might be back to keep you company." He nodded to the woman, touched his hat, and raced for the door. "Hurry up! Move yourselves!"

Shaughnessy shoved Westlake hard across his shoulders just as musket fire erupted from streets close by. Westlake stumbled forward across the road, and when he looked up, at least twenty men in green jackets were waiting just inside the tree line. If he had tried to fight Tasker and Shaughnessy inside the cabin, he'd probably be dead by now. Maybe he wasn't so unlucky today. After all, he'd found the man who identified the traitor in York garrison and perhaps held further answers to his questions. He had to survive, waiting for a chance to speak privately with Sterling.

Musket balls suddenly zipped past his ears as redcoats poured into the street behind him. He began to scramble with the others for the forest.

"Return fire!" Tasker screamed the order at his men as he ran for the treeline. The riflemen blasted away in unison and the redcoats sprang for cover.

"Hurry," Tasker demanded, "into the trees."

Once well inside the safety of the forest, Tasker allowed the party to catch their breath behind a thick stand of cedars. He held his riding crop under Westlake's chin. "Ever been to Sackets Harbor?"

Westlake didn't reply.

"No? It's where you'll be tried for espionage," Tasker explained. "Perhaps then I'll get to shoot you myself."

11

......

THE RESIDENTS OF PLATTSBURG, New York, had never seen anything like it and probably never would again. The United States Fifteenth Infantry was invading Canada — or so everyone thought, except Colonel Zebulon Montgomery Pike.

On a snow-covered field at the outskirts of town, one hundred and thirty-six horse-drawn sleighs were lined up, jammed with soldiers, muskets, and ammunition. Packed in beside each man were supplies necessary to survive a one-hundred-and-seventy-five-mile journey: food, blankets, wax for the sleigh runners, axes, knives, feed for the horses ... the list went on.

A column of soldiers formed, all wearing snowshoes, waiting behind the loaded down sleighs. In total, five hundred determined men and more than a hundred and fifty horses exhaled and snorted an icy breath, anxious just to get started. Pike rode his own horse to the front of the column where he waved to the crowd of Plattsburg residents gathered in a circle around the assembly field. The colonel had planned this moment for weeks, right down to the spare leathers straps provided for sleighs and snowshoes. Exuberant to be in good health again, he decided that the crowd and his men would enjoy a speech to mark the occasion, and he had just the words for them.

"The Fifteenth Infantry is here practising for a march of superhuman proportions," he announced in a raised voice. But on the word "practising," a murmur ran through the ranks. Already, the usual grumbling had begun after only a few words into his address. "We will soon be marching to invade Upper Canada and thus save the honour of our great nation." A few residents cheered and Pike smiled. *Honour, they like that word.*

He decided in that instant to keep to himself the details of the twenty-mile rehearsal trek planned for that day. Instead he'd quote from his favourite book, *The Economy of Human Life*: "I offer this advice to all of you: Preserve your honour free from blemish. Be always ready to die for your country. The sod which covers the brave shall be moistened by the tears of love and friendship." He nodded his head curtly to indicate that he'd finished and waited for the applause. Silence. The troops groaned again. *Anxious to get started; that's a good sign.*

Pike whipped his hand forward in a grand gesture that pointed straight ahead. "Forward," he commanded. The entire force lurched into motion. The horses began tugging and the sleighs jerked into a start. The runner of one sleigh shook itself loose immediately so it had to stop. Not used to walking in snowshoes, the men awkwardly lifted their feet and leaned into the wind. A man tumbled over, cursing as he fell. Pike turned his horse and rode back alongside him. "Now you see why we need this training exercise," he asserted. "Keep trying. You will get the hang of it. You'll be thanking me before long."

Private Fred O'Reilly helped a friend to his feet. "Sweet Jesus, I'd like to strangle that idiot. And I bet even the other officers would thank me for it."

A recent transfer to the Fifteenth, Private Bill McKnight struggled to stand, brushed the snow from his greatcoat and swore. "Aye. Born here, that's his problem. Thinks he knows everything. Never had to live under a tyrant king. Without us Scots and you Paddies, the lot of them would be finished and that's no error."

McKnight pushed forward harder on his snowshoes to catch up and regain his place in the column. Eventually, he understood the timing needed for pushing and lifting simultaneously, just like the colonel had promised. Yet, he still disliked the man. Pike used words like *honour* and *country* in the same breath as *glory* and *dying*. Long ago, Bill McKnight had determined he wouldn't die for any king, and the same held true for any country.

Officers like the zealous colonel got ordinary men like him killed, and McKnight wanted no part in satisfying this preening idiot's quest for glory. The man still thought of himself as an explorer, an adventurer seeking honour and fame. Except this was war, and one needed to survive not just climbing some mountain in Colorado but evading some bugger with a musket trying to kill you — or worse, an officer planning to march twenty miles a day, for ten straight days, in the middle of winter.

McKnight reached around into his pack and drew out a foot-long narrow piece of wood. "O'Reilly, I hear you're good with an axe." He grinned and held the stick up in front of the other man's face.

"Scotsmen who use bullshit flattery always want something, so why not just come out and say it."

"I can see there's no deceiving you, laddie," McKnight said.

"There you go, again, talking bullshit," O'Reilly replied.

"I have plans for us!" He raised his eyebrows and kept his feet moving.

McKnight debated with himself on whether to tell him his secret. Fred O'Reilly was the closest being that he had to a friend. Even if the man was Irish as a shamrock, McKnight knew he could trust him with his life. "O'Reilly, my friend, this stick is going to save our lives from that asshole of a colonel. And I'll tell ye how *if* you'll just mind your manners."

The column came to a halt on orders passed down and shouted from a sergeant.

"That stick?" O'Reilly laughed. "Are you sure you weren't born on the English side of the border."

"English, am I? You Irish bastard." McKnight took a fast step forward, swinging the stick at his friend. He had forgotten about his snowshoes and toppled clumsily to one side. "Goddamn these things." Meanwhile, the stick had snapped in half.

"We're doomed," O'Reilly announced, chuckling.

After the short pause, the column began marching again.

"You'll soon see." McKnight dragged himself to his feet and continued his struggle to march.

Westlake waited for his first chance to be alone with Sterling, but the trek they were undertaking on the southwest trail through the forest was arduous. None of the men wore snowshoes and in places the snow drifted knee-deep. By the time they reached Forsyth's main column, eight miles away at Thurber's Tavern, their twenty guards were verging on collapse.

They halted, and Westlake fell back onto the snow. Even Tasker dropped to his knees and closed his eyes. Sterling limped along and simply rolled down on the snow beside his guard. At no time during their eight-mile hike had Sterling been close enough to even whisper to.

"Don't get used to that rest," Major Forsyth ordered. "I see you made it through our pickets all right?" He gestured to the surrounding forest.

"Didn't see our pickets, sir," Tasker replied, getting to his feet. "Useless buggers are already drunk, no doubt," he added. "Maybe I should shoot one of them to make an example."

"Any sign of the British chasing you?" Forsyth asked.

"None, sir."

"Good show," Forsyth congratulated. "Afternoon, Mr. Sterling."

Sterling sat up ramrod straight and Forsyth turned to look down at Westlake. "Who the hell are you?"

"A friend of Mr. Sterling," Westlake replied quietly.

"Westlake's his name," Tasker interrupted. "Visiting Sterling ... so birds of a feather, I'd say."

Westlake stood up without a word.

A light snow began to fall as Forsyth studied Sterling's impassive features. Sterling peered up and a few snowflakes melted on his cheek. With no warning, Forsyth bent over and slapped the man on the side of his head, sending him in a sprawl. "You've been seen too frequently in the company of Joseph Rosseel and his buddy Ross. Seems you're used to midnight callers from the other side, aren't you?"

Sterling rubbed his temple and sat up again. He held his head in his hands and replied softly, "You'd have to arrest most of Ogdensburg if visiting Mr. Rosseel's store is a crime. I'm no traitor."

"You're a liar as well as a traitor — you deserve hanging." Tasker spat out the words in disgust.

Forsyth walked along behind the prisoners. Sterling ducked low, but no blow was forthcoming. The snow fell harder. "But not all the residents of Ogdensburg make frequent visits to Sackets Harbor," Forsyth continued. "They don't know the details of the goings-on there like our Mr. Sterling."

"My business provides the items that make a ship into a home: teapots, kettles, lanterns, and blankets."

"Goddamn English teapots!" Forsyth yelled. "And how do you get hold of them? Smuggling!" With an effort, he appeared to calm himself. "Otherwise known as trading with the enemy."

"That's not true," Sterling pleaded. "I buy all my stock from Boston and have bills of lading to prove it. Ask Commodore Chauncey."

"You can ask him yourself 'cause we're heading off to Sackets Harbor. Better count your time left on earth, because if he can't vouch for you, you'll hang the day we arrive." Forsyth then turned to Westlake. "State your business."

"Westlake Trading Company deals in furs. We have offices in New York and Upper Canada. Your war doesn't concern me." Westlake spun around to find Tasker standing directly behind him, raising his riding crop to strike. As Westlake seized the stick in mid-air, Tasker drove his fist into Westlake's unprotected gut.

"Does our war concern you now?" Tasker snarled. "Still think we're not smart enough for you, Mr. Westlake?"

Westlake doubled over, gripping his belly in pain. He could barely breathe. His first thought was to strike back with the riding crop. *Just accomplish your mission, no sideshows,* the words came to him. An image of Brock jumped into mind, and he remembered that big hand clasping his shoulder.

He threw the crop far enough away to annoy Tasker before turning to address Forsyth. "Like I said, I trade in furs." He groaned. "I'm sure someone in Sackets Harbor must know of Westlake Trading."

"Pray for it, Mr. Westlake," Forsyth advised. He gestured to Sterling. "Because if he's guilty, then you'll hang together."

Sergeant Shaughnessy then arrived and held his hands out to the side, asking if he'd missed anything.

"Guard these two men," ordered Forsyth. "We march for Morristown once I get something to eat. And, Tasker …" Forsyth paused.

"Sir?"

"Take that knife from his boot," Forsyth commanded sharply. "He could have killed you at any time he chose."

Tasker's face slowly reddened and he gestured to Shaughnessy. "Search them both."

"Suits me, sir." Shaughnessy grinned.

Westlake pulled the knife from his boot, flipping it around to offer it handle first to the sergeant. "It was a gift to me so don't lose it."

"I'll shove it straight up your ass if I get any more lip from you. Turn around and raise your arms overhead."

From behind, Shaughnessy roughly probed beneath Westlake's coat, and then in his pockets. "Lookie what I found." He held up Willie's two charcoal sketches. As Westlake lowered his arms, the sergeant drove a fist into his kidney. He collapsed to the ground, wincing in pain.

"Y'all look particularly nasty, sir." Shaughnessy chuckled. He put the sketches in Tasker's outstretched hand.

Tasker viewed the two images, imitated his sneer depicted in his picture, and snorted a laugh. "Waste of time, this rubbish." He tore both of them in half and threw them up into the breeze.

A half-dozen soldiers were given the job of guarding Westlake and Sterling: two in the front and back and one on each side. In the four-mile hike to Morristown, escape was therefore impossible. No one runs away easily in two-foot drifts of snow. Westlake peered behind the last of the marchers to see only trees bending in the wind under a slanting snowfall. But there was no sign of any British rescue.

He inhaled deeply and then breathed out slowly. The soldiers to either side, struggled under their packs and muskets, as they advanced knee-deep through wind-blown snowdrifts. The dash for Captain Nelles would have to wait, and in the meantime, he would save his strength as best he could. Westlake kept right to the trail behind the others where the snow was trampled hardest.

At one convenient point, he grabbed Sterling by the arm, aiming to continue their earlier dialogue. "There can be no mistake? Your man was sure?"

"He's not *my* man. Anyway, he'd never met this winky fellow before or since." Sterling shook his head in gloom. "He sends others to do his business 'cause he can't get away so easy. But that's just a guess on my part."

"Others?" Westlake queried in astonishment. "You can't be serious. There are others involved?"

"I've no idea who they are."

The two guards behind caught up with them and shoved Sterling ahead with a musket rammed in his back. He tumbled forward, sprawling in the snow. Westlake stepped quickly to help him to his feet.

"No more yapping, just march," the guard ordered.

Westlake mouthed the word *later* to Sterling, who just looked away. The questions would have to wait.

They passed several well-kept farms on their trail to Morristown. Westlake listened as Sterling audibly recited the name of the property and who owned it: the Wallaces, the Rousseau farm, and so on. The names he mentioned were mainly Scots and Frenchmen. Obviously, he'd travelled this way many times before.

Forsyth must have feared encountering the British Army even more than the weather because he regularly forced his weary column to increase the pace. By the time they finally reached the village of Morristown, the light snow had become a howling blizzard and the sun had long disappeared. Having not eaten since breakfast, Westlake was aware of his stomach grumbling, and worse, his feet and hands had gone numb with the cold.

Where they halted, it was under an inn's sign half dislodged by the wind so it now swung and twisted from only one hook. Westlake caught the words, neatly painted in white capital letters that identified the establishment as DELANEY'S TAVERN. The familiar name gave his spirits a lift. Assuming Joe Delaney remembered him, perhaps he'd offer assistance and a chance at escape.

Inside, the tavern appeared like every other of its kind. The long bar was lit in the dimmest of light by candles at each end. Covered in straw, the dirt floor was clean as could be expected in winter. A fire at one end burned bright enough to take the frost off the customers and Westlake began to strip off his outer garments, praying for time to get warm.

He immediately recognized Joe Delaney, the proprietor, brother of Sean back in Elizabethtown. Now that he thought about it, their two taverns were almost replicas of each other. Delaney gave him only a cautious nod while the two guards stared longingly at the fire.

Tasker burst through the entrance, talking to Sergeant Shaughnessy. "Forsyth will demand revenge for this. I couldn't believe the roll-call myself." Tasker put a hand to his forehead. "Twenty-six killed and sixty taken prisoner. All our artillery, eleven pieces of it, plus almost seven hundred muskets." He bounded up the stairs two at time, and paused on a landing where the steps changed direction. Westlake guessed that Forsyth must have arrived here earlier, and Tasker had the unenviable job of reporting the butcher's bill for the rout at Ogdensburg.

As he turned on the stairs, Tasker noticed Westlake and Sterling standing by the fire. "Those bastards sleep there where they stand on the floor," he commanded the guards. "And just be thankful I don't put the pair of you outside in a goddamn tent. They get half-rations until I say otherwise," he instructed Delaney.

Later that night Delaney threw in a fresh bale of straw for Westlake and Sterling to spread out on the floor. At least the damp would be kept to a minimum. The proprietor even risked his life by serving them each a full plate of hot stew.

"Can you help us escape?" Westlake whispered hopefully.

Delaney looked over at the guards a few yards away and shook his head slightly. Westlake passed the rest of the night peacefully, but at all times two guards remained present. He had no opportunity to even whisper to Sterling.

In the morning, he asked one of them permission to relieve himself. Heading out the back door, he counted no less than six other guards on the way to the outhouse. Presumably the front of the tavern would reveal at least as many. More snow had fallen overnight so that he could barely open the outhouse door. On his return, the guards were hovering, so again there was no chance of interrogating Sterling.

As Westlake sat and stared at the fire, he tried to imagine Puffer's game. Intelligence of some kind would reach the quartermaster in the form of payroll lists or new supplies for incoming troops. But being perpetually on call at York garrison, Puffer would have to slip his traitorous reports to others to convey elsewhere. What Sterling had said made sense: whomever he gave those reports to would either be the courier or he'd have someone else able to travel across the border to visit the enemy.

Puffer had been in Niagara back in October, which must have been the only time he'd crossed the border himself. Something had gone awry for the chief mole to come out of his hole. Unlike the larger St. Lawrence, there were places on the Niagara River where the gorge narrowed to only a few hundred yards. With thousands of soldiers jamming into Niagara, desertions every day heading both ways across the river, Westlake surmised that Puffer had rowed himself across and back in the same evening.

"Y'all on your feet." Sergeant Shaughnessy interrupted his thoughts with a jab from his bayonet.

"Where are you taking us?" Sterling asked.

"Never mind. Just move." The sergeant butt-ended Westlake's shoulder hard with the musket.

Within minutes, Westlake and Sterling had joined others busy chopping wood for the firepits scattered throughout the camp. Guards remained at the prisoners' backs. The snow still fell thick and heavy, and the men around them grumbled openly about rumours of another forced march ahead. Some riflemen had already suffered frostbite, and they were damned if they'd risk more of the same.

A scouting party that retraced their steps for five miles had found no sign of the British. Finally, orders filtered through the troops chopping firewood that the entire force was to set up a permanent camp and that led to a small cheer from the axemen. Forsyth clearly wasn't keen to set off in a blizzard again.

No sign of the redcoats meant Red George was content with seizing Ogdensburg. Westlake swung his axe in anger, giving up hope of any rescue. Captain Nelles and the news of the traitor would have to wait a little longer.

12

......

CAPTAIN NELLES HELD the inventory board in his hand and stretched out his arm. Though still in his mid-twenties, his eyes seemed to see better far away than close up. But whether close or far, the inventory records of Sergeant Puffer tallied to perfection. Incoming canteens, one hundred and forty-four; requisitioned canteens for the York Militia, sixty; balance remaining on the shelves, eighty-four. Nelles checked the shelf, and sure enough there were the eighty-four canteens. General Brock had once proclaimed Sergeant Puffer to be the best in the business.

During the captain's inspection, Puffer stood at attention to one side, ready to answer any questions should the need arise. Nelles continued up and down the aisles, checking and rechecking the numbers. It had always amazed him how Puffer kept such a neat storeroom even while his personal deportment was disgusting.

The man's thinning hair was greasy and forever appeared as if he just pulled his head out of a windstorm. His filthy-looking jacket reeked of sweat, and usually it had at least one button missing. General Brock had only tolerated his slovenliness because of his exemplary history on the job. Then there was that nasty pink scar above his right eye, which invariably produced an annoying wink — and that damn quirk drove Nelles to distraction.

Yes, Sergeant Puffer was a strange man but a competent one. "You've been in the army a long time, Sergeant," Nelles remarked.

"Joined when I was fifteen, sir." Puffer winked and swelled his chest. "Aged forty-two today, so that makes it twenty-seven years, I reckon."

"Happy Birthday." Nelles offered his hand. "Always been so good at sums, have you?" He counted the haversacks and, finding the total perfect, moved on to the blankets, listening to Puffer as he checked the count.

"Asked to leave school when I was a youngster, sir." Puffer made it sound like an apology. "Got caught, bit of trouble, but it's never happened again," he boasted. "Everything I've learned, I had to learn the hard way, sir, on the job." He winked again and accepted the inventory board back into his own hands. "I protect the King's resources and that's an honour my old father would be proud of."

Nelles gave a last glance down an aisle. "I too have found no mistakes, so your record appears intact. Good job, Sergeant."

"Thank you, sir. By the way, rumour has it that the Royal Newfoundlander Regiment is coming up from Kingston in March. That means one hundred and sixty of those funny talkers on their way to York garrison. Should I ask Quebec for a further supply of boots?"

"I've heard the same rumour so it's probably true. Go ahead and stock up on the boots. They'll never go to waste."

"I hope that doesn't leave Kingston short of men, sir. 'Specially if those American buggers get wind of it."

The back of Nelles's neck tensed at the thought. "What's one hundred and sixty from eight thousand, Sergeant?" Nelles demanded. "Come on, give it quick."

Puffer at first appeared shocked and clearly didn't appreciate the humour. "Why, that would be ... let me see." He looked up at the ceiling. "Seven thousand, eight-hundred, and forty. Are you saying that's how many men are now in Kingston, sir?"

"That's my understanding of how the math works." Nelles laughed. If Puffer was hunting, he'd just been given an elephant. Now the captain would see where that elephant landed.

A week after their arrival, the order to move out finally came during the small hours of the morning. Westlake took it as a positive sign — perhaps a chance to escape? The blizzard had ended, and the temperature soared to the point where the snow melted and icicles around the tavern's roof broke off and speared the bank below.

Lieutenant Tasker trotted down the stairs with a fresh spring in his step, the crushing defeat at Ogdensburg seemingly forgotten. He dressed in an immaculate green jacket and wore a hat with three white plumes attached to the side. Clamped under one arm, the familiar riding crop travelled with him. And, on this fine morning, his demeanour radiated an outward calmness that hid the potential violence lurking underneath.

"On your feet, you two. Get outside and join the column." Tasker beckoned the guards. "This time tomorrow you'll be swinging from the hangman's noose. By the way, your friend Delaney is upstairs with two welts on either side of his head and a sore belly for disobeying orders." He gave two sharp strikes at the air with the crop. "I hope you enjoyed your full rations."

Westlake took his familiar place in the column with the guards spread out around him and Sterling. Again there was no chance of running without receiving a bullet in the back, but at least their watchdogs eventually kept a greater distance. After a week of imposed silence, he got a chance to speak to his fellow captive. "So how exactly did you get your information, Mr. Sterling?" he whispered.

"I'm not obliged to tell you anything more." The man tightened his lips and stubbornly shook his head. "You received what you came for. Did Shaughnessy find the money you had for me?"

"Remember when Tasker's thugs first burst through the door? I slipped the package under your wife's dress." Westlake looked away, slightly embarrassed. "She squealed, you may recall."

"Brilliant." Sterling's face brightened. "I'm beginning to like you a bit more, Mr. Westlake."

"I need to know how reliable your courier is," Westlake insisted. He held his breath, waiting for an answer.

"He's not my courier. He's theirs." Sterling looked at Westlake and smiled. "Listen to the story and judge for yourself. Name's Robert Lywelyn, and he's drunk in the Eveleigh Hotel and Tavern in Sackets Harbor ... a local Republican bar. Says Niagara Falls is the most amazing sight he's ever seen. So my friend says, What you doing there,

Robbie, seeing how you don't like to travel away from the Harbor? Says he was helping his best buddy, who got sick … and I happen to know that his buddy works for Commodore Chauncey. Doing what? my friend asks. Picking up a package from the other side that he can't talk about. Lywelyn's acting a big man now, working for the commodore and all. Then he says that not only was he a substitute, but so was the other courier. Instead of just handing over the money for the valise, they had to have a conversation to prove who they were to the other guy." Sterling laughed. "Weird things happen in this business, Mr. Westlake, because during the conversation, the other courier winks after every sentence and it's driving Lywelyn crazy."

There couldn't be many people that winked all the while they were talking. Some fluke caused by a mix-up had led to Puffer collecting the money and passing the intelligence himself. "Thank you, Mr. Sterling. That will do nicely." The story made perfect sense, and afterwards Puffer would doubtless think he was home safe. But it proved that Puffer worked with others.

Westlake had now found one piece of the puzzle, only to find an even bigger puzzle. His chest heaved and a general gloom settled over him. If he couldn't inform Captain Nelles soon, Puffer would continue his treachery. And at some point he'd disappear, taking the other conspirators with him.

Except for a short break midway, they marched all day in the sunshine and into the fading light of evening until they could barely see a hand in front of their faces. Westlake considered making a run for it, but as night descended the guards moved in closer. The column's pace had slowed to an exhausted crawl, and Westlake was obliged to support Sterling under one arm. By the time they reached Sackets Harbor, the guards, the riflemen, even Westlake collapsed where he stood.

There were no indoor accommodations for more than half the men and that meant tents for everyone else, including the prisoners. Westlake helped the guards raise the tent while Sterling lay motionless in the snow. The guards even fashioned a few logs to act as benches right outside the tent's entrance.

Sitting on the floor inside the tent, Westlake whispered to Sterling his plan to steal a horse and run that same night.

"The guards?" Sterling gestured to the entrance.

"They'll be fast asleep in an hour."

"So will you. As for me I'm exhausted ... can't do it." Sterling shrugged.

"In the last year, I've hiked more miles than you can imagine. I just need a short rest."

"You'll never make it." Sterling rolled over.

"Thanks for your confidence." Westlake laid back, put his hands behind his head, and closed his eyes. One hour later, he woke to the sound of a guard snoring. He pulled himself silently to his feet and poked his head through the tent flap. A sharp crack on the top of his skull sent him reeling back inside, the pain exploding in his brain. He staggered backward and flopped down, holding his head with one hand while steadying himself on the ground with the other. He wondered if he'd been shot.

"I had a hunch you'd try to make a run now," Tasker sneered. "It's exactly what I would do. Kind of proves your guilt, though."

It was the riding crop that had slashed him across the head. Westlake reopened his eyes and winced. "I assume you guys need to piss in the American Army like the rest of us."

"You're a liar, Mr. Westlake, and if you weren't trying to escape, then you're stupid. Come out and do your business."

Westlake pulled back the flap to confront the muzzle of a pistol. A few steps away from the tent he urinated, then wished Tasker an insincere good night. "I may have to go again, so you'd best keep yourself awake all night." Westlake said it boldly, though aware that he'd been defeated.

"It was fun cracking you on the head." Tasker laughed. "Must have given you a surprise. Why not poke your head out and let's do it again."

Westlake laid back down with a ringing in his ears. Tasker had obviously won and there would be no escaping tonight.

The order to march from Plattsburg to Sackets Harbor, a distance of one hundred and seventy-five miles, arrived as no surprise to Colonel

Zebulon Montgomery Pike. As usual, he was mentally and physically ready. And he'd also made sure that his regiment was prepared down to the last detail.

He said his goodbyes to Clarissa and warned her to expect glorious news of victory — but also perhaps of his death. She began to sob, and he apologized, but reminded her that he was the sort to become a man of history. After kissing her on the cheek, he placed his hat on his head and marched out the door.

Five hundred fit men of the Fifteenth Infantry had formed in columns in the centre of the field. The men continually lifted their snowshoes and stomped their feet like bulls in the ring, anxious to charge. Arranged around the field in a semicircle waited one hundred and thirty-six horse-drawn sleighs. The residents of Plattsburg had long ago stopped coming to see the military men off only to have them return again the same day, but no matter, the sight exhilarated Pike. These were his men and they would follow him to the ends of the earth if he so commanded.

He rode his horse to the centre of the circle and declared. "We march for the honour of our beloved country." He cleared his throat, and heard a familiar murmur run through the ranks. "Today we leave on a one-hundred-and-seventy-five-mile journey in treacherous conditions and difficult terrain. This is no practise drill."

In a cloud of white breath, a great cheer rose from the column, followed by a wonderful round of applause. He hadn't yet finished his speech, but Pike smiled, waving both hands for the commotion to subside.

"Forward," someone shouted from what sounded like the centre of the column, and the entire expedition lurched into motion.

Pike frowned; there was more he intended to say. He hadn't given the order nor waved his arm to signal the advance, yet everyone was already marching. The horses jerked the sleighs ahead and the column surged into its stride. How could he stop the entire enterprise so he could resume a speech? Even his own horse curbed around, sensing his agitation.

"Well, Montgomery, that's what happens when you bring men to a feverish pitch," Pike murmured to himself. He spurred on his horse, determined to remember his undelivered speech for another time when the men needed encouragement.

"I can't believe you did that." Private O'Reilly laughed and slapped his friend on the back as they lifted and pushed their snowshoes over the snow. "I wouldn't have the balls to do it."

Private Bill McKnight thought back to a different occasion during the war of independence when he learned the trick from a chum. General Washington had kept them freezing in the goddamn foul weather while he gave a speech about honour. As soon as the general paused, someone yelled, "March!" and that was the end of the waiting.

"You have to time it right, see, so he can't just stop the whole parade and start speechifying again." He chuckled to himself and wondered whatever became of his old comrade. "Been stamping my feet to keep warm for almost an hour. We're lucky it's a sunny day, but I'd be damned if I went on listening to another idiotic speech."

"Christ Almighty himself couldn't have cut off that bastard better." O'Reilly sniggered.

"Asshole talks about dying like it's an honour," McKnight said. "The problem is it's always one of us who dies. Think of how many lives would be saved if we didn't have officers seeking glory."

McKnight glanced over his shoulder, happy to get out of Plattsburg. Men were dying there every day from the ague's fever. The Fifteenth itself had been reduced from seven hundred to five hundred soldiers on active duty. "And good riddance to that dammed place," he said.

The key idea now was to stay alive and something good would come your way. It always did. *Staying alive.* He reached behind to his back and touched the split pieces of wood. Then he reached into the top of O'Reilly's pack and felt for the sticks.

"I have them," O'Reilly complained. "Thirty-six, just like you said. Though for the life of me I don't know why I need to have them with me all the time."

"Let me tell you a secret, laddie, the key to my plan," McKnight said. "The hardest thing on this trek will be keeping warm. Not while we're walking, I mean, but after we stop sweating and camp for the night. The man who builds a fire fastest, if he can build one at all, will stay alive to reach the end."

"So why was I keeping the sticks with me back at camp?" O'Reilly asked.

"'Cause you were inside and dry the whole time, and I need dry kindling to start the fire," McKnight explained. "Twelve from each of our packs each night. During every fire, we dry out another twenty-four, so we're prepared the next night — and we always have twenty-four extra each, just in case we need them." McKnight smiled, pleased with himself. If the other men of the Fifteenth couldn't manage to start a fire tonight, he thought he might try charging them for the privilege of sitting around his.

And if the weather changed for the worse, he could charge whatever he wanted for access to a warm fire. He peered up at the blue sky and felt sure it wouldn't last. It was the beginning of March after all, and once the weather turned, old Bill McKnight figured they'd all be begging to sit at his fire.

Outside the tent, Westlake rested on a stump to take in the panoramic view. Sackets Harbor sat below in the bowl of a hill that rose gently from Black River Bay. At the southeast corner of Lake Ontario, a great sweep of land, like the left arm of a giant, curled out into the water from the hill's base to form a barrier against the worst of the lake's ravages. This natural harbour had elevated a village of forty dwellings, with a population under two hundred and fifty, into the most important U.S. naval base anywhere on the Great Lakes.

Westlake jumped up and put a hand to his forehead in disbelief. More ships than he had ever seen lay locked in the ice. An entire squadron with their masts in the air like so many sticks, surrounded a larger ship under construction. On the brig *Madison*, men hammered and sawed away as if their lives depended on it. He compared the intensity here to the snail's pace of building the *Sir Isaac Brock* and he shuddered. Rumours in the taverns of York were correct; if this fleet sailed, no town on the lake was safe.

Personally, he had been given a reprieve of sorts, since Commodore Chauncey was not due back in Sackets Harbor for at least a couple of days. There would be no trial or hearing, or whatever Forsyth had in mind. For Westlake, it meant a little more time to figure an opportunity for escape.

On the first day, he and Sterling were assigned to building sheds for the troops who otherwise spent the night under canvas. Westlake marched with two dozen other prisoners along a road high above the water. Their guards were no longer Tasker's riflemen but common militia from the local area.

The work bored Westlake, but at least it kept him warm. A pleasant surprise also greeted him when that same afternoon Joe Delaney drove by in a sleigh on his way toward town. There was something odd in the wave he gave that made Westlake take notice. The guards were watching so Westlake made no effort to move closer. The rest of the day passed without Delaney showing himself again.

The next morning, after a breakfast of thin gruel, Sterling was ordered back to building sheds while Westlake struggled through the snow to chop firewood out in the bush. On the outskirts of town, he had worked for an hour in the light of dawn when Delaney reappeared, driving his sleigh. He exchanged words with one of the four guards and then passed the man four bottles.

Suddenly Delaney was heading over to Westlake's woodpile. "Load up this sleigh, damn you," he yelled at Westlake. Then in a whisper, he added, "Give them a half hour to drink all that wine, then run like the blazes for the trees yonder. There's a trail beyond." He swivelled his eyes to indicate which direction.

He must have seen the surprised look on Westlake's face. As Westlake loaded the sleigh with wood, Delaney continued, "You asked me to help you escape, so here I am. Remember, I hate the bastards."

Delaney turned his head to one side to show Westlake the welts where Tasker's crop had broken the skin. "I'll be waiting."

The loaded sleigh then moved off slowly for town, heading in the opposite direction to Westlake's escape route.

Although the prisoners worked in the forest, with the trees felled, it was still ten long paces to reach somewhere under cover in the woods where a direct line of musket fire would be hindered. Hoping the wine would impair their aim, Westlake thanked his lucky stars that these guards weren't trained riflemen whose aim at such a short distance would almost certainly mean a bullet in the back.

As the minutes passed, he had more time to think about his escape. One horse pulling a sleigh with two men on it could only go so fast. He hoped that Delaney had thought to get another strong horse or his escape might be short-lived and Tasker would be acquiring another prisoner for his collection.

The four guards downed their bottles of wine in fifteen minutes. Soon it was time for Westlake to start looking toward the trees. He could see no further sign of Delaney but why would he? Delaney would be a fool to show himself so he had trust that the man would somehow be there, waiting for him.

My God, what am I doing? His heart was pounding in fear before he'd even started to run.

Westlake swung the axe and with a thud he split a block of wood. One of the guards began to unbutton his pants, ready to urinate. The other three all stood facing away. One more swing of the axe and it was time to run. Westlake's back tensed as he thought of a musket ball piercing between his shoulder blades.

The axe struck the block — then he ran for the trees.

He was six paces into his dash for freedom before the urinating guard yelled, "Hey! Hey, you stop!" The other guards jerked their heads in his direction, their eyes following his pointing finger. Just as Westlake reached the trees, he heard three cracks of the musket; one after the other, three balls slapped into a tree behind him. Then a single shot banged out and the sound of a ball whizzed overhead.

Where was Delaney?

Westlake kept running until he reached a narrow trail heading north. If Delaney didn't appear soon, the guards on horseback would catch him. He was running so fast that his heart thundered against his ribs. They would be on him any second. His body went stiff at the sound of horse hooves directly behind. He'd run as far as could manage and so doubled over, dropping to his knees in the snow. He threw his hands in the air in surrender, his chest heaving for breath.

"Get on!" Delaney hissed from atop his horse. "You can't bloody well run all the way."

Westlake spun around to look as Delaney handed him the reins of another horse. The sleigh was nowhere to be seen. He put one foot in the stirrup, swung a leg over the mount, and nudged the animal with his heels. They were flying off in seconds. He heard men shouting on the trail behind.

Four muskets exploded in unison. The guardsmen, drunk and out of breath, must have fired in haste. The balls shot by overhead, but didn't come near their quarry. The wine had done its work.

Westlake galloped in Delaney's wake, his head down and his rear end barely touching the saddle. With an occasional glance over his shoulder, he saw no sign of his pursuers, but for a short time he heard them calling out to each other along the forest trail. Soon the voices faded and Delaney slowed his horse to a trot before the animal was completely blown.

"Christ, you run fast, Westlake," Delaney panted. "It took over a hundred yards for the horses to catch up with you."

"I can run fast when I'm scared." Westlake grinned. His chest was still heaving as he asked Delaney which way they were going.

"Cape Vincent first, then across the ice to Wolfe Island," Delaney explained. "We'll be crossing plenty more ice before we hit Kingston. Tasker won't follow us that far because he'll risk capture."

Westlake smiled, picturing Tasker's face when he discovered their escape. He was sure to follow fast on their trail, maddened with rage and seeking revenge. Westlake rubbed his head where the riding crop had left a bump. The man could be vicious, and a knot grew in his stomach as the realization came to him that this time Tasker would be out to kill him.

Delaney continued, "Forsyth reneged on his promise to pay up for eating me out of house and home," he snarled. "That scum is without a shred of honour."

There was that word again. Westlake wondered about the contrast between Willie's idea of honour and Sterling's or, for that matter, Forsyth's ... if he even had any. Yet Willie was dead and Forsyth was no doubt already planning his next attack. Honour could not protect Willie from a rifleman's bullet, but a little common sense might have done the trick. "You realize that they'll find your sleigh and know you've helped me escape."

"This is the least I could do after the way you helped my brother," Delaney shrugged. "Since I'm flat broke, I'm going to live with him now until this ridiculous war is over."

Acutely aware that they needed to pass Cape Vincent before Tasker, Westlake interrupted him. "I think the horses are rested. Let's go." He urged his mount into a trot while pondering when Tasker would pick up the trail. The guards had chased after them on foot for a quarter of an hour, and it would take them at least that long to get back to their horses. Another twenty minutes to report to Tasker, then twice that time for him to organize a search party. Altogether this should give the escapees about an hour and a half head start. However, Westlake knew it still wasn't enough if Tasker decided to bring a change of horses.

13

· · · · · ·

Lieutenant Tasker stood to attention, his hair tussled and his jacket out of place. He'd run to the newly constructed cabin to beg Major Forsyth for the use of a half-dozen extra men. Together, he promised they'd chase down the escaped prisoner. The major paced the little room, rubbing his hands in agitation.

"Stand easy," he said at last. "You're even making *me* nervous."

Tasker smoothed his hair and tugged his green jacket into place. His breathing grew calmer, though his heart still pounded as he waited for Forsyth's decision. The longer the man took, the farther away Westlake would be when the chase began.

"That Delaney character told me the British have pulled back across the river from Ogdensburg," Forsyth recalled, rubbing his chin while he thought out loud. "If we all went back there, I suppose they'd only attack again."

Hurry up and make your decision.

"More militia and regular infantry are currently on their way to Sackets Harbor." He pointed dramatically to the floor they stood on. "Something big is going on here. Either Kingston intends hitting us soon, or our superiors are planning one hell of an invasion. Unfortunately, I don't know which."

Tasker realized he'd lost. There was no way Forsyth would let him go off somewhere on the eve of a battle.

"However, you would have to head toward Kingston." Forsyth moved behind a small table, plunked himself in a chair, and studied the remains of his breakfast. "If you did some valuable scouting for us, that might be counted as a feather in our caps. Even finding no

evidence of an impending attack up there would be something worthwhile to report."

"I'd take special care once across the river from Kingston, sir."
Tasker gripped the back of an empty chair opposite the major as his
excitement rose again.

"Go get your six men and take Sergeant Shaughnessy," Forsyth
ordered. "At least it'll set an example to the other prisoners that
attempts to escape won't be tolerated. You had better requisition supplies for a full week."

"I'd ask for one more thing, sir, if you please." Tasker knew he was
pushing his luck, but this might make the difference between success and failure. "May I take an extra horse each for the sergeant and
myself, so I can be sure to make Cape Vincent ahead of the bastard."

"You still might not make it."

"I will if I ignore the trail and instead cut across the bay and over
the ice," Tasker stated.

"You'll freeze against that wind."

"It will be a sacrifice worth making when I beat that fellow to a
pulp."

Westlake and Delaney galloped the horses hard along a narrow trail
until the animals needed a rest. The two men leapt down on to the
well-used path and trotted along beside their mounts. They had travelled miles inland, skirting the open ice while staying hidden in the
bush, and had turned north only during the hour previous.

"Cape Vincent is the closest available crossing to Upper Canada."
Westlake voiced the thought out loud. "It's exactly where he'll head for."

"We'll be fine." Delaney smiled. "We have a good head start."

"No, we don't. With extra horses, he will go straight north, cutting
across the ice. That means he'll be there to blast us to hell as we make
a run for Wolfe Island."

Delaney frowned but kept moving. "How do you know that?" The
optimism evaporated and his voice grew serious.

"Because it's exactly what I'd do. Tasker said we think alike, so he'll
be waiting at Cape Vincent."

"Then where do we cross the river?"

"We use all this time spent travelling inland to our advantage," Westlake explained. "Listen," he stopped trotting along and grabbed Delaney by the arm. "Instead of heading northwest, we go northeast, stay away from the river, and cross at Morristown."

"That's miles out of *your* way, but it suits me just fine. It's still on the route to Elizabethtown."

Westlake gestured to the northeast, tugged his horse to the right, and resumed trotting again. A couple of hours later, they came upon the trail that Forsyth himself had used in coming into Sackets Harbor. The snow remained packed solid from the impact of hundreds of pounding snowshoes and horse hooves.

He wondered if he'd guessed right about Tasker, even though it made sense. The lieutenant would have a few soldiers follow the trail inland, making sure the escapees didn't double back, but he'd be keen to race across the ice himself. Then at Cape Vincent he'd be waiting with the rest of the men to take the first shot. *Bastard.* Westlake remembered his uncle's cloak and how Tasker had been flaunting it like some kind of ship's captain.

Westlake's thoughts wandered to Puffer and Nelles, and his pace quickened unconsciously. Every day that Nelles continued unaware of Puffer's guilt, vital intelligence would keep flowing out from York garrison like blood through a gash in a wounded patient. He thought next of his mother and father at home on Maple Hill. They'd be preparing for the sugaring-off season, when the sap flowed from their forest of maple trees — but totally unaware of the traitor just to the south of them who was endangering all their lives.

He shook his head in frustration and imagined Morristown lying to the northeast. With each step they extended the distance between themselves and their pursuers. Tasker would be furious on realizing that he had waited in the cold for nothing.

Westlake pressed on, tugging his horse along behind him. There would be no rest for them until he and Delaney reached Upper Canada, and he worried if his partner could stand the strain. The wind picked up speed out of the north and he felt the temperature dropping. He raised his collar and pulled his black woollen hat farther down over his ears.

Soon they'd have to eat. "I hope you know someone hereabouts that will feed us and the horses," Westlake said.

Delaney pulled two thick biscuits from his pocket and threw one to Westlake. "One each, courtesy of Major Forsyth." Delaney raised his eyebrows with a laugh, meaning he had stolen them off Forsyth's table. "Yes, I have friends along the river who will help us."

With his belly grumbling, Westlake ate three-quarters of the biscuit and then holding it in the flat of his palm, put the remainder under his horse's mouth. "Time for us to mount up and ride for your friends. Only a short visit though and we're on our way. Was there any food remaining at your tavern?" Westlake asked, staring back along the trail as if expecting their pursuers to appear at any moment.

"Just some cheddar cheese and biscuits I hid away. Enough to see us through. Forsyth took everything else — without paying me a cent."

Lieutenant Tasker had made steady progress over the white expanse of Three Mile Bay and now galloped the last miles to his destination. He'd changed horses three times, and his current mount was already breathing heavy. As the anxious lieutenant approached the St. Lawrence River, a biting wind picked up speed to slash him across the face. His cloak billowed behind him, his eyes stung, but the thought of shooting Westlake drove him on. Just the idea of that young bastard having the audacity to run and make him look bad pissed him off. He looked forward to seeing the surprise on Westlake's face before he shot him.

"Where did you come from? And bang," he said out loud to himself. Then he laughed heartily at the thought. He glanced over his shoulder but could no longer see the three mounted soldiers trailing him. He'd have to remind them that he got to take the first shot.

Tasker imagined Sergeant Shaughnessy and the three men accompanying him now making their way through the snowdrifts in the woods. It would be much tougher going, but if the sergeant caught up with the escapees, it would only make them run faster into his own waiting ambush. He prayed Shaughnessy knew enough not to kill Westlake, just to chase him.

Tasker skirted the fringe of the little town of Cape Vincent, continuing on his way down to the river. The trail leading to the docks was clearly marked but also something to avoid. A vast expanse of ice and snow stretched before him. He tucked himself and his two horses under an overhang fronting the riverbank. Pleased with his speed and confident in his plan, he drew out his rifle and waited to kill Westlake and Delaney.

An hour and half later the three soldiers following him appeared farther along the river's edge. Tasker stepped out from his hiding place and waved them over. "You stay with me, and you two hide yourselves beyond the wharf. Do not attempt to shoot until you hear me fire."

The men nodded their understanding.

"Are we going to eat soon, Lieutenant?" one of the soldiers asked politely. "We're starving."

Tasker hungered for food himself. He looked up at the grey sky to locate the sun and give him a better sense of the time. "I doubt they'll stop to eat before they hit Cape Vincent."

"No, sir."

"Then they could be here at any minute. Go hide yourselves," Tasker ordered. "This could be over sooner than you think."

He waited for another hour, then crept out on foot to scan the trail approaching the docks. Far down the trail, the only riders visible were Shaughnessy and his three men. *Where the hell was Westlake?*

Tasker ran forward, motioning his men up onto the shore. While the others tugged their horses behind, Shaughnessy rode hard to the docks and jumped down from his mount. "Didn't see him, sir," he said, shaking his head. "I trust you have."

"Not a goddamn sign of the rotten shit." Tasker kicked hard at the snow with the toe of his boot.

"I'm sure we didn't pass him." Shaughnessy was almost pleading. "And if he doubled back, he would have run right into to us."

The lieutenant walked away from the others, thinking. There was no way that his escaped prisoner could have reached the Cape before him. He couldn't have doubled back either or Shaughnessy would have .... Morristown! Westlake had guessed that there would be an ambush reception waiting for him here at Cape Vincent. "Shit!"

"Mount up, again. He's crossing at Morristown," Tasker announced. He gestured to the sergeant's men. "You three stay here just in case he tries coming back this way. If there's no sign of him after two hours, then catch up to us."

"Morristown?" Shaughnessy echoed.

"We'll take the river route and still beat him there," Tasker said. "Bastard thinks he can outsmart me. We'll soon see about that."

Tasker fastened the reins of the second horse to his saddle and then mounted his own horse. He looked around to find Shaughnessy, who waited for him. "Let's go," Tasker ordered. "You other men follow."

The lieutenant spurred his horse, three men trailing behind and Sergeant Shaughnessy bringing up the rear with his own extra horse. With the wind at their backs, they headed northeast along the river for about half an hour, galloping as fast as the horses could take them. Then Tasker and Shaughnessy changed mounts, leaving the others to trot slowly along behind. After thus changing horses again and again, they reached the riverside at Morristown, where they halted under a copse of overhanging cedar trees.

Tasker quickly dismounted and lifted a blanket from behind his saddle. Closer to the riverbank, he unrolled the blanket and threw himself down, utterly exhausted. Shaughnessy perched on one corner of it, his head hung between his knees.

"We did it." Tasker laid face up and spoke directly to the darkening sky. "Remember this spot?"

The sergeant shook his head.

"This is exactly the same place where Delaney led the company across the ice to raid Elizabethtown. You can be sure he'll cross here again." Tasker lifted an arm from the blanket and pointed down toward the horses. "Fetch the rifles, and remember I get the first shot at Westlake. You can kill that swine Delaney whenever you like. Let's eat while we wait. I'm bloody well starving."

Westlake left the farmhouse with a full belly and apologized to Delaney's friends for departing so soon after enjoying their hospitality. Over the meal, the husband announced that the British had evacuated Ogdensburg and marched back to Prescott. Life had returned to normal here in the St. Lawrence River Valley once Forsyth's gang and the British invaders retreated. The man reported how the raid that swept Forsyth away had left eight dead and fifty-two wounded on the British side. Westlake remembered young Willie Robertson and his dreams of becoming an artist. *"I'm counting on you, Mr. Westlake."*

With their horses watered and fed, the two men mounted up, setting a steady pace to the northeast. The five-hour ride strained every muscle in Westlake's body. By the time they reached Morristown, the lower edge of the sun's orb touched the treetops in the western sky. Westlake peered out across the ice to Upper Canada.

"We pass my tavern on the way to the crossing," Delaney explained. "I'll grab the cheese and biscuits, and we'll be on our way again, right quick."

"Let's go in the back door," Westlake suggested.

Delaney glanced at him with a questioning frown.

"Just to be careful." Westlake shrugged.

The two men entered through the rear of the tavern, where Westlake motioned upstairs. "Mind if I visit Tasker's old room?" Not waiting for answer, he took the stairs two at a time. He opened the door and ran over to the side of the window, cautious not to show his face.

Westlake scanned the shoreline. Under the overhang of some trees, three men had stopped on their horses. They seemed to be chatting to someone below them on the ice. Then a flapping cloak stepped into view. Tasker!

Westlake raced down the stairs, jerked Delaney by the arm and ran for the back door. "They're already here! Quick, man, to the horses!"

In seconds, Westlake was mounted and galloping away, Delaney following close behind stuffing the food in his pockets. They soon passed the outskirts of Morristown, where Westlake slowed his animal's pace to a walk.

"Now what — on to Ogdensburg?" Delaney asked. "When we don't show up at that crossing, they'll know that's our only option."

"I need to think," Westlake replied.

Tasker had guessed Westlake's plan and taken the river route to arrive ahead of them. He'd probably do the same again, or perhaps he'd already sent men on ahead along the river, who were now waiting at Ogdensburg. With the British gone, there was nothing to stop them from laying in ambush there on the ice forever. It was as if Tasker could read his mind, one step ahead, or a half-step just behind.

Westlake's body quivered and he told himself not to panic. Even in the cold he began an unnatural sweat. The stable boy in Whitby had said in awe, "You weren't even scared." If the same lad could only see him now, near sick with panic.

There were at least five men following them along the ice, with more of them probably on the road to prevent any chance of doubling back. The question was what they should do when they got to Ogdensburg. He had to assume that Tasker and his crew would be waiting for them, hiding on the ice somewhere up against the riverbank. Westlake glanced over his shoulder and back down the trail. So far they were not being followed.

The twelve-mile trip to Ogdensburg ended in semi-darkness, but by the time they reached the town, Westlake had developed a plan. It depended on a great deal of co-operation — and not a little luck — but it would shock the hell out of Tasker. For that reason alone, Westlake knew it was the right one.

He went to the first house they came to in southwest corner of the town and knocked on the green door. It opened a crack. Mrs. Sterling poked her head around the gap. "You!" She immediately stepped back, allowing the door to swing open. "Come in. Where is Silas?"

Westlake stepped into the cabin and immediately felt the inviting warmth of a blazing fire. A wall divided the back half of the building into two bedrooms, and with the curtains drawn aside, their interiors were clearly visible from the front door. He stepped to the centre of the room from where he could see the baby sleeping in a crib in one bedroom. All appeared safe and quiet here, and Westlake breathed out a long sigh of relief.

"This is Mr. Delaney, a friend of mine. Mr. Sterling stayed behind when we escaped, but he's well enough," Westlake explained. "He'll be interrogated, of course, but seems unafraid. Claims he sells teapots to Commodore Chauncey."

"That's true," she pleaded. Her mouth lowered at the corners and she looked like she was about to cry.

"Teapots from Boston?"

She stared down at her shoes. "Silas claims he knows the commodore very well. The documents confirm the teapots come from Boston, but I suspect he also sells the commodore information. At least that's what he told me." When she looked up again, her face was filled with concern.

"Then have no fear, Mr. Sterling is perfectly safe."

She tilted her face skyward, clasping her hands together as if to thank God.

Westlake paused, feeling puzzled. Sterling never showed the fear of a man about to be hanged and now he knew why. The man who had revealed to him Brock's traitor was selling secrets to both sides … and just for the money. If he'd known that earlier, he might have killed him for it.

Yet why were trading teapots to the enemy acceptable but exchanging secrets a sin? He turned this question over in his mind while the young woman watched him intently. Because trading in teapots never got anyone killed, while spewing secrets to the enemy led to people dying. For a moment he wondered what Sterling might reveal to save his own skin.

"Mrs. Sterling, we face a serious problem." Westlake then described to her how they were being chased from Sackets Harbor by the same men who seized her husband. "What was the signal Mr. Sterling used for telling Captain Jenkins it was time to come across?"

She glanced toward a lantern. "I'm not sure of the number of times he showed the flame."

"Does he have a favourite number?"

"Four."

"What time did he go out at night?"

"In the winter, it was earlier — about ten o'clock, I think. Then someone would come to meet him before midnight."

Westlake smiled. "I need you to do me a favour."

"We're going to Ogdensburg," Lieutenant Tasker informed Shaughnessy. "I've waited here long enough."

The sergeant's shrug revealed a lack of enthusiasm. The cold had no doubt dampened his spirits. For the first time Tasker was feeling the conditions himself, as his feet and hands grew numb the longer they remained in the weather. "They're not damn well here, are they?" Tasker spit out the words angrily. "Mount up. You two stay here." He indicated a couple of men with his finger. "And follow on after two hours. If he shows up in the meantime, just shoot him."

"Sergeant, take a man and scout the inland trail, but be careful as you go. Before you reach the old fort, head back toward the river and meet me there." The balance of the lieutenant's party mounted their horses and galloped after him, heading northeast along the river. It was as if Westlake knew his moves before he did. It was going to take something special to catch him.

On the snow-packed ice along the river's shoreline, Tasker and his troop made good speed. As he reached the bank beneath the wall of the old fort, Tasker let his tired horse slow down. A luminescence, the reflection on the river's snow from a bright moon, allowed him a clear view across to the Canadian side. Although there were plenty of tracks visible heading in both directions, there was no trace of his escapees. He prayed that he wasn't too late.

Tasker motioned his men to dismount, before walking his horse to where the embankment began sloping down to the river. "We'll split up, two on each side. Another sixty paces farther along you two." He gestured to his men. "Tie up your horses under the trees and take up position on the ice along the riverbank. Build yourselves a snow wall at least four feet high so you'll be invisible if you stay down."

"Happy to do so, sir," a burly rifleman replied. "It'll keep this blasted wind off us as well."

Tasker slid his rifle from its sheath on the horse, handed the reins to the fellow beside him, then gestured toward the trees. When the soldiers had tethered the animals and returned, they began to build their little fort of snow.

"Reminds me of when I was a kid," one man remarked as he packed the snow higher with each handful.

"Only back then you weren't trying to kill anyone," Tasker observed grimly. "Our friend has to make a mistake sometime."

The little snow fort grew rapidly on the dark shoreline, and when they were finished, Lieutenant Tasker sat down to rest behind the wall. Almost immediately he heard the faint hoof beats of a horse trotting across the ice. He slowly raised his head above the parapet of snow.

A single rider approached from the Canadian shore and then stopped. Down near the docks, a woman stumbled out onto the ice, her dress rippling in the breeze. She reached up to hand the rider what looked like a letter, and then with determined strides she ran back toward the docks. The rider waited, watching her run for cover, and then slowly turned his horse and trotted back toward the Canadian side.

"Goddamn spies. If it wouldn't give us away, I've half a mind to shoot the bastard. Even the women are part of it."

One hour later, Sergeant Shaughnessy quietly rejoined the lieutenant to report that they had spotted no one on the inland trail: no Westlake, no British soldiers, and no American militia either. Tasker ordered the sergeant over to the other side of their ambush, but kept his man close by. Now they were three on each side, with sixty paces between them, and a good match for anything that a conniving Westlake might throw against them.

The lieutenant had meanwhile plenty of time to consider his adversary. The fellow's traitorous friend Sterling was known to frequent the homes of Ross and Rosseel, two well-known smugglers. Westlake had admitted trying to trade with Sterling, but there was something else that Tasker couldn't figure. The bastard was altogether too fast with his hands and too slick with his words to be an ordinary fur trader. He was more than ever convinced that Westlake was a spy of some kind. Otherwise, why would he run — and know how to run so well. What did he know that was so secret? Perhaps the answer rested in Sterling. Tasker couldn't even guess at it, but he was determined about one thing. The young man couldn't be allowed to return to Upper Canada, and that meant Westlake had to die.

14

* * * * * *

HOURS AFTER MIDNIGHT, the two men left behind to guard the Morristown crossing finally arrived at Lieutenant Tasker's fort of snow and ice.

"No sign of him, sir," a man said. "We even searched inland a ways to make sure he wasn't waiting us out. We came straight here as ordered. Be dawn soon."

"I know the damn time," Tasker snapped. "Join Shaughnessy down the shore and keep low," he ordered. He turned to the other man. "You stay here. Four aside, the more the merrier."

But Tasker was now beginning to worry. To remain on the ice during daylight would invite capture by the British. He shivered and rubbed at his shoulders, realizing his own men would be frozen through like himself. He'd give their ambush until dawn, then withdraw to start a search of the town and maybe pay a visit to Sterling's wife.

The sky soon brightened and the moon's glow faded over the snow. A rumble sounded from the Canadian side, causing lines of puzzlement to appear on the brow of the man sitting beside Tasker. The lieutenant stretched his neck up, peering over his homemade wall. The sight shot a lightning bolt of fear down his spine. His hand gripped hard on the cold rifle.

Two columns of British soldiers marched straight toward him, the fife and drum pounding a beat that echoed clear across the flat surface of the ice. The redcoats split into two columns as they had done on the day of the invasion, only this time they lined up in double ranks directly in front of his two little groups hidden behind their vulnerable ramparts. Tasker sucked in his breath. To the far right, he spotted four dragoons. They would try to cut off his retreat.

"Oh, Jesus save us," a man blurted. "We should run now, sir, while we still can. There must be five hundred of them."

"I can count, you blithering idiot," Tasker snarled. How the hell did the enemy know he and his men were here in the snow forts? He looked across to the other fort only to see Shaughnessy and his men toiling up the riverbank and then scrambling for their horses. There was obviously nothing to do but run while they had a chance. Failure amounted to one word: "Go." The word, spoken quietly in the face of defeat, barely passed his lips when he heard a British officer shout the order, "Present."

Aware that he had only a few seconds to make good his escape before the British fired weapons, Tasker turned and clambered up the riverbank along with his men, running desperately for his nervous horse. The crash of musket fire echoed down the St. Lawrence River as the snow forts were pierced with musket balls. He leapt onto his horse and spurred the animal inland. The dragoons would be coming fast and that meant no visit to Mrs. Sterling.

Tasker held on to his hat, twisting round in the saddle first to see two figures on horseback already well on their way across the ice-covered river. Then Westlake turned his head as he rode to freedom and with a grin gave him a mock salute.

"Bastard. You won't escape me next time."

Westlake galloped hard against the wind across the ice to the waiting ranks of British infantry, never so glad to be home. His pursers having gone to cover, there was no need for the infantry to fire again. He burst through a gap at the centre of the British line in time to see dragoons charge the snow forts. They'd pursue Tasker's men until they were far gone from Ogdensburg.

Westlake reared back on his horse in front of a smug-looking Lieutenant Colonel Macdonell. Under the man's hat, strands of red hair blew in the wind as his red-rimmed eyes stared at the visitor with a glint of mischief.

"Good to see your face again, sir." Westlake offered a nervous smile.

"We're even now. My debt to you for charging against those cannons is cancelled," Red George said. "Which one of you played the woman?"

"Let me introduce, sir, Mrs. Joe Delaney," Westlake teased.

"Bugger off," Delaney replied.

"I tried on the dress borrowed from Mrs. Sterling, but it just didn't suit me." Westlake began to laugh. "Joe, on the other hand, looked ravishing in it. It was him who *skirted* the enemy to hand you that note."

"That's an awful pun," Red George replied with a chuckle. "I should *dress* you down for that."

"Thank you for the demonstration out on the ice, sir," Westlake continued. "A lifesaver, for sure."

"Couldn't see the snow forts from our side, so showing that lantern behind each one did the trick," Red George congratulated. He turned his horse for the Canadian side and then raised his voice to bellow an order. "Captain, march them home now and dismiss."

He continued conversing quietly with Westlake as they made their way across the snow-covered ice. "I couldn't resist the chance to capture that bloody Tasker, but it appears he's escaped me again. Come on back and have tea with me, I have a gift for you. Did you discover the traitor's description?"

Westlake nodded firmly. "I'm destined for York soon, sir, but both Delaney and I need food and some sleep first. Hot tea would be great." He paused with a frown. "I'm assuming you found my uncle?"

"He left us days ago for his farm. I didn't mention your presence, as I thought it best to leave that to your own discretion."

Westlake stepped onto Upper Canadian soil and his chest heaved a long sigh. Home. He glanced toward the American shore briefly before turning his back on the river. Something to eat, a welcome nap, and he'd be on his way to York.

"If you don't mind, I'll say me goodbyes here," Delaney said. "I have plenty of cheese to eat, and my brother's probably wondering where the hell I am. I'll sleep better once I reach his tavern." He gestured south with a nod of his head. "Wouldn't want Sean wandering over to Sackets Harbor looking for me."

"Thanks for all your help," Westlake replied, offering his hand. "I couldn't have got away without you."

"Happy to be of service." Delaney took hold of Westlake's hand while gazing at the double column of marching redcoats. "Just wait till I tell my brother how I crossed the St. Lawrence River." He saluted Red George, pulled his horse around, and set off on the ride for Morristown.

The mug of steaming tea at Red George's cabin quickly warmed Westlake's innards. He hadn't realized how chilled his body had grown. After being awake for more than twenty-four hours, the heat of the cabin's blazing fire made him feel drowsy. His head involuntarily dropped onto the arm he had rested on the table.

"You're exhausted," Red George observed.

"Did you catch hell, sir, for attacking Ogdensburg?" Westlake inquired as he straightened up again.

From inside his jacket, Red George produced a note that he slid across the table. His entire face lit up with a grin. Westlake scanned the note for the salient message contained in its neatly formed handwriting:

"Although you have rather exceeded my orders, I am well pleased with what you have done.
Governor-in-Chief
Sir George Prevost"

"Congratulations, sir. And what was Colonel Pearson's reaction?"

"His plan in the beginning." Red George's smile broadened. "He's only jealous that it was I who got to carry it out. You'll find, in the British Army, that victory makes allowances for almost anything but failure."

"I should tell you, sir, that I witnessed enemy troops flooding into Sackets Harbor. When the ice retreats, there's a whole squadron of ships waiting to launch an attack somewhere. Also, the Americans are expecting an assault from some eight thousand soldiers at Kingston."

"Not bloody likely, if the governor has his way." Red George shook his head. "You heard him: defensive measures only ... Besides, there're not eight thousand men available at Kingston."

Westlake rubbed his eyes to keep them open. He put a hand to the back of his neck and squeezed.

"Before you fall asleep, let me get you that present I mentioned." When the colonel returned, in one hand he carried an enemy rifle. This he placed in Westlake's lap. "Courtesy of Major Forsyth," he explained. "We captured six hundred and seventy-two muskets, plus a few abandoned rifles, along with eleven cannons. The schooners locked in the ice, the *Niagara* and the *Dolphin*, we burned."

"I don't know what to say except thank you, sir." Westlake slid his fingers along the smooth barrel and balanced the sixty-inch rifle in both hands. "Weight feels about the same as a Brown Bess." He put the butt to his shoulder and peered down the length of the barrel to the sights.

"Eleven pounds, but they take longer to load," Red George replied. "They're deadly accurate up to two hundred yards, three hundred with practice. The grooved barrel inside will foul if you don't keep it clean." He passed two pouches full of rifle cartridges across the table. "Sixty .45 calibre bullets in each pouch, packed in a cartridge of fine grain powder. It's the perfect weapon for the type of work you're doing."

"Thank you again, sir. A surprise, indeed." Westlake spoke in a tired whisper. "It's been a long couple of weeks for me. I should sleep now."

Private McKnight stretched his numb hands out over the fire until he could feel the heat penetrate his worn mittens. He sat and brooded, watching from the corner of his eye as other soldiers, all of them cold and damp, crept around the blazing logs for warmth. The idea of collecting a coin as the price of sitting at his fire hadn't worked well. Very few of his fellow sloggers in the U.S. Fifteenth Infantry had any coins to offer.

Although disappointed, he settled instead for other items: a biscuit, a bit of thread, or a leather strap he could use to fix his snowshoes. His

friend O'Reilly acted as the collection agent and now passed from soldier to soldier holding out a leather bag that contained the evening's
take. Tonight, O'Reilly saw there were more biscuits contributed than
he needed, but he refused to turn away any man who paid a fee.

"Damn unfair of you, McKnight," an infantryman complained,
"to charge us like this, night after night."

"You don't have to sit with me," McKnight replied sternly. "Freeze
your ass off with others if you choose, but if you think I'm building
you a fire every night, playing Maid Marion for you lot, then you're as
dumb as cow shite, so you are." McKnight jabbed his staff hard into
the embers.

Out of the five hundred infantry who had begun the long march,
three men had since actually frozen to death, but McKnight and
O'Reilly had suffered frostbite the least of everyone. Another man
reached for a warm stone at the fire's edge, but as he touched it,
McKnight rapped the back of the intrusive hand with the staff. "Warm
stones cost extra. O'Reilly places them careful. They're reserved, and
you know it." He raised his staff as if to strike again. "So hands off."

The soldier shook his head.

Every evening, McKnight instructed O'Reilly to place large stones
around the burning logs so they grew hot from the flames. At evening's end, O'Reilly carried these stones to the tent to warm their
blankets during the night. Even still, both men woke up shivering
from the winter weather by the next morning.

After ten cold days of marching and sleigh rides, Zebulon Pike's
weary column finally reached the outskirts of Sackets Harbor. At the
very top of the hill, on the northern edge of the bowl sheltering the
harbour, Private McKnight slowed his pace to survey the fleet of ships
below, locked in the ice of the harbour. To him and to every man
that saw them, the gathering of this many ships and men could only
portend something dangerous. And, if that sight didn't impress the
visitor, McKnight knew that the sharpshooters perched on platforms
high up in the trees meant that someone of real importance camped
inside the town.

He heard the banging of hammers and noticed a dozen men toiling at what appeared to be a new barracks. His column was dismissed in front of its temporary quarters, a connected series of low-ceiling huts each with three bare walls and a flat roof. Every man present began to grumble simultaneously. *Damn the officers!* McKnight stared at his new home in disbelief.

"They treat us like shit," a soldier complained next him. Others joined in the moaning.

"There's no front door." O'Reilly blurted out the obvious. "Looks to me more like a damn animal stall."

"No door! You mean they're missing an entire wall!" McKnight answered. He peered back at the men constructing the barracks. They had hammers, axes, planks, logs, and a two-handled saw, all the necessary tools he'd need to convert his shed into a proper home. A plan started to form in his mind.

"You have that look on your face again, when you're up to no good," O'Reilly said. "Am I involved in your plan?"

"I didn't tramp one hundred and seventy-five miles just to sleep in a blasted cowshed. We need planks for our floor, logs for the front wall, and somehow we have to cut a hole in the roof so we don't choke to death on the smoke from our fire."

"And you plan to steal all that?" O'Reilly asked. "Everyone will see our shed is the only one with a front wall."

"You and I are carrying more biscuits than we can eat in a year. Now look at those poor devils with the tools; they appear mighty hungry to me. Perhaps a fair trade would be in order?"

"But we'll still stand out from the rest."

"Then we'll build everyone a front wall," McKnight announced with a grandiose wave of his hand. "For a small fee, mind you."

The panoramic view from Commodore Chauncey's dining room impressed seamen and landsmen alike. The commodore surveyed his squadron now frozen in the ice, marking time until spring thaw. Even on this winter's day, men hammered at gun carriages or cut and sewed sailcloth preparing for the battles sure to follow the receding ice.

Not long to wait.

He selected two cigars from his humidor and returned to the parlour where Major General Henry Dearborn awaited his return. Named by President Madison as commander of northern land forces, Dearborn had served on George Washington's staff during the Independence War. The man was a known patriot and politician, serving two congressional terms. However, since war was declared on June 18, 1812, this old patriot had achieved nothing but a series of defeats.

Dearborn's considerable girth overflowed his chair. "Thank you, sir," he said as he clutched the cigar in his fingers. "So Kingston it is. It will be a grand victory."

"We're already sorting out the details," Chauncey replied, letting the other man know that he, and he alone, would plan the invasion until the infantry was ashore. "Nothing will be left to chance. Every ship, every officer, indeed every single man will know precisely what to do."

Dearborn held up the cigar for a light just as an aide interrupted by knocking on the closed door.

"Enter," Chauncey called out.

"A Major Forsyth, sir, of the Rifle Company," the aide announced. "I told him you were occupied, but he insisted that he has an appointment."

"He's correct. Show him in," Chauncey said. He poured wine into two glasses as the newcomers entered.

Clad in an immaculate green uniform buttoned down with silver, Major Forsyth sported his trademark white vest underneath the open neck of his jacket. Accompanying him was Lieutenant Tasker and a man identified as Mr. Silas Sterling, who was held tightly by the collar.

"Major General Dearborn, this is a pleasure," Forsyth said, smiling as he shook hands with both men. "Thank you for approving my promotion."

"We needed a victory. The rifles raid on Elizabethtown provided one, however minor," Dearborn said, but there was no hint of congratulatory joy in his voice. "I warned you about undertaking further antagonisms along the St. Lawrence, but you didn't listen. Now the British have booted you out of Ogdensburg and have their run of the place." He took a sip of his wine and looked again toward Chauncey in silent request to light his cigar.

"But consider the smuggling, sir," Forsyth pleaded. "We had to make them aware of our presence."

"Is there more or less smuggling there with you gone altogether?" Dearborn asked the obvious question, not waiting for an answer. "Exactly."

Chauncey cleared his throat. "State your business with me, Major Forsyth, and let's get this unpleasantness over."

"We seized two enemy agents on our departure from Ogdensburg." Forsyth gestured toward Sterling. "We've tracked this man consorting at late hours, usually midnight, with Messers Ross and Rosseel, who are well-known smugglers throughout the region. We caught him red-handed in possession of one hundred and forty-four iron frying pans, cases of teapots, and a host of other cooking utensils. I'm assuming that trading with the enemy remains illegal?"

"I have papers, sir," Sterling blurted out, "showing the pans to be imported legally at Boston harbour."

"Shut up," Lieutenant Tasker interjected. He put his riding crop under Sterling's chin. "You'll speak only when spoken to."

"Take that stick down," Chauncey snapped. "This man works for me and those pans belong to the navy."

Tasker appeared puzzled, yet left his riding crop pressing hard under Sterling's chin.

"Put it down immediately or you'll be the one behind bars."

Tasker slipped the crop back under his arm. "I'm sorry, sir."

"Where are those cooking utensils now?" Chauncey demanded, jumping up from his seat to take a step around his desk. He lifted Sterling by one arm and guided him to a chair next to his own.

"We have them stored safely at our camp, sir," Forsyth replied softly, aware that he'd made a colossal blunder.

"You two bunglers will deliver them to the commissariat forthwith," Chauncey ordered. "But I believe your message reported another prisoner?"

"The one named Jonathan Westlake escaped, sir," Forsyth explained. "We caught him at Mr. Sterling's home and believed the two were in league together."

Chauncey looked to Sterling for an explanation.

"It's true," Sterling admitted. "In this job, Commodore, I do have to associate with some unsavoury characters. But even here I have more information. Westlake knows the name of your source in York."

"This is *all* I need." Chauncey took a gulp of his wine. "Is he any relation to the Westlake Trading Company that has offices in New York?"

"So he claimed, sir," Tasker replied.

"Then I know the man's father," Chauncey said, "as does everyone else who ships furs to the continent. Still, the lad must be stopped, you understand? Eliminated, if necessary."

"I sent three good men to head him off at his uncle's place south of Elizabethtown," Forsyth asserted. "They'll get 'im for sure."

"You may yet redeem yourself. Although from what his father once told me, this lad got himself tossed out of school and then lived with the Indians for some time." Chauncey explained, holding his cigar between his fingers as if it was lit. "We'd best hope your men don't end up on the wrong end of a scalping knife. You're dismissed gentlemen. You can give your apologies to Mr. Sterling outside."

"I should add one more thing, sir, if I may," Tasker said in an obvious effort to make amends.

Chauncey frowned, but nodded curtly for him to continue.

"Our pursuit of Westlake took us along the river from Ogdensburg to Cape Vincent, and we found no sign at all of any pending attack from Kingston."

"Thank you Lieutenant, that is worth noting," Chauncey replied. "Now leave us."

General Dearborn stayed seated. "Commodore?" He held up his cigar, which Chauncey finally lit for him before lighting his own. "You have to get word to your man at York." Cigar smoke streamed between Dearborn's lips. "Or they'll hang'im as sure as I'm sitting here."

Chauncey began enjoying his own cigar as he sat back in his chair. Odd that Richard Westlake's son should need to be put down. He waved away the smoke surrounding him and sipped his wine. He had to send a runner immediately to warn his agent in York as Dearborn suggested. It would indeed be a great blow to his organization to lose Sergeant Puffer. However, if the man got himself hanged, there were others to replace him, others willing to sell out their fellow citizens for a few pieces of silver, having no sense of duty or honour to their home. If Chauncey had his way, he'd hang all the traitors on both sides. Until then, he'd continue paying Sterling good money to sell him information that only a traitor could provide.

"Damn fine cigar, Isaac."

"I'm happy you appreciate it, Henry."

15
. . . . . .

WESTLAKE SLEPT a full twelve hours and woke to find the moon shining once again on the town of Prescott. He left a brief note on the table, thanking Colonel Macdonell for his exceptional assistance and gift of a rifle. The officer had arranged for some food to be packed in a bundle that Westlake scooped up from the table. He stuffed his belongings in his haversack, picked up his new weapon and cartridge pouches, and hurried over to the stables.

Under a full moon and stars, and back astride the same horse he arrived on, Westlake trotted southwest out of Prescott, heading to Elizabethtown. He sighed deeply, enjoying the quiet and safety of Upper Canada. With the thought of Puffer behind bars and his mission complete, he looked forward to enjoying the warmer weather at Maple Hill. The sap would be running soon, and he'd help his mother collect every drop to produce maple syrup. Then springtime, and green buds on the trees, something to look forward to. A quiet life, at least for a while, is exactly what he now wanted. For whatever reason, young Willie Robertson's eager face jumped back into his mind. "I'm counting on you, Mr. Westlake."

"Look where it got you, Willie," Westlake said out loud. "And what the hell do you want *me* to do?" A sparrow flew overhead, drawing his eye to the near by trees. He stared around him at the forest of pines and their branches laden with great pillows of snow. "Christ, now I'm talking to a dead boy." Westlake shook his head.

Best just to ride away and forget about Willie Robertson. He didn't have to stop the Taskers and Forsyths of the world. Let them do their worst; why should he care. He'd seen the results of revenge, individuals so damaged by the past they couldn't let go. His duty was done with Puffer's identity revealed.

Westlake rode on, but the farther he travelled from Prescott, leaving Willie physically behind him, the more he knew his duty was not finished. *Perhaps it's never complete, never discharged.* Mere months ago, he'd announced to Brock that he wanted somehow to make a difference. Today, this very instant, he couldn't honestly convince himself that was no longer true. His own sense of honour would not let him deceive himself.

Clouds drifted over the face of the moon, so for a short while the trail disappeared. The horse pressed on, following the ruts in the road. By the time the sun was rising, Westlake was on the street to Sean Delaney's tavern. Joe had gone back to bed but Sean wouldn't allow Westlake to depart without breakfast and a confirmation of his brother's wild story.

Once on the trail again and for the rest of the day, Westlake used every muscle to press against fierce winds out of the west. At times he was forced to stop and rest for the sake of himself and his labouring horse. As the day wore on the sun disappeared and the temperature dropped rapidly. Finally, the moon's glow lit the path ahead to the snow-covered lane swooping down to his uncle's farm. Within minutes of turning toward the farmhouse, the dog ran out barking, its tail wagging furiously. The golden retriever adored Westlake and wouldn't stop yapping until he dismounted at the stable and gave her a hug.

"Cherry, how are you, old girl." Westlake scratched the excited dog under her chin, then patted her on the head as the animal licked his hands. "Quiet girl, shh!" He led his horse to the stable where he unsaddled and fed her before closing the heavy stall gate. Another mare whinnied and shuffled sideways in the adjoining stall. His uncle must have purchased a new horse to replace those stolen by Forsyth. He hauled up his rifle and haversack, ready to head to the house.

Cherry had dug a two-foot burrow running under the barn wall so she could come and go at will. It was half filled with straw and out of the wind. Here she wriggled down on her makeshift bed where she stuck her head out under the wall. Westlake whispered goodnight to her with a pat on the ear.

He hurried to the farmhouse, but the door opened before he could even knock. In the entrance stood a scowling middle-aged man, legs apart and a musket pointing at the intruder. The moon reflected off the top of a bald head.

"Uncle, it's me, Jonathan. Lower the musket, please."

His uncle squinted in surprise, then smiled. "Good to see you, young man! Come in," Adam exclaimed. "I heard the dog barking and then nothing. The buggers won't take me by surprise again. What time is it, now?"

"Sorry for the lateness of the hour. I'm half frozen through. I was passing by on my way from Prescott." While his uncle held the door open, Westlake stepped past into the warmth of the kitchen.

"Your old room hasn't been touched so you can sleep there." Adam quickly closed the door to shut out the winter air. He held out his hand and Westlake clasped it firmly. "Your aunt will be happy to see you, after your last visit. Our talk can wait until morning if that's okay. You won't believe what I went through."

"I have some idea," Westlake replied, "but it can wait for a few hours."

The two men made their way upstairs where they quietly said goodnight. Westlake took his old room at the back overlooking the stables. From the window, he saw Cherry's head rise from her burrow to sniff the air. She'd been the best of companions during those long summer months spent away from school, when any human friends were miles away on scattered farms.

The room still held that remembered smell of a comfortable quilt and maple furniture. The bedposts were smooth to the touch, familiar, like the patterns in the quilt. He placed his rifle atop the dresser, laid the haversack down by the bed before pulling out his nightshirt. Once his head hit the pillow, it felt like he'd never been away.

Westlake slept lightly even though the dozen hours of deep sleep at Prescott had only left him wanting more. He tossed in his bed for hours until Cherry barked unexpectedly. He heard the dog growl and then it suddenly stopped. Westlake leapt to his feet and peered out the window from one side.

A man held something in his hand that Cherry had begun licking. Another scoundrel stepped beside him and slammed the butt end of his musket onto the dog's head. Cherry collapsed to the ground, limp, perhaps even dead. The man glanced up at the windows.

Shaughnessy! He pointed hard toward the house. Both men turned to run for the back door that Adam had guarded only an hour earlier.

Westlake thrust his legs into his pants. He snatched his rifle from the top of the dresser, then grabbed a half-dozen paper cartridges from his box. As he dashed down the hall to his uncle's bedroom, he loaded the rifle. He burst into the room and swiftly put a hand over his uncle's mouth to prevent the man speaking. Fortunately, his aunt remained soundly asleep.

"There are men breaking in downstairs," Westlake said in an urgent whisper. "Place yourself at the top of the stairs."

His uncle nodded his comprehension, eyes the size of plums. "I'll shoot the first bastard who puts a foot on the stairs." He pointed to the musket leaning against the far wall.

"Loaded?" Westlake asked as he heard the back door jiggle once and then again only harder.

"Yes," Adam whispered. "There's also my hunting knife on the hearth downstairs."

"Let's go." Westlake raced down the passageway to the staircase. Someone next tried the front door. *Another man or perhaps there was more.* Westlake took the stairs two at a time and heard the lock on the back door give way. He ran to uncle's favourite chair in a darkened corner of the parlour and sat perfectly still.

At the other end of the room, the doorway from the kitchen lay in shadow. To his right, the embers of last night's fire burned low and gave off almost no light. To his left was the same wall that continued along to the front door.

He reached over from the chair, his hand quickly searching along the hearth. When his fingers touched the sheath, he snatched up the knife and slid it inside his right boot. Sweat moistened his palms and his heart pounded like an iron fist against his ribs, but with the knife in his boot he also felt ready. Westlake cocked the rifle, pointing toward the kitchen, and silently waited for the right moment to pull the trigger. He took a deep breath and tried to relax. His nightshirt stuck to his spine with sweat.

A kitchen chair banged suddenly against the table. Shaughnessy and his comrade were coming closer. What was their plan? Just another random raid or were they specifically after him? He decided on the latter. They'd probably hold his uncle and aunt to ransom for Westlake himself, and then kill him — maybe them too. His thoughts jumped around like a madman, but he'd made his decision now. Once the opportunity arose, he'd kill them all.

A figure crashed through the front door, snapping off the lock. Rifle in hand, the intruder looked left and then right, directly into the parlour. Westlake tensed in anticipation, sure he'd be spotted, but the man didn't seem to register his presence. His two partners entered the parlour through the other door, their shapes silhouetted against the kitchen's dim shadows, their weapons clutched at chest level.

"Sergeant, is that you?" the man at the front door called in a whisper to the moving shadows at end of the room. "I can't see me hand in front of me face in this damn place." The other men crept forward.

Shaughnessy. Sergeant bloody Shaughnessy was here in the parlour. The three men met in the middle of the room. "Upstairs and grab both of them," he ordered. "We'll wait to kill the young bugger down here."

Westlake eased the knife out of its sheath. The three men turned toward the stairs. A swish of air. The knife tumbled twice before catching one man between the shoulder blades. He groaned and slumped hard to the floor. Westlake remained still.

"Christ! What was that?" The man with his foot poised on the stair jerked around to stare straight into the corner, finally catching sight of Westlake's silhouette. He lifted his weapon to fire. Westlake pulled the rifle's trigger first. The weapon exploded in noise and flame as his would-be assailant dropped to the floor, gripping his chest.

Aunt Evelyn screamed from the bedroom.

The third man spun round and fired blindly at the corner. Westlake felt something tear at his ribs. Adam was halfway down the stairs before he pointed the musket and fired too. The man shot backward as if hit by a shovel to the shoulder.

"Uncle!" Westlake cried out, leaning against the chair for support. The right side of his ribcage burned like it was on fire. His uncle stepped cautiously down the rest of the stairs, brandishing his musket like club.

The three men were lumped together on the floor at the foot of the steps.

"Are they dead?" Adam asked.

"That one's just wounded." Westlake pointed to the man shot by his uncle. He felt himself fading, his nightshirt clinging to his body drenched in sweat and blood. "Pull your knife out of that man." He gestured limply with a finger. "Then slit that bastard's throat and call Aunt Evelyn. I fear I've been shot … messed up your favourite chair and …" Then for Westlake, the room descended into darkness.

Captain Nelles stepped carefully over the debris in York's shipyard. Loose planking, empty buckets, great stacks of squared timber, even cooking utensils littered the ground. Looming overhead, far above him rose, the beautiful hull of his majesty's ship the *Sir Isaac Brock*.

He found Captain Francois LeLievre, deputy assistant quartermaster, directing a dozen militiamen on a special clean-up duty. The numerous teams of horses that dragged in the heavy timbers had dumped more than just the load they transported here for the shipwrights. Horse dung had been left everywhere to disgrace the worksite.

"You've come to assist us no doubt, Captain Nelles," LeLievre chided as he kept walking. "See what I'm starting from. Give me less than a week and all this will be a proper place of work." He waved an arm at the construction site.

Nelles surveyed the mess all around him and now understood why the complaints grew daily about Superintendent Plucknett, the officer in charge of building the new brigantine. Prevost should have sacked the man.

However, if anyone could re-energize the dockyard, it was the sixty-year-old, Captain LeLievre. Despite the leathery face, he had the enthusiasm of a youngster combined with the competency of a veteran. After a cold march from Kingston, he'd arrived in York with one hundred and sixty officers and men of the Royal Newfoundland Regiment.

"The little issue regarding the magazine is cleared up, I hope, *monsieur*," LeLievre inquired. "There, Sergeant." He pointed out a mound of horse droppings and the men ran toward it with their shovels. "Something about loading barrels of powder onto racks that hadn't yet been built."

"Not your fault, Captain. The racks are now up, and the militia is loading the extra inventory of cartridges," Nelles replied with some satisfaction. "The barrels in the old magazine shed come next. One has to take care with three hundred of them filled full of fine-grain powder."

"*Mon Dieu*, to turn this place into a marine depot is crazy. How are we supposed to defend all that powder — " LeLievre threw his hands in the air and then pointed to the unfinished hull. "— as well as this ship?"

Nelles had the same concerns, but if the ship could be launched, then it had a chance of escaping a potential attack. He peered up at the hull's skeleton: the great timbers that would complete the keel had yet to be inserted, and the oak planking on the starboard side of the hull was just beginning. "I agree, Captain, but if she could be made capable of floating, then —"

"By when? The end of April? Not going to happen. Beams to support the decks aren't even in place. No steering yet either: no gunports and no magazine." He pointed to the different sections of the ship as if he could see the details clearly in his mind's eye. "I'm sorry to tell you that little has been accomplished by this man Plucknett."

"Any possibility of building the ship without him?"

LeLievre gestured to the steps ascending the embankment, set well back from the water's edge. "I plan to work directly with the master shipwright himself. He and I, together with the rest of his shipwrights, will complete this ship," he explained. "I'll get the materials delivered to this dock whenever they need them, and they'll do the building ... but it still won't be finished until some time in May. And that's too late."

Nelles had to agree. As soon as the ice went out, every town around Lake Ontario's shoreline became vulnerable to the American fleet, including York. That meant LeLievre had only a month to finish building the vessel. At the top of the embankment, men worked on the lower masts, which were up to ninety feet long. The two officers carried on walking until they arrived at the sailmaker's shop, where they inspected the main topsails.

LeLievre continued his account. "All is not lost yet, but we need a little more time. You've doubtless heard discussions about an attack on Sackets Harbor." He gestured southeast toward the harbour. "If you could use your influence with Sir George, such an attack would give us the time we need."

First he had been Brock's man and now he was Prevost's. It would never end. "Let me see what I can do with all my *influence*." He grinned, and LeLievre nodded his understanding. "I do agree with you about buying time." Nelles said.

The nimble fingers of Captain Nelles tapped a nervous beat on the armrests of Brock's great leather chair. Major General Sheaffe had never graced this spartan office, and yet in a few minutes time Sir George Prevost himself would be sitting in the chair opposite him. There had to be a special reason the governor wanted to see him.

Nelles surveyed the map of Lake Ontario that lay spread on his desk, held down with a pistol at either end. At the eastern tip of the lake sat the naval town of Kingston, in Upper Canada. Sackets Harbor to the south, on the American side, rested no more than thirty-five miles away. Upwards of a dozen ships in that anchorage waited for spring's warmer air to thaw the lake's ice and give the enemy control of the lake.

Nelles jabbed his finger hard on the word *Sackets*, as if he could damage the enemy squadron just by striking the map. An armed force had to attack those ice-bound ships before they could affect the war's outcome. Even burning just the two brigs, *Oneida* and *Madison*, would bring an end to the immediate threat. He leaned back in his leather chair, satisfied in knowing what he wanted from this meeting. Now all that remained was to find out what the governor needed.

An aide knocked, poked his head in, and the swung open the door. "Governor Prevost to see you, sir."

Nelles stood and saluted when Sir George strolled into the office. The salute returned, Prevost offered his hand and a broad smile. "Pleasure to finally meet you, Captain Nelles. General Brock was always effusive in his praise of you and your insightful advice."

"That's very kind of you to remark, sir, but I gave him less advice than everyone seems to think," Nelles replied as the two men sat down across the desk from each other. He caught the governor's eye scanning the outstretched map, the business of the meeting already flowing through his mind. Nelles had expected an imposing and powerful man, but Prevost's chin was dimpled and small, giving an overall impression of softness. However, there was nothing weak about the governor's light brown eyes that seemed to take in everything.

"Now *I* need your thoughts," Prevost explained, "and that's why I've asked to meet with you alone ... without General Sheaffe present. A couple of days ago in Niagara, I put an end to the cabal forming against him at Fort George." The governor leaned forward and rested his elbows on the desk, his face serious, almost grim. "I'm well aware Mr. Sheaffe's style does not engender personal loyalty, but we need to get on with winning this war together."

"I couldn't agree more, sir. If I can speak freely ..."

Prevost nodded in encouragement.

"General Sheaffe starts from a position of weakness, sir, simply because he's not Sir Isaac Brock. Even his loyalty is questioned because of his Boston birthplace. Add that to his imperious style with the officers under him, and it's no wonder they agitate for a change in command."

Prevost remained silent.

Nelles wondered if he'd gone too far in his first meeting, but the governor just continued nodding his head. Then Nelles remembered that Prevost had been born in New Jersey and so might identify with Sheaffe's predicament. The governor had known Sheaffe from his school days in England, and probably sympathized with the man in other ways. Nelles decided to stop talking.

"You've seen our shipbuilding problems first-hand?" Prevost changed the subject.

Nelles nodded.

"Mr. Plucknett's second-in-command complains too much, and progress is at a snail's pace. Perhaps Captain LeLievre will finally get things moving." Again he glanced down at the map.

"It's Plucknett that holds things up, sir, not any complaints about his lack of organization. Even with Mr. LeLievre's efforts, the *Sir Isaac Brock* will not be ready for the spring thaw. There's only one way to save that ship." Nelles leaned forward to point at a location on the map.

"You too wish an attack on Sackets Harbor?" Sir George spoke the words that Nelles was thinking.

Aware that Brock's orders had always been to defend, and undertake no offensive operations, Nelles spoke carefully. "If the enemy's ships are allowed to escape that harbour, sir, they can bring to bear overwhelming firepower anywhere on the lake." He tapped several targets around the northern edge of the water. "If we lose Kingston, the rest of Upper Canada will wither. They will then concentrate every man they have for an attack on Montreal and Quebec. The best defensive move is to take out those ships before the spring thaw."

Prevost stared down at the map, and Nelles wondered what he was thinking. Orders from London had urged a defensive posture, but surely they did not expect Prevost to do nothing. This type of limited offence that Nelles proposed now had been Brock's way of thinking.

"Perhaps it's time to broaden the definition of defensive. You don't think York can hold against a full American attack," Prevost asserted.

Nelles sighed and shook his head.

"Making York a provincial marine depot was Brock's idea, and I encouraged it so as to get away from Kingston."

"General Brock always looked for ways to win, sir," Nelles stated. "Keeping a marine depot here, at this time, is a sure way to lose. He'd have changed his mind, concentrated everything at Kingston, and attacked Sackets Harbor *now*, sir."

"I see why Sir Isaac valued your opinions. You have a straightforward manner." The governor stood up to leave. "Expect my confidential communications from time to time." Prevost held up his hand as Nelles began to protest. "General Sheaffe is aware of my wish and it's fine with him. Also, he has the paperwork raising you up to the rank of major. Congratulations, Major Nelles." Prevost offered his hand.

Nelles jumped up, his chest expanding with joy. "Thank you, sir." He grinned. "It's very much appreciated."

"Leave this Sackets Harbor business with me. Thirty-five miles is a long way to march in winter and then expect the men to fight. The Americans would be waiting for us." Prevost opened the door, but before departing he turned back to speak. "I met that young fellow, Brock's agent, in Prescott. Seemed an honourable young man ... very loyal to you. The both of you will make a good pair in the intelligence business ... that is if he doesn't get his head blown off."

16

. . . . . .

WESTLAKE OPENED HIS EYES in his old room. He ran a finger along the familiar pattern of his quilt and, for a brief moment, imagined that school had ended and it was now summer. Then the night's events travelled through his mind and brought him back to reality. A dark room, one man taken down with the knife, one shot through the chest, and the other through the shoulder.

He moved to get up, but searing pain shot up his right side. "Shit," he cried out. His head flopped back on the pillow as he tried to keep his breathing shallow and hold his ribs still. Footsteps clumped down the hall outside, and he closed his eyes, aware of the bandages wrapped around his ribcage.

The footsteps stopped beside his bed. "You've lost a lot of blood, sport," Uncle Adam said. "You'd best try not to move."

Westlake slowly opened his eyes to see his chubby-faced uncle shaking his bald head sadly and staring down at him.

"This here is Doctor Acker," Adam explained. "He's actually an animal doctor, but he's bandaged you up real good and tight." He stood aside to let Acker step forward in front of him.

The doctor reached over to feel Westlake's forehead, the tips of his pudgy fingers feeling cold to the touch. "Like I thought, not much different than with an injured calf," he declared. "After a few days the fever's gone down."

"A few days!" Westlake jerked up and was punished again by the pain shooting through his side. "I need to be in York, immediately." He fell back on the pillow. *Shaughnessy?*

"That bullet went clean through you but nicked a couple of ribs," the doctor explained. "You would have lost the rest of your blood if your auntie hadn't staunched the bleeding. Stay perfectly still and you'll heal up fine, but go riding and that wound will re open just as sure as a pig loves muck."

"The third man, Uncle, did you kill him?" Westlake gritted his teeth with eyes closed.

"I couldn't do such a thing to a wounded man. I kept the musket trained on him the whole time he laid there. He wasn't hit so bad as you and managed to slink off as soon as your aunt finished bandaging him up."

"You should have killed him," Westlake declared. "There's a traitor operating in York and I know his name. Those men will be back for sure. All of us have to get away from this farm now." He winced again as he tried to sit up and swing his feet over the bedside.

Uncle Adam paused as if considering Westlake's decision and then he slowly nodded his head. He peered up at the doctor. "The lad's probably right. Evelyn won't like this one bit."

"Best to be on the safe side," said Doctor Acker. "Take my sleigh for the patient and your wife. I'll ride the lad's horse home. While you and your wife pack whatever you need, I'll change these bandages a last time." He frowned and lifted Westlake's shirt. "This wound will reopen as likely as I'm standing here, but that's better than having the three of you stay and get shot to death."

Adam shrugged, resigned to the course of action that seemed best. He left to tell his wife the bad news.

Doctor Acker rebandaged Westlake. "You're better off than Cherry at least. Poor dog probably died on the first blow to her head." Anxious to return to his other duties and get some distance between him and the farm, the doctor departed forthwith.

Within the hour, Aunt Evelyn reluctantly snapped the reins and the horse jerked the sleigh carrying herself and the patient forward. Westlake winced at the sudden movement but made no sound in case she changed her mind and remained at home. She stared down at him lying in the sleigh, and he smiled back as if they were just setting off on another family outing. Adam rode his own horse beside them.

Westlake stared straight up at the grey sky, listening to the muffled sound of horse's hooves as the sleigh runners cut through the snow. Large flakes had begun to fall before noon, and that suited his purpose. Their tracks from the farmhouse would soon be covered.

"You brought some kindling, Aunt Evelyn?" Westlake asked, thinking of the fire they would need to build later that night.

She nodded, gazing back one last time toward her farmhouse over a white expanse of snow. "I could've slit that evil man's throat for what he did to you and Cherry, but your Uncle Adam wouldn't hear of it. Now I have to leave my own home on account of his foolish kindness." She jerked her head angrily in Adam's direction.

"It was me who brought this on you. Uncle Adam has a code of honour that wouldn't allow him to kill a wounded man."

"There's honour and there's stupidity," Evelyn asserted. "One has to behave honourably, but one does not have to be stupid. Men, especially, get confused where honour is concerned."

Westlake nodded in agreement, thinking of Willie Robertson trying to rush the cannons. Then he remembered Brock charging up the hill in the face of American musket fire. Doing the right thing might be honourable, but if it got you killed there was little point. He took a deep breath and watched the snowflakes floating down to land on his cheek and then melt. His eyes closed as he imagined the surprised look on Captain Nelles's face when he heard the identity of Brock's traitor.

Less than seventy paces from the water's edge, near the bottom of Sackets Harbor's hill, the white-painted Eveleigh Hotel and Tavern stood out as a singularly respectable establishment. The Eveleigh family, it was common knowledge, determined to maintain their hotel to the highest standards, no matter the onslaught of war. On entering its front door, guests knew they were visiting the high point of village civilization.

Straw covering the planked floors of the barroom was changed every other day. The plates and cutlery glistened from constant washing in fresh water drawn from Lake Ontario. The quality of the food, cooked by Mrs. Eveleigh herself, showed no diminishing standard, regardless of the increased number of meals she had to serve daily. And for this reason, on Monday, March 15, 1813, the hotel would boast the most important guests that it would ever entertain.

From an upper-floor window in his corner suite at the Eveleigh Hotel, Commodore Isaac Chauncey surveyed the litter lying about in the cratered roads leading into town. Flooded by an influx of thousands of seamen, soldiers, and their horses, the lakeside village of Sackets Harbor had quickly deteriorated into a place of sprawling squalor. Around the construction sites for new buildings, the refuse and waste material spewed onto the streets.

He shifted his gaze to the harbour where a flotilla of frost-covered ships lay still in the ice, all of them at the mercy of the weather. *My ships. And by God I'll use them only to my liking.*

Commodore Chauncey, his stomach grumbling, looked forward to the meal. Even up on the second floor, the wafting aroma of roasting lamb filled the commodore's nostrils. But despite the temptation of a good meal, Chauncey was feeling wary.

At the invitation of Major General Henry Dearborn, the midday fare would be lavish. The general maintained a bulky frame, and news not only of his appetite but also of his bullying manner preceded him. Commodore Chauncey, however, was determined to stick to his own plans for the war. And, answering only to the secretary of the navy, Chauncey *was* rightly his own man and knew that Dearborn could not order either him or his ships into harm's way. This meal, then, by Chauncey's way of thinking, was somewhere between a political peace offering and a bribe.

There was a certain class of individuals who knew how to win in the affairs of men, and Commodore Chauncey included himself in that company. Planning the first combined operation of major naval and army forces in U.S. history, Chauncey decided that no second-rate old general would imperil his chance of success. The requirements for victory would not in any way be subordinated to politics. Granny Dearborn, so nicknamed for his age and his girth, would therefore have to be convinced regarding the merits of Chauncey's new proposal for winning this war.

The commodore strolled across his hotel room to peer out of the front window. Below, Granny Dearborn arrived in a horse-drawn sleigh escorted by six dragoons and a dozen riflemen on foot that quickly encircled the hotel. Two soldiers dismounted before reaching up to lend a hand to the major general as he managed one slow step down followed by another. A few well-dressed onlookers waved to him from the other side of the street. He paused at the foot of the stairs leading to the hotel, as if to catch his breath, nodded to them politely, and then disappeared from view as the dragoons hoisted him up to the front landing.

The old hotel steps creaked as Chauncey descended to the main floor. He turned to his right and entered a formal dining room with walls panelled in dark oak. A full-length mirror allowed him to study the reflection of himself in his dress uniform. He straightened the gold braid on one shoulder and tugged down on his smart blue jacket.

Surrounded by ten high-backed chairs, a white linen cloth covered the dining table. Two candelabras stood in the middle of the table, each with six lighted candles that flickered as he entered. The table had place settings for three diners. *Another guest at dinner?* That meant Granny was stacking the odds against him.

Apart from the occasional clinking pot in the kitchen, the normally bustling hotel held an eerie quiet. All the guests had been asked to leave and not return until early evening. The front door of the hotel opened to let in a chill breeze. At the far end of the room, a fireplace sparked with new life. The major general had arrived.

"Good afternoon, Commodore," Dearborn wheezed as if out of breath. "I take it the hotel has made you comfortable." He stamped his feet to let the snow fall from his boots.

"I'd have been just as pleased to meet you up the hill in your personal quarters as down here," Chauncey replied.

"Neutral ground this. One is less inclined to defend one's interest in the pleasant atmosphere of a tavern. I've always liked the warmth of this room." Dearborn smiled while gazing around at the oak panels.

"Besides, you would have missed a fabulous meal from Mrs. Eveleigh. Colonel Pike will join us, if you don't mind. He's marched his men a full ten days from Plattsburg and so deserves special treatment this afternoon." Dearborn rubbed his hands together in anticipation.

"Very nice of you, sir," Chauncey complimented. In fact, this venue suited his purpose well. He now had only to wait for the appropriate opportunity during the forthcoming meal to present his plan.

At that moment, Pike himself hurried into the room, his face flushed and his hair dishevelled. He apologized for his appearance, explaining that there had been a problem with the living quarters for his men, but that all was settled now. Dearborn waved away his concerns and claimed the winged armchair at the table's head. Pike took the seat opposite Chauncey.

Over the next hour, Mrs. Eveleigh's staff served the various courses described on a neatly written menu. The lamb came direct from Albany, the steaming vegetables from the Carolinas, and of course the warm bread was homemade. Mrs. Eveleigh, a portly woman, eventually entered to deliver the chocolate cake herself. The major general thanked her profusely and then asked that the dining room be off limits to the hotel staff unless summoned. The woman curtseyed, turned, and departed the room.

General Dearborn proceeded to offer his congratulations to Pike on his successful march from Plattsburg, and Chauncey added his own compliments.

"Thank you, gentlemen." Pike leaned back in his chair, and Chauncey hoped they were not in for a speech. "Just give my men a chance to rest and we'll be ready to seize Kingston," Pike bragged.

Chauncey sensed the moment and decided to initiate the debate before Pike could continue. Excitement rose in his throat and he tried to swallow, for Granny Dearborn was a man used to getting his own way. "Not Kingston. York ... I'd like to attack York first, sir."

The commodore calmed himself while Dearborn continued to shovel cake into his mouth as if nothing had been said. At that second, Chauncey hoped the comforting food and ambience would soften his suggestion of moving the battle away from the original target and instead to the little town of York. He was sure Dearborn would not favour a change of plan.

"Kingston has already been approved" — Dearborn pushed back a little from the table, and counted off by holding up one finger at a time — "by the president, the secretary of war, the secretary of the navy, and me."

"So?" Chauncey asked bluntly.

"So why the change?"

"The ice," Chauncey replied.

Pike stayed quiet, but the expression on his face was one of surprise. At the end of the dinner he'd be told his mission and would no doubt enthusiastically agree. As for where the man would stand in this argument, Chauncey knew it would be with his boss. *Politics, there was always damn politics.*

"The plan to strike as soon as the ice goes out is still a good one," Dearborn claimed. "The sooner we get at them, the less chance they have to bring any new ships against us. Our superiors in Washington demand progress. We need a victory sooner than later." Dearborn returned to another spoonful of cake.

So the problem was political. The coming elections meant that the Republican Party was pushing Major General Dearborn for an early victory, something that the candidates there could boast about on the hustings. They couldn't even wait for the ice to clear Kingston.

"On that we agree, but the ice will go out later this year than most," Chauncey added. "It will jam up at Kingston as usual, creating a further delay."

Dearborn didn't seem to listen as he continued. "But if we gain Kingston — the trunk of the tree — the branches will die, and there would be no need to lose ships and men in battles fought for York, Niagara, or the rest of Upper Canada, for that matter." He'd been holding his knife in the air and now threw it down on the table. "Kingston is still the key."

Chauncey decided on a demonstration. He held up his empty

wineglass and then swept all the dishes on the table, including the white table cloth, into a great pile directly in front of Dearborn. Now, with the general's eyes wide open, he finally had his full attention.

"Let's, for argument sake, say I agree with your point on early timing," Chauncey said. He leaned forward on one elbow. "You are Kingston, and that's the ice." He gestured to the pile. "Mr. Pike here is York. This is my flotilla." He slid his glass easily across the table's polished surface, where Pike caught it before it fell. "And remember also that we'll capture the *Sir Isaac Brock* before she's completely finished. You've seen the intelligence … enormous supplies in the quartermaster's storehouse. In fact, a small fortune! Don't forget the new powder magazine. And the schooner, the *Duke of Gloucester*, is also docked there."

Dearborn sat back in his chair, hands on his lap. His expression turned to one of puzzlement. He stared down at the pile of dishes representing the ice jam at Kingston harbour.

The intelligence regarding the supplies was paying dividends. The argument to attack York would swing on that information.

"Please, Henry, listen to me." Chauncey continued. "Even in respect to timing, I can give you an earlier victory at York than at Kingston. The ice will be gone at York long before Kingston, and the victory is more easily assured."

Chauncey let Dearborn consider his points for a moment and then added, "York would be like a practice run for the bigger prize of Kingston. Adding a British brig and schooner to our fleet can only make things easier. And we know for sure that York is far less well defended than Kingston."

Pike sat up straight as if to say something and then thought better of it. He remained silent until Dearborn invited him to comment with a wave of his hand.

"Well, gentlemen." Pike cleared this throat, "I really don't have a card in this game. All I would say is that the Fifteenth and Sixteenth Infantry are so well trained that we could attack any place you chose and expect to win. Just give us a ride there, Commodore, and let us go to work." Pike rose up on his own accord and strode over to place another log on the fire.

He returned to the table and sat down. Both men stared at Dearborn for an answer. The commodore knew that Dearborn would not go back to upper management without a firm understanding of the proposal. He waited.

Dearborn unfolded his hands in order to grip the table's edge. "Timing is critical." He nodded his head firmly. "Sooner is better than later. So suppose that I agree ... York is first."

Chauncey breathed a sigh and jabbed a thumb toward Pike. "Remember, I run this invasion, top to bottom, until he's safely on land."

"They're your ships." Dearborn nodded his agreement.

"Then let's get started on the change in plans. Inform the secretary of war and the president, and I'll inform the secretary of the navy — we attack York."

17
. . . . . .

THE STREETS OF YORK bustled with sleighs as Westlake approached. The morning air chilled his lungs, but the freezing winter winds that had accompanied their party for much of the trip had subsided. Spring wasn't too far away. Westlake had pressed his uncle and aunt onwards as fast as they could travel. They arrived barely able to sit up straight from fatigue after their journey. Whitby's Lynde Inn and Tavern had been the only decent lodgings along the way.

"You've pushed yourself too hard." Aunt Evelyn held the reins tightly in hand as she turned to shout at her nephew lying in the sleigh. "When we reach this Captain Nelles, wherever he is, I'm taking another look at those bandages."

She spoke to him as if he was only twelve years old again. Westlake laughed but didn't mention that the wound in his side continued to burn like hell. One complaint from him and he knew she'd insist on stopping.

Government House lay farther along the lakeshore, and the horses kept up a weary pace until reaching the guards posted on duty at the southern entrance. A sentry took the reins from his aunt while another placed himself in front of Uncle Adam and his mount.

"State your name and business," the sentry demanded.

"I'm here with an urgent message for Captain Nelles. Name's Westlake. Let us through."

"There's a war on," the guard replied with a contemptuous smirk. "You can pass, but the others must wait here."

Westlake looked at his uncle and shrugged. He eased down slowly from the sleigh, his wound making every step a struggle. "Give me your shoulder, man." He gestured to his escort and the man offered his arm to lean on.

The escort then led him through the entrance hall and down a corridor. He stopped outside the office of Captain Nelles. A redcoat standing in the outer doorway raised an arm to bar the way. "The major is in conference and has asked not to be disturbed."

"Major?" Westlake frowned. "I've come a long way with vital news. Please tell him that Jonathan Westlake is here." The wound in his side throbbed painfully and he leaned more heavily on his escort.

"I have my orders, sir," the sentry said. "You will have to wait." He nodded back down the corridor.

Westlake clenched his jaw in frustration. He couldn't take on two of them with a burning rib. He let go of his escort's arm, as if to turn away, then charged like a bull for the door ahead. His escort snatched for his arm, trying to stop him, but grabbed only air. Westlake collided with the redcoat sentry, hurling him backward into the door. It crashed open and they hit the floor with Westlake landing on top of the sentry.

"What the devil's the meaning of this?" demanded an angry voice from inside the room.

Westlake's body convulsed with surging bolts of pain. He glanced up from the floor to catch a glimpse of gold braid. Major General Sheaffe stood over him, a hand resting on his sword.

"Jonathan." A hand touched his shoulder and Westlake peered up into the concerned face of Major Nelles. The sentry pinned underneath him groaned.

"Winky, sir. Sergeant Puffer's the traitor." Nelles grabbed him by the shoulders to help lift him to his feet, but the pain around his ribs proved too much to bear. "Congratulations on your promotion, sir," Westlake gasped. A further jab of agony overwhelmed him, the blood draining from his head. The room went dark.

Major Nelles gently lifted Lieutenant Westlake off the sentry and dragged him unconscious to a bearskin rug in the centre of the floor. He laid a hand on the lieutenant's forehead to discover the lad's burning temperature. The sentry was on his feet again by the time Nelles grabbed a sword off the desk. The map it had held open rolled shut with a snap. Nelles strode toward the door.

"Puffer, a traitor?" Sheaffe asked. "He was always one of Brock's favourites. Before you kill the fellow, find out who he works with."

"Get the doctor," Nelles ordered. Then realizing to whom he was speaking, he added, "If you please, sir." He pulled Westlake's escort by the arm. "Come with me and be prepared to use that." Nelles gestured to the musket as he ran.

Directly outside Government House, he saw two individuals huddled together in a sleigh. "You brought Mr. Westlake here, no doubt."

The man nodded. "He's shot through something terrible, sir."

Nelles turned to one of the redcoats on duty. "Take these good people to my office and then return to your post ... on guard." To the other sentry he ordered, "You're with me."

He now had two armed soldiers at hand to seize Puffer and who ever might be with him. Nelles hastened east from Government House, along Front Street, toward the quartermaster's storehouse. Puffer! To think, all this time he'd operated under their noses, selling secrets to the enemy. The bastard had lied, winked, and questioned every bit of supplies passing through his hands. Nelles had entertained suspicions about Puffer for some time. He was the only one he'd told about the eight thousand troops garrisoned at Kingston. When he heard this echoed to him by his American friends, he realized Puffer must have blabbed to someone. Now he was going to wring the traitor's neck like he would a chicken.

Nelles approached the garrison palisade at a run. The sentry at the front gate stood to attention and saluted. "Stand aside," Nelles panted, gesturing with his drawn sword. As soon as the sentry swung open the gate, Nelles and his couple of guardsmen charged on through.

Nelles hurried straight to the storehouse, where a lone sentry stood on guard. "Open the door and step away," Nelles demanded. "Is Sergeant Puffer here, man?"

"No, sir."

The door swung open, but there was no one to be seen inside. Nelles took cautious steps toward the quartermaster's counter, his sword extended at the ready. "Straight to the back door," Nelles ordered the two men accompanying him.

The guardsmen ran to the rear while Nelles began checking the aisles of racking in search of Puffer. Nothing. The red coals in the grate burned low, so the building had assumed a distinct chill. The supplies looked in perfect order, but there was no sign of Puffer himself. The sergeant was gone.

The rear doors of the storehouse were constructed high off the ground and built to open like a barn. Supplies could thus be off loaded directly from carts onto a dock with two lines of labourers ready to move the goods inside. Each guardsman now slowly opened a door. Again, no Puffer.

Nelles ventured out to the loading dock. A guardsman turned to him and shrugged. "Nothing out here, sir."

"Goddamn his skin!" Nelles stared out toward the garrison gates. Someone had to have got past the guard to warn Puffer in time to make good his escape.

He glanced down at the snow from the edge of the dock. Fresh sleigh tracks led away heading straight for the gates. "I know how they did it," Nelles said out loud, talking to himself. The sleigh would have normally delivered supplies. This morning it passed through the gates as it always had. Only this time it came not only to deliver supplies. It came to warn Puffer to run.

"Off to the gate, man," Nelles ordered. "Ask the duty officer for a list of every sleigh that entered and departed this morning. It shouldn't be a long one. Bring the list to my office." The guardsman ran off.

Nelles jumped down from the dock and bent over to touch the snow. A fine white powder ran under his fingers. *Flour*. The garrison's miller on the Don River had driven here to warn Puffer to run.

By the time Nelles returned to Government House, the sentry informed him that Westlake had departed in the company of the garrison doctor. Nelles hurried down the hall past his broken-down door to Sheaffe's office and knocked.

"Come in."

Nelles entered the room to find Sheaffe standing in his shirtsleeves behind the desk. "Puffer's gone, sir," Nelles announced. "I believe our flour supplier tipped him off, and they ran together. The gate's log has confirmed that the miller paid a visit this very morning. Horses are being readied now to pursue them. What of Lieutenant Westlake, sir?"

"Doctor rebandaged him right there on your office floor," Sheaffe replied. "Says the lad's been shot and mustn't try to move for at least a week. All of them went off together to the young man's residence at Maple Hill."

"I know the family well. I'll pay the lieutenant a visit in a few days … find out exactly how he came to identify our traitor."

"He's that same agent, isn't he … from Queenston Heights. Bloody awful business, playing the impostor half the time."

"You'd best add Fort Mackinac and Fort Detroit, sir." Nelles felt himself grow defensive. "He seems to get the job done wherever he goes."

"He scared the hell out of me, bursting through that door." Sheaffe wiped his brow. "Didn't get his man this time, though. Puffer's got away."

"The game's not over, sir." Nelles's face flushed with anger. *Inconsiderate* was the word used by fellow officers to describe Sheaffe. Over any length of time men would grow to despise Sheaffe, and for good reason. He left everyone feeling unappreciated, the exact opposite of the sentiments inspired by the general he was trying to replace. "We'll pay a visit to the miller and with any luck, we'll figure out how Puffer managed to send intelligence across the border."

A guardsman ran the length of the hall to announce the horses were saddled and ready.

"Do it quick, by God," Sheaffe added. "The enemy most likely knows our strength right down to the number of toothpicks we have in storage."

The newly promoted Major Nelles and a dozen dragoons set off at a gallop toward the lower Don River and arrived at the flourmill twenty minutes after leaving Government House. The sleigh that had appeared to warn Puffer earlier sat empty near the front porch. Nelles sent three men down each side of the mill toward the river, to watch out for an attempt at escape across the ice. The rest of the grenadiers stepped through the open front door with their fixed bayonets at the ready. The grinding wheels stood quiet inside the darkened mill. Nelles drew his sword.

A young apprentice appeared, his hair covered in flour dust. Seeing the bayonets, the boy's mouth dropped and he threw up his hands.

"Where's your master?" Nelles shouted.

"At the back, sir, just behind the wheelpost." The lad pointed to the stout post that rotated the great stones.

The miller must have heard something because his head showed itself around one side of the post. Nelles beckoned him forward. At first the man stood frozen still, then he inched closer, barely moving his feet.

"Hurry along, damn you. Step outside where I can see you." Nelles grabbed him by the collar and ushered him out through the door into the daylight. "Where is Sergeant Puffer?" Nelles demanded after letting go the collar. He held the point of his sword to the miller's chest. "We know how you warned him off this morning."

"Warned him, sir?" The miller looked puzzled. "I was merely given five pounds to take him a new saddle and horse and tell him that the battle of the Nile was fought in 1806. Since I was making a delivery to his storehouse anyways, I thought, Why not?" He lowered his hands and took in a deep breath.

Nelles shook his head. "When was that?"

"Two hours ago. I delivered him the full measure, went on to my next stop, and came straight here. Is the sergeant in trouble?"

"Who was it that gave you the money and horse?" Nelles asked.

"That's the strangest thing. You know the old drunk Forbsy what hangs around the Jordan? Shows up at my door just after dawn — smelling something awful, I might add — and asks if I'd do him this favour. Then he looks back toward the woods."

"Mr. Forbes had brought you the horse and money?"

The miller nodded. "See those trees." He pointed.

Nelles turned around to study a stand of maples and oaks some fifty yards distant. "So what then, man. Get on with it."

"I had my boy deal with Forbsy while I ran upstairs to sneak a peek out the window." The miller touched his temple twice with a finger. "Sure enough, two men on horseback were waiting there just inside the fringe of that forest."

"That was smart of you. Describe them," Nelles demanded.

"Dawn's light, sir. Can't see a man's face who doesn't want to be recognized at fifty yards," he pleaded. The miller shrugged, slapping his flour-covered hands together. "I thought it a strange request, but Sergeant Puffer's always been perfectly fair to me. Do you want that five pounds Forbsy gimme?"

Nelles waved his hand in frustration. "Keep it. You earned it." He looked again at the treeline and grimaced. "I suppose we have to speak to bloody Mr. Forbes himself now."

"Say hello to him for me and you might tell him that the battle of the Nile wasn't 1806. The Nile was 1805, and everyone knows that."

That signal from friends outside the garrison had told Puffer that something was wrong. Nelles frowned as he gestured to his men to mount their horses. "Next time, be more careful who you work for." He waved the back of his hand at the miller to go back inside and led the way to the Jordan tavern, wondering if the man had told him the honest truth. Perhaps old man Forbsy held the answer he sought.

A dozen travellers and hotel guests sat in the Jordan's barroom ordering their late-morning fare, as Nelles entered with a single redcoat at his side. That the soldier carried a fixed bayonet would not be lost on the patrons.

The room's conversation ceased immediately so the only sound was the crackling fire. Dim light from a few candles forced him to squint through the smoke. He made eye contact with the barman, who rushed around from behind the counter to greet personally his new customer wearing a major's uniform.

"Lucy," the barman called out and gestured for the barmaid to hurry over. He peered around Nelles through the open door to see mounted grenadiers. "Where would you like to sit, Major?" He spoke quickly with a nervous pitch, like a man guilty of some small crime. "I can get these scousers to shift themselves for you, sir. There's a warm bench by the fire."

"I'm not here for a drink." Nelles surveyed the room, looking for Forbsy but also taking in the characters staring at him from each table. Two men sitting at the middle one hunched over their mugs of ale and kept their heads down. He studied the men standing at the bar before they slowly turned their backs to him, one by one. "I'm looking for a Mr. Forbes," he announced.

The barman looked to the maid.

"Haven't seen him here for more than an hour, Major," she answered. Her brown eyes were calm. "And he was three sheets to the wind by the time he left. Usually Mr. Forbes is begging the other customers for a drink, but this time he had more money to spend than his belly could hold."

Nelles was immediately attracted to the slim figure. "Do you know where he went?" he asked. "Quickly, girl!"

"He staggered through the back door, probably on his way to the outhouse." Lucy shrugged.

"Anyone else come in after Mr. Forbes departed — say within the last half hour?" Nelles asked.

Lucy looked to the barman, who slowly shook his head. Nelles guessed they were probably both lying, but he didn't understand why. He ordered a sentry to stand guard at the main door, then shouted out for his troop of men to meet him around the back of the building. "Everyone stay in your seats," he bellowed to the customers.

With a hand placed firmly under the barman's arm, Nelles escorted him out through the back entrance, where numerous footprints marked the path to the outhouse. The door had been left open, showing the latrine to be empty. A few drops of blood in the snow led to rear of the outhouse.

Nelles spotted Forbsy's feet first, then his crumpled body, with one arm splayed at an odd angle. The fierce odour of the latrine matched the sight of Forbsy's battered corpse. The back of his skull had been crushed in, and blood stained the snow all around him. Nelles gently rolled the body over. Forbsy's battered features stared up at him. Under the body lay a broken bottle, its jagged glass fragments standing upright in the snow. Nelles reached down and closed the dead man's eyes.

His stomach wrenching, he jerked his head away. This scene reminded him of the worst sights at Queenston Heights and the butchery that men could inflict on each other. Forbsy's face looked like it had been hit full-on by an axe. The barman's retching broke through his concentration. Nelles didn't blame the man.

"There was no need," the barmen gasped. "He may have been a drunk, but he didn't deserve this."

"Who were the last men to enter the barroom after Mr. Forbes left it?" Nelles inquired.

The barman looked away. "I don't know, sir." His hand was shaking as he rubbed his forehead.

Nelles stared at him in angry disbelief. He knew the Jordan Hotel held American sympathies, but this was the murder of a harmless old man. "Then you are no better than those who did this."

The barman glanced down again at Forbsy. "They'll kill me too. I've come to know those men. Promise me you'll question everyone in the tavern equally, not just the two men at the centre table. That's the only way I'll be safe."

Nelles nodded in agreement. "Their names, barman?"

"Hendrickson and Archer."

18

. . . . . .

BRIGADIER GENERAL ZEBULON MONTGOMERY PIKE peered out his Sackets Harbor window to watch the snow dripping from the branches. The ice of Lake Ontario appeared soft to the eye, and he'd ordered a halt to the daily drills on its surface. He dipped his quill in the ink and finished the letter to his wife with a favourite passage.

> *Preserve your honour free from blemish. Be always ready to die for your country. The sod which covers the brave shall be moistened by the tears of love and friendship.*
> *Yours in love,*
> *Montgomery*

What a thrill to be writing to Clarissa, informing her of his promotion to brigadier general. *Clara, God, how I love her.* He imagined her beautiful face and touched his cheek with his fingers. Pike leaned back in his chair, peering out the window and chuckling to himself. He was about to make history, on the verge of greatness; he could feel it in his clenched fist.

His thoughts drifted to plans for invasion. The largest combined naval and army invasion ever undertaken in the history of the United States. While no decision had been made on who would lead the invading army, he felt sure that Major General Dearborn would place the responsibility in his hands.

He'd already advised Commodore Chauncey that the first men to hit the beaches of York had to be skirmishers, men who were both nimble and used to fighting independently. Casualties might be high so the company had to be battle-tested and that meant Major Forsyth,

Lieutenant Tasker, and their company of riflemen. They had proved themselves before and now yearned for a chance to redeem the reputation of their company after that disaster at Ogdensburg. Forsyth had responded with enthusiasm when told of the honour to lead all invading forces, an enthusiasm that diminished on hearing that any of his men caught for looting private property would be shot.

Although he didn't like Forsyth personally, Chauncey had agreed immediately and like a dyke that had suddenly opened, the commodore's orders went flooding out to ship captains, and their senior officers. Every regiment now knew their place on every ship. Every officer knew how and when his men were to take action. Nothing was left unplanned, nothing left to chance.

Pike folded the letter to Clarissa and slipped it into a valise. Glory and immortality beckoned so close that his heart beat faster the more he thought about it. No one could forget the man who successfully led this invasion. What an honour! Congress would have to give him a special medal and promote him to major general. Perhaps he'd even replace Granny Dearborn as commanding officer of the northern armies. Pike smiled.

A day off for the troops was his idea, and the men loved him for it. Two men of the Fifteenth Infantry staggered arm in arm past his view from the window. They had marched with him from Plattsburg during ten days of freezing hell and, since he'd always made a point of remembering the men's names, these were two characters he'd never forget. Privates McKnight and O'Reilly actually made some money for themselves on that march. Somehow they always managed to have comfortable quarters and lots of food. He nodded, proud that his men were survivors, and knowing he could win anywhere with them. Yes, he loved men like that and knew that they loved him. *Wait till they hear my speech before we embark on those ships. They'll crave glory by the time I'm finished with them.*

Dressed in their greatcoats, two soldiers staggered along the rim of the bowl leading down into the harbour. Private McKnight slung his arm over O'Reilly's shoulder and sang along with him. The questionable Irish ditty told of stupid officers and the constant hope they didn't get you killed. McKnight continued at the top of his lungs.

"Keep it down, fella," O'Reilly advised. "You'll have us both in the brig."

"There was never a bigger asshole than zealous Zebulon," McKnight replied. "He'll get everyone killed yet, but not you and me, old chum. I'm too smart to get myself sucked into his quest for glory. And anyway I have plans." He yanked a canteen out from under his jacket and pulled its stopper with a sharp twist. The rum slid down his throat a little too fast, making him cough.

"They're giving away hundred-acre parcels in Upper Canada, with implements and seed to start you off. We work it for a few years, sell it, and move back south with cash in our pocket." McKnight slapped his friend on the back. "Maybe we slip away from Zebulon after we land."

"Old Pike got us this day off," O'Reilly reminded him as he accepted the canteen from McKnight and jerked down a swig before handing it back. "He's not so bad and I don't like the idea of running."

"Just the calm before the storm, laddie," McKnight replied. "He can't drill us out on the ice without risking us all plunging through. And besides, he wants the men well rested before shovelling us into those damned ships." McKnight gestured to the harbour with the canteen. The wind still held a nip, as it swept over the frozen surface of the lake but nothing like the bone-chilling bite during February or March. Exposed water could be seen in spots around the edges of the lake, and it wouldn't be long before the ice was gone and the ships were free to sail.

McKnight rested his foot up on a stump and a hand on his knee while staring at the anchorage. Shipwrights were busy working on every ship, preparing for the minute the ice released them from its grip. By his count, there weren't enough of those ships to carry all the soldiers below decks, which meant that some of the invaders would have to sleep above decks, under the stars ... in the open weather.

His eyes widened at a sudden realization. The last men loaded on to the ships would have to be the first unloaded at the other end. The first men to hit the beach were guaranteed little more than a forlorn hope. Pike's glorious death waited somewhere on the northern shores of Lake Ontario.

"We have to be first on to one of those ships," McKnight blurted. "Get ourselves a bunk below decks."

"The less time spent on the water, the better for me," O'Reilly replied. "I get seasick too easy. We should go last."

"Every landsman here is thinking that way. But last on is first off to face the enemy's fire." McKnight nodded his head knowingly. "See. When have I ever led you wrong?" He felt slighted by O'Reilly's opposition. Maybe the drink talked too loud in his head. "Think of it this way: you're better seasick than dead."

O'Reilly was looking puzzled so McKnight explained his theory further. "And last on board sleeps on the open deck … in the cold weather. You know they'll make a right hash of this bloody invasion. We have to be first on those ships, and take all our extra food with us so we don't starve."

"Pack it around our bodies, under our jackets," O'Reilly suggested. "We'll just look a little fat."

"Now you're thinking with the Scottish half of your brain." McKnight grinned and slapped his friend on the back. "That calls for a drink, I'd say. We got this whole invasion thing planned in less than a single canteen. I'd promote you to being an officer if it wasn't so demeaning."

Lieutenant Westlake sat up in his Maple Hill bed and winced. Several days had passed since he'd burst open the door to Major Nelles's office. His ribs had stopped throbbing unless he moved or took a deep breath. By the end of the third day, even the persistent fever had disappeared. He tugged up his nightshirt to peer down at the clean bandages. No blood seeped through. *A good start to the day.* "Now, if only to get out of this room!" he said to himself.

Uncle Adam appeared in the doorway, followed by Aunt Eve. "It's time for us to say our goodbyes," his uncle said. "The sleigh is packed and your father has generously donated new furs to keep us warm on the trip home. If we don't go soon, the snow along Kingston Road will melt and we'll be travelling in mud."

"I can't thank you enough for what you did," Westlake replied. "I wish I was going with you." He gazed around the room.

"Rest in bed." Aunt Eve shook her finger at him. "A few days and you'll be back at it."

He hugged his aunt with his left arm, shook hands with his uncle, and then they were gone. At the front door of the house, he heard voices and laughter as his parents said their goodbyes. He laid back and closed his eyes. The house grew silent for a moment until through his bedroom doorway stepped Major Nelles, with hat in hand, dressed in his finest red jacket.

"Good morning, Lieutenant." Nelles grinned. "Hope I'm not disturbing your sleep."

"Sir." Westlake grimaced while trying to sit up without showing his discomfort. "The faster I can get out of this room the happier I'll be." He shook hands with his senior officer.

"You were once reluctant, as I recall. Didn't want any part of this war, you claimed," Nelles chided him.

Westlake slumped back down, flinching as the bandages pulled at the wound. "That's before they killed a young friend of mine, wrecked my uncle's house, and shot me. Evil buggers even killed his dog." Westlake shook his head, thinking of Cherry. "I'm told the ice is going out."

"Not long before American ships will roam Lake Ontario," Nelles said. "How are you healing up?"

"I just want to jump in the lake and heal my side. Did we get him ... Puffer?"

"Ah, yes, the lieutenant's secret remedy for healing everything ... jump in the lake." Nelles held up his arm that had broken after taking a ball at Queenston Heights. "I must admit the swelling went down in my arm ... though I bloody near froze to death in the damn lake."

"Sir?"

"He was warned we were coming. I fear Puffer's got clean away." Nelles told Westlake the entire story. "We questioned two men at the Jordan who might have killed Mr. Forbes. But we have absolutely no proof."

"Forbsy! No." Westlake sat up to protest and winced in pain. "And after all this, Puffer's escaped."

"I believe that on their behalf, Mr. Forbes bribed the miller to warn Puffer," Nelles explained. "With Forbes dead, there's no link to their wrongdoing."

"Old Forbsy wouldn't hurt a fly." Westlake gestured his visitor to the only chair in the small bedroom. "Who are these men?"

"Ever heard of either a Mr. Hendrickson or his pal Archer?"

"I caught those two bastards threatening the Jordan's barmaid. She was paid to give them tidbits of information overheard at the tavern."

"They told us nothing and we have no witnesses." Nelles sat down and shook his head. "Let's start at the beginning of your journey and tell me about it, all the way through. Leave out nothing."

Westlake began his tale when he stopped at Whitby, the Lynde Inn and Tavern, and from there moved on to his Aunt Evelyn's run-in with Forsyth and Tasker. He mentioned his meeting with Prevost and watched Nelles smile without understanding why. "On top of the dresser right beside you is my report on Red George Macdonell and the battle for Ogdensburg. After that, I met Sterling, who gave me Winky's description. Then captured, escaped, and ended up at my uncle's place, which is where Forsyth's thugs turned up."

"But why follow you all the way there?"

"There's only one reason I can guess." Westlake noticed that Nelles took note of his every word. "The only person aware that I knew about Puffer's treachery was Sterling himself. I think the swine sells information to both sides, to whoever will pay him the most. Sterling should die."

"Don't say that. He's useful to us. There are many who play both sides, Lieutenant."

Westlake grimaced in disgust. "So now what?"

"Hendrickson and Archer are too stupid to manage Puffer on their own. And the money he's rewarded with probably comes in from outside the province. According to the miller, Puffer rode away on a fresh horse and new saddle." Nelles stood to leave and straightened his jacket. He picked up Westlake's report from the dresser and brandished it in the air. "Someone is directing and financing this little ring of murderous traitors, and it sure wasn't Mr. Forbes. I don't think the miller was lying … but then again, I could be wrong. He was able to come and go from the garrison as he pleased. How well do you know the barman at the Jordan?"

"Not exactly the most loyal fellow around, but I reckon he tries to avoid trouble rather than look for it." Westlake shook his head. "I'd go see him myself but the doctor says it's another few days at least before they'll take the bandages off. You could do me a favour and look in on the barmaid, Miss Lucy Dunbar. She's had trouble with Hendrickson and Archer."

Nelles paused and stared at him. "She has a certain attraction."

"No advances on my part, sir." Westlake shrugged his false innocence. "I think Miss Dunbar can help us." He remembered her embrace and the feel of her slender body against his own.

"Just get better soon." Nelles inclined his head to wish Westlake well, "And let me bother about the Jordan's barman. I thought our Miss Dunbar knew more than she said on my last visit."

Westlake gave a half salute and Nelles was gone.

The warm days and cool nights of early spring start the sap running in the maple trees of Upper Canada. This viscous liquid is collected in buckets placed under spouts tapped into the trees' trunks. It's then transported to a shack where the sap is boiled down to form the sweet topping known as maple syrup. On a brisk morning in mid-April, 1813, two men were approaching a sugar shack located north of York.

From inside the shack itself, through cracks in its logs walls, a third man scanned the arrivals' progress and then intently studied the forest right behind them. No one followed.

He saw both men wore wide-brimmed hats and long overcoats. One cradled a musket as he constantly looked over his shoulder at the winding trail they had travelled. The other man left his coat hanging open to reveal a pistol tucked in his belt. He walked with a limp and stumbled before he reached the shack's door.

"That's far enough. Hands in the air, both of you." The man inside the cabin kept himself hidden.

"It's Hendrickson and Archer, sir," Hendrickson called out, as if their identities should be obvious.

Archer cleared his throat and spit.

"Put the musket and the pistol on that bench by the door. Check the forest once more, and if it's clear you can step inside."

The two men did as instructed before tugging open the door to the sugar shack. On this crisp morning, a fire of birch and maple in the stove filled the interior with warmth. Archer rubbed his hands and smiled. "Don't you think you're being a little cautious, governor."

"If anyone's followed you, I'll be apprehending a couple of intruders who tried to ambush me as I did a little sugaring off." He kept a musket pointed at the visitors. "What did you tell Major Nelles?"

"Nothing," Hendrickson replied. "He hasn't a clue and you can put that musket down, if you please, Mr. Westlake."

Richard Westlake lowered the musket. These two had worked for him in the Westlake Trading Company for years doing whatever nasty business was required. But their loyalties extended as far as they got paid, and he had to wonder if Nelles might have paid them extra to turn against him. In a world without honour or loyalty, the highest bidder won the prize.

"Puffer's safely away, then," Richard said.

"Just as you planned it, sir. The miller only met old Forbsy, no one else. Now that stinking drunk can't tell anyone anything no more." Archer twisted his squeezed fist with delight.

"Forbsy was a bloody mess and the whole town is talking about it," Richard replied.

"Don't you complain. It's done and this is what I got for my trouble." Hendrickson tilted his head to show the thin gash along his neck. "Another inch and that old geezer and his bloody bottle woulda had me done for."

"What about the girl?" Richard asked.

"She'll be delivered to Puffer, as requested. Another few days." Hendrickson grinned. "What's next?"

Westlake senior peered out between the crack in the log wall and caught sight of a white-tailed rabbit racing down the trail, but no humans stirred in the forest to cause him anxiety. In addition to Sergeant George Puffer, these two thugs were the only men in Upper Canada who knew he was a traitor, playing off both British and American sides. He'd thought of inviting Hendrickson and Archer to his former sugar shack, a mile farther north, deeper in the bush, and killing them there, but he had decided that he might still need their services in the coming days of turmoil.

Richard Westlake grinned. "What's next is that we wait for the Americans. They'll need some good people they can count on." He poked a finger hard into Hendrickson's chest. "Think of the business opportunities to rebuild little York after they wreck the place. In the meantime, you two should make yourselves scarce. Don't be seen in York. Puffer can wait for the girl."

Hendrickson glanced at Archer and nodded. Richard peered out through the crack again.

If the Americans attacked York in force, the town might be destroyed. Public buildings would have to be repaired and in some cases, he hoped, rebuilt entirely. He had acquired the sawmill to move the Westlake family business out of furs and into construction. A good destructive battle was exactly what he needed to increase his profit from this war. Loyalty to one side or the other was a fool's game. War was only about making money.

"Meet me back here in a week," Richard ordered. He clapped his hands, rubbed them together, then bent to throw another log on the fire. "My fur trading business is going to hell in a hand-basket, so we'll move right into construction or whatever else the Americans need."

"What about your son?" Hendrickson asked. "He's going to end up dead if he's not careful."

"He's the reason for this bloody limp." Archer lifted his pant leg to show the gash where the edge of Lucy's door caught his limb. "If he hadn't been your son, I would have killed him," Archer snarled.

"My son is my business." Richard clenched his jaw. "Don't either of you dare touch him. You're lucky he hasn't killed the pair of you." He took a step toward Archer, and the man backed away.

"How can you be so sure they'll attack York?" Archer asked before clearing phlegm from his throat.

Richard glanced at him and grimaced. Both of these men disgusted him, and right then he decided that when the time came, he would do the world a favour by killing them. "No one knows for sure where they will attack," he conceded. "We may not be lucky the first time since that honour may go to Kingston, but sooner or later they have to attack York because it's the capital of the province. And you can bet your life they won't ever let the *Sir Isaac Brock* float."

And whenever they did come, the Americans would undoubtedly wreck the town and guarantee Richard Westlake another fortune. He grinned.

19

. . . . . .

COMMODORE ISAAC CHAUNCEY, hands clasped behind his back, paced the quarterdeck to the port side of the new brig, *Madison*. He stared out across the heaving anchorage of fourteen ships. The ship tilted, and he reached out, gripping the rail to steady himself. Long-boats laden heavy with supplies slowly plied their way against the swells from the shore to their designated vessel. He tapped his foot impatiently, then shouted for some rowers in the harbour water directly below to shift themselves. This was all taking too long.

Embarkation had begun on April 20, and now two days later, munitions, supplies, and men were still loading. Eight heavy field guns, their limbers and caissons included, had to be manhandled into the boats and rowed out to the waiting ships, where they were hoisted and tethered into place. "Swing the chains out, man!" the commodore ordered. "Lieutenant, see to it."

"Sir." A young officer ran over to where a crane worked to haul a waiting cannon barrel up and into the ship.

The weather worsened by the minute, the wet wind soaking the boat crews with a bone-chilling spray off the lake. Chauncey slammed one fist into the other. If the flotilla did not get under way soon, the whole north shore of Lake Ontario would know what they were about. He glanced westward to see drifting grey clouds darken the sky as the last of the longboats returned to shore.

Including his own eight hundred seamen, he would hit York with a combined force of twenty-six hundred officers and men. The flotilla carried eighty guns to assist in the assault. His flagship, the *Madison*, by itself carried more than six hundred crew and soldiers above and below decks, packed in rows like fish in a box. He prayed that his seamen would have enough room on deck to sail the damn ship.

Early in the day of April 23, the commodore finally gave the order to up anchor, but by mid-afternoon, with waves washing over the side of every ship, he signalled the convoy to shorten sail and search for safe harbour. Comment from below decks arrived sooner than he had expected. From the time Major General Dearborn took the bucket to come on board, Chauncey had not heard a word from the great man, but now he was being asked to report to his quarters.

"We'll never get there at this rate," Dearborn proclaimed while chewing on a piece of apple. "The enemy will be waiting for us. We have to push on."

"Do you think I don't know that, but push on now and we won't get there at all," Chauncey argued. "We've got torn canvas, broken spars, and injuries throughout the entire fleet. Without anchoring immediately, we'll merely sink our own ships. Can you swim?"

Chauncey watched Dearborn's face as he considered the implications of another campaign failure, and perhaps even a slow death by drowning. Just then a series of cruel waves crashed against the ship's side as the sailors above them changed tack again. Someone on deck screamed a curse after a loud thud.

The general shook his head. "It's hard to believe our bad luck." He waved his hand dismissively. "Very well, anchor if you so choose."

Chauncey hastened his way to the companion ladder. "And I don't need your damn permission," he muttered to himself. He passed soldiers retching in their hammocks and realized that none of the infantry born in the United States had ever been on a ship before. The damp rails of the ladder slipped through his hands as he climbed aft. Two men at the wheel, soaked to the skin, were fighting to keep the ship on course. He glanced up at a bitter sky but couldn't see any chance of a break in the weather.

All ship captains in the convoy had received orders to sail at least two hundred yards apart. No accidents through collision would be tolerated. If any one of the inexperienced commanders lost his way, he was to head straight for Fort Niagara. Chauncey used his glass to search the not-too-distant shore for a suitable anchorage. Each ship contained a five-week supply of stores for the crew, so no one would go hungry just yet, but he did wonder how long this storm would hinder their progress.

"I told you they'd bugger it up," Private McKnight remarked, swaying in his hammock below decks. Only twenty-three inches directly above him, Private O'Reilly lay in his own hammock, and McKnight poked a knuckle in his friend's backside. "We've been three days on this ship, matey, and I could still swim back to Sackets Harbor." McKnight laughed. "That's how bloody far we've gone."

"Knuckle my ass again and you'll be over the side to begin that swim. Can't blame the officers for the weather," O'Reilly replied. "'Sides, you wanted to be on this ship before anyone else. Got your wish now, so don't whine."

"And aren't you lucky I did. Poor bastards above decks are freezing and soaked to the skin. Probably die from exposure, the lot of them." McKnight slid a broken biscuit out from under his overcoat and proceeded to chew on it. His mind wandered while his hammock rocked to the ship's movement.

The thought of the free hundred acres in Upper Canada gnawed at him. He'd have to run from the army with his possessions. He checked off again the gear he had hauled on board and stored under his hammock: knapsack and haversack containing his extra clothing and blankets; musket and cartridge box; his issued rations of several days' food; plus his own stash of rum canteens and extra biscuits. Although warmer beneath decks than above, he wore his greatcoat while lying down to keep off the damp.

McKnight thought of all the men he'd met on shore. The Fifteenth Infantry joined in with companies of the Sixth, Twenty-first, and Fourteenth. There were many more he hadn't met, and those he had avoided like Major Forsyth's rifle battalion dressed in their greens — a nasty lot who kept to themselves. He tried to think of what all these men on board might need that he could supply. His extra food would be of no value because seasickness prevented most of the men from eating. And they couldn't pay for it anyways with the little money they had.

The ship shuddered underneath him, the waves smashing against the hull hard enough to rock his hammock to and fro. Perhaps he was looking at this the wrong way around, so McKnight cleared his mind and started over. The men on deck desperately wanted out of the weather, but they had food that they couldn't eat. He and O'Reilly had warm bunks that he could trade for that same food. One day's rations for a single twenty-four hours in a warm bunk! He could sell that to anybody.

"O'Reilly, you've been complaining about the smell down here." The odours of men puking mixed with those of cordage, sweat, and damp. It took some getting used to and even then O'Reilly complained that the stink left him nauseated. "Well, I've got a plan just for you."

McKnight explained his proposition as the ship rolled and his hammock swung. By the time he'd run through the details of the plan, the waves hammering the decks above had spilled onto the grating and now dripped below. He heard the bilge pumps begin at a steady thump.

"I'll sleep on it," O'Reilly replied. "I'm in no rush to get soaked and I'm not that hungry myself. It's this filthy stink that bothers me most."

For another full day and night the waves of Lake Ontario crashed against the Madison's hull. McKnight listened from his hammock to the water surging alongside the ship, knowing that this rain and driving wind made sailing impossible. Once started, the bilge pumps below decks never stopped.

April 25 dawned with the storm abating and the ship almost at rest. "That's our cue, Sonny-Jim." McKnight swung out of his hammock and almost slipped on the puke from the man in the hammock next to him. He nudged O'Reilly to get moving. "Let's make our deal up top while they're still soaked."

The very first couple of men from the Fifteenth Infantry that McKnight approached readily agreed to change places for twenty-four hours. They offered up a day's rations of pre-cooked food that they had been unable to eat. McKnight shook his head, wishing he'd asked for more.

Crowded with soldiers, the main deck offered few empty spaces. Before running off to their newly acquired hammocks, the pair pointed out two narrow spots under a cannon's barrel that gave the false impression of offering protection from the elements. But at least it offered a space away from under the feet of the sailors who cursed as they worked their way around a deck packed with infantrymen, in an effort to get the vessel under way.

McKnight heard an order barked out near the great wheel. "Signal to make more sail," a lieutenant yelled at a midshipman to thus inform the whole fleet. They were sailing north, with a wind out of the west, Kingston being the obvious destination. McKnight wondered if he'd struck a sensible bargain, remembering that those on deck would be the first disembarked to assault the beaches.

"Get the t'gallants on her, Lieutenant."

McKnight turned to see for the first time Commodore Chauncey himself directing orders.

"The t'gallants you'll have, sir." The lieutenant cupped his hands around his mouth, shouting the order up toward the main mast, where it was repeated above the courses.

McKnight stretched out one arm to lean on the cannon while under the other he held on tightly to a thick canvas bag. The deck tilted as the sails spread, and he steadied himself against the steel barrel. After several days of putrid atmosphere, the breeze filled his lungs and he felt the freedom that attracted so many to the sea.

"I'd forgotten what fresh air tasted like," O'Reilly said, taking one deep breath after another. "So clean." He sighed.

A flock of gulls soared overhead, screeching as they dove for scraps in the *Madison*'s wake. McKnight glanced skyward to see black clouds blowing in from the west. He thought of those two men below, probably swinging comfortably in the hammocks.

"What's in the bag?" O'Reilly asked.

McKnight gave him a wink. "I was hoping not to use it, but it looks like we'll have no choice." He gestured at the sky. "My plan was to hoist this roll of canvas over our heads if it rains, but let's drape it over the cannon instead … only if we need it, mind you."

"By the Jesus, you think of everything." O'Reilly grinned and slapped him on the back.

A seaman hurried by, tugging a line of fresh cordage behind him. Others would splice and haul it to the upper yards, repairing damage caused by the previous storm. A cool rain began to fall, and McKnight quickly spread the canvas over the cannon barrel so that it fell on his own and O'Reilly's shoulders after they ducked into their temporary abode.

The swells grew larger, the wind rocking the ship to one side, while the fresh rain kept a steady tap on their canvas. O'Reilly slid sideways, bumping into McKnight's head, who grimaced as he pushed O'Reilly upright. The ship dove into a swell, righted itself, and then dove again. Lake water splashed over the side and ran along the deck, soaking the bottom of their pants.

"So much for keeping dry," McKnight muttered. Every spar and sail creaked under the strain, until he thought the main mast would pull right out of her.

"Shorten sail, Lieutenant." Chauncey sounded despondent. "You'd best signal the flotilla while they can still see us through this damnable spray." The lieutenant passed on the order at the top of his lungs. McKnight peered out from under the canvas to see men scampering up the ratlines and a young midshipman changing the flags so as to signal the rest of the convoy.

Like a turtle, McKnight drew his head back under the protective shell of his canvas. The patter of the rain was all he heard until a surprising order was given.

"Change course to west by southwest, Helmsmen," Chauncey bellowed. "Bring her around."

"West by southwest it is, sir."

The *Madison* swung ponderously into the wind, her deck tilting, her progress slowed almost to a stop until the bow dipped onto the new setting. In an instant, the entire ship realized that Kingston was no longer their destination, if it ever had been. Under the canvas cover, McKnight smiled to himself while listening to the strain on the cordage and sails. This new heading meant they would be attacking either Newark or York, and he didn't care which town, only that he'd be back below decks long before the order came for them to charge the enemy shore.

Brigadier General Pike gripped the *Madison*'s slippery rail to steady his balance. Along the upper wall of Fort Niagara, American soldiers enthusiastically waved their arms. Overwhelmed at the sight of the fourteen tall ships flying American colours, a few men jumped up and fired their muskets skyward. Pike lifted his hand toward the wall and another cheer went up. Now the enormous spread of tilting sail tacked the convoy slowly north, away from the mouth of the Niagara River and from the enemy stronghold of Fort George.

Monday, April 26, and black smoke from the chimneys of York, the remaining target, gradually appeared on the northern shore of Lake Ontario. Pike silently prayed for Major General Dearborn to put him in charge of the land forces in the battle to come. But after months of planning, Granny Dearborn had yet to tell anyone who would lead the American Army ashore.

By mid-afternoon the screaming wind and treacherous waves dropped to a whisper. Commodore Chauncey signalled the commanders of every ship in the convoy. *Repair onboard flag.* Within minutes of the order, longboats carried all the captains to the *Madison*'s side. These commanders, young and agile, climbed the numerous ladders flung over the side to enable their ascent.

Down in the congested wardroom, General Pike took his place at the front of the crowd. He saw Major Forsyth pick up a glass of wine from a tray only to stand and bang his head on a ceiling beam, spilling much of the wine on the green sleeve of his jacket. The commodore quickly dismissed the servants and then turned the meeting over to General Dearborn.

The general didn't bother to heave his body out of the chair but requested Pike's assistance in explaining the details of the forthcoming attack. The brigadier rose from his chair and stared across at Forsyth. "Tomorrow morning, you and your men have the honour of leading the largest amphibious landing onto a foreign shore in American history. You will be followed by elements of every regiment under my command and with the Third Artillery pushing right behind. As infantry units arrive, Major Forsyth, your men will provide covering fire in skirmish order."

"Thank you, sir," Forsyth replied. "My men will meet the challenge, on that you can rest assured."

"No one will attack the fortifications until we have formed up in proper column and the artillery is ready," Pike continued. "Again, Mr. Forsyth, your rifle regiment will continue to provide cover for that exposed column."

"Sir." Forsyth stood, careful not to bang his head, and saluted.

The brigadier looked to Dearborn for permission to continue and received the general's go-ahead nod. Pike's heart leapt at the prospect that Dearborn was now giving him the command of his dreams. He continued with vigour, warming to his subject. "Any man quitting his post must be put to death." A general murmur of agreement ensued among the officers present. A few cowardly deserters could spook a column of soldiers into a rampaging herd. Cowards would not be tolerated.

"Let me speak about honour and glory. The American Army will show humanity after our victory, despite whatever examples of savagery the native allies of our enemy have given us." Pike sensed the room grow distant. "As for unoffending citizens, their property must be held sacred, and any soldier who shall be guilty of plundering the inhabitants, shall, if convicted, be punished with death."

He raised his voice for the finale, his words uttered in quick succession. "You are liberators of these people from the yoke of monarchy. The American Army brings not theft and immoral behaviour, but rather freedom and justice for all. That is your challenge. That is your destiny. Are you with me?"

The officers jumped to their feet, the room reverberating with the sound of scraping chair legs. Jubilation and applause! *They're cheering my speech!*

"Are you with the United States of America?" Pike shouted.

Commodore Chauncey himself stood up to lead three cheers for America, his fist pumping the air. Dearborn cheered from the comfort of his seat while Pike picked up his glass. He then proposed a toast, and the officers raised their glasses to repeat after him, "To honour. God save the United States."

Chauncey continued briefly with detailed instructions regarding the order in which each of the vessels would disembark to support Pike's plan of attack. The meeting drew to a close, and everyone waited for General Dearborn to announce the land expedition's leader, but instead he only offered the barest few words of encouragement to the officers present. As they departed the wardroom, a few confidants looked to Pike and shrugged, wondering why his appointment hadn't been announced. Surely the overstuffed Granny Dearborn wasn't considering waddling ashore himself.

Pike, although unsettled, returned to his quarters satisfied with his performance. There was no one of his stature that Dearborn could rely on to produce a victory, and he was confident that Dearborn himself knew it. Afternoon wore into early evening, and Pike decided to write a brief letter home to his wife.

My dear Clara,

We are now standing off the harbor of York, which we shall attack at daylight in the morning: I shall dedicate these last moments to you, my love, and tomorrow throw all other ideas but my country to the wind. General Dearborn has not yet announced that I shall lead the assault but he has acted honourably so far, and I feel great gratitude to the old gentleman: My sword and pen shall both be exerted to do him honor.

Should fate decide that I perish on the morrow, defend my memory
and know that I die aspiring to deeds worthy of your husband.
Think of me with a father's love, a father's care, to our daughter.
Warmest sentiments of love and friendship,
Montgomery

His letter written, the general folded the page and sealed it with wax. He grabbed at the edge of the small writing table to hold himself upright as the ship tilted under way, surging toward the enemy village.

How would its residents be feeling right now?

Pike snatched up his spyglass and headed for the deck. The rails of the *Madison* were already packed with infantry staring out at the enemy shoreline. He climbed the stairs to stand by the wheel and extend his glass. Out of the west, the wind blew fair, and the lack of spray allowed him to see the log houses of York in distinct clarity. On the bluffs to the east of the town, a solitary rider brought his massive horse to an abrupt halt. Pike chuckled to himself.

"Surprise, we're here," he sang to no one.

20

......

WARMAN, THE GREAT STALLION presented to Westlake on his tenth birthday, stretched out his legs and ran with abandon. The windswept top of a hill proved dry compared to the lowlands where melting snow soaked the ground. Lieutenant Westlake had made his way directly east from Maple Hill but now turned to cross the road to Kingston before continuing on south toward Lake Ontario.

For the first time in more than a week, the doctor had cleared him for a ride. His ribs remained tightly bandaged and pained him only slightly when he twisted round in a certain way. The young lieutenant breathed in the fresh air and exhaled a slow, whistling sigh. Relieved to be free of his bedroom's confines, he had decided to extend his ride far enough to scan the lake from high up on the Scarborough Bluffs.

Horse and rider crested a rise to look back down on the chimneys of York and the western shore of Lake Ontario as it curved south toward Niagara. Westlake slid his spyglass from the saddlebag and turned his head, slowly swinging the glass from west to east. What he saw caused him to yank the instrument away from his face. His knees must have jerked involuntarily because Warman bolted forward before Westlake could rein him in. A mile or so off the shores of Upper Canada, the sinking western sun glinted off the lake to light up a flotilla of American warships. The war had come to York; a battle was only hours away.

Any hope that a British attack on Sackets Harbor had destroyed the American fleet, vanished in an instant. At first sight, he counted eight ships, their spread of white sails tilting with the wind — and then another, and still another, floated into the circle of the spyglass's lens. Westlake refocused the glass on the largest vessel, its sharp lines cutting smoothly through the water. The *Madison*, the ship he'd seen them constructing at Sackets Harbor, came about into the wind. Near the wheel stood a man in uniform, gold braid on his shoulder. He held a telescope to his eye, scanning the shoreline intently. *Looking for a place to land.*

Westlake searched the water for longboats that would bring the enemy's soldiers ashore but found none. That meant time was still on his side. His heart raced as he snapped the glass shut and pulled out his timepiece. Five o'clock. Perhaps three hours of daylight remained. He took a last look at the ships, almost to make sure that his eyes weren't playing tricks, then spurred his mount into a gallop.

The softer ground forced Warman to labour for every step, but the animal steadfastly plowed ahead. Westlake wondered exactly how many ships were in the flotilla and how many men did it carry. He pressed his horse on toward Government House and Major Nelles.

Along the road he thought of what the enemy landing might bring. If the attackers could somehow be contained on the beach, the town might be saved. Much depended on the number of enemy soldiers that could land at one time. General Sheaffe would surely have devised a plan to overwhelm and push any landing party back into the lake. Westlake slowed Warman for a while to allow the horse to catch its breath and cross the bridge of planks over the Don River.

The sacking of Ogdensburg came to mind and Westlake began to worry about the vulnerability of his own home on Maple Hill and of what his mother and father might do. His chest tightened when he thought of them running north to the sugar shack or worse, staying to defend their property. His father would never give up their home to invaders without a fight.

He glanced over his shoulder to the lake, but no longer saw any ships. The curvature of the shoreline had put them out of sight. Near the lake, the Union Jack fluttered from the peninsula lighthouse, the signal that enemy ships approached from the east.

By the time Westlake reached Government House, his side was aching and Warman neared exhaustion. The guns of the fort boomed out a warning to tell the town of approaching danger. He slid out of the saddle and raced to the office of Major Nelles. In answer to his knock, Nelles himself opened the door, his hat under an arm.

"Enemy ships, sir, off the Scarborough Bluffs," Westlake reported in a huff.

"I've already heard. How many?"

"I counted ten, but there could be more." Westlake panted. "I think their new ship, *Madison*, is in the van."

"Come with me."

They walked down the hallway passing several doors until the major stopped at one and knocked hard. An aide to Major General Sheaffe opened the door, and inside, the general himself sat behind Brock's old desk. Officers stood around the desk pointing out locations on a detailed map of York's shoreline.

Westlake remembered this office well, and it seemed only yesterday that here Brock had asked him what he wanted to do with his life. "Make a difference. Do something significant," he'd replied flippantly, not realizing what those words would mean and how they would change his life. He recalled Brock's responding smile, and now he grinned at the memory as he surveyed the room.

Facing Sheaffe, Major Nelles came to attention and saluted. Westlake followed his example. Sheaffe merely gave them a nod.

"Lieutenant Westlake here reports ten ships off the Scarborough Bluffs, with the new ship *Madison* in the van, sir."

Sheaffe looked back to the maps and his expression barely stirred. "At least he didn't break down my door this time." He must have caught sight of Westlake's grin, for he continued. "Something amuses you, Lieutenant?"

"No, sir. I was remembering the last time in this office ... with General Brock." Every officer there raised his head and stared at Westlake as the room went silent and still. His mouth went dry, and he guessed that no one ever talked about the deceased general in front of Sheaffe. "And he asked me to help him."

"Asked *you* to help him, did he?" Sheaffe repeated skeptically and then smiled at his officers.

Something in Sheaffe's style grated on Westlake. Either he had no idea of the effect his words had on people or he didn't care. The other officers hadn't budged likely expecting Westlake to back away from his claim, but his side ached and he resented the general's inference. "It was *his* way, sir. Yes, he asked for my help and then offered me a mission."

"Hmph. How do you know it was the *Madison*?" Sheaffe asked.

"I was in Sackets Harbor ... saw the ship being built, sir."

"Ten vessels in all, you say?"

"There could be more, but that's all I counted within view at that moment."

Major Nelles interrupted. "That other matter we discussed, sir. Should I proceed to Mrs. —?"

"Yes." Sheaffe lifted his hand to dismiss them. "Take him with you."

"Sir." Nelles departed the general's office with Westlake trailing behind.

On returning to Nelles's office, the major closed the door but did not make his way to Brock's old chair. "Christ Almighty, Jonathan, you didn't have to wave a red flag in front of a bull."

"Been too long in bed, sir," Westlake replied laughingly. "And he rubbed me the wrong way. What's this other matter, sir?"

"Ride with me." Nelles gestured with his hand. "We're off to visit the receiver general. His young daughter may feel more comfortable with someone around that's her own age."

"Want to know what I think of General Sheaffe, sir?"

"No. Let's go."

To Westlake's surprise, there were four soldiers waiting alongside Warman as he stepped out the back of Government House. Two were perched on a horse-drawn wagon and two mounted on horseback. Apparently, these men were to act as an escort, although Major Nelles did not explain why until they got near their destination.

In his two-storey framed home on Frederick Street, Mr. Prideaux Selby was too ill to come out of his room on the second floor. As auditor and receiver general, he kept the proper order of accounts for

Upper Canada. His pretty daughter, Mrs. Liz Derenzy, had just married in late January before her father grew ill. At the time, she sent word to Major General Sheaffe that Mr. Selby held funds of two thousand five hundred pounds, plus many official papers all locked away in a heavy iron chest. Why Sheaffe hadn't squired them out of York months ago, Nelles had no idea, but with American ships threatening off the coast, it was clearly time to hide the chest.

Westlake thought back to a Christmas of laughter and lighted candles when the same Mr. Selby and his daughter had dined at Maple Hill. Two years older than Westlake, Liz Selby had always seemed out of reach. Now she stood before him as a married woman. He bowed his head politely.

Liz fondled a handkerchief, thankful to rid herself of responsibility for the money and papers. Nelles signed a document taking charge of the chest and modestly bowed goodbye. Two burly guards grabbed hold of the leather straps on each end and carried the chest outside to the waiting wagon.

On the steps to the veranda, Nelles closed the door and delivered new orders for Lieutenant Westlake. "Find Major Givens and tell him that General Sheaffe wants him and the Ojibwa at Government House by first light. You too, for that matter."

"Very well, sir."

Liz Derenzy re-opened the door. "Mr. Westlake, before you go, I have a small note for your mother." She gestured for him to come back inside.

"I will leave you," Nelles said. "See you at dawn … armed."

"Sir." Westlake saluted and watched the major with the wagon and the escort trundle off down the road.

He stepped back inside the Selby home to the aroma of fresh bread that must have just emerged from the oven. On hearing Prideaux Selby groan from his upstairs room, Liz glared at the ceiling and asked Westlake to sit down and wait. She scurried upstairs, to return a full fifteen minutes later carrying saddle bags in one hand and a small note page in the other.

"I'm sorry for the delay," Liz said. "This is a note, thanking your mother for the maple syrup."

Westlake slid the note inside his coat, wondering what was in the leather bag.

"Unfortunately, Father had not assembled these bags in time for the chest. Six hundred dollars on one side, as well as official papers on the other. Please take them away to safety." She thrust the bags into Westlake's hands.

"It's getting dark now, and I still have to find Major Givens."

"Just take it to the clerk's residence, a couple of streets over," she insisted. Lizzy was no longer the little girl that he remembered. She had grown into a woman who was fully capable of taking charge. "That's where he resides, on Toronto Street."

"I know where the clerk lives," he said.

"Now sign here." She pointed to a spot for his signature and handed him a quill. "Make sure the man signs this page for you too." She held up another sheet of paper before putting it in his hand. "His signature is proof you gave him the bags."

"Yes, *sir*," Westlake replied with a grin and made for the door. "It's only a few minutes ride, but I should be off." He gave a token salute and waved goodbye from his horse. "Stay safe, Mrs. Derenzy."

"You could always make me laugh, Mr. Westlake." She waved her handkerchief.

By the time he reached the residence of Donald McLean's, the magistrate and clerk of the assembly, the sun had started its descent. The air grew cool, and Warman reared his head as McLean greeted them from the porch, gripping a musket in his hands.

"Just running through the prime-and-load drill, Mr. Westlake. I can fire better than twice a minute." McLean smiled as he raised up the weapon, the barrel clipping him under the chin. He jerked back his head. "Still not used to the damn thing, but I'll do my bit. Do you suppose they'll attack tonight?"

Westlake quickly dismounted and carried the leather bags up the few stairs. "You should be at Government House at first light, sir.

That's apparently when they will attack, and everyone is assembling there." Westlake handed him the bags and pulled out the receipt for the clerk to sign. "Six hundred dollars in government bills as well as some official papers from the receiver general."

McLean looked at him with a frown. "Why give them to me when I'm going off to fight?"

"Mr. Selby's too ill to carry out his duties, and his daughter doesn't want the responsibility for money or documents."

McLean shook his head and gestured Westlake inside. He put the bags under a small desk benefiting from the light of a window. Next to a few bottles of wine, he picked a quill from a jar and spread out the receipt on the desktop. After scrawling his signature, McLean handed the document back to Westlake and stared at him in silence for a moment.

"Sir, there's something else?" Westlake asked.

McLean hesitated but obviously wanted to add something. He stepped forward, his features taut. "None of this needed to happen if only we had attacked Sackets Harbor, but Prevost and Sheaffe don't seem to know how to win. I'm telling you, young man, Sheaffe will make a cock-up of this too."

Westlake recalled the dinner and Prevost's explanation of his orders from London, knowing that he could interpret them according to the circumstances. After all, British forces had successfully attacked Mackinac and Detroit, and now there was Ogdensburg. He decided to keep his thoughts to himself.

"When the fighting starts, Mr. McLean, make sure you do not expose yourself, unnecessarily. Fire your two rounds a minute, but stay well concealed. Thanks for doing this." Westlake nodded toward the bag and then shook McLean's hand. "I have to be off."

Westlake set his horse at a gallop into the wind, heading west along King Street. At the Ojibwa encampment somewhat northwest of York, he hoped to find Major James Givens. The sun had dipped below the horizon, and after ten minutes of hard riding he reined Warman into a steady trot as he considered Donald McLean's comments. No one could question the man's loyalty, but here he was complaining openly about the management of the war by those in authority. Perhaps he'd been too hard on his own father about similar comments criticizing the upper command.

At the west end of town, King Street gradually tailed off into not much more than a wide pathway and luckily Major Givens was coming back into York from the native village. "Good evening, Mr. Westlake," Givens called out. "I suppose you too are here to tell me to assemble at first light on the morrow." His horse breathed heavily and circled Warman.

"Sir." Westlake saluted, and supposed others had delivered the same message before him.

"You may advise the good Major Nelles, whenever you see him, that all my Indian fellows will be at Government House anxiously waiting for their orders. Let's hope the orders from the general staff will be ready."

Westlake swung his horse around and headed back into town beside Givens. He wondered if he should raise McLean's comments about Sheaffe with Givens. Since they could both be dead the next day, it didn't much matter. "Major, there has been talk, while I was prisoner in Sackets Harbor, about an attack on the place. How do you feel?"

Givens made no reply, and Westlake figured that he had somehow offended him. A full minute passed before Givens next spoke.

"It doesn't matter at this point. We do our duty to the King and defend our homes. Things are simple for a soldier," Givens said. "The question now is on which side of York will the Americans land?" Givens glanced at him expecting an answer.

Westlake considered his reply. "Reminds me of a joke, sir. Where does a bear shit in the woods?"

Givens frowned and then shrugged.

"Anywhere he wants," Westlake said. "With ten or more ships, the enemy can land where it pleases him."

By now they'd reached Yonge Street, where Westlake turned north. "I'll be on my way home, sir," Westlake explained. "Should be an interesting morning tomorrow." Westlake saluted and kneed Warman into a trot.

Maple Hill sat in darkness by the time Westlake lead Warman to his stall. Joseph, the stable hand came running into the barn to strip and feed the horse. "Be on your way inside, sir. I'll look after this for you," he said, smiling. "Tomorrow's a big day for us. Remember I joined the York Militia, so I'll be gone before first light. Do you want me to tack up your horse before I leave?"

"That's kind of you, Joseph, but tomorrow I'll manage by myself. Good luck and keep your head down." Westlake stroked the animal's nose once, before turning to hurry into the house. Entering through the kitchen door, he found no one present there but the fires still burned in the oven. A single loaf of bread and an apple pie sat on the table, but he didn't stop to savour the smell before heading for the parlour.

"I suppose you must know the Americans have been sighted just offshore," Elizabeth said quietly. She sat on the sofa by the fire, with Richard beside her. His father stood on seeing Westlake enter.

"Saw them from the bluffs," Westlake replied. "And I've been trying to get back here all afternoon. Ten ships at least, with the new *Madison* in the van. Everyone is assembling at Government House tomorrow morning." Westlake handed his mother the note. "From Mrs. Derenzy."

"You should delay your departure, then give yourself up to the Americans," Richard advised. "No more fighting then until you're exchanged."

"I can't believe you'd suggest giving my parole to the enemy," Westlake proclaimed, glancing at his mother, who looked away. "I'll fight and defend my home, which is nothing less than what you yourself should do." His stomach growled, reminding him that he hadn't eaten since midday. "I'm hungry." He turned back to the kitchen.

"Come back here while I'm talking to you," Richard ordered in a raised voice. "I'll protect Maple Hill in my own way. Ten or more ships mean the Americans are here in force. You'll be killed for absolutely nothing. Your mother and I need you to stay here at home." He pointed hard at the floor with a finger.

Westlake continued to the kitchen table to tear off a chunk of bread and pour some water from the pitcher into a cup before returning to confront his father. The fire sparked and crackled, providing him with a necessary pause. He breathed in deeply. "Is this true, Mum? You want me to hide? If every man thought that way, there would be no one to defend York. What would General Brock have thought of me?"

Richard answered. "Brock would just get you killed."

"But I'd have my honour still and I'd have done my duty." Westlake stared at his mother, but she didn't budge in his father's presence. "And your premise is wrong," he continued. "There is nothing to say I will be killed or that our side may not be victorious. Never count the redcoats lost until the final musket fires." He swallowed the last of his bread and took a sip of water.

Richard Westlake turned to face the fire. "What about loyalty and duty to your own family?"

"I'll serve my family when I stand and protect my home ... not by running away," Westlake declared. "If we are finished, I'd like to sleep. Whoever wakes first, please get me up before first light. Goodnight."

He strode off to his room and placed the empty cup on the dresser. On top lay the knife his uncle had given him. He picked it up and fingered the blade. Lighter and somewhat smaller than the one Sergeant Shaughnessy had stolen from him, it was evenly balanced and had a thick handle. He spun round, tossing the weapon across the room, aiming at a vertical post. Two tumbles in twelve feet and the knife stuck home with a thump. "It will do nicely." Quivering, it remained embedded in the wood.

As he undressed and climbed into bed, he realized all the riding had stressed his wound, but no fresh blood showed around the remaining few bandages. The idea of staying here at home, of hiding out, seemed so tempting, but where was the honour in that? On the wall hung the American rifle, the gift from Red George and the weapon he'd be using in the morning. His stomach gave him a twinge just thinking of the killing that would occur on the morrow.

Head on the pillow, he closed his eyes and thought again of young Willie Robertson's hopeless charge into the cannon's mouth. Was honour foolish at some times and yet noble at other times? The answer he figured was yes. But why was Willie's run any more foolish than what he himself would undertake in the morning? Poor Willie's chances had been slim to none, whereas his own chances of living through the day … He took a deep breath, shut off his thoughts of the battle to come, and instead thought of the sun glistening on the lake.

Soon he drifted into sleep.

21

······

WESTLAKE FELT HIMSELF gently rocked from side to side. The nudging of his shoulder got stronger until he opened his eyes. As his mother took her hand away, he smelled pancakes from the kitchen.

"If you get up now, there's still time to eat," Elizabeth said. "I've made breakfast, and this year's maple syrup is light and sweet."

He groaned, feeling the aches from the previous day's ride. "There's no time." He sat up and yawned.

"You can't hope to save York on an empty stomach." His mother smiled. "Joseph has already left, but I asked him to saddle up Warman for you."

"Then you want me to go? What about father?"

"You're my only child." She grimaced. "But if you don't go, you'll never be able to live with yourself." She turned and left the room.

Westlake ate his breakfast quickly and gulped down some hot tea. His mother watched him but did not speak. He rushed back to his room and hitched the knife's sheath through his belt. He grabbed the rifle and ammunition pouches, then made for the stable. As he rode out, his mother waited at the barn's door. "A few of those enemy soldiers are very bad men," he explained. "If things go poorly for us, dress loosely and wear a hat." He reached down and squeezed her hand goodbye.

"Make sure you come home, Jonathan, but give 'em hell."

Westlake raised his eyebrows. From the time he was born, he couldn't remember his mother swearing — except when she'd urged him to find Brock's traitor. He coaxed Warman into a trot through the growing daylight, then looked back once to see his mother standing alone, waving to him. He offered her a salute.

Elizabeth Westlake stood in the barn's well-worn path and shivered. She clenched at the heavy shawl wrapped around her shoulders and fought to take a breath. Her headache had returned and she felt it pounding in her temples. She watched Jonathan's back ride away in the semi-darkness until he had disappeared from view. She whispered, *Goodbye* and kept a hand raised, using every bit of will to hold back her tears. "Oh, Isaac, if you are looking down, take care of my boy."

At five o'clock in the morning of Tuesday, April 27, 1813, Major Edward Nelles stood on the crest of a hill at the edge of Lake Ontario, just west of Government House. Officers on the staff of Major General Sheaffe, resplendent in their red coats and gold epaulettes, gathered around to see for themselves the earliest glimpse of the American fleet. Blocked by cloud, the first dull rays of the sun began to brighten the surface of the water.

Nelles held his telescope steady and out of the lake's shadows the first enemy ship crept into view. He moved the glass left and like ghosts taking shape, three more square-sailed vessels grew into solid form. The Americans were coming, slowly, but they were coming. He turned and nodded good morning to Major James Givens, who puffed with each breath after his morning ride.

"Deck there," another officer shouted, as if surprised to see a ship. He pointed to everyone's right, where six ships now eased out of the darkness.

Nelles held his breath and waited, peering into the lake's gloom. The chance of an American victory was increasing with the addition of every ship in view.

"I count ten." Major General Sheaffe had joined them and now adjusted his bicorn, its red and white ostrich plumes waving in the wind. "No, make that twelve." He pointed west to where two — then four — more ships floated into view. "Fourteen warships. They've brought the entire house."

"Until they anchor, they won't attack," an officer observed.

"See the men scrambling up the rigging," Nelles said. "They're preparing to take in sail. Sooner or later, they'll bring their bows to the wind and drop anchor."

He surveyed the ground lying to his left. The townspeople of York had turned out in numbers to locate the position of the American ships. At least the general and his staff now knew that the enemy planned to land about a mile west of York garrison. The sky had brightened during the last hour, and even with the naked eye, the ship decks were crowded with soldiers and seamen waiting along the rails.

"What do you think, Major Nelles?" Sheaffe asked.

"Fourteen enemy ships are not here for a friendly chat, sir," Nelles replied, "They will drop anchor soon, lower boats, and attempt to seize the beach near old Fort Rouille, or just west of there." As he spoke, the *Madison* dropped her anchor. Nelles looked down at his timepiece: six o'clock.

"I meant, what do you think about a course of action on our part?" Sheaffe repeated.

The other officers stared at Nelles, wondering why Sheaffe solicited advice instead of issuing orders. On this morning of high drama, standing in a blustery wind, Nelles could do without the Brock hangover. He considered his reply and then, in typical Brock spirit, he said, "Oppose them with everything we've got, and crush them at the point of landing, sir."

"If the first landing is a feint, we'll have all our forces at the wrong place," Sheaffe replied.

"Boats lowered, sir," an officer yelled above the wind. Precious minutes were slipping by while Sheaffe debated his first move.

"All the enemy ships are to the west, sir. Our men can easily be shifted from one beach to the next, but we will have defeated the initial landing no matter whether it's a feint or not," Nelles argued.

Sheaffe put the glass to his eye again. The longboats started to fill with enemy oarsmen. The officers crowded around him expecting orders for each of them. "Major Givens, take your Indians along the beach and oppose a landing there until I decide who else to send to you."

"Sir." Givens stepped forward and saluted.

Sheaffe turned and marched back toward Government House, the officers behind him creating a mass of redcoats trundling along the crest of the hill. One young fellow stayed back, dressed in grey pants and a short fur coat, unbuttoned so his buckskin jacket showed beneath. He had a black tuque pulled down over his ears and carried an American rifle.

"Morning, Mr. Westlake," Nelles greeted. "Go with Major Givens and help out, but let me know if things go bad. I'll try to get you more help." Nelles shook his head. "If the man thinks the major and sixty Ojibwa can hold off that lot, he'll lose us the day."

"Sir." Westlake saluted and started running for his horse.

"And Jonathan, don't get yourself killed," Nelles continued. "I don't want to give your mother bad news later today."

Lieutenant Abraham Tasker sat in the wardroom of the *U.S.S. Conquest* and spooned a mouthful of what the sailors called burgoo. The porridge of oatmeal and hot water, slid down his throat to help warm his stomach. He sipped his "Scottish coffee" made from burnt toast, boiling water, and a pinch of sugar. "No wonder the Scots are such miserable buggers," he grumbled, wiping the side of his mouth with his hand.

"Just get me off this damn ship and onto firm land where I can get a decent meal," Major Forsyth replied. He had paled again, and it appeared to Tasker like the man was about to puke.

Tasker felt the *Conquest* swinging around and he put a hand on the bench to steady himself. Most of the men were in Forsyth's condition, and had been so since they'd first boarded. From the deck above an officer shout orders to shorten more sail followed a few moments later by the command, "Helm down."

"The longboats will be coming for us," Tasker said.

"Get the men up top," Forsyth ordered. "I want all our boats landing together. No stragglers."

"Let go!" The ship's commander ordered the anchor dropped off the bow.

By the time Tasker had everyone moving onto the open deck, longboats from all the other ships in the fleet were rowing toward the schooners *Conquest* and *Ontario*. He worried that the effort would exhaust the rowers so they'd have nothing left for the pull toward shore. A brisk wind made him thankful for his stolen boat cloak, and he turned up the collar before hunching down. Out of his pocket, he pulled a small spyglass to scan the shore. As the ship tugged at her anchor, he lost his balance and swore.

Tasker scanned for beaches to assault, where the shore might be flatter and thus easier for a charge inland, but an embankment seemed to stretch across the entire coastline. He focused his glass on a group of redcoats studying the fleet. They abruptly turned and marched away, leaving only two men behind who continued to stare out at the ships. One wore an officer's dress coat and the other ... Jonathan Westlake, dressed just as he was when he escaped. *I was right, he was a spy.*

"Sergeant Shaughnessy, here!" Tasker called out harshly. "There's our target. If we're forbidden plunder, then I'll still have my revenge."

The big man stepped in beside Tasker, who handed him the glass. The ship rocked violently and Shaughnessy banged his left arm against the rail. "Christ be Jesus, that hurts." He rubbed his shoulder where the bullet had grazed the bone, then raised the glass and focused along the line of Tasker's pointing finger. "Westlake, the bastard — and him acting so innocent like. Next time I won't miss him. 'Sides, I owe him for this and it still hurts like bloody hell." Shaughnessy put down the spyglass, then lifted his left arm and grimaced. "No plunder at all, sir?"

"I wouldn't be able to save you from Pike's wrath." Tasker gripped his own throat. "He'll stretch that neck of yours if you so much as steal a chicken."

"Doesn't seem fair, sir. What's the point of us going in first if we all don't get first dibs on the plunder?"

"Strange things happen in the course of battle, Sergeant," Tasker said. "You'll get your chance. Just have patience."

"Signal from flag," the *Conquest*'s commander shouted to Major Forsyth. "You may enter the boats, gentlemen."

Forsyth nodded for Lieutenant Tasker to begin. "I'll never take firm land for granted again!" the major said.

"Over the side, you loafers," Tasker bellowed. "The pleasure cruise is over. Time you lot earned your keep."

"I've puked more than I've loafed," a man barked as he swung his leg over the rail. "This navy owes me," he added before his head disappeared down the side.

The cool winds of April whipped the waves into whitecaps, and the longboats dipped and bobbed with every swell. Tasker grinned to himself and watched the lead boat, where Forsyth and a few other men stood in the centre trying to keep their balance. If old Forsyth thought the schooner was bad, that longboat was going to be a rolling menace. The lieutenant peered skyward to see scudding grey clouds but nothing dark enough to threaten their assault.

"Sit down in the hull, you stupid bastards, or we'll all end up in the drink," the longboat's master demanded. In each boat there were a dozen oarsmen and up to twenty-four riflemen. Having never taken part in an amphibious assault, the soldiers didn't know what to do with themselves.

Tasker followed the master's orders and sat down with a thump, gesturing for the others in his boat to follow his example. The boat pitched downward in a violent swell and his queasy gut rolled with it. A rifleman made to sit, instead tipping over onto the legs of a rower.

"Get off me, you oaf," the seaman yelled.

The two men glared at each other, but Tasker knew nothing would come of it. His men were tired and ill and the seamen exhausted from their pull. Lucky they were attacking today or they'd be at one another's throats instead of the enemy's.

The first shots rang out from Upper Canada, and everyone instinctively crouched down. Men who previously wanted to stand up in the boat now lay flat, clawing the bottom of the hull. At three hundred yards from shore, Forsyth cupped his hands around his mouth and shouted, "Rest easy on the oars."

The order was passed back to the other longboats, and soon all the boats drifted, twisting with the current, while the men kept low, catching their breath. Tasker nodded to himself, watching the seamen fall forward, resting on their oars. Old Forsyth was smart. The rower's pace had slowed due to their strenuous efforts. By drifting for a few minutes, it would allow that final push for the shore to be much quicker … and safer.

The easterly wind pushed them farther along the shoreline, where Tasker saw Indians running past the evergreens, keeping parallel with the drifting vessels. The boats began to bunch up, which was exactly what Forsyth wanted. They would all go in together. The ten boats were now spread across one hundred yards. The musket fire from the shore was unceasing and a lucky ball clipped the rail right beside Tasker's hand.

Forsyth stood again. "You will fire in half-boats, every other man. Stand, pick a target, and fire. I don't care if you hit anything so long as you keep firing." His idea was to prevent the enemy from killing everyone before the boats hit the beach. The seamen nodded in agreement.

Again, his order was shouted along to the last boat in line. The men counted off their numbers.

"Commence rowing for the shore." Forsyth waited a few seconds while the long, sweeping oar strokes of the seaman got them underway. "Commence firing."

"That's us, lads," Tasker ordered. "Odd numbers first. Stand, pick your target, fire." The rifles cracked out in ragged bangs down the line. "Now the even numbers. Stand, target, fire." The rocking of the boat made it almost impossible to hit anything, but the previous musket fire almost came to a stop.

For the first time in history, the American Army was firing on York. The forces of liberty had come in strength to Upper Canada.

Lieutenant Westlake galloped Warman westward along the lakeshore but cut inland when he reached the ruins of old Fort Rouillé. Hundreds of soldiers had slowly disembarked from the fourteen invading ships into the white-painted longboats. His chest heaved at the sight.

An easterly breeze carried the drifting invaders gradually west. Major Givens, on horseback, shouted for Westlake to join him farther along the shore. "We have to move with those boats." He pointed toward the lake. "I hope General Sheaffe is sending more men. We won't hold them off with sixty natives and just the pair of us."

"Major Nelles is trying hard to persuade him, sir," Westlake replied. "We should stay in the trees." He urged his horse to cover behind a curtain of cedars and maples on the eastern curve of the treeline. A brisk wind stirred, rocking the treetops, and Warman whinnied, sensing the danger from his master's gripping knees.

"They can't shoot accurately on those rolling waves," Givens said.

At that very moment, half of the riflemen in every boat stood and fired. Some of the bare branches above Westlake's head splintered under the impact of lead striking wood, and he crouched in the saddle. A scattering of twigs fell on his shoulder, and Westlake looked up to see an entire branch hanging by just a strip of bark.

Major Givens trotted in beside him. "See what I mean? They're shooting wild, but perhaps I'd be wise to take cover ... just a precautionary measure, mind you." Givens laughed, nudging his horse quickly out of harm's way.

Soon the other half of the men stood and fired from the boats. Again, their shots sailed overhead. The lead boat dipped out of sight in a swell a hundred and fifty yards away. When it reappeared, the oarsmen were pulling with renewed strength in a dash for the shore. Westlake knew the first lot of riflemen were meanwhile frantically reloading to fire again, and keep the Indians in hiding instead of shooting back. He looked over to the woods, where flashes of musket flame and smoke appeared as the Ojibwa began to return a sporadic fire. A native dressed in buckskins stepped out to take aim, his face painted blood red.

Westlake slid down from his saddle, pulled his rifle from its ring, and began to load. He aimed at the closest boat, peering along the barrel to find a target. The boats fell with the waves and then rose again, clearly into view. Westlake could see the individual faces and uniforms of the soldiers. The same bloody rifle regiment that had lost Ogdensburg was now leading the invasion of York. He shifted the point of the rifle from one boat to another. *Forsyth, Tasker, Shaughnessy.* Anticipation took an iron grip on his heart. "Stay calm," he told himself.

He aimed the rifle at Major Forsyth standing in the lead boat, and squeezed the trigger. The man sitting in front of the major immediately jerked backward and disappeared. The rifle had fired too low. Westlake reloaded and heard Major Givens draw his sword.

"Only a fool would make a charge against those Harper Ferry rifles, sir," Westlake said. "There is no honour in trading one's life for nothing." The rifle was loaded and Westlake handed it to Givens. "Try it, sir. A gift to me from Colonel Red George Macdonell … the same kind that they're using."

Givens put the rifle to his shoulder, the walnut stock against his jaw, aimed, and fired. Another man dropped down in the lead boat that was now only fifty yards from shore. "My God, I'd never make that shot with my old Bess. They'd cut to us to ribbons if we showed ourselves."

Westlake snatched back the rifle. "Good shot, sir. I'll strike the second boat if your men can hit the first." He looked up to see the sailors frantically heaving on their oars with every stroke.

Givens rode out from the trees to shout orders to the Ojibwa. "Concentrate on the closest boat." He gestured with his arm. Rifle shots rang out, and the major turned his head to stare at the boats with disdain. Westlake winced, expecting at any second to see the man blown off his horse. The major kneed his horse and trotted back to the safety of the cedars.

Westlake scanned the second boat and aimed directly at Tasker's heart. He fired just as Tasker turned to sit down. The shoulder of his Uncle Adam's cloak puffed out, and Tasker brushed at his sleeve as if to rid himself of a fly. The bullet had only clipped some threads.

A man rose up in the lead boat, peering past the rail to discern the lake's bottom. A few muskets cracked out and then he simply keeled over the side to float face down. Seconds from shore, every rifleman stood up, thus making easy targets of themselves. Westlake fired, taking off a man's lower jaw. As the man collapsed, other soldiers leapt over the boat's rails. Their boots splashed in shallow water and then they ran for the safety of the embankment.

The Indians fired at the second boatload. A single rifleman slumped. Again, the soldiers leapt into the water, following their comrades in a dash for safety. When all the riflemen in the third boat stood and fired together, Westlake watched the natives run wisely for cover. The boat crunched in onto the stones and the men jumped over the side to rush up the beach.

He wiped his forehead with the back of his hand while quickly reloading. "I'm sweating," he said.

"Just fear. Ignore it and it'll go away," Givens replied.

"We can't hold them, sir," Westlake yelled. "After a few more boatloads, those men will come charging over the bank with rifles blazing."

"I was one of the officers who refused General Sheaffe's suggestion to retreat in Niagara," Givens announced proudly, "but you're right, this is madness." He coaxed his horse out of the trees and gestured with his free arm to his Indians allies. Immediately, they began to shift through the woods toward him. Natives with black spiked hair, wearing silver earrings and bracelets, their faces painted in fierce red stripes, emerged out of cover.

Westlake heard Forsyth scream the order to charge. The riflemen scaled the embankment, paused, fired, and ran again. One Indian collapsed to the forest floor, but the others scurried to safety. Tasker ran between the trees in front of Westlake, ordering his men to scatter into the woods. Dressed in their green uniforms, they soon blended with the dull forest until Westlake couldn't spot a single man. The rifle regiment had secured a foothold amid the trees.

Givens ordered a gradual retreat along the shoreline, but the growing rifle fire hastened their withdrawal. They'd rolled back only a few hundred yards when, behind Westlake, a loud crashing through the bush made him turn his head. The grenadiers of the 8th Foot, dressed in sharp red coats with their deep blue facings, came marching to confront the enemy. He breathed a sigh of relief. Givens rode to greet one hundred and twenty officers and men, battle tested and appearing angry.

"Their commanding officer has been shot dead," Givens explained on his return.

The grenadiers quickly formed a front to stop the further advance of Forsyth's riflemen. Soon they were joined by York Militia from the town. Among them marched the handsome face of Mr. Donald McLean, magistrate. Dressed in a suit and neckcloth, and wearing a tall black hat, on seeing Westlake he pumped his musket above his head, obviously his civilized imitation of a warrior.

"Told you I'd be here, young man," McLean declared.

"Take cover, sir," Westlake replied, lowering his arm. "Those are sharp shooters we're facing, not country bumpkins."

The continuous firing of weapons brought with it the acrid smell of burnt gunpowder. Grey smoke hung in the air and then swept upwards with a gust of wind. McLean fired his weapon into the forest where the enemy riflemen were taking aim. He grinned, seeming pleased with himself and began to reload in a slow but meticulous fashion. Westlake shook his head in disbelief. Here was a man full of his sense of duty, but clearly meant for something other than fighting.

A booming sound from the lake made Westlake instinctively crouch. A split second later the treetops crashed together, with the ripping noise of grapeshot. A ship's cannon had joined the battle. Westlake stared out toward the water and saw more white longboats pulling for the shore right in front of him. Others must have seen the same thing, because the grenadiers swung men toward the lakeside and engaged the incoming attackers.

"The day will be lost if we aren't reinforced again soon," Westlake said.

McLean fired a second time. "What did I tell you? Sheaffe isn't up to it. Sir Isaac set up the Queenston victory and everyone knows it."

"Get down, Mr. McLean," Westlake shouted, as a rifle cracked out.

Too late to comply, the clerk crumpled to the ground, gripping his chest. McLean eyes stared straight ahead as Westlake peered over his body. Another blast of the cannon's grapeshot shook the trees above them, and Westlake dove flat to the forest floor beside him. McLean reached slowly into his pocket and pulled out a key attached by a small metal ring to a piece of wood the length of a finger. "Yours … the six hundred."

Westlake took the key from his grasp and McLean closed his eyes as his breathing stopped. "What a waste of a good man." He shuddered and bowed his head. The continuing sound of the battle brought him quickly back to reality. Westlake gripped the rifle tight, stood, and fired at one of the men in an incoming boat. A bullet zipped overhead and Westlake jerked his head around to see Tasker and Shaughnessy grinning at him from not forty yards away. *Bastards.*

The enemy continued advancing toward the houses of York. Westlake glanced at the key still held in his hand and thought of the clerk's home. *The official papers … the six hundred in cash.*

"Lookee who's hanging over the one you shot with the tall hat." Shaughnessy pointed out Jonathan Westlake.

"Shoot him!" Tasker yelled. "Now! I'm not loaded. Shoot, damn you!"

Shaughnessy stepped out to take his shot but a sudden volley from the newly arrived redcoats forced him back into safety. The balls whistled through the air, smacking into the trees around Tasker. A schooner fired its cannon again, and the trees above the enemy shattered with the sound of impacting grapeshot. The instant his rifle was loaded, Tasker jumped out again to take his shot. But the schooner's missiles had forced Westlake to hug the ground so Tasker's shot sailed over his quarry. "That bugger is luckier than a rooster in a hen house. Shoot him!" he screamed at his sergeant.

Shaughnessy stepped out and fired. He'd hurried at Tasker's urging, and the bullet merely clipped the tree beside Westlake's shoulder. "I'm going to fillet him with his own knife," he rasped, caressing the handle of the long hunting knife that he'd stolen from his target. "Do you even think he knows we're here?"

"We sat out in the lake in those damn rowboats in full view for an hour," Tasker replied as he continued reloading his rifle. "Of course he knows – and we're lucky not to be shot through, for Christ's sake." Despite a cool morning breeze, Tasker was sweating and had to wipe his clammy palms on his green jacket.

He watched as Westlake jumped up to fire at an incoming long-boat. *That bugger has one of our rifles!* An officer keeled over the side, to splash in the water, but by the time Tasker looked back to take aim, his enemy had already disappeared into the bush. Major Forsyth shouted something behind him, his white vest prominent under the green jacket. He advanced, waving his sword to signal an attack just when the line of redcoats broke. The British Army was falling back, easy targets for his sharpshooters. A spontaneous cheer erupted from the American riflemen.

Particularly happy to be on firm ground again, Lieutenant Tasker had run forward to the cover of the trees along with the rest of the green-clad riflemen. The Indians scattered through the bush, falling back toward York. Normally he carried only a sword and his riding crop, but today he'd decided to kill some self-righteous British bastards himself. Since the time he was forced to run from Ogdensburg, Tasker had sworn revenge. He aimed at a retreating native, pressed the trigger, and shot the man in the back.

"Like shooting fish in a barrel." Shaughnessy laughed. He fired too, and another Indian dropped to the ground. "Redcoats, sir." The sergeant nodded toward the trees standing between themselves and York.

"Good, that's what we came for." He stepped out from behind a tree and fired. A redcoat collapsed, screaming and gripping his shoulder. "Do these fools not understand we have rifles?" He heard Shaughnessy grunt as the man fired.

"Take Shaughnessy and two dozen men," Major Forsyth ordered him from the cover of a stout maple. "Swing north and try to get round behind them and then kill as many as you can. Watch out for those damn savages." Forsyth removed his great plumed hat and used a finger to draw a line across his forehead where an Indian might begin to scalp him.

"We can't get ourselves too far from the town, sir," Tasker reminded, rubbing his hands together with an eager grin.

"I won't be able to protect you from General Pike if you and your fellows are caught plundering," Forsyth replied, readjusting his white plumes. "His army is God's sword for liberty, and he'll hang you just as sure as I'm standing here. Are you listening to me?"

"No worries, sir." Tasker laughed. "I was thinking more of the women. Perhaps one might like to try a real man rather than these British fops."

"Just don't shoot them this time before you proposition them. Get going and do some damage," Forsyth ordered.

22

. . . . . .

"THE INVASION IS YOURS TO LEAD, GENERAL PIKE." Dearborn didn't lift himself from his seat. "Best of luck."

Brigadier General Pike took a deep breath of cool morning air, his arms stretched out to either side of him as he leaned against the *Madison*'s rail. After weeks of praying to hear those same words, Dearborn had finally given him command of the attack a mere hour before Forsyth's riflemen had climbed down into their boats. Pike had watched the first white longboats pull away, ferrying the soldiers to the stony beaches of Upper Canada. He heard the discharge of weapons on shore and put a spyglass to his eye. Yellow flashes of musket fire had ringed the forest where Forsyth's longboat landed. The men had soon charged to the cover of the forest.

The enthusiasm was infectious. A company of his old regiment, the Fifteenth Infantry, gave a cheer and climbed over the *Madison*'s side, right beside him. The wind gusted, jerking one soldier from his grip on the rail. Pike grabbed him just in time or the man would have fallen headlong to the boat waiting below.

"Thank you, sir," the man said, now clutching the rail with both hands. "I was a goner for sure."

"You won't survive this day by being careless, good fellow," Pike said. He listened to the man chattering to himself in excitement all the way down into the waiting longboat.

The staff officers gathered around Pike and clapped their hands, rejoicing. After weeks of planning, they had finally landed in York. Commodore Chauncey arrived at Pike's elbow, grinning and pumping a spirited fist in the air. "Well planned and well executed," the commodore said.

"By God, I can't stay here any longer!" Pike informed him. He tightened his belt and took hold of the *Madison's* rail, then turned to beckon his staff. "Come, jump into the boat."

Private McKnight glanced up from his seat in the longboat's hull to see at least four officers swing over the *Madison's* side. They were no doubt joining him and his fellows in the assault on the beaches of York. "We're doomed," McKnight muttered, tugging on the sleeve of Private O'Reilly beside him.

"What?" asked O'Reilly.

"I said we're doomed." McKnight gestured at the officers climbing down into their boat.

"Don't be daft," O'Reilly replied.

"Have I ever led you wrong?"

O'Reilly stared at him but didn't reply. The longboat crunched against the *Madison's* hull, and a few sailors reached out to steady the vessel until the officers stepped in. McKnight squeezed closer to O'Reilly to help make room for the additional bodies aboard.

"Look here, laddie, all these officers with their fancy uniforms will attract the attention of those fellows who don't want us to come visiting them," McKnight said quietly, nodding toward the shore. "Crouch low in the hull, my friend, or that stupid Irish head'll get blown off."

General Pike stepped carefully toward the bow of the longboat and then stood in the centre right beside McKnight. His staff of officers followed him as best they could. "Good day, gentlemen," Pike said, rubbing his hands. "In for a glorious day?"

"Sir," McKnight replied. "Glory, sir, yes, that's what I look for." He tried his best to hide any cynicism and offered Pike a fake smile.

"Away boat," the longboat's master shouted. "Oars!"

McKnight sat straighter to scan the shore where grey smoke drifted amid the trees and constant flashes of flame marked the spot when a musket fired. He watched carefully as Forsyth's riflemen charged through the trees. He spotted redcoats firing a volley at the oncoming greenjackets. A ship's cannon boomed, and the same redcoats turned their attention to the incoming boats — more specifically *his* boat.

McKnight could now see the faces of the men firing at him. Two other boats approached the beach on a parallel course. He ducked farther into the hull and pulled O'Reilly alongside him. The oarsmen swept their oars like mad fiends, despite a steady rain of musket balls chipping at the rails. Strangely, for almost a full minute, all went quiet.

"Not much farther now lads," Pike shouted. "Fix bayonets but be damn careful not to stab one another."

McKnight poked his head up quickly to survey the landing beach, his heart pounding in his chest. A blonde-haired young man wearing a black tuque stepped out from behind a tree, aimed his rifle, and fired. An officer standing beside Pike pitched overboard immediately. More balls pounded into the boat's hull as it scraped onto the stones of York's beach.

"Up and at 'em," Pike ordered.

"Here we go," McKnight said to O'Reilly. "To glory." Rolling his eyes, he stood and jumped into the shallow water. His guts churned and he urgently needed to find a quiet place where he could drop his drawers.

Twenty feet away, an embankment rose up beyond the beach. McKnight ran while balls peppered the stones around him. Under the shade of the embankment, Pike shouted orders to form up in platoons. At Pike's instructions, a third of the men had only long pikes instead of muskets. McKnight fell in beside O'Reilly, still puffing from the run. "Just watch this fiasco," he said.

"We are climbing the embankment to attack them with the edge of our steel," Pike shouted. "Company will advance and charge."

McKnight shinnied over the bank and immediately a volley of fire exploded from the tree line. The man beside O'Reilly fell backward before the rest of the Fifteenth fired as one. Behind the spitting flames and rising smoke, redcoats emerged from the trees to take a few cautious steps, all huge men carrying fixed bayonets. As they screamed "Charge!" the Fifteenth retreated fast to the cover of the embankment.

"Christ, that was stupid," gasped McKnight, so fearful he could barely breathe. "Did you see the size of those fellows? They have to be grenadiers."

Pike ordered his small reserve back to the rim of the embankment whence they soon fired on the advancing redcoats. The grenadiers then retreated to the trees, neither side having achieved a thing. O'Reilly was lying oddly still beside McKnight, with a look of pain on his face. "Are you hit?" McKnight asked.

O'Reilly didn't speak, merely nodded.

"Let me see," McKnight urged. O'Reilly just shook his head. "Come on, show me quick."

O'Reilly pointed to his groin and began unbuttoning his pants. He peeled them off slowly and glanced down. "Burns like hell, but it's not what I thought." His groin showed a red line across the unbroken skin.

"Another two inches and no balls." McKnight laughed. "All those beautiful Irish girls would have had to go without."

More boatloads of Fifteenth Infantry arrived to join in the withering fire of their comrades, but this time they brought two field guns with them. The guns were manhandled over the side as the lake boiled with musket balls around the straining artillerymen. Slowly they made the cover of the embankment.

The British grenadiers were meanwhile taking casualties from the rifle fire. McKnight heard the rifle regiment's trumpet blare, the signal for advance. He didn't care for them personally, but today he was happy to have the greenjackets on his side. He poked his head above the embankment to watch some of the Fifteenth rushing for cover in the woods. Pike was shouting above the din for them to form up in platoons as the grenadiers retreated.

"Here we go again," McKnight said. "You'd best pull your pants up now or you'll scare both sides to death."

Major Givens bellowed for everyone to fall back. The grenadiers needed no encouragement and quickly showed the enemy their heels. Westlake leapt onto Warman and followed along with the natives in a fast withdrawal. He rode hard until reaching the ruins of old Fort Rouille, to find Major Nelles with of hundreds of redcoats who were marching at the double in the opposite direction. To stem the tide of defeat, the Royal Newfoundland Regiment, the rest of the 8th Foot, and yet more of the York Militia were stomping to the rescue.

"The Americans have gained the beach, sir, and are advancing north, as well," Westlake reported. "They've even landed artillery."

"They'll try to outflank us," Nelles huffed. "Either along the shore or farther to the north."

"Just a half-hour ago we could have stopped them on the beach," Westlake said matter-of-factly. "Now ..." He shrugged.

"The general wouldn't budge until he'd assured himself there was no landing to the east of us." Nelles shook his head in despair.

Westlake heard the crack of rifles to the north of the clearing. It meant Forsyth's men were trying to get behind them exactly as Nelles predicted. Directly in front of Westlake, in the centre, the redcoats advanced. By the lake to Westlake's left, the 8th Foot marched forward into the withering fire of the U.S. Fifteenth. But in less than three minutes, the entire front reeled backward.

The Glengarries in their green coats under command of a Captain McPherson marched in to provide support, but all they could do was cover the retreat. From a schooner a cannon boomed, spraying the shoreline with grapeshot. Westlake felt something pluck at the leg of his pants. He looked down to see a rip in the cloth but no blood. Clouds of burnt musket powder hung in the air until a gust of wind wafted it up into the trees. Westlake buried his mouth in the crook of an arm, the smoke clawing the back of his throat.

Major General Sheaffe waved his arms to halt the withdrawal, just as the Americans tried charging along the beach. The 8th thus rallied in line for a volley that stopped the enemy where they stood. A British cheer went up but faded fast at the sound of American fife and drums playing "Yankee Doodle." When the Fifteenth Infantry charged straight for the centre of the British line, Sheaffe realized he was outnumbered and had no option but to order a withdrawal.

"Come, Mr. Westlake," Nelles shouted. "Let's make a dignified retreat before we become one of them." He pointed to the bodies of several grenadiers lying dead on the ground, as he spurred his horse.

Westlake edged Warman around and set off at a gallop. No one had given any orders as to where they should reform so Westlake simply slowed the animal to a walk once there were enough trees between himself and the enemy to offer sufficient protection. Some militia paused in a clearing on his side of the western battery, and Nelles held up his hand. "We'll wait for the rest of them here."

Westlake dismounted and hitched Warman's reins to a tree. As the two sides disengaged, an eerie silence descended along the shoreline, until a thunderous boom let fly a hundred yards behind his position. The men serving the British cannon of York's western battery let out a cheer.

Nelles pointed to the harbour, where the *Conquest*, a U.S. schooner, had been blasting grapeshot at anything that moved within the British lines. Westlake removed the glass from his saddlebag and focused on the ship. A large hole had appeared in her side at deck level. Sailors lay among the shattered timbers, their up-stretched hands seeking help, ignored by others scurrying across deck to contain the damage.

The guns of the *Conquest* returned fire, flames shooting from the cannon mouth. The ship must have been rising with a wave because their shots sailed far overhead. Westlake handed the glass to Nelles. "The *Conquest*, sir, she's taken at least one direct hit from the western battery."

"I hope they sink the bastards," Nelles hissed, peering through the glass.

The next boom from the battery immediately preceded the whoosh of an explosion. The ground shook beneath Westlake's feet and a great veil of black smoke rose in the heat of the blast above the cannon's emplacement. Westlake pointed skyward, staring at this rising cloud.

"What the hell was that?" Nelles exclaimed. "Check on the battery, Lieutenant, and report back immediately."

Westlake remounted his horse for the short ride and galloped off. Where the cannons were once mounted, men on the ground with blackened faces and torn garments gazed up at him in bewilderment. A man in a smouldering coat rolled over to face upward and cried out for his mother. Another stood wavering, as if the slightest breeze could knock him over. Body parts littered the area around the cannons.

The devastation was like a stiff punch to the gut and Westlake retched where he stood. Beside a displaced eighteen-pounder, a huge blackened circle appeared on the ground. Those still standing backed away together in stunned silence, shrinking down, not knowing what to do.

"What happened here?" Westlake asked.

A boy with powder burns on his scalp and little hair remaining choked out the word *cartridges*. Another said lucky shot and gestured with a sleeveless arm toward the schooner. Others shook their heads with hands cupped around their deafened ears. Westlake counted the torsos near the hole: three men of the Royal Artillery and two others he couldn't identify lay dead.

"*You men*, get ropes around this cannon," Westlake ordered. "Remount it." He leapt back on Warman. Those men who remained alive began to move themselves slowly, quietly, staring straight ahead with listless eyes. He galloped the entire way back to Major Nelles. Retreating soldiers flooded around him, marching to form up in line.

"Battery's taken a direct hit, sir, or else the charges have blown up beside the eighteen," Westlake reported. "I can't tell exactly what happened, but they need more men to remount that cannon. At least five dead." He grimaced.

Nelles peered through a glass toward the enemy gathered along the shore. They had stopped their drive forward in order to reorganize themselves for a final assault. Wheeled cannons pushed their way forward through the ranks. *Methodical.*

"We're falling back to the battery," he said to Westlake. "Take a dozen men and remount it as quickly as possible. Seems we have a respite, but for how long …" Nelles shrugged and threw up his hands.

23
· · · · · ·

FROM HIS PLACE at the very head of the column, Private McKnight studied the skirmishers ahead that dashed in and out between the trees. He'd already pleaded with the officer in charge that a grave mistake had been made. He and O'Reilly were not part of the Sixteenth Infantry here at the front, but rather they should be with the Fifteenth Infantry at the rear. The damn officer simply laughed at him.

"Bugger," McKnight said under his breath before he kicked at the dirt. "This will come to no good." McKnight loathed presenting himself as the first available target for any enemy sharpshooter. At least General Pike had thought to send a full body of scouts forward of his main force. *That should keep the column's nose safe.* McKnight appreciated the general's extra caution, especially when it came to risking his own tender neck.

Pike stepped in front of the main body to greet an officer returning from the line of skirmishers. The other man came to attention and saluted.

"Ruins of an old fort up yonder, sir," the officer reported. "Seems the enemy's already high-tailed it out of there."

McKnight glanced over his shoulder to view six field guns rolling along the road to catch up with the column. "They'll help us nicely." He nudged O'Reilly in the ribs. "Getting everything prepared before we attack," McKnight continued. "Knows his business, this one. I prefer men with plans." He touched his temple with a finger.

"You said earlier we was doomed," O'Reilly replied.

"Just don't stand too close to him." McKnight grinned. "They always try to kill the officers first."

Another officer marched up to stand directly beside the column. "The Sixteenth will advance at the ordinary." He turned smartly and stared straight ahead. "March!"

Advancing along the road, McKnight soon passed the enemy dead and dying. One man cried out for aid, but the marchers didn't stop. McKnight turned his head away to glance out at the blue expanse of Lake Ontario, aware that the schooners in plain sight would remain on station to evacuate the army should they run into trouble.

The column halted. Twenty yards ahead, a small bridge over a narrow stream had been knocked away.

"The first dozen men will fall out, lay down their muskets, and put those planks back in place," an officer shouted. A single shot banged out and the ball plucked at the man's sleeve. McKnight hesitated and no one else moved either. "Come on! Our cannons can't fly over the water on their own. Sergeant, take control." The officer ran off, hand on sword, trying to catch up with Pike's other staff that had jumped the stream and were now struggling on all fours up the opposite bank of the small ravine.

"We shouldn't be here," McKnight explained to the sergeant yet again. "We're in the Fifteenth Infantry, not the Sixteenth." The sergeant gave him a shove forward with the staff. "I could have been shot if I'd been standing beside that officer," McKnight protested.

With the bridge replaced and McKnight reluctantly in the van, the column of men jolted forward again, the wheels of the cannon creaking behind him. It didn't take too long to realize that the enemy had begun retreating in disarray. Not only were many of their wounded left behind, but the roads ahead remained clear. McKnight wondered why trees had not been felled to block their path or a nasty rearguard left to impede them.

"This seems too easy," he muttered to O'Reilly as they marched straight toward the town. "I don't like it."

"You complain when it's hard and now you're complaining 'cause it's not hard enough," O'Reilly replied. "Make up your mind."

They halted twice more while Pike sent scouts ahead to reconnoitre cannon emplacements that might check their advance. At one such stop, McKnight stared at the men of the Sixth Infantry making a frontal-assault on the guns. Crazy, he thought, until finding out the enemy had abandoned the position after spiking their guns.

Arriving at the second abandoned battery, the column came into view of York's garrison wall. With the Union flag atop waving in the breeze, one large building stood some four hundred yards away across open ground. The blockhouse presented itself as a wonderful target for Pike's cannon.

"Major, bring up the artillery and open fire immediately," Pike ordered. "That's your target." He pointed straight ahead. Once again, he sent skirmishers in front for safety. From the direction of the garrison, a cannon fired, sending a ball whistling overhead.

McKnight dove for the ground, jarring his chin. He looked up to see Pike staring down at him. "Damn good idea," Pike said. He turned and said something to his staff that McKnight couldn't hear, but soon the officers were ordering all the other men to get down close to the ground.

"He cares about the soldiers under his command, so he does," McKnight said, approvingly to O'Reilly. "I'm beginning to like this fellow. Knows his business. Do you think he'd let the both of us move to the rear?"

Westlake had ridden Warman back alongside some retreating troops from the Royal Newfoundland Regiment. The officers had barely formed their men into line when the order came to fall back again, only this time to the Half Moon Battery, located several hundred yards in front of the York's garrison walls. He listened to the crack of muskets and rifles echoing through the forest. Major Nelles rode in beside him.

"Is there any plan to this retreat, sir?" Westlake asked. "The men are grumbling that we keep falling back, but there's no orders to ever stop and fight."

"I've given up asking," Nelles replied. "We should have blocked the access roads and fought them at every ravine. At least make them pay."

"So we just keep falling back, sir?"

Nelles nodded, and the instant he did so an officer rode by announcing a further withdrawal toward the garrison. Westlake looked at his superior, who shrugged. "There's nothing I can do," Nelles said sadly.

"It doesn't take a major general to keep telling the men to turn tail and run, sir," Westlake replied. Elements of the York Militia streamed by, heads hung on their chests. Their homes in town unprotected, they wanted to put up a fight. Once the order arrived to abandon York's garrison, Westlake knew for sure the town was lost and he began to think about the safety of Maple Hill.

He rode in beside the 8th Foot and heard the men complaining. They had been ordered to march straight past the garrison without even stopping to pick up their greatcoats and packs. A few militiamen had disobeyed orders and run into the blockhouse to grab some warmer clothing. The sight of a defeated army in retreat sickened Westlake and everyone else who had the resolve to resist.

They'd reached John Street and the Half-Way Tavern when the Reverend Strachan appeared, galloping toward Nelles and then pulling back on his reins to come to a halt. "You're leaving the wounded behind. Disgusting." Strachan's brow furrowed and his eyes narrowed in the anger that Westlake had seen many times during his school days. It still alarmed him even though Strachan no longer had a hold over him. But for once he agreed with the man: the entire battle had been poorly conducted.

"Our mighty general declares that he won't lose his precious army to save this little town," Strachan continued with obvious disdain in his voice. "What did I tell you, Major Nelles?" Strachan shouted. "The man does not know how to win, but you wouldn't listen."

Nelles looked away.

Strachan turned his agitated horse in the enemy's direction, his black garments flaring out at the side. "You should do your duty and come with me now to save a few of our wounded."

"I need no lessons from you about duty, sir," Nelles replied tersely. "I have my orders."

"I could help, sir," Westlake interjected. "I'm no use here." Warman pranced to one side sensing Westlake's excitement.

Nelles pulled out his watchpiece. "Twelve-forty. Fine, be back here in an hour. Don't do anything foolish to get caught. And then let me know how far the enemy has advanced."

"Sir." Westlake saluted and rode off alongside Strachan in a strange turn of events. Only two short years ago, the man had thrown Westlake out of his school in Cornwall. Now the churchman and the secret agent rode together in common cause to save the wounded. Westlake was willing to work with the man he hated, but it didn't take long for Strachan to cause offence again.

"What do you do for Major Nelles?" he demanded, his stern voice already grinding on the lieutenant.

"Nothing that concerns you." Westlake would not be bullied.

Strachan glared at him, setting his lips in a tight line.

They'd almost reached Government House by the time he spotted a couple of wounded York militiamen assisting each other to stumble away. One was using his musket as a crutch while the other hobbled on one foot. A cannon blast crashed out from the garrison battery, the vibration reverberating through Westlake's shoulders. The arillery men then spiked their gun and ran to catch up with some retreating stragglers of the 49th Regiment. The enemy's gun fired in reply, and Westlake heard the ball zoom directly overhead.

"The York Militia have certainly done their part today," Strachan announced, viewing the wounded with concern.

"Remember that fact the next time they petition you for implements to work their land," Westlake replied. "I've heard nothing but complaints about you and your committees. It's a wonder they're prepared to fight for our side at all."

"God will damn your impudence!" Strachan shouted.

"Let's hope He saves these two fellows first." With bloodstained pants, one of the men leaned against a comrade who had blood trickling from a gash on his cheek. They limped and dragged their way forward.

Arriving at the eastern wall of Government House, Westlake bent over from atop Warman and reached into his bag for a small telescope. He could clearly discern several blue-coated officers standing in a cluster around the Half-Moon Battery, with spyglasses of their own. One officer sat down on a stump as the artillery fired from a battery of cannon set some ways behind them. The ball shot well above Westlake's head. Clearly, the enemy cannons had yet to find their range.

Westlake yanked his rifle from its ring and swung his leg over Warman to dismount. He helped each of the two wounded men into his saddle, one seated behind the other, and then handed the reins to Strachan. The cannons crashed out once again, and a ball smashed into the blockhouse mere yards away.

"Take these men to the Half-Way Tavern," he instructed Strachan. "And look after my horse there." He didn't wait for Strachan's reply before he slapped the clergyman's mount on the rear end and it bolted off with Warman trailing. Strachan tried to say something but could barely hang on. Westlake laughed. "Serves you right."

He turned back to observe a well-formed column of American soldiers that stretched down the road as far as he could see. Some men sat over to one side, but most lay flat trying to avoid the cannon fire from the garrison. A smartly uniformed general was giving directions, and it was clear to Westlake that General Sheaffe was outmatched.

Three men stood as an officer pointed them along the shore. They left the rest of the column, and Westlake watched as they reached the stony beach and then headed in his direction. An enemy scouting party, no doubt. They had travelled a hundred yards down the beach when Westlake raised his rifle, aimed, and fired. The sergeant leading them fell dead. Westlake turned to run.

He'd gone twenty paces before Captain LeLievre approached him at a run with Lieutenant Alex McMullen trailing. "We must blow the main magazine!" the captain shouted. "Orders from the general. Seems he forgot about the powder and shot falling into enemy hands. Three hundred barrels of it!"

Nelles had given Westlake orders to return immediately with his report, but at sixty years of age, LeLievre would have a tough run to beat the fuse to the barrels. "I'm with you," replied Westlake. "But there's enemy patrols approaching so we have to be quick."

The magazine stood about a hundred yards from Government House. McMullen had the keys in hand and opened the great oak door while LeLievre stood to one side, chest heaving. "Crack open two barrels," the captain ordered. A cannon fired from a schooner and grapeshot peppered one wall of Government House. "Hurry!" LeLievre urged. "The next shot could hit us directly and we'll go up with the damn barrels."

McMullen stove in the side of a barrel and a thick trail of gunpowder poured onto the floor. He did the same again to another barrel and crossed the powder trails so they connected. He rolled the second barrel away, spilling the powder as the barrel shifted. "A bloody shame, this is." McMullen gazed up at the ceiling's arch. "All our damn work, up in smoke."

Westlake helped him roll the barrel out through the door and along toward the beach. A long fuse was inserted, stretching a distance away from them. LeLievre drew a pistol from his belt. "Longer. Make the fuse longer," he said. "I need lots of time before it explodes." He pointed to the wrinkles on his aged face and grinned. Two cannons fired again from the schooners, one right after the other, the deadly balls plowing up the beach nearby.

"Here! Here! What are you up to there?" The small enemy patrol that Westlake had spotted leaving the column had approached within a hundred yards.

"Light the fuse," Westlake urged. "I'll deal these two fellows."

Captain LeLievre bent down and snapped the unloaded pistol. "Good luck to you, Mr. Westlake." The first spark didn't ignite the fuse. A second time, still nothing. "Third time lucky," he said. The pistol sparked. The fuse caught and hissed. The captain and McMullen darted away.

Westlake ran toward the patrol, brandishing his rifle above his head. "Run for your lives. The magazine's going to blow." He didn't stop when he reached them but kept running right toward the enemy column.

O'Reilly stared wide-eyed at McKnight. "Go after him," McKnight ordered. "He'll be our damn prisoner." McKnight glanced over his shoulder to see the other two men dashing in the opposite direction, away from sparks and smoke expanding on the ground. He ran.

The pair passed the dead sergeant and kept running. The prisoner stopped ahead once he saw the American column. He kept his rifle raised above his head in surrender. McKnight rammed him from behind with the butt of his musket and motioned for O'Reilly to take the rifle. "Your name?" The young man didn't reply but continued to march quickly along at McKnight's direction.

Their patrol had been ordered to have no enemy contact, but with their sergeant dead McKnight wondered what their reception would be when he reported to the officer in charge. The small group of officers parted to allow the prisoner through. The officer who had dispatched the patrol on their mission stood beside General Pike who sat on a stump.

"Our sergeant is dead, sir!" McKnight announced. "Caught blondie here lighting a fuse yonder." A crack of thunder shook the air and he swung around to stare along the beach.

"The main magazine is blowing, sir," the prisoner declared.

"What!" General Pike leapt to his feet. Then the ground began to shake. Everyone turned to stare at the explosion.

"Holy Mother save us," O'Reilly whimpered, gazing up at a giant fireball rocketing into the air.

"This is not good." McKnight's voice trembled as the sky darkened.

"My God!" Pike exclaimed in astonishment.

Something struck O'Reilly, pitching him violently backward. McKnight raised his arm in protection against a sky that now rained chunks of wood and fragments of rock. Something sharp struck his head, and he toppled into the prisoner.

24

· · · · · ·

WESTLAKE STARED UP at this rising balloon of yellow flame. The initial crash of the explosion had sounded like the crack of lightning directly overhead. Even at four hundred yards away, his legs shook with the ground's vibration, as if the earth itself had suddenly split apart. The officers around him crouched in alarm. The flame quickly turned into a rising gush of black vapour expanding larger than anything he'd ever seen. His first reaction was to run, but he couldn't take his eyes off the billowing cloud of heat and smoke.

Everyone kept staring skyward until the first rocks and rafters from the magazine hit the earth. Something struck one of his two guards and the man pitched sideways into him, groaning. Westlake dropped to the ground with the fellow's body sprawled on top of him. He listened to a storm of debris hitting the dirt all around him. His capturer jerked twice in silence under one hard thud after another. Men screamed and called out for help, as they were pulverized by raining timbers or bits of stone and clay. Finally, a wooden post slammed into the ground like a spear, just inches from Westlake's head. Then the unnatural storm ceased.

Westlake rolled his guard to one side and felt the man's warm blood on his own face. Cautiously, he sat up to look around him. Bloodied officers lay scattered about, their limbs at odd angles. A few men cried quietly to themselves, while others lay completely still. The entire surface of the ground appeared to be littered with the ruins of the magazine. Great shafts of timber, and boulders larger than a six-pound shot spread out as far as he could see.

"Bastards blew a mine," whimpered an officer directly behind him.

"General Pike's been hit!" another man shouted.

On the ground, Pike himself lay moaning. He rolled on to his back, his arms lying limp across his torso. "I am mortally wounded … my ribs and back are stove in." Any officers capable of standing rushed to his side.

"McKnight! What's happened?" The bewildered voice belonged to the other one of Westlake's guards. "Bill, wake up!" The comrade held McKnight's hand, but the injured man lay still on the ground. Blood pooled slowly in the dirt under an ear while his face had turned the colour of chalk. Slowly his eyes fluttered open.

"O'Reilly. Bad plan." McKnight managed a grin. "Standing close to officers is never good." His head lolled to one side and he was dead.

O'Reilly leaned forward, and rested his head on his friend's chest. He uttered a loud wail as he began to rock back and forth. "All his plans," he cried. "What will I do now?"

Westlake climbed to his feet, his shoulder paining him where the guard's head had struck. Aware that he needed to get away during this moment of confusion, he took a few cautious steps, expecting to be challenged. O'Reilly merely stared up at him in anguish, the tears streaming down his face. "I'm sorry," Westlake said.

An officer standing at least thirty yards away from the carnage shouted back an order for the Sixteenth and Sixth Infantries to form in column. "Come on, up, all of you! Let's charge these dogs." The men began to jump to their feet, uttering groans of outrage. Another soldier somewhere screamed out in pain.

The enemy was already preparing to advance on the garrison. Westlake picked up his rifle beside O'Reilly and crept his way down to the shore. Once out of sight, he began to run.

Where the magazine had once stood now remained a great black gaping hole. Columns of smoke drifted straight off the ground's surface, as if the earth itself was on fire. The heat emerging from the crater was like a furnace and didn't allow him to stand too close to the hole itself. Huge trees once standing nearby had vanished or were flattened, with their roots upturned. He began running full out again, hugging the shoreline, and didn't stop until well past the garrison.

There he slowed to a walk, trying to breath normally, before turning north to the Half-Way Tavern.

By the time he reached the tavern, more men were flooding into the streets, bloodied from the explosion. British troops were carried wailing to the upstairs rooms where a single doctor worked his miracles with a saw. The wall clock read one-forty, so he'd made it back within the hour Nelles had given. Sheaffe's general staff had long departed, as well as the Reverend Strachan. Tethered to a tree near the back porch, Warman tossed his head on seeing his master. Strachan had left him properly secured as requested.

Westlake mounted up and eased the horse into a gallop, heading east along King Street, in the hopes of catching up with the retreating army. A man and woman scurried along with their worldly goods on their backs, heading northward out of town. Another townsman drove a team of oxen pulling a wagon full of children. Otherwise the empty streets quietly waited for the invaders.

He had travelled only five minutes before being stopped by the Reverend Strachan and two militia officers coming in the opposite direction.

"General Sheaffe is running with the army for the Don River. Disgraceful," Strachan sneered. "It's the worst-planned battle that history has ever recorded. He's gone off and left the surrender of York to the local militia — and its citizens to the mercy of the Americans." Strachan spurred his horse and trotted off with his companions toward the garrison to find the enemy.

Westlake couldn't disagree and determined to catch up with Major Nelles. He galloped on until he reached Parliament Street, and the two red-bricked buildings that housed the government of Upper Canada. Captain LeLievre and Lieutenant McMullen careened around the corner on the horseback.

"You again!" The captain grinned. "Follow me, Mr. Westlake," he ordered, as he passed. "Our general has now forgot to burn the ships."

Westlake grimaced in disgust and turned his horse south toward the lake. After a five-minute ride they'd reached the beach and the shipyard. Captain LeLievre pointed to the storage sheds that surrounded the dry dock holding the giant hull of the *Sir Isaac Brock*. A little schooner, tied to a second dock, rocked gently only yards away. Westlake stared at a beach strewn with planks, cordage, tools, and even a wagon wheel. He peered up at the unfinished ship and remembered the men complaining about the slack pace of its construction. *They had been right all along, but neither Sheaffe or Prevost had reacted to solve the problem.*

"Break open those sheds, Mr. McMullen," the captain ordered, indicating two large wooden structures. "I want every oil lantern and all the cordage you can find carried into the hull. Mr. Westlake, chop some kindling out of these planks. You'll find an axe in the nearest shed."

LeLievre then rode to the other side of the dock, where a solitary building stood with chains across the doors. He leapt out of the saddle and seized a sledgehammer. With two roundhouse swings, the lock tore from its hinges and the chains fell to the ground. The captain disappeared inside.

Ten minutes later Westlake and the others had climbed the ladder into the hull of the ship with LeLievre carrying a bucket of black powder.

"Below decks, quickly!" he ordered.

McMullen had shredded some cordage and dropped it in a heap on the planked floor. Westlake now placed his armful of kindling on top and raced out with the lieutenant to bring up the four lanterns. Both he and McMullen made another trip to fetch more cordage and the axe. Westlake had broken the wagon wheel into pieces, and now threw it on top of the kindling. He next chopped at the loose planking lying about inside the hull, until there was a mound of extra firewood beside the unlit bonfire.

"Now, run the lantern oil as far as it will go down the length of the ship," the captain ordered.

Westlake and McMullen each tipped a lantern over, allowing the oil to spew out in two parallel streams as they walked away backward. LeLievre meanwhile poured his gunpowder on to the pile of cordage and kindling. With the empty lanterns, Westlake and McMullen returned to see the captain draw out his pistol.

"He'll have to snap to it," Westlake said straight-faced. McMullen grimaced at the pun.

This time the first snap of the unloaded pistol produced the spark that ignited the gunpowder. In a brief whump, the waiting pile burst into flames and smoke. Once the kindling caught fire, immediately the veteran captain threw on more cordage. "Mr. McMullen, bring some more planking. Mr. Westlake, check outside for anyone approaching. Go, now!"

Westlake climbed the companion ladder and leaned over the rail. He scanned the shoreline leading to the docks and saw no one, but when he looked farther along toward the garrison he noticed a sight that made him ill. The Union flag had disappeared and in a stiff wind the Stars and Stripes fluttered above Government House. *How did it come to this?* What about *Maple Hill?* He still had not been home to inform his parents nor had he reported back to Major Nelles.

At the far end of the beach, below the garrison, enemy soldiers were forming into a column. An officer pointed his sword toward the docks and the column marched off. Westlake's heart began to race. He had no more than ten minutes to make his escape. He dashed below to see the two lines of flaming oil speeding away from the fire. "Enemy approaching in column, sir," he shouted.

Captain LeLievre waved his arms at the smoke rising from the inferno blazing in the centre of the floor. McMullen threw on an extra armful of cordage and jumped back. Westlake followed by tossing the rest of the chopped planking into the flames. He could no longer see LeLievre clearly for the smoke.

"Up! Up!" the captain ordered. "With the tar in the planking it's enough. Now to the schooner." The smoke billowed up the companionway.

Westlake scrambled up the ladder with LeLievre directly behind him. He pointed to the enemy's direction. "That column's too close, sir. We're too late to burn the other ship."

"Fine. Our main job is done," LeLievre conceded, shaking his head. "They can have that little bugger."

Down the ladders they clambered and ran straight on to their horses. Westlake swung Warman around to take a last look at the smoking ship. *What a waste.* A blast of musket fire made him crouch as the balls smacked the hull above him. LeLievre and McMullen had spurred their horses and were racing ahead.

The enemy column must have seen the smoke and now they came charging along the beach. Westlake gave Warman his heel, and the animal lurched into a gallop. On the Sir Isaac Brock something collapsed in a crash, and over his shoulder Westlake watched a plume of smoke and ash rising above the ship. It would burn itself into a smoking hulk and the enemy would be denied their prize.

Sergeant Shaughnessy shoved open the door to the Half-Way Tavern and barged in, followed by a half-dozen riflemen. Lieutenant Tasker and Major Forsyth followed them. "Check both upstairs and down," Tasker ordered. "Make sure there are no weapons." He tossed his cloak over one shoulder and strolled into the barroom.

The table and chairs were pushed up against the walls, and on the exposed floor lay dozens of wounded soldiers. Redcoat lay side by side with bluecoat. Upstairs he heard a man call out, "Please, oh, God!"

Tasker pointed with his riding crop to a man on the floor. "Is that man dead?" he asked. A rifleman reached down, touched the man's neck for a pulse, and nodded.

"Drag him out for the burial wagon," Forsyth ordered.

Ignoring the screams and mayhem around him, the tavern keeper stood wiping off the top of his bar counter around a single lit candle.

"Barman, do you have *one* empty room?" Forsyth asked him.

The man hesitated. "Only my quarters behind the bar." He gestured with his head to the door directly behind him.

"That will do," Forsyth said. "Two tankards of ale and give each of my men a single drink too. Perhaps it'll drive out the damp."

Tasker opened the door behind the bar to find a bed and a small table with two chairs. At the head of the bed stood an open-faced wood stove. In the excitement of the day, the tavern keeper had not yet lit a fire. Now he scurried to put a candle to the paper and kindling, and within seconds the room glowed in the firelight. The man placed a few mid-sized pieces of wood amid the flames, then Forsyth took his candle and ordered him out of the room before closing the door.

"It's too bad about General Pike." Major Forsyth kept his expression serious. He glanced around the empty room. "There'll be no one to enforce his ban on looting now." He placed the candle in the centre of the table and sat down, gesturing for Lieutenant Tasker to take a seat.

Tasker eyed him carefully, knowing that there was more news to follow. The thought of pillaging the town had his attention. He lifted the tankard to his lips for a sip of the Half-Way Tavern's ale and to hide his growing smile. All day he had shot at and killed British soldiers, inflicting as much damage on the retreating army as he could manage. He plunked himself down and leaned back in his creaking chair, wondering about the nature of the real news that Forsyth was about to tell him. The clock chimed five o'clock and already the town was in a panic about the occupation.

To guard against a British counterattack, the army was surrounding the town with patrols. A platoon had been sent east to guard the bridge over the Don River. Those wounded by the magazine's explosion had overwhelmed the garrison's hospital so that the tavern's upper floor rooms were full of groaning men and their attendants. Tasker glanced at the ceiling, annoyed when a patient screamed.

The American army had taken over the soldiers' quarters in the garrison blockhouse. The holes in the roof caused by the shower of rocks would do little to keep out the rain, but it was still better than sleeping on a ship's open deck. No one had yet given him orders regarding the Rifle Company.

"With the regular army busy, someone has to protect the town's welfare." Forsyth shook his head and stared him in the eyes. "I know it's an imposition, but would you and your men mind looking after the town's property … keeping the riches safe."

Tasker realized he was holding his breath and now exhaled a deep sigh. "You're not joking, sir?" he asked, tilting his head. He took another gulp of ale and kicked impatiently at the straw under his feet.

Forsyth's face broke out in a wide grin. "The fools have just put the foxes in charge of the henhouse!" He pounded the table and chuckled. "The Rifles' orders are to ensure public safety — you know, guard the town's jewels and money." He pulled a folded sheet of paper from inside his breast pocket and spread it out on the table. A list of names and addresses appeared beside a map of York.

"Post guards at these locations," Forsyth said. The bottom of the page showed a single black star and the word *protection*. One at a time, Forsyth placed his forefinger over the black stars that marked storehouses and residences that were not to be touched. However, the long list gave the name and location of every officer and militiaman's home in York.

"But all of these houses belong to us!" Forsyth smiled, tapping his finger on specific buildings. "Remember that you and I divide the cash and jewels equally. And find us some damn horses so we don't have to go everywhere on foot." Forsyth motioned to the wood stove that had begun to dim.

Tasker stood up quickly and threw a couple of dry logs on the flames, all the while trying to remain calm. Riches awaited here, and there was nothing to stop him. He'd waited for this opportunity all his life. "Can I start now, sir? I really wouldn't want the houses of York to go without protection."

"Wait at least until the sun goes down. Then free everyone currently in the jail. Thereafter we'll direct any complaints toward the escaped criminals."

Tasker grinned and nodded his approval. Forsyth had carefully thought through the plan, and he felt confident working with such a professional. He surveyed the marks on the map. "We'll protect the stars first. No mistakes will be made, sir. All these names … " Tasker said in wonder. "I suppose the list is reliable and I shouldn't ask where it came from."

"It doesn't matter now." Forsyth shrugged. "The agent is uncovered and we've won the day." He grinned and raised his glass in a toast to their victory. "We had a man inside the garrison quartermasters providing a who's who. He's long gone now. He worked with others outside the garrison to transport his information across the border to Commodore Chauncey in Sackets Harbor. Hence this list." Forsyth laid his finger on a star.

Tasker scanned the list of names again. "Westlake! That's not —"

"His father. I said there were others who helped. What better than to have a fur trader whose people regularly crossed the border?"

"His son tried to kill us today!"

"So kill him if you catch him, but leave the old man alone. I'll go and pay a visit to this Maple Hill place myself. Give me Shaughnessy and a few men." Forsyth pointed to the star on the Westlake residence.

"Send the guards out in pairs," he continued. "Government House, these storehouses, this sawmill, the dockyard sheds ... those'll make the commodore happy. And once the sentries are posted, here is a good place to start searching for treasure." Forsyth ran his finger over the words *Frederick Street*. "The home of the receiver general, Mister Prideaux Selby. Should hold lots of government cash. Turn half of it in so Granny Dearborn can crow, but keep half for ourselves. I'm told he has a beautiful daughter who looks after him."

"I'll protect her, sir, as if she was my own." Tasker offered a sly laugh and pushed his chair back in place. He leaned over the map, running his eyes along the streets. "What about this clerk of the legislature, McLean on Toronto Street? He may have some cash too."

"Just the task for you. Make it your second visit — after you see the receiver's daughter."

"If she'll let me out of her embrace, I'll be there, sir." Tasker downed his ale and strode off to protect the citizens of York.

25

. . . . . .

WESTLAKE AND HIS COMPANIONS slowed their horses to a trot and he glanced back over the Don River bridge. As usual, traffic in the Don Valley packed the river that measured twenty yards across. Three canoes flew south with the river's current, while a dozen boats of various kinds, stuffed with belongings, paddled north against the flow. York's citizens were evacuating by every means available ahead of enemy soldiers.

Westlake stared back down a road lined thick with trees. A platoon of bluecoats marched into view, shouting obscenities that were lost to the wind. The Americans halted on the west side of the bridge and raised their muskets ready to fire. Westlake kneed Warman into a gallop around the next bend and crouched in the saddle just before the enemy let go with a volley that tore through the trees behind him. With Lieutenant McMullen in the lead and Captain LeLievre in the middle, the three men continued their ride to catch General Sheaffe's retreating army.

After a few miles they halted at the approach of a light company of redcoats. The 8th Regiment of Foot had arrived from Kingston too late to join the battle, but was now being used by Sheaffe as the rearguard. LeLievre warned them of the enemy platoon at the Don Valley bridge and waved them forward. The bulk of the British Army was not too far ahead.

McMullen spotted the stragglers first; men too weak to walk by themselves were supported under their arms by comrades. Most of them journeyed without coats or belongings of any kind. Three old grey wagons, loaded with wounded, jerked and bounced behind the main column, which was marching four abreast. Major Nelles rode slowly behind the wagons.

"I'll say my goodbyes here, gentlemen. It's been nice destroying everything in sight with you." Westlake saluted. "I have to report to Major Nelles."

"Snap to it, sir." McMullen laughed.

"Our pleasure, *monsieur*." LeLievre returned his salute. "*Merci*."

Westlake urged Warman on until he could ease in beside Nelles. The expression on the man's face told Westlake of his frustration. "I returned within the hour, as ordered, sir, after blowing up the magazine with Captain LeLievre. I believe that explosion may have killed General Pike with falling debris."

Nelles turned his head to look at him but did not speak.

"Actually, they have a great many wounded and are as mad as hell about it," Westlake added. "And then we burned the *Sir Isaac Brock*, sir, again with the help of the good captain."

"I'm happy you've had a fine day, Lieutenant," Nelles said flatly.

"It's not *so* great when the best thing you've done is blow up your own powder magazine and burn your own ship, sir," Westlake said. "Do you know where we're going now?"

LeLievre and McMullen rode by at that moment on their way to make a formal report to General Sheaffe. They saluted but didn't stop.

"Kingston, we're running away to Kingston," Nelles explained.

"I can't leave York, sir." Westlake tried not to sound insubordinate. "I want to go back to Maple Hill and see my parents before it gets too dark. Besides, you'll need someone to report on the situation here in town."

"I should have told you, but with all this it slipped my mind. The barmaid, Lucy Dunbar, has disappeared from the Jordan. First Puffer, now days later Miss Dunbar." Nelles held up his hand and snapped his fingers. "Just vanished. Hendrickson and Archer have gone into hiding as well. The four of them are connected, but I don't understand how."

Westlake tensed on hearing the news of Lucy's disappearance. "I'd say Puffer vanished in the wink of an eye, but I don't feel like being funny today, sir." Westlake turned his horse. "I should go."

"Don't get yourself killed. I have to stop at the Lynde Tavern in

Whitby to wait for the report of the rearguard. Good luck." Nelles reached over and shook Westlake's hand. There was still no smile on his face.

"Today's disaster is not your responsibility, sir. The blame rests with others."

"Major Givens often advised me to attack Sackets Harbor. My duty was to convince those *others*, as you call them." Nelles shook his head despondently.

"There is no honour lost in trying your best, sir."

Nelles shrugged and looked away, the discussion over.

"At least you have a warm coat for your journey, sir." Westlake unstrapped his coat from the saddle and handed it to him. "Many soldiers have no coats for the march. Give mine to Major Givens, please." Westlake saluted and coaxed Warman around toward York.

Well before he reached the Don River, Westlake had time to think about Lucy. He couldn't deny the physical attraction, but he wondered if there was more. In the crazy rush of events, sorting his emotions seemed impossible. Still, his guts twisted thinking of her under the control of Archer.

He swung north along a narrow trail that led up the east side of the water. The enemy patrols seemed content for now to use the river as the eastern boundary of their day's conquest. He remembered the shallow crossing where the waterway widened below the sawmill and proceeded there directly. Warman waded across the river without incident.

Heading north, now in enemy territory, he set his horse to a cautious walk. He felt for the old wound in his side, but the bandage held firm. His hand rubbed against something in his vest pocket. He drew out the key given him by Donald McLean as the man lay dying. *The papers and the money.* Then he spotted the bluecoats: two men standing at ease some thirty yards in front of the sawmill. A group of horses stood tethered to the trees outside the mill's front entrance.

Westlake slowly backed Warman away. Quietly, the horse moved south to reach an overgrown path that turned in a great semicircle away from the mill and toward Maple Hill. In the twilight with the wind at his back, Westlake encountered no more patrols.

He approached his home from the rear and dismounted well out of sight. The clouds had covered the moon and a thin rain began to fall. Westlake unslung his rifle and crept along Maple Hill's side wall. Again, two bluecoats stood at the bottom of the hill sloping up to the front entrance. He shook his head in disappointment. He raced around the house to enter through the back porch.

Westlake pressed gently on the kitchen door's handle and quickly stepped inside. All appeared normal with his mother standing by the table. "Where's Father?" he asked.

Elizabeth squealed. "Where did you come from? Thank God you're safe." She lunged out to hug him. "Look at your face. Where have you been cut?"

Westlake touched the dried blood on his temple. "Not mine. It's from the man who saved me." The familiar aroma of baking cookies reached his nostrils and he inhaled deeply. *Home.*

His mother dampened a cloth and wiped his face and forehead. "Some men came here looking for you. At first they were friendly, but your father ended up arguing with them." Her brow furrowed until the lines around her eyes made her look like she was about to cry. "What have you been up to, Jonathan?"

"What colour jackets?"

"Green. They're protecting the town. We even have two sentries down at the bottom of the hill." She gestured to the front window.

"Mother, they're the same men who robbed Aunt Evelyn and beat up Uncle Adam. They shot me at the farm." Westlake gripped his mother's shoulders. "Back in Ogdensburg, we placed sentries at the front of our friends' houses — allies or traitors, depending how you look at them, the same ones who sold us information. I saw sentries at the mill as well. So what does that tell you?" Westlake slung the rifle over his shoulder and stepped back toward the door. "Is it possible that Father is —"

"I don't know what to believe anymore," Elizabeth interrupted. "And where are you going now, in the dark?"

"You won't have to lie to Father if I don't tell you."

She held her hands out to the side. "I don't know where he is either." Her tired and drawn features reminded him of how she looked during the period after Brock's death. "Have you eaten anything since breakfast?"

He shrugged, feeling the pangs of hunger.

"Then at least have some soup and fresh bread." She didn't wait for an answer but set a bowl on the table and ladled it full of soup.

Westlake sat down in a chair, tore off a piece of bread, and began eating. In minutes, he'd finished and stood ready to leave. "Thank you for that and don't worry." He smiled to reassure her. "I know the streets of York even blindfolded." He closed his eyes and took two steps, then gave his mother a hug goodbye. "I'll be fine."

Lieutenant Tasker had spent hours sending off pairs of sentries to guard his list of protected sites. He organized two sets of relief so that each location received twenty-four hour protection. His men had found him a sturdy mare, and he departed to inspect Government House, the naval storage sheds, and the garrison storehouse. The more he could perform in order to endear himself to the major and commodore, the better his prospects for future promotion.

Riflemen marching in front of him led the way with two lanterns. The deserted streets, eerily quiet, remained in total darkness. The town felt like everyone in it had died during the battle. At each corner, Tasker slowed down to survey the side streets.

The shock of such rapid defeat had surprised not only the residents but also the victors. Exhausted from spending days on board ship, most riflemen happily bedded down in a dry bunk at the earliest opportunity. Near Government House, the unlucky burial parties of the Fifteenth and Sixteenth Infantries busied themselves with digging shallow mass graves for their fallen comrades. After reassuring himself that his sentries were in place to guard the protected sites as decreed, Tasker decided it was time for the more pleasant job of visiting the receiver general's daughter.

He passed Major Forsyth and Sergeant Shaughnessy on their way back from Maple Hill and learned from them that Jonathan Westlake had vanished. They assumed he must have fled with the retreating army. The major then ordered Shaughnessy to accompany the treasure party consisting of Tasker and three riflemen.

The drizzle continued until the lieutenant and the sergeant arrived at the two-storey framed residence inhabited by Mr. Prideaux Selby and his daughter. Tasker posted the three riflemen out in the street and then knocked loudly on the door. The sergeant stood ready behind him with a loaded rifle.

A minute later a woman's soft voice called out from behind the door. "Who's there?"

"Lieutenant Tasker, ma'am, of the United States Rifle Company. I'm here to post a guard outside your home and to ask you a few questions." Tasker breathed in deeply, straightened his jacket, and using the step, wiped the mud from the soles of his boots.

The door opened slowly, just a few inches, enough for Tasker to see a beautiful face.

"Really, madam, you have no need to fear," he assured her. "I won't let anything happen to you, you have my word."

The woman swung the door wide open and Tasker stepped into a small hallway. Liz Derenzy led the way into the parlour.

"Wait outside by the door, Sergeant," Tasker turned and ordered sharply. "Make sure there are no intruders."

He followed the woman into the warm parlour, where she indicated a chair by the fireplace. Tasker untied his cloak and sat down, wondering how he was going to begin. He folded the cloak across his knees. She smiled briefly and her face grew even lovelier. He gripped his riding crop, suddenly aware he was at a loss for words. Tasker could only grin foolishly at her in the silence.

"Well, Lieutenant, how can I help you?"

He regained his composure and blurted out, "I'm here to protect your house, Miss Selby. Criminals have escaped from the jail."

"Mrs. Derenzy, please." Liz held up her left hand to show the wedding ring. "I'm a married woman now."

"Ah, I would never leave my wife alone if she were as pretty as you." Tasker forced a smile wondering if he'd been lucky that day and perhaps shot her husband. The woman's expression remained impassive. He cleared his throat and continued. "Well, we have three men posted outside to guard your house. Meanwhile, I've been ordered to inquire about the funds and official papers in the care of the receiver general. Is your father at home?"

"He's ill and delirious." She gave a shrug and pointed upstairs.

"Sorry to hear that." He couldn't believe himself when he felt a reluctance in asking, "And the funds, ma'am?"

"Major Nelles and a troop of dragoons arrived and took most of it away, goodness knows where. I'm sure someone can tell you." The young woman stood up. "Mr. Westlake carried the rest in saddlebags over to Mr. McLean's. I'm making tea. Would you like a cup?"

"You mean, Jonathan Westlake?" Tasker stood up with her. She didn't back away. Unlike other women, this one seemed not in the least afraid of him. Suddenly, he imagined himself coming home to her and waking up beside her in the morning. He breathed in deeply.

"Yes. I've known him since he was a boy." She smiled to herself. "Let me take your cloak."

Tasker followed her to the front door. "Westlake carried the bags to McLean's house on Toronto Street?"

"You know it then." She smiled right at him and he could barely think.

"Thank you, I'll take that tea, if you don't mind. Just give me a second," Tasker said. She walked away from him as he opened the door. "Sergeant." The drizzle had turned into a substantial rain and the men had gathered under a tree. Shaughnessy came running.

"Up to King Street and back west." Tasker pointed. "Then north on Toronto. McLean's house is the framed building. Take a lantern and two guards. Bring back the money and whatever jewellery he has … all of it. Look for saddlebags."

"I can handle that, sir."

"And be careful, for Christ's sake," Tasker cautioned. "Leave Mercer here to stand guard."

The sergeant grinned and tapped his rifle. "Not coming with us, sir?"

"Still have work to do here," Tasker said, but there was no sly grin or hint of insincerity in his voice. He enjoyed the comfortable feeling of being with this woman even if only for a few moments more.

Westlake's shirt stuck to his skin under the sheeting rain. By the time he reached the periphery of York, the growing expanse of dark cloud made it easy to hide himself from an American patrol heading out of town. The enemy hovered there on the outskirts in anticipation of a British counter-attack.

Westlake took a trail leading down the back of Yonge Street's east side. Only once did he hear a cry, but otherwise silence prevailed. After heading far enough south, he cut over to Toronto Street and crept up on the McLean residence from the back. No light showed itself from the interior as he slipped around to the front veranda. He stood on tiptoes to peer through the window but all remained dark.

Westlake slid the key into the lock and pushed open the door. He remembered the writing table under the window to his right and took three steps in that direction, his outstretched hands feeling the way in front of him. *Leather. Leather straps.* On the same small table sat a pair of saddlebags. His eyes adjusted to the dark and he saw the outline of the bags silhouetted beside a several wine bottles. Westlake's hand searched through each bag in turn. On one side he felt sheaves of documents and on the other were government bills, as good as cash. Lizzy had said six hundred dollars worth.

Westlake unslung his rifle, threw the bags over his shoulder, and turned for the door. He took two steps and then froze still the instant he heard voices.

"Where is everyone, Sergeant?" the rifleman asked.

"Asleep — which is where I'm going after this," Shaughnessy replied. "Hold up that damn lantern."

"Door's open, Sarge," another voice said.

Shaughnessy, and two others. Three men in all.

"I can see that for myself."

Silence.

Westlake retreated two steps toward the table. The men outside had paused, obviously deciding what to do. A shadow moved past the window. He lowered his rifle, pointing it at the door.

Silence again. Shaughnessy wasn't sure what to do. *But he won't stand out in the rain for long.* Westlake tensed and tried to breathe normally. He couldn't tell if it was the damp or fear that sent a shiver running down his spine.

A rifleman lunged through the door with a lantern in one hand and a rifle in the other. He raised his rifle to shoot. Westlake fired. Both the man and his lantern were blown backward out the door. The gunshot echoed around the room like a cannon going off. Again there was darkness.

Westlake could hear nothing except the ringing in his ears. The saddlebags slid off his shoulders as he began to reload the rifle. He searched for some place to go but could barley see a few feet in front of him. His heart pounded in his chest. He looked back toward the window. Nowhere to run.

"Y'all get in there," Shaughnessy urged. "He's shot his bolt!"

"What if there's another? It's dark inside," the rifleman replied.

"Get in there, now!"

Before Westlake could reload, the silhouette of a rifle appeared around the frame of the door, followed by what must have been the second soldier. The man looked to the left of the room and Westlake crouched low. That faint sound of movement prompted the rifleman to fire in Westlake's direction.

The bang reverberated throughout the room, but the man's bullet sailed overhead. The room briefly lit up from the rifle's flame like it had been hit by a flash of lightning. The soldier hurled his weapon, at

Westlake, catching him in the forehead. He fell backward and pulled out his knife even as the man charged. Westlake could only see his approaching shadow and quickly moved to one side. He stabbed upward as the man flew by. The soldier cried out before slamming into the table. The wine bottles clinked and fell to the floor.

Shaughnessy stood in the doorway and fired his rifle in the dark at the source of the noise. The rifleman groaned and collapsed to the floor. Again, the brief flame from the end of the rifle lit the room, showing Westlake on the floor gripping his knife. He saw the surprise on the sergeant's face as he recognized his enemy.

"You again," Shaughnessy spit the words. "I'm going to gut you with your own knife this time."

Westlake rolled away from the table. In the enveloping darkness, Shaughnessy stood silhouetted in the open doorway. Westlake threw his knife and heard a thud. He jumped up and raced toward the sergeant. There was no need. The sergeant had fallen to his knees, clutching at the knife's handle sticking out of his chest.

"Bastard, I don't deserve this," Shaughnessy moaned as the rifleman lying by the table whined for help.

"You beat up my uncle, killed his dog, and shot me," Westlake said, standing over him. "Just a horse thief, a common criminal. Can you handle that?"

Shaughnessy keeled over flat on the floor. "You won't stop Tasker now," he gasped. Then his head rocked to one side, his body gone limp. Sergeant Shaughnessy was dead.

"We'll see about that."

The other man on the floor whined again. "Where's Tasker?" Westlake demanded. He picked up his stolen knife by Shaughnessy's corpse and yanked his uncle's knife out of the dead man's chest. Finally, he groped around on the floor for the two saddlebags.

"Bugger off," the rifleman rasped. "Oh God, I can't feel my hands."

"Suit yourself. In that case, I'm going to slit your throat." Westlake pressed the knife blade under the man's chin.

"Wait, stop!" the wounded man's voice was barely above a whisper. "The framed house on Frederick."

Tasker's at Lizzy's house? Westlake gripped the man by the shoulders. "How many sentries."

"Just Mercer." His voice was fading.

Finally, the man's body went still.

Westlake jumped up to grab his rifle laying on the floor where he had left it. He placed it with the saddlebags by the open door and stepped warily outside. The soldier who had taken the rifle blast in the chest lay face up on the porch. He dragged the corpse inside, feet first. The dead man and him were both about the same size, and Westlake stripped off his green jacket and put it on over his own. He then threw the fellow's rifle and shattered lantern into the house. Remembering the bottles of wine gave him an idea.

The key slid in easily to lock the door and Westlake mounted the sergeant's horse. From the outside, no sign of a struggle was evident. He took a deep breath, fastened up his new jacket — and galloped off to confront Lieutenant Tasker.

26

······

WESTLAKE RODE PAST Frederick Street to approach the Selby residence from the lane behind. He dismounted, tethered his horse to a tree, and crept along the side of the house. At the corner, he leaned his head out to scan for any sentries. The dying rifleman seemed to have told him the truth: only one man stood guard on the veranda.

"Mercer!" Westlake whispered loud enough to hear.

The rifleman jerked his head toward the sound of his name and raised his weapon.

"Mercer!" Under the light of a curtained window, Westlake stepped into view, waving the wine bottle above his head. "Y'all want some wine?" He pulled back into the darkness, and shivered in anticipation.

"Shh! Keep your voice down." Mercer glanced back to the Selby's front door and tiptoed off the veranda, heading to the side of the house. He rounded the corner. "Can't see my hand in front of my face here. Where the hell are you?"

Westlake pressed the bottle against Mercer's chest. The sentry took hold with one hand and Westlake stepped quickly to one side. With a full swing of his rifle, he clubbed the back of Mercer's head. The guard grunted and crumpled to the ground. Westlake crouched on his haunches and felt under the man's head. Blood oozed from the back of his skull. He hadn't meant to kill him.

"Sorry, fella."

He ran around to the front veranda steps, past Tasker's horse, and approached the front door. Westlake took a deep breath and pounded. "Lieutenant, Lieutenant Tasker," he called out in a hoarse whisper. "Come quick, sir!" He pounded again and repeated his words.

Seconds later he heard footsteps. The door jerked open.

"This better be ..." Tasker's eyes widened.

Westlake hammered the lieutenant's forehead with the butt end of the rifle. Tasker's knees buckled and he collapsed to the floor. The riding crop lay beside him. "I'll take that. Bastard." Westlake pushed the man's feet clear and shut the door. He reached down and pressed two fingers to Tasker's neck: the lieutenant lived.

Liz Derenzy rushed in from the parlour, her hands on either side of her face. "Mr. Westlake, what have you done? We were having tea!"

"Evening, Mrs. Derenzy. Have no sympathy for him. These riflemen killed our fellows today, including Mr. McLean."

"Oh no, no. It shouldn't be," she sighed in despair. "Such a good man."

"When the authorities come here looking for Tasker, tell them you sent him to McLean's house for the saddlebags you gave to me."

"That's what I did," she said.

"I thought as much." Westlake paused to look into her face. "Liz, he never stayed for tea with you."

"No." She shook her head.

"Stick to that story no matter what. The other men he came with are all dead. Do you have any rope?"

Liz stared at him for a moment and then nodded.

"One more thing, I'll take that cloak, thank you." Westlake smiled.

Having gagged and tied Tasker, he dragged him outside and hoisted him over the horse's saddle. He tied the unconscious man's hands and feet together under the horse's body, then did the same with the dead sentry on his own horse. Again the rain was pouring as he swung the boat cloak over his shoulders and slowly led both horses along the back lane leading out of town.

The rain proved a blessing that kept most of the enemy off the streets. Occasionally, he heard shouts of anger, but on this, the first night of occupation, Westlake guessed most soldiers were too exhausted to bother pillaging. If challenged, he'd say that the men on horse were returning drunk. In the darkness, he hoped it would be enough.

Westlake needn't have worried, for the streets and lanes were deserted. He swung wide, north east of York toward the waters of the Don River. Hugging the path along the riverbank, he led the horses to the back entrance of the sawmill. Around the corner of the building's north wall, he could see that the sentries guarding the gate had made themselves a lean-to of sorts. The roof probably leaked, but it was better than enduring open weather. Between cracks in the structure's wall, Westlake spotted the glow of a small fire.

Built on a hill beside where the river level dropped and picked up speed, the sawmill had two floors. As his father had shown him, the basement housed the gears and machinery of the water wheel that powered the blades on the cutting floor upstairs. Westlake dumped the dead man on the floor just inside the basement door before carrying Lieutenant Tasker inside too. He first secured the bindings on Tasker's feet and hands and checked the gag around his mouth. Then he sat him up, binding him to the main beam that supported the floor above. If the lieutenant woke up and tried to escape, he'd bring the entire building down on himself before getting free.

Westlake searched Tasker's breast pocket. He pulled out a page listing the names and home addresses of every official and militiaman residing in York. Across the top in scrawled writing read the words *Ours for the taking*. It seemed their houses and property would be plundered in turn.

However, according to a note on the page's bottom, those storehouses and sheds marked with a star were earmarked for protection. He spotted a star beside Maple Hill and the sawmill. The Americans were protecting property belonging to his father, a man who also collected intelligence for Major Nelles. He frowned and pressed his lips together. Could it be true that his father was a traitor: that he worked for both sides when it was convenient?

Westlake picked up a shovel and headed back into town, with the other horse in tow. From somewhere in the distance, he heard smashing glass followed by a shout. The drizzle had not let up for a moment. The rooftops dripped, the trees sagged with damp, but he splashed on through the puddles and shivered.

Well after midnight, he reached the McLean residence, where the dead men laid as he had left them. He piled their bodies on top of the two horses and set off at a walk for the cemetery. Burying parties had been working all day to cover up the dead. Most other men stayed well away from the digging, fearing they'd quickly be called to help shovel if they interfered.

A few minutes away, the Episcopal Church sat in a field surrounded by a farm fence. The cemetery behind the church was the safest place to bury the bodies of the enemy soldiers and meant he wouldn't have to make his way through town again. Like so many others had done that day, he started to dig.

By the time Westlake had finished filling in the joint grave and had ridden back to the sawmill, the light of a grey dawn began lighting the forest. Smoke from the sentries fire curled slowly above their lean-to. *Good, the American Army will protect me while I sleep.*

He opened the basement door and crept inside. The dead rifleman wasn't going anywhere and Tasker remained passed out, sitting tied to the beam. Wondering again if the lieutenant might be dead, Westlake felt the man's neck for a pulse. Tasker was still alive, but he'd wake with an awful headache.

Westlake returned to the horses and brought the saddles and the saddlebags inside. He cleared the workbench quickly and he threw a saddle up on one end of it for a pillow. He'd now been awake for more than twenty-four hours and felt exhaustion overtaking him. He climbed up on the bench and lay down with his loaded rifle across his chest. Immediately he fell asleep.

The Reverend Strachan, in his customary black robes, stood before the seated Major General Dearborn. The garrison wharf was an odd place for them to meet, but it had taken until Wednesday morning for the general to finally come ashore. A group of officers in greatcoats accompanied him, including Commodore Chauncey. The commodore offered Strachan a curt nod.

The looting that had been sporadic on Tuesday, the day of conquest, had started in earnest the following morning. Livestock and poultry rapidly disappeared. Riflemen had broken into one house and stripped it of clothing, jewellery, and one hundred and fifty dollars in government bills. A soldier was seen running along the street carrying two drawers while his friends trailed him clasping a bundle of women's clothes and a silver candlestick.

A light rain began to fall and Dearborn's party moved indoors to Government House. The general sat behind Sheaffe's former desk, and Strachan accepted a chair on the other side of it. The rain turned into a deluge, and both men looked up to the ceiling as if this was a sign from God.

Strachan gripped the edge of the desk. "We signed the terms of capitulation yesterday, but it remains incomplete on your side," he complained, his jaw clenched in anger. "If those terms are not signed immediately, we will not receive it. The delay is clearly a deception calculated to give your riflemen time to plunder, and as God is my witness, the world will know about it."

Dearborn did not reply forthwith. Indeed his expression appeared almost uninterested and his overweight frame didn't budge. Strachan judged him to be slovenly of both body and mind. Gluttony was a sin made much worse when many others had so little to eat.

"The magazine explosion injured and killed over two hundred of our men," the general finally responded. "We've been busy attending to them." Dearborn looked to the commodore for support, but Chauncey made no sign. The general sat up straighter in his chair and continued, "You then burnt the brig *Sir Isaac Brock* after surrendering, thus provoking the very same riflemen who should be protecting your town."

"Some of our own men died in that accidental explosion and we had no knowledge of the burning ship," Strachan pleaded. "But does this excuse your men stripping Elmsley House down to the bare walls? It's just a public library, for goodness' sake!"

Commodore Chauncey interceded. "I give you my word that any books stolen will be returned."

"Thank you, sir," Strachan said. "An honourable offer."

"On the other hand," Dearborn continued, "we have reports that some of your own people have been joyfully pillaging their betters. Don't blame the American Army for all the looting."

"What can you expect when your forces do not impose order on the disgruntled? This is your responsibility." Strachan replied. "We're currently moving the injured — your men as well as ours — from the garrison and into the town, where they will be better cared for. The surgeons, again yours and ours together, have worked all night in saving as many wounded as humanly possible." Strachan stood and glared down at Dearborn. He shook one finger in the air as he next spoke, a pronounced quiver to his voice. "God looks favourably on the compassionate, but otherwise on those who oppose his work."

"I'm told that Major General Sheaffe took York's two surgeons away with him, also a medical kit, and many of the medicines," Dearborn claimed.

"One surgeon returned with those same supplies to help the wounded of both sides," said the Reverend Strachan.

"Sheaffe is therefore completely ruthless or a bumbling fool," Dearborn declared with a wave of his hand.

"On that you have my complete agreement," Strachan replied. "However, don't think you can trifle with me. His conduct does not excuse your own." He began to make his departure without the customary goodbyes.

"Stop!" Dearborn shouted after him.

Strachan turned around slowly, his red face drawn taut.

"You'll have your terms of capitulation signed early this afternoon," Dearborn said. "Good day to you, sir."

The Reverend Strachan nodded his approval and left to supervise the wounded. Once outside, he scanned the remains of the blockhouse and barracks. Every rooftop in sight had craters, the effects of the exploding magazine. Most of these structures would have to be rebuilt. He wondered about the safety of the farm implements in the government storehouse on Gibraltar Point. He had not heard of local residents turning on their fellow citizens, as Dearborn reported, but it didn't surprise him. The devil worked his way whenever evil triumphed.

Major Forsyth spent the better part of Sunday afternoon scouring the town for Lieutenant Tasker. The man and his entire party were missing: three riflemen, one sergeant, and one lieutenant, gone, vanished with no trace. Mrs. Derenzy, the last person apparently to see Tasker alive, had reported that the lieutenant went off to the clerk's house, chasing the money she'd handed over to Westlake. Hers was an entirely believable story.

Standing inside McLean's modest home, Forsyth found some evidence of a struggle: a broken lantern on the floor, an upturned table, and a smear of blood by the doorway. Something had happened here, but no one in the neighbourhood admitted having seen a thing, or else they were lying. On the other hand, with the rotten weather and darkness, how much could anyone see? He scanned the ground by the front of the porch, searching for hoof marks, but the torrential rain had washed clean any traces that might have been there.

Mrs. Derenzy could be lying, of course, but he discounted that as unlikely. She had even found out who had hidden the larger chest of money given to a Major Nelles and now she was trying to have it returned. Old man Selby was clearly too sick to plan anything sinister. Forsyth couldn't think of any explanation.

Commodore Chauncey appeared in the doorway and held up his hand. "No need to explain, I've already heard."

"Strangest thing, sir," Forsyth said. "I'm baffled."

"Think they might have deserted, the lot of them, gone?"

"For six hundred dollars, sir? Not damn likely." Forsyth shook his head. "Sixty thousand maybe." Forsyth chuckled, knowing that for sixty thousand he himself might desert.

"What about young Westlake and this Maple Hill house?"

"Lad's been missing since yesterday morning. I could go and burn the place down," Forsyth volunteered.

"Half the town's gone missing since yesterday morning when the whole British Army retreated. And anyway, you'll do no such thing, Major," Chauncey ordered. "I meant to just question them. You will do well to remember that Richard Westlake provided those lists I've been giving you over the past few months. He's risked his neck to help us." Chauncey walked out to the veranda and down the steps to his horse.

"I did question the parents, sir," Forsyth pleaded. "They too claim they haven't seen their son since yesterday morning, and while the old man might turn the kid in, the mother would rather die first. I got nothing from her."

"It's likely that the son retreated with the army," Chauncey suggested. "After the big explosion, a fellow named O'Reilly in the Sixteenth reported a lad matching Westlake's description running along the beach back toward their army." The commodore mounted his horse. "By the way, Major, every stolen library book must be returned to my ship without fail. We're Americans, not barbarians." Chauncey saluted and wheeled his horse away.

Tasker and Shaughnessy missing and still no sign of the money. Anger welled up inside him. Forsyth didn't know what to do so he drew his sword and smashed the window with its point.

His officers had waited on the veranda while Chauncey was inside. Now that the commodore was gone, he turned to them, his faced flushed in anger. "I want every building not marked for protection stripped of valuables. And our men have to hurry. The terms of capitulation have been signed hours ago."

"What does that mean, sir?" an officer asked.

"That private property is to be protected," Forsyth replied. "So get on with it before the army starts posting sentries on every street. And break open the doors of that damn shed full of farm implements on Gibraltar Point. And leave them open. That'll set the citizen thieves on fire. Then we'll blame everything on them."

Wednesday afternoon Westlake opened his eyes to the sound of rain beating heavily against the mill's basement door. His stomach grumbled from hunger. He raised his head off the saddle and sat up to see

Tasker was still unconscious. The prisoner had toppled over from his sitting position and Westlake bent down to straighten him up. Inches from Tasker's face, Westlake jerked away as the man's eyes opened and glared at him.

"Christ!" Westlake blurted and stumbled backward. "You scared the shit out of me!"

Tasker made a grunt as if to speak and pleaded with a face contorted in pain.

Westlake sat up and placed the point of his knife under Tasker's chin. "I'm going to pull the gag off. Raise your voice just once above a whisper and I'll slit your throat as easily as you stabbed Willie's leg."

Tasker nodded and the gag slid off. "Water, please. Oh God, my head." The lieutenant bent forward as far as the bindings would allow. Westlake put a canteen to his lips and Tasker gulped down the water. He coughed and gasped a breath through his mouth. "Where are the others?" Tasker groaned quietly.

"Shaughnessy's dead and buried with the rest of them."

"But the town surrendered. You had no right, you bastard." Tasker's voice rose in protest and then groaned again from the pain in his head.

"Quiet, now. It's the second time your men have tried to kill me. Shaughnessy wasn't so lucky this time. You're fortunate I didn't finish you." Westlake spit the last words. He raised the canteen and Tasker took another sip.

"There's been no killing since the surrender — other than yours," Tasker added tersely.

"Very honourable, indeed. I guess you forgot to tell Shaughnessy and your men." Westlake offered a last sip of water and jerked the gag back over Tasker's mouth. He pressed the knife against the lieutenant's throat. "I'm going to be outside that door. Any sound from you will be the excuse I need to kill you. Understand?"

Tasker nodded.

Westlake stared out through the side of an upstairs window as he ate some bread and cheese he had taken from the family kitchen the day before. The two sentries hid out of the weather in their lean-to by the sawmill's gate. As he watched, one of the men walked out, unbuttoning his trousers, to urinate on a fence post before hurrying back inside the shelter.

Time now to bury the dead rifleman.

Westlake ran downstairs to the basement, hauled Mercer's dead body outside, and slung it over a horse. He picked up the shovel and led the animal north a quarter-mile into the bush, well out of the sentries' earshot. He dug, soon feeling the aches of yesterday's battle and his efforts throughout the night. Two hours later he was on his way, wondering where his parents might be and feeling guilty for not being home with them. As he rode and thought about his situation, it became plain that he couldn't stay at the mill very long with Tasker. The idea struck him that while he had supplies, travelling east was the safest course and he knew just where to head.

The clouds grew darker as the mill loomed ahead so that by the time he dismounted and peered out again through the upper floor window, he could barely see beyond the sentries and their makeshift shelter. All appeared calm. The rain descended in a torrent and then returned to a thin drizzle.

Westlake had just saddled the second horse at the back of the mill when the sound of voices rose faintly above the rain. He snatched up his rifle and pouch and raced upstairs to see that a group of men on horseback had joined the sentries, including a stout man wearing a white vest under his open green jacket. Major Forsyth slapped one sentry roughly on the side of the head and started toward the mill. Westlake almost flew down the stairs, slinging his rifle over a shoulder. He untied Tasker and heaved him over the nervous horse. *The saddlebags.* He darted back inside, grabbed the bags and ran out to the horses. Quietly, the animals started away.

The front door of the mill crashed open. Voices hollered, but Westlake couldn't make out what they were saying. Along the north trail heading into the bush, he urged the horses on faster, but Tasker slid off the saddle and fell to the ground, groaning.

Westlake jumped down again, pulling a rope off his saddle. "Make no sound!" he ordered as he threw the lieutenant over the animal and slipped the rope through the bonds on his feet and hands. In two bounds, he remounted and began spurring the horse onward.

Behind him he heard men at the mill's back door. They would soon see the hoof prints and know the way he was heading. Two minutes, that's all he needed to reach the river crossing. The darkness deepened to hide his escape, but the riflemen would be running for their horses by now. He pressed on and heard Tasker groan.

A minute later he heard the thud of the troop swinging onto his trail. Aware that the Don River to his right broadened and slowed its pace well north of the mill, Westlake decided to chance a crossing while he still had a good lead. The two horses entered the water, feeling their way cautiously in the darkness. Here the river was just more than a dozen yards across, but with the horses taking their time it felt like twice that distance. On the other side, the riverbank dropped low and he spurred his horse up and into the dense trees, easily hiding in the blackness beyond.

Westlake dismounted and quieted his own horse. Then he turned to Tasker's animal and stroked its nose. "Just stay quiet now," he whispered. He stepped around to inspect Tasker, whose eyes glared at him. The enemy approached at a gallop toward them on the opposite bank. He pulled up Tasker's head by the hair. "Give me an excuse. Please. I'll slit your throat if you make a single sound."

Westlake unslung his rifle and watched through the trees, his heart pounding in his ears. The other horses trotted by and then slowed to a stop. He looked back at Tasker and in warning held up his rifle like a club.

"Can you see him, sir?" a man asked. "I can't hear anything."

"I can't see or hear a goddamn thing," Major Forsyth replied angrily. On the other side of trees and the river, he was less than fifty feet away.

"Did he cross over, do you think?"

"I have no idea," Forsyth replied. "If he did, whoever it was is now long gone."

Westlake shivered, watching Forsyth's shadowy figure dismount. The major peered across the river right in his direction.

"Let's get out of this rain." Forsyth mounted his horse, but as the others departed, he remained there, staring and listening.

Westlake stood absolutely still, holding his breath, except for a glance over his shoulder at Tasker.

After five minutes in the rain, Forsyth swung his horse around and headed off south. Westlake himself waited another five minutes before moving into the bush. Trails ran along his side of the river too and one quickly revealed itself. He continued south slowly, peering into the dark for another path that led east. After a short distance he found it and was immediately on his way.

Riding in the dark meant slow going, but he kept up a steady pace, never quite believing that Forsyth wasn't in pursuit. After riding all night, by the time he hit the Lynde Tavern in Whitby in the early hours, he fell off his horse, exhausted. He had to drag himself up to knock on the door. In a few minutes, his old friend the barman opened it, still in his nightshirt.

"Not you again," the man protested. "It's five o'clock in the damn morning."

"Is Major Nelles here?" asked Westlake.

"Who wants to know?" Nelles stepped out from behind the barman with a pistol gripped in one hand. "My God, Jonathan, I didn't even recognize your voice. You're white as a sheet."

"Lieutenant Tasker of the Rifle Regiment." Westlake gestured with a thumb over his shoulder. "Probably has several broken ribs riding like that all night." Tasker was still wrapped around the horse, bound hand to foot. Westlake handed to Nelles the pages he took from Tasker's breast pocket. "Lists of names and addresses ... of everyone." Westlake felt himself growing faint. "You can guess how the bastard got them. God, I'm tired." He collapsed to the floor.

27

. . . . . .

RICHARD WESTLAKE WAITED in the sugar shack for the arrival of his two henchmen. He had dimmed the light to conserve oil on three of four lanterns sitting on the table. Thursday morning had dawned with continuing rain, and his irritation grew the longer Hendrickson and Archer remained late. He opened the door to the wood stove and threw in another split log, letting the escaping heat linger on his face.

Rumours swirled through York that the Americans had plans to evacuate the town soon in preparation for another attack somewhere along the lake. Before departing, they would burn Government House, the barracks, a blockhouse in town, and the storehouses — plans that suited the purpose of his sawmill. At some time in the future, he'd make a fortune on York's reconstruction. He rubbed his hands together for warmth, thinking of the money to be made.

Money! More than a million dollars' worth of food and military supplies seized by the invaders were now headed for their vessels anchored offshore. Commodore Chauncey complained that the ships couldn't carry all the loot. He even began distributing the garrison's barrels of flour and salt meat to the villagers, like a latter-day Robin Hood. The receiving citizens loved him for it.

For smuggling out those lists provided to the Americans by Puffer, Richard received an entire wagonload of supplies for himself, a few thousand dollars, and most important, protection for Maple Hill and his precious sawmill. Chauncey had even patted him on the back. He had a friend for life.

Richard thought back to their brief meeting just after the invasion. At first the commodore had railed about the ineptness of his own side. They'd lost the *Sir Isaac Brock*, one of the main reasons for attacking

York. But his tune soon changed when Richard explained that the giant sheds at the dockyard held all the material and more required to build two new ships. Chauncey had grinned from one ear to the other, declaring that his own ships would sail by the end of the week.

Richard nodded at the thought. He hadn't much time.

One last job.

Through the partially opened door, Richard spotted Hendrickson and Archer slowly trooping up the path to the shack. Both men carried muskets across their shoulders and hung their heads as they walked. Apart from Puffer and Chauncey, who were utterly reliable, only these two characters could identify him as a traitor. But they would die at midnight, after completing their last job. Richard picked up his musket, swung open the door, and stepped outside.

"Do you always have to point that thing at me?" Archer asked. He turned his head and spit.

"You're late ... again. Put your muskets against that tree and step inside," Richard ordered.

"Flints'll get wet out here," Hendrickson said.

Richard peered down the path behind the two men but could see no one trailing them. "Fine. Put them over your heads and come in."

"You're too cautious." Archer shook his head. "There ain't no one out here in the bush."

Richard ignored the comment and studied the trail behind them. "Lay the muskets here. Careful. You're going to need those lanterns."

"For what?" Archer asked. He flopped down in an old chair by the stove and stretched out his hands to warm them.

"Tonight we burn down the Parliament buildings," Richard announced.

Neither man moved, except Archer stared up at him from his seat. "We could face a hanging," he said.

"And the American Army is posted on every street corner," added Hendrickson. He rubbed at his neck where old man Forbsy had nearly slit his throat.

"They won't suspect men who are carrying their own lanterns,"

Richard said. "Make your way between the buildings … where they almost join. Use those lanterns to light up the curtains. Enter and leave through the side doors and no one'll know until it's too late."

"How much?" Hendrickson asked in a tone that suggested the reward had better be high.

Richard pulled out a folded page from inside his jacket and held it up. "There's a hundred dollars inside for you. When it's done, come back here for another hundred. That's more than a good year's wages for the likes of you."

Archer snatched the money out of his hand. "Double it," he demanded. "I'm risking my neck here to keep your damn sawmill busy."

Richard paused. He had no intention of paying the bastards the second half. His plan to murder them on their return meant such promises didn't matter, but he couldn't make it too obvious. "Why should I? That's fair pay for dangerous work."

"'Cause your mill will make thousands when they start rebuilding." Archer cleared his throat and spit on the floor. "Always need some place for those politicians to gather and yap." His pal Hendrickson laughed and spit like his partner.

The two men were quickly getting out of his control. "Hear me well." Richard pointed a finger at each man in turn. "Both those buildings had better burn. I'll be watching from a distance." Richard nodded. "All right, I'll have the three hundred ready on your return." Their meeting over, he gestured to the entrance.

The two men picked up their muskets and headed for the door.

"You're forgetting." Richard glanced back at the lanterns. This pair was dumb as tree stumps and he would be soon well rid of them.

For the second day in a row, Jonathan Westlake woke up in the afternoon, but this time to someone pounding on his door.

"Lieutenant Westlake. Wake up, man." The knocking continued. Major Nelles could be persistent.

"I'm awake, sir," Westlake called out.

"Splash some cold water on your face and get downstairs. I'll give you fifteen minutes. Count yourself lucky."

The lieutenant rolled over on one side, feeling the aches of his long journey. Last night and into the early hours of the morning, when he wasn't banging into trees in the dark, he'd travelled a good deal of the time feeling lost. Westlake shook his head in wonder that he'd even found the Lynde Inn and Tavern. He pulled on his pants before washing his face and hands. The basin's cold water jarred him, but now at least he could think clearly.

In his mind's eye, he could still see the face of Red George. "We protect their traitors," Westlake had asserted. "Our allies," Red George had replied.

Having seen enemy guards protecting Maple Hill and the family sawmill, there could only be one explanation. *My father is a traitor.* He clenched his fists. Just the thought of it made him feel ill.

Once he considered his father in this new light, it was easy to guess at the rest of the puzzle. Puffer had handed the intelligence to a go-between, probably someone employed by Westlake Trading. This trader, being a regular traveller, delivered those secrets to the other side.

The question formed in Westlake's mind as to where he owed his primary allegiance: to his country and King or to his family? The enemy seemed to know the name and address of every officer, administrator, and militiaman. His father must have turned over lists that even included the name of his own sister and brother-in-law, Evelyn and Adam.

Westlake recalled Major Nelles counting off the motives for treasonous behaviour: money, ideology, sex, and ego — MISE. His father easily fell into the first and last categories, for there was no honour in selling out one's country. *What did that mean, selling out one's country?* "Someone is telling tales," Aunt Evelyn had said. In this case, selling out amounted to turning traitor on one's neighbours and relatives just to save your own home.

Honour and *duty*, two common words that Sir Isaac Brock had lived and died by. Looking back on it, his death now seemed so foolish: a wild charge up a hill against unknown odds. It didn't have to end that way, but Brock had stayed honourable to his life's finish.

Westlake considered the similarities between Brock and his father, both men fighting for their separate causes — one risking everything for his country, the other for self-interest. It wasn't his father he hated so much as the injustice that the man had caused. He remembered the terror in his aunt's eyes and the broken dishes scattered on her kitchen floor. As if he were watching again from that window, he saw those militiamen prisoners of war marching through the main street of Elizabethtown, their hands held over their heads. His father surely couldn't have realized all the consequences that his treason had set in motion.

Westlake's duty to his country and family forced him to oppose and fight his own father... but how? His own battle was for justice. To fight against his own family was to do his duty *for* his family.

I need proof that he's a traitor.

Westlake suddenly remembered the saddlebags of official papers and the six hundred dollars. The beginnings of a plan formed in his mind. He'd reveal all to Major Nelles, calculate the odds and reduce the risks — no reckless dashes. He reached for his boots, so excited he could barely hold a thought in his head.

Unlike the other hostelries in York, the Jordan Hotel's owner had refused to take in any wounded prisoners. That business decision made perfect sense to Richard Westlake for now the barroom stood packed with evening customers clamouring for spirits. His pocket watch read ten o'clock. Time for him to go.

After consuming a single mug of ale, he departed the hotel. Its proximity on King Street to the Parliament buildings suited his purpose. He squeezed past the five armed guards of the Twenty-first Infantry standing under the porch, out of the drizzle, and wished them goodnight.

Richard coaxed his horse a block south and waited in the shadows of the trees surrounding a small field. He shivered and hunched down inside his fur coat. From astride his horse, he had a clear view of the two target buildings where Hendrickson and Archer were due between ten o'clock and ten fifteen. By eleven o'clock, however, there was still no sign of them.

He peered over his shoulder to check for approaching patrols but found none. If passing guards scanned the field carefully, they'd discover him and he'd need an excuse for lingering there. Just taking a piss, he'd say and hope they wouldn't interrupt his two conspirators from their activities across the road.

Well after half past eleven, he spotted the four lanterns swinging up from the beach. Arriving late as usual, Hendrickson and Archer were singing some filthy song as they staggered along, obviously drunk. It seemed they were already spending their reward money before they finished the job. Richard's body went rigid when he saw the two American sailors singing along with them. His horse shifted forward a few steps under the pressure of his knees. *Christ, what were the bastards thinking?*

The four of them reached the gap between the buildings, surveyed the area in front and behind them, then disappeared into the alley's darkness. Richard held his breath, anxiously, praying that they'd find the side doors. Almost immediately, the five soldiers from the tavern turned the corner just ahead of him. He waited to hear a smashing of the lanterns that would alert the patrol, but no sound came from inside the buildings. The guards moved on quickly past his darkened field to return to the comforting shelter of the hotel.

Wondering what was causing the delay, he gripped the reins tighter, fearful that they had been found out. They'd spill their guts to the authorities in an instant and blame him. Finally, he heard a faint smash, then two more. Seconds later, four figures appeared at mouth of the alley. The two sailors set off running back toward the lake, while the other two dashed across the road into his field.

Hendrickson and Archer were running right toward him.

He stepped his horse forward to intercept them. "What the hell are you doing coming near here?" he demanded.

Both men hauled up, breathing heavily. "Didn't know you'd be here," Archer puffed. "Give us our money now."

Richard stared over at the targeted buildings where, except for a few traces of smoke, nothing unusual could be seen. "You were behind time again so it's too late to meet at the shack now. First thing tomorrow morning, eight o'clock sharp, and make sure you're not followed." Suddenly flames followed by billowing smoke shot out through the shuttered windows. Richard smiled on seeing what he'd been waiting for. York's legislature would need a new building, and his mill would make him another fortune. But for now, he had to get away.

"We're drinking late tonight," called out Hendrickson. "Eleven's better tomorrow." He slapped Archer on the back as they headed off.

Richard spurred his horse on, glad to get away from them. *Suit yourself. You can die at eleven as easily as eight.*

Lieutenant Westlake reached the relative safety of Maple Hill just as the last curve of the sun's red ball dipped beneath the treeline. It had been a long ride here from the Lynde Inn and Tavern, and he couldn't help but think how easier it was riding in daylight. The aches and stresses of the last few days had wearied him and now, most of all, he needed a good night's sleep.

The sentries remained posted at the bottom of the long path leading up to Maple Hill's front door. He smiled, thinking it odd that the enemy protected the very man they searched for. Westlake crept in through the back door, clutching the precious saddlebags, to find his mother bent over the kitchen table. "Hello, Mother."

She jolted upright. "You have to stop scaring me like that. How did you creep in so quietly?"

Westlake grinned and pointed to his bootless feet. "Boots covered in mud so I left them in the porch." He sat down at the table.

"I have some roast pigeon and fresh bread ready for your father, but he won't be home till later." She prepared a plate and slid it in front of him, then wiped her hands clean on her apron. 'I'll make you some hot tea; that'll warm you up."

Westlake slowly gazed around the kitchen. "My God, it is good
to be home." He broke off a piece of bread and put it in his mouth.
"Where's Father?"

"He doesn't tell me such things anymore, only that he'll be home
later." Elizabeth replied. "You were right in what you said. Ours is
one of the few houses the Americans protect. Something *is* suspicious
about that, but he won't tell me anything." She turned away, hiding
whatever emotions showed on her face. "A Major Forsyth and some of
his men were here looking for you, again."

"It doesn't surprise me," Westlake replied. "I'm leaving at first light
for the sugar shack. I have saddlebags the enemy is looking for …
official papers and six hundred dollars. Tell father that after I've gone."
Westlake continued eating calmly, as if it was an everyday request.
"We'll see how he reacts."

Elizabeth poured him a cup of steaming tea and then leaned back
against the cupboard facing him. "You want me to deceive my own
husband … your father. He could be violent with you and he'll have
other men to rely on as usual."

Westlake let the disappointment settle over their conversation as
he reflected on what to say next. "You will not betray him; if he's
working with the Americans he'll betray himself. As for violence …"
He took a sip of scalding tea and looked at his mother with the same
emotionless expression he'd worn before he had killed Shaughnessy.

His mother stood up straight, not quite alarmed, but unsure.

"Don't worry about me, Mum."

She walked over to where he sat and put a hand on his shoulder. "If
anything ever happened to you, I would die myself."

Westlake reached up to pat his mother's hand. "I have to bed down
Warman." He sipped some of his tea and stood. "And I can't wait to
sleep in my own bed again. Thanks for this, goodnight." He gave her
a hug. "Don't forget, tell Father about the bags as soon as you wake."
He slipped out through the back door.

Before first light, Westlake woke to the weight of his thick quilt
twisted around his feet. All night he had turned in his bed, dreading

the day to come. He yawned, burrowing deeper under the blankets. His emotions wavered as he anticipated the day ahead. The excitement of catching one or more of Brock's traitors was counterbalanced by a reluctance to find out the truth about his own father. In his letter, Brock had surmised correctly that there was a network of traitors in York working closely together. Reading the dead general's note now seemed so long ago.

Westlake forced himself out of bed and he dressed in a hurry. Over his buckskins, he put on his everyday homespun garments. His old knife with the foot-long blade he sheathed and strapped to his boot. He jammed his uncle's knife and a tomahawk through his belt. The pouch of rifle balls swung over his left shoulder. By the time he threw on a fur coat, slung the saddlebags over his other shoulder, and picked up his rifle, he had become a walking armoury. On his way through the kitchen to the back door, he spotted his father's riding boots beside his own and wondered what he'd been up to the previous evening.

Westlake rode Warman out of the barn and headed north. His hands gripped the reins too tight and his chest felt like it was held in a vise. He began to hope for some wild explanation that would absolve his father from any crime or dishonour.

The sun lit the trail briefly until strong winds and building clouds brought back the inevitable drizzle. The three-mile ride offered time to think what to do if his father's behaviour *was* treasonous. Giving him up to be hanged was hardly an option. Better to banish him from Upper Canada to his American friends farther south. There were worse fates than that, and his mother would still have a husband and he himself would keep a father.

Westlake caught the whiff of a fire long before the sugar shack came into view. Clearly someone had got there ahead of him and lit the wood stove. He nudged Warman eastward and circled the building before dismounting a hundred yards north of it. A thin ribbon of black smoke curled up from the shack's chimney as he crept through the trees and descended a slight incline to the rear.

His heart drumming in his chest, a few paces from the back door, he crouched down and surveyed the forest around him. Everything held still except for the brisk wind. A few damp leaves turned over on the ground, but he saw no one except a horse tethered to a tree in plain sight. The animal shifted sideways, sensing danger from this prowling visitor.

Obviously the intruder inside the shack felt no fear of discovery, and Westlake tried to figure who it might be, friend or foe. The only person who even knew he'd be coming here was Major Nelles, and he doubted the major would light the stove. A crow squawked directly overhead, breaking the silence and making him jump. He hesitated, wondering.

Westlake loaded the rifle and stepped up quietly to the back door. He couldn't believe his ears as he listened to the occupant snoring. The wooden latch lifted without a sound, and the opening door produced only the barest creak as it swung to one side. Westlake stepped inside, the rifle to his shoulder ready to fire. He drew in a sharp intake of breath.

Lying on the bench before him, Sergeant Puffer slept.

28

......

RICHARD WESTLAKE WOKE to sunshine streaming through the bedroom window and the sound of rustling at the back of the house. He had returned to Maple Hill well after midnight, while the rest of the household slept. Tempted to wake his son, he decided that his own sleep was more urgent and that any questions could wait until morning.

Now, listening from his pillow in the early light of dawn, the sounds from the back door made him curious. The sentries at the bottom of the hill had their instructions to let no one pass. Daily rations of rum encouraged them to protect his interests, and he felt assured that no pillagers would be allowed on the path to his house. Richard sat up in bed, straining to hear.

The sound of departing horse hooves faded away through the log walls. He leapt out of bed and rushed to Jonathan's room to find him gone. "Christ, that lad tries my patience."

By the time he returned to their bedroom, Elizabeth was sitting upright and gave a small yawn. "Morning," she said.

"Your son's already left for God knows where," Richard replied. He didn't return her greeting because already this didn't feel like a particularly good morning. Elizabeth stared at him impassively and, those blue eyes no longer kind and loving, made him feel like a stranger to her. "I should have spoken to him last night."

Elizabeth slowly laid her head back on the pillow and faced away from him. "He's taking saddlebags of documents and six hundred dollars to hide at the sugar shack." She drew the covers up around her.

"What! Why didn't you tell me earlier?" Richard demanded as he began pulling on his pants.

"When? You weren't here to tell. Anyway, why do you care?"

"Half the bloody American Army is looking for those damn bags, and the other half is looking for him. It's a wonder they didn't break down our door in the middle of the night." Richard buttoned up a shirt and pulled on a pair of socks. "An entire patrol sent to look for those bags is missing. Your smiling son may have killed them all. Do you know anything else?"

Elizabeth rolled on her side and closed her eyes. "Makes sense then that he wants to hide them," she said, uninterested. "I just hope he's careful."

Richard greeted her comment with a dismissive wave from the doorway. At the back door of the house, he jammed both feet into his mud-caked boots and picked up a musket. His son carried the very saddlebags that had driven Major Forsyth into a frenzy. Any citizen that returned them would be a hero.

Puffer would have slept at the shack, waiting to carry out their plan to kill Hendrickson and Archer. But, if Jonathan had really wiped out an army patrol, he'd have no hesitation in killing the quartermaster. On the other hand, what kind of reception would the sergeant give his son? Puffer would be prepared to eliminate the lad if Jonathan threatened his life.

Richard shook his head. He should have brought his son into the game long ago. Now all this could go terribly wrong. The thought of losing Jonathan would mean the end of the world as he knew it. He put a hand to his forehead, realizing that Elizabeth would leave him. *Damn the boy!*

And the last thing he needed was a bloody commotion to scare off his unsuspecting prey. The thoughts tumbled through his mind. How loyal Puffer would stay if he found the money in those saddle-bags? *Christ, that's half the value of my sawmill.* Richard spurred his horse into a gallop. He needed that money for himself, for his mill, then he'd shoo Jonathan away and kill the two bumbling accomplices when they arrived. Finally, like a hero, he'd turn the bags and their papers over to Forsyth. Maybe this would turn out to be a good morning after all.

Jonathan Westlake remained standing in the back entrance, rifle in hand, scanning the sugar shack's interior. Two large vats stood against the one wall. The wood-burning stove threw off enough heat to warm the single large room. Other than the snoring Sergeant Puffer, no one presented themselves. A musket rested against the wall right beside him. He grabbed it by the long barrel and leaned it between the two vats.

Except for his heaving chest under the blanket, Puffer hadn't shown any sign of movement. The man must have felt himself safe here, to fall asleep without protection. Such was the relationship between this traitor and his father. Westlake fingered the knife in his belt, considering whether to simply slit Puffer's throat.

Puffer, Hendrickson, Archer, all missing ... and so was Lucy Dunbar. *Where was she?* In case he had answers, Puffer would live for now.

Westlake stared down at Puffer's face, wondering what would make a long-term sergeant in the British Army betray his fellow soldiers. The usual: money, ideology, sex, ego? Puffer was too base for ideology and ego. That left money and ... a sharp intake of breath seized him when an idea struck that made his stomach churn. He turned his head at the faint sound of galloping hooves. His father had taken the bait.

Westlake crept outside to grab the saddlebags off Warman. He re-entered the shack and stood in the gap between the two vats, directly facing the back door. Puffer continued to sleep on the table to his left. Westlake stared at the back door and then dropped the saddlebags at his feet. As the horse stopped outside the front entrance, the rider jumped to the ground and ran around to the rear. Westlake gripped the rifle tightly to his shoulder.

Seconds later the back door flew open to reveal Richard Westlake, musket in hand. His eyes cut to the saddlebags on the floor and then to Puffer still asleep on the work bench. "I want those bags." His father glared at him.

Westlake inhaled in slowly. "Put the musket down, Father." He aimed the rifle at his father and felt his hands tremble. *I must be near crazy. This is my father.* "Your friend and I have been waiting for you. Move up next to him, if you please." The sergeant had stopped snoring.

Richard chuckled, his hard lips curling into a sneer. He leaned his musket against the wall by the door and walked over to Puffer. "What will you do, shoot me, or turn me into the authorities?" Richard laughed again. "Put the rifle down."

"You were off in Europe too long, Father." Westlake kept his own face impassive, looking on the man as a stranger. "I *am* the authorities."

"And your duty to your own family?" His father's expression turned sombre and he grabbed Puffer's shoulder, shaking him, "Wake up."

"You've been identifying militiamen and their officers to the Americans, for their little raids. Your own brother-in-law was on those lists. So which family are *you* protecting?"

Puffer began to stir. Sensing the danger, Richard gave him a hard shove. "Your Uncle Adam was a mistake. Mistakes happen in war. You have a duty above all to your mother and me, Jonathan."

Westlake thought of Willie Robertson, dying in the street, then of old Forbsy, and now Lucy Dunbar. "I have a duty to justice."

"What the hell?" Puffer sat up suddenly. He saw Richard first, then stared at Westlake with the rifle. "Where'd you come from?" He winked involuntarily and climbed down from the bench, eyeing the musket by the back door.

"You'd never make it, Sergeant, and I'd have a good excuse to shoot you," Westlake said. "Where's Lucy Dunbar?"

"Go to hell!" Puffer shouted, then winked.

"I won't ask again," Westlake said quietly. He held the rifle steady in his left hand, his anger rising. Winky's insulting manner grated on him like a sword scraping against bone. The sergeant laughed again. In one swift motion, Westlake pulled the long knife from his boot and threw it hard.

Puffer screamed and dropped to the floor, the knife sticking straight out of his left arm.

"Christ almighty, Jonathan." Richard bent down to help.

"Don't touch that knife," Westlake ordered his father. He pulled the other knife from the sheath in his belt. Puffer groaned. "Still think it's so funny, Sergeant? You have three seconds to tell me Miss Dunbar's location or die. One, two —"

Richard stood up and took a step away. "A mile straight north of here. You know the place ... the original sugar shack."

"You knew!" Westlake exclaimed. "You're as disgusting as this filthy excuse for a human being. Don't ever speak to me again about honour and duty." He slid the knife back in his belt.

Richard pulled the blade from Puffer's arm and tossed it on the floor to Westlake's feet. He tore a strip from Puffer's shirt and tied it around the wound. "I did what was necessary to protect Maple Hill and our family," Richard shouted, shaking his fist in the air.

The back door facing Westlake burst open. Hendrickson lunged through the entrance and swung around with a musket. Westlake pressed his rifle's trigger. It seemed as if time stopped, waiting for the weapon's firelock to snap forward, the frizzen to open as flint and steel sparked together to ignite the powder and propel the ball down the barrel.

It took only a second. The bullet's impact lifted Hendrickson off his feet, pushing him back out the door. The blast left Westlake's ears ringing when at the same time, the front door banged open too. Archer stood on the threshold, with a musket to his shoulder. Westlake tensed to leap but the musket spit flame and ball. Richard bawled out a painful cry. Another shot cracked from somewhere outside, and Archer grimaced.

Westlake dropped his rifle, tugging the tomahawk and knife from his belt. He lunged at Archer, hooking the musket to one side and stabbing into the man's belly. The weapon fell easily from Archer's hands and his limp body collapsed to the ground. Twenty paces behind him, visible now through the open front door, stood a man in civilian clothes.

Major Nelles held his musket raised, smoke trailing from the tip of the barrel. "Afraid I've arrived too late," Nelles called out.

Lying motionless on the ground, Archer's eyes stared up blankly at

Westlake. He reached down to feel for a pulse in the man's neck and pulled back on his knife. Archer was dead.

Westlake turned to see his father slumped on the floor. Horse hooves began to pound away. Puffer was gone through the back door and with him went the saddlebags.

Westlake dropped the tomahawk and rushed to father's side to support his head. "No."

Richard moaned and stared up at him, his face flushed.

"Why, Father?" Westlake asked in despair.

"They came too early for our meeting. I was the only one who could identify them as traitors," Richard whispered. "Puffer and I would have killed them both if not for your interference."

"I meant, why did you start down this path?" Westlake pleaded, gripping his father's hand. Nelles came running into the shack to look down over Westlake's shoulder.

"Ah, the British Army has arrived to save us." Richard moaned again. "My lungs are filling. I can feel the blood." He coughed and raised his hand to touch his son's arm. "The sawmill is our future."

The hand slid down Westlake's arm. His father tried to say something more and Westlake bent over to hear.

"Tell your mother ... tell," Richard's voice whispered, "tell your mother ..." He closed his eyes and his hand fell out of Westlake's grasp. If he died, Westlake would have to take the news to his mother, and he wondered how she would react. He leaned forward to hear barely a sigh in his father's breathing.

Westlake stood up and glanced at Hendrickson and Archer lying dead on the floor, one man in each doorway. "They came here to kill him, not me."

"They got what they deserved, Lieutenant," Nelles replied.

Westlake felt the urge to throw up as he stared at his father. "This has all gone so wrong." He shook his head. "Please stay with him, sir. I have to go." Westlake wiped the blood off his knife on Hendrickson's coat and sheathed it. He picked up his tomahawk and rifle. "I know where they hold Miss Dunbar, sir. Puffer could kill her."

"Be careful, Lieutenant," Nelles ordered, holding Westlake's shoulder. "Puffer knows he'll hang so he has absolutely nothing to lose."

The horse galloped hard, the wind lifting Westlake's hair behind him. Every time he rode to the old sugar shack, he remembered the freedom of a young boy riding away from his parents' supervision. Today that feeling of elation disappeared with the thought of his father's imminent death. Weighing heavy on his mind and heart was the realization that he would have to tell his mother. His chest ached, he could barely swallow, and he prayed it wasn't too late to save Lucy Dunbar.

Westlake slowed Warman to a walk as soon as the small shack came into view. No smoke swirled up from the old chimney pipe. He scanned the trees around the building: nothing. No sound, not even a horse. He dismounted and tethered Warman to an old maple tree. The forest floor, soft with damp leaves from the previous fall, muffled his approach on foot.

Before touching the door handle, he crouched down and peered back into the forest. It seemed just like Puffer to sit there somewhere among the trees, waiting for a clear shot at his pursuer. Westlake carefully surveyed from tree to tree but could see no one. He stood upright, stepped to one side, and yanked open the door.

A stifled whimper greeted him. Westlake peered around the doorframe to see Lucy all alone in the room, bound and gagged on a bed. Her torn blouse revealed a naked breast and her face was bruised and streaked with dried tears. He took one last look over his shoulder before stepping inside and closing the door.

Westlake quickly drew his knife and sliced through the cloth gagging Lucy's mouth. She gave an audible sigh, then dropped her chin to her chest as Westlake slit the bonds restraining her feet and hands. Immediately, she yanked up a blanket to cover herself. He sat down beside her on the bed, cradling her in his arms, wondering what to say, feeling her body shiver against his chest.

"I don't want you seeing me like this," she sobbed.

"You're safe now. They're all dead, Hendrickson, Archer, probably my father too … all except for Puffer."

At the sound of Puffer's name, Lucy gripped him closer. "You warned me to stay away from them in the beginning." She cried and coughed. "I'm sorry. Now look what I've done to myself." She turned her head away from his chest to stare at the floor.

Westlake took hold of her shoulders and held her away from him so as to look directly into her eyes. "You did what was necessary to survive," he said. Lucy wouldn't look at him. "There is no shame in that. We must leave this place now. One day, you can come back here and burn it to the ground."

Lucy rode on Warman while Westlake walked in silence back down the path leading to the newer shack. Major Nelles had dragged both the dead bodies inside in order to close the shack doors. He'd begun digging a grave.

"My father?" Westlake asked.

"Gone." The major shook his head and quietly added, "I'm sorry."

"Oh no." Even though he had expected it, Westlake couldn't believe his father had really died. The man had filled such a large space in the world, his plans so intense. It was difficult to believe his life was ended. Westlake held back his tears, surprised at his own emotions. And what of his mother? He wanted to go home.

Westlake asked Lucy to stay astride Warman, not wanting her to see the corpses. He stepped through the back entrance to the cabin to see his father lying still. Nelles followed him and closed the door.

"Puffer?" Nelles whispered.

"Vanished, sir."

"Then he's travelled twenty miles west by now," Nelles reckoned. "You'll not catch him today."

"There will be time for Sergeant Puffer on another day, sir," Westlake said with assurance. "He may have gone straight to the enemy, but I doubt it. His arm's bleeding, and most of all he wants distance between us right now."

"Still, we should leave here quickly" — Nelles rubbed his chin — "just in case he's informed the American authorities."

"We have time, sir." Westlake shook his head in disagreement. "He'll need to hide that money before he approaches the enemy. My guess is he'll make for the border first. Let's dig. I can't risk taking my father's body back home with the Americans now crawling all over York." He grabbed a shovel leaning in the corner.

As Westlake dug, his anger rose with every shovel-full of dirt. What a waste of lives. When the pair of graves was deep enough, the two men rolled the bodies of both Hendrickson and Archer into one of the graves and covered them. On the far side of the shack, Lucy stayed silent.

Westlake returned inside to carry his father's body out to the second grave. He lifted Richard's head and shoulders while Nelles gripped the legs and feet. It reminded Westlake of holding Brock's head in his hands as they had slowly descended Queenston Heights. Then, there had been a sickening sense of loss and sadness that churned his stomach; now, only anger and remorse invaded his heart at the stupidity of his father's actions.

Westlake carefully lowered the corpse to rest at the bottom of the grave. He lay at the graveside to reach down and fold his father's arms across his chest. "Goodbye, Father," was all he managed to say before filling in the hole.

The two men leaned their shovels against the wall of the shack and walked around it to where Lucy stood patiently beside Warman. She remained staring at the ground, and Westlake put an arm around her. "I'll come to see you in a day or so. I have an idea," he said to the girl. "Things will turn out. Meanwhile, take Warman along with you. He's a good friend."

Then he turned to Nelles. "Can you escort Miss Dunbar to Lynde Tavern, sir?" Westlake asked, eyeing the sky to gauge the weather. "She can't risk going back to the Jordan. I'll be along later, but I have to tell my mother about all this." He nodded to his father's newly covered grave and then looked to Lucy for approval.

She shrugged and nodded but still did not catch his eye.

"I'll see her safely to Whitby," Nelles agreed. "The Americans may be preparing to leave York, but no one knows for sure. Be on your guard, Lieutenant."

The two men shook hands. Westlake gathered up the reins of his father's horse and strode off homeward to give his mother the sad news.

29

· · · · ·

WESTLAKE STAYED OVERNIGHT at Maple Hill after telling his mother about her husband's death. Elizabeth didn't cry or even turn pale on hearing the news. In her black dress with white lace cuffs and a white lace collar buttoned up to the neck, she remained stoic throughout the tale, sitting upright in the parlour, her hands folded on her lap, while the fireplace radiated a warm glow.

"I once said to you there was something false about our family," she declared. "It started with the love between your father and me, lost long ago. We stayed together out of duty to each other and to you, but it didn't make things any easier. In the end, I'm not sure what he thought he was fighting for."

"Maple Hill, the sawmill, a semblance of a family perhaps," Westlake replied. "Unfortunately he lost his way." There was only sadness in his voice.

His mother remained quiet. Westlake sat watching the fire for a time. He stood, threw on a few extra logs, and walked to the front window. There was no hurry now. The drizzle had returned, and the guards at the bottom of the hill hunched miserably into their great coats. He reminded himself to have the stable hand deliver them some extra rations of rum.

Westlake told his mother about Lucy Dunbar and the part she'd played in the treacherous game with Puffer. He explained the lesson received from Major Nelles about the four motivations for treason. He paused on sex and his mother understood. "Father knew. We ... our family has a responsibility."

Elizabeth nodded in agreement. The conversation continued thus for a while and then Westlake announced he was off to an early bed. He kissed his mother on the cheek and bade her goodnight.

A short time later, as he dozed off to sleep, he heard a sound coming from the parlour. His mother was weeping and he wondered for what ... her husband's death or the fact that their marriage had died many years before? Perhaps she cried for her own life, not lived to the full. He wasn't sure. He knew only that the future ahead seemed less certain without his father.

The two-storied Lynde Inn and Tavern loomed ahead as Westlake approached it on horseback. He had risen before first light and, after a small breakfast, ridden off at dawn. A couple of York militiamen challenged his arrival at the British perimeter, but he had no problem getting through.

Entering the inn, he knocked on the door of an upstairs room.

"Enter," Major Nelles called out from within. Westlake opened the door and peered inside to see Nelles working in shirtsleeves, a quill in his hand poised over a sheaf of papers spread out on a table. "Good morning, Lieutenant." Nelles gestured to the chair across from him. "How is your mother today?"

"Considering the circumstances, she's doing rather well, sir. And Miss Dunbar?" Westlake sat down.

"We'll see her shortly. Take a look through these names."

He handed Westlake several sheets of papers that listed names and addresses. At the top of the first page the heading read THOSE GIVING THEIR PAROLE. These were men who, for their freedom, promised not to fight until they were exchanged for American prisoners held by the British. Westlake knew some of the men listed, mostly men he had not seen anywhere on the day of the battle.

"Strange how a man from Markham too ill to fight for us on the day of battle could walk more than fifteen miles into York to sign his parole, then travel another fifteen miles back home," Nelles said. "Read the last page."

Another list showed the names of fellow citizens who had joined in the pillaging of York's homes, and also those thought to have conspired with the enemy. The last name on the list was Richard Westlake. "Once the Americans leave, the Reverend Strachan will be demanding the arrest of everyone who conspired with the enemy. Some of the influential folk in York — their committee — are calling for a charge of treason to be laid."

Westlake sat down. Obviously no one yet knew of his father's death. The establishment of York was now turning against the citizens who had turned against it. Looting could not be sanctioned, but a charge of treason for merely stealing seemed rather severe. "Is there not some middle ground, sir?"

Nelles shook his head. "The outrage is too deeply felt." He held a letter in his hand that he passed to Westlake. "This is the draft of a letter regarding Sheaffe and Prevost's conduct, that's going to the Prince Regent himself, to the London and Montreal papers, and to anyone else who'll listen."

Westlake scanned the letter vilifying General Sheaffe for not better supporting Major Givens and the natives at the first point of attack and for not counterattacking after the magazine blew. Westlake could hardly believe that the criticisms levelled were so bold, although he couldn't disagree. On Sheaffe the letter concluded that he had "lost entirely the confidence of the regulars and militia, and his very name is odious to all ranks of people."

"Although not named, the last section concerns myself and Governor Prevost," Nelles said.

Westlake read on:

In the capture of York, behold the first fruits of the imbecility which prevented a vigorous attack upon Sackets Harbor, an attack which ... would have secured this Province during the whole war.

"I don't know what to say, sir, except that a lack of leadership at the top is hardly your fault," Westlake said.

"The Reverend Strachan seems to think I didn't put the case strongly enough to those in power." Nelles shrugged. "I may in fact have to leave Upper Canada permanently on account of it."

"God's teeth, that man always goes too far!" Westlake exclaimed. "I'm sorry, sir, but my influence with Strachan is less than yours."

"And it will be even less now that your family's name appears on that list." Nelles sighed, pushed his chair back, and stood. The meeting was over. "Let's visit Miss Dunbar. She's waiting in the landlord's parlour."

Lucy looked away as soon as she saw Westlake enter. She slumped on a couch near the fireplace, where Westlake took the cushion beside her and held her hand in his. "Miss Dunbar, won't you look at me."

Slowly her brown eyes met his.

Nelles cleared his throat and stepped to one side.

"While you are considering your future, my mother would like you to stay with her at Maple Hill ... for as long as you like. She has no one there now that my father is gone and I'm away so much. Would you think about keeping her company?"

"Will you be there at all?" Lucy almost whispered. "I'd like to start again."

Westlake paused before making any other commitment. "I'll be travelling, but I should be there to begin with, yes."

"Then that's a start," she murmured.

"I suppose so, yes, a new beginning ... like spring." He smiled and looked over toward the window.

Lucy nodded but did not speak.

"That's settled then," Westlake said as he stood. "I'll have Warman readied immediately. Just sit tight here and we'll be off." He walked back toward the major.

Nelles was staring at the fire. "That was the right thing to do, Lieutenant," he said. "But what's this about you travelling?"

"I'm assuming that whether you're stationed in Upper Canada or not, you'll still need my services, sir."

"I thought you were tired of all this."

"Me, sir? Must be someone else you're thinking of," Westlake said. "There's something about losing that doesn't sit well with me."

"You think we're supposed to win every time?" Nelles asked and then answered his own question. "War isn't like that."

"What the Americans don't understand is that they will have to kill every single person in the Canadas who is loyal to the Crown, or else they will never win. I'm sure their patriots feel the same way about the United States."

Nelles held up a sheet of paper. "These are my orders to meet Governor-in-Chief Prevost. I'm off to Lower Canada." Nelles held out his hand and smiled. "Goodbye, Jonathan. You'll probably hear from me soon."

Westlake grinned and shook his hand. "Say hello to him for me, sir. Surely between the two of you, you can think of something destructive for me to do."

On Sunday morning, six days after the invasion, Westlake stood and watched the guards at Maple Hill marching away. He announced to his mother that he was travelling to town. Elizabeth began to say something, then shrugged. "We've been through this conversation already. I know I can't stop you." She smiled. "Never could."

"Don't worry," Westlake replied. "I'll be right back." He slid on his boots and went off through the back door. Two robins chirped on the barn roof, a sure sign of warmer weather to come. In the barn itself, he found Lucy patting Warman on the nose.

"He's beautiful," she said. "May I take him out for another ride sometime?" The horse snorted as if he understood her request.

"Of course ... once the Americans are gone. We'll see them go soon enough. I'm off to York now."

"No! What if he comes back?" She reached out to grab his arm. "Don't go." As the horrific events at the old sugar shack distanced themselves, Lucy's conversation had grown less muted, but this was the first time she'd gone out of her way to actually touch him.

Westlake gently put his hand over hers. "Puffer is miles from here so you'll be fine. Besides, Joseph is around back, and my mother is deadly with a musket."

She still did not release his arm. "You said we could begin again."

Westlake looked straight into her eyes. She wanted acceptance, needed it for what had happened. He pulled her closer and kissed her firmly on the lips, and then again. He felt her body sigh. "Now we've really begun, again." He smiled.

American soldiers surged through the muddy streets of York, as the last of the wounded were carried on stretchers to waiting longboats. On Yonge Street, three infantrymen ran by clasping stolen silverware and carded wool in their arms. One rifleman lugged all the crockery he could carry, items dropping to the ground as he rushed toward the boats. Just seeing that green jacket again made Westlake's stomach twist.

A column of black smoke curled up in the west. The garrison buildings had been set alight. Government House, the symbol of British authority, would be one of the first to go. Brock's old office would burn too. Destruction and chaos reigned.

Well back from the waterfront, Westlake leaned against a tree and looked around. In front of him, the naval storage sheds burst into flame as torch weilding sailors ran from one to the other. Smoke blew toward him by a stiff on-shore breeze. The bastards would have a difficult time leaving in this wind, he reflected.

He felt a nudge on his elbow and turned to see the familiar face of Lieutenant Alex McMullen.

"Mr. Westlake." He touched his hat and Westlake nodded. "They're doing exactly what they did to the Parliament buildings," the lieutenant observed.

"There's been no rapes and after the surrender, no killing. Did you actually see them set those buildings on fire?" Westlake asked.

"There were only American sailors around," McMullen replied.

"You're sure."

"That's the rumour." McMullen shrugged. "As for damage, you helped old Captain LeLievre and myself blow up the magazine and burn that ship." McMullen grinned and gestured in the direction of the *Sir Isaac Brock*'s burnt-out hull. "I remember you running directly toward the enemy so me and the old man I could get away. That was an honourable thing to do."

"Honour? Once, I knew what that word meant, or at least I thought I did." Westlake shook his head. "Now I know it's a slippery term that changes sense according to the circumstances."

"Are you even a member of our militia?"

Westlake paused, wanting to tell McMullen everything, all the secrets buried inside him. "Did some odd jobs now and then for General Brock," he replied. "Not much, really." Westlake swung around to leave. "I've seen enough." Some schooners had set sail against the wind and were pulling away from the others still anchored.

"Say hello to your parents for me. Wish I'd kept hold of that mill. York will have to be rebuilt." He poked his thumb at the smoke billowing above the garrison.

Westlake turned back to see the burning sheds along the beach and a few other ships trying to set sail against the stiff wind. It meant the Americans were finally leaving. The smoke from the sheds obscured his view. "Perhaps you can help us manage the place, Mr. McMullen. My father's now out of the picture."

"But who'll finance the business?"

Westlake considered the one hundred dollars he'd left in the saddlebag, now in the possession of Puffer. With his right hand, he reached inside his jacket to finger the other five hundred. "You've got five hundred in cash to start."

"That's more than enough." McMullen held out a hand, slapping Westlake on the shoulder with the other hand. "You're an honourable man, Mr. Westlake. It's a deal."

"Nobody's perfect, Mr. McMullen." Westlake smiled and tried peering through the smoke toward the lake. "But I do my best. Deal."

The End

HISTORICAL NOTE

GO TO THE NEW WATERFRONT park in Gananoque, Ontario, and stroll beside the great St. Lawrence River. Up the highway, visit a wonderful town now called Brockville, but in 1812 named Elizabethtown. Imagine the Americans in their white longboats crossing the river in the dark, and then months later charging over the ice to storm up those low banks toward the town's centre. Major Forsyth's riflemen were hated by the settlers on the British side of the river and not much liked on their own side either.

Of course, Brock's letter to Jonathan Westlake is a fiction, as is Westlake himself. However, in the major general's personal letters [available online] Brock was often concerned about the many disgruntled citizens only too ready to aid the enemy. Militia duty, lack of farm implements, and the clergy reserves of valuable land were only a few of the problems faced by the residents.

The Americans, too, had their problems with their own citizens who had been deprived of their livelihoods sustained through trading and were now opposed to the war. American historian, Alan Taylor, has described the conflict as "a civil war" between Federalist and Loyalists on one side, and Republicans on the other. [*The Civil War of 1812*] It was little wonder that New England's newspapers eventually even discussed seceding from the new union. The Republicans under President Madison had just declared war on their largest customer — Great Britain — and New England's farmers came to detest the conflict, the president, and the Republican Party alike.

The War of 1812 was a strange occurrence in that many combatants on both sides were American. About 60 percent of Upper Canada's population were Loyalists, settlers who had escaped the United States after the American Revolution to take up free farmland being offered north of the border. Even British Governor-in-Chief Prevost and Major General Sheaffe had both been born in the United States.

Next on your journey, you can't miss Kingston's Fort Henry, with a fantastic view of Lake Ontario and the St. Lawrence River. You might see in your mind's eye Commodore Chauncey in the *Oneida* chasing the *Royal George* into the harbour. Or imagine the rim of the steep banks lined with redcoats peppering the American flotilla with musket balls, and the shore batteries blasting cannon shot and yet missing almost everything!

Finally, Fort Wellington in Prescott has finished a federal government makeover for your enjoyment. In the new visitor centre, speak to the knowledgeable staff about the raid on that cold morning in February when Red George, against Governor Prevost's orders, stole across the ice to attack Ogdensburg. There's a note to Red George displayed on one of the centre's walls that readers of *Brock's Traitor* will recognize. Guess who it's from?

If you have time, drive a little farther on toward the Quebec border and visit the spectacular Upper Canada Village. Among many other worthwhile attractions, it has the working sawmill on which I based the one that became Westlake's. The employees at this mill can tell you all you need to know about pricing, construction, and the technical skills required to work with lumber in the early part of the 1800's.

As you continue over the border bridge from Prescott to Ogdensburg, New York, look down to envisage Red George in command of five hundred redcoats and militia, storming across the ice to attack the town. You will recognize some of the street names — one commemorating the smuggler Rosseel, for instance. Did you know that President Madison sent federal customs officials to Ogdensburg, where Judge Nathan Ford, a local magistrate, had these men arrested and thrown in jail for trespassing? Prevost once admitted that the Canada's would starve without the produce of the American farmer. According to Lieutenant General Jonathon Riley [*A Matter of Honour*], a million bushels of grain and beef were sold and shipped from New

England to feed Wellington's army in Portugal, the British troops battling Napoleon's forces! No wonder New England's farmers were livid with their president.

After driving from Ogdensburg to Sackets Harbor, you might fancy a drink, and there are lots of excellent restaurants and colourful bars to serve one. If you check into the Ontario Hotel and Spa, like I did, staff can recommend a man who will take you on a tour of the battle sites. He has some fine stories to tell!

By the time Governor Prevost had organized himself sufficiently to attack Sackets Harbor, the US flotilla under Commodore Chauncey had long departed to invade Upper Canada at York. The debate continues today whether British forces should have risked an attack earlier across the ice from Kingston. It would have been tough to haul cannon thirty-five miles in the dead of winter and then expect the exhausted men to fight. But they didn't have to seize the town itself, just destroy a few ships there, preferably the brigs *Madison* and *Oneida*. Bishop Strachan and the elite residents of York never forgave Sheaffe for deserting them, and they never forgave Prevost for not attacking Sackets Harbor before the ice broke in the spring of 1813. The draft letter that Westlake reads near the book's end is word for word what Strachan wrote to the prince regent.

Remember that General Pike had marched his men one hundred and seventy five miles from Plattsburg that same winter. I should mention that I have no historical evidence for that meeting at the Eveleigh Hotel between Chauncey, Dearborn, and Pike, but it seems to me inconceivable that the three men did not convene at some point in Sackets Harbor.

Walk down to Sackets' pier and visualize the harbour filled with tall ships and their great sails. The soldiers will march down the hill to the pier to enter the longboats that will take them out to the waiting ships. Granny Dearborn will be hauled up in a basket chair and you might dare to laugh at the thought. And don't miss the military cemetery. There is a monument at the grave of Brigadier General Zebulon Montgomery Pike — yes, that's the same Pike as the mountain named

Pike's Peak. The letters Pike writes in *Brock's Traitor* are edited versions of his own.

Now you can cross at Cape Vincent by ferry [where the fictitious Lieutenant Tasker waited to kill Westlake] or you can retrace your drive, but somehow you must get yourself over to Toronto. Did you know that York was called Toronto first, then York, then back to Toronto? It's my hometown and I visited Fort York when I was a young boy. I knew about the American invasion, the Western battery exploding, and the magazine blowing up much as I describe in the novel. According to Robert Malcomson's wonderful book *Capital in Flames*, the battery blew up not because of a lucky shot from the *Conquest* but rather from a self-inflicted wound. Someone had placed a box of cartridges too close to the guns!

What I didn't know until I read Malcomson was that no one ever actually saw the Americans set fire to the Parliament buildings. We were taught in school that the enemy plundered and pillaged our town and then set fire to the legislature. This turns out to be partially unproven. Also, it is important to note that unlike the war in Europe, after Dearborn signed the surrender, all the killing stopped and there were no reported instances of rape. Carl Benn, a Ryerson University history professor, pointed out to me that this still does not excuse the Americans from the damage done to public and private buildings because they were then the civil authorities with the responsibility of maintaining law and order.

The victory at York by the largest combined American Army and Navy operation in history [up to that time] gave the administration in Washington a much-needed boost. But in the grand scheme of the war, the battle didn't amount to much. The Americans couldn't hold the place, and it was surely a distraction from the main prizes at Kingston and Montreal.

For the British, with the burning of the *Sir Isaac Brock*, it meant that their naval superiority on Lake Ontario had vanished. However, for the residents of Upper Canada, the defence of York and its destruction sewed together the myths needed to build a foundation for a nation. Even if one dislikes Reverend Strachan's bullying style, one has to admire his courage and ability to weave a tale supporting the interests of the Anglican Church.

Like the good Reverend Strachan, all of the senior officers on both sides in *Brock's Traitor* were historical figures except for Major Nelles. Of course, Jonathan Westlake and his family — along with Lucy, Willie, McMullen, Tasker, Shaughnessy, McKnight, and O'Reilly — are all fictitious too. As for the bag of official papers and the six hundred dollars in Army Bills, the bag itself was eventually recovered, along with the documents, but the money had gone. This fits in nicely with my story. You can still visit the Lynde House on Tauton Road in Whitby at Cullen Park.

Meanwhile, fed up with these upstart Americans, the British are secretly planning something big to put them in their proper place. As for Westlake, he has travelled a lot over the last couple of years so he may need a rest. Then again, he may be travelling soon; we'll just have to wait and see if there is another mission in his future.

ACKNOWLEDGMENTS

I would like to offer sincere thanks to a team of individuals who assisted me in bringing *Brock's Traitor* to fruition: my writing circle friends, Andrew Varga, Colleen Zoellner, Suzanne Robinson, Sharon Overend, Fred Ford, Sandra Clark, Cryssa Bassos; fellow writer Lory Kaufman; Brian Henry; Tom Fournier for his military historical advice; Sarah Maloney of the Niagara Historical Museum; Major John R. Grodzinski, of the Royal Military College for his historical advice; Val Bunbury for her invaluable support; Shelly Macbeth, Blue Heron Books; the Humber School for Writers; Joan MacKinnon of Fort Wellington, Carl Benn of Ryerson University for his historical advice, Joseph [the Chandler] Lischka; Robert Henderson; Keith Butterley; Debbie Kellogg and Stephanie Taylor. Bill Fowler and Pierre Geneau of Upper Canada Village for taking the time to explain the workings of their beautiful sawmill; Tania Craan for her striking book covers; Elizabeth Woodley-Hall for her award winning photos; Bernard Cornwell for showing the way; Bill Hanna; my editors, Peter Lavery and Heather Sangster; and Debbie Taylor, who allows me to escape household duties so that I may take the time to write.

One last mention: There would be no novel, and perhaps no Canada, without the extraordinary efforts of Sir Isaac Brock. To him, and to all the soldiers on both sides who fought at the Battle of York, we honour your memory.

Ontario, Canada
March 2013

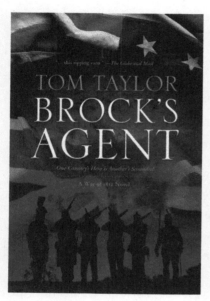
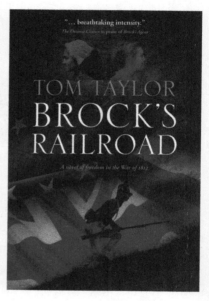